Julie Miller is an award-w[illegible] author of breathtaking roma[illegible] Readers' Choice Award and [illegible] Award, among other prizes. She ha[illegible] earned an *RT Book Reviews* Career Achievement Award. For a complete list of her books, monthly newsletter and more, go to juliemiller.org

Amber Leigh Williams is an author, wife, mother of two and dog mum. She has been writing sexy small-town romance with memorable characters since 2006. Her Mills & Boon miniseries is set in her charming hometown of Fairhope, Alabama. She lives on the Alabama Gulf Coast, where she loves being outdoors with her family and a good book. Visit her on the web at amberleighwilliams.com

Also by Julie Miller

Kansas City Crime Lab

K-9 Patrol

Decoding the Truth

The Evidence Next Door

Sharp Evidence

The Taylor Clan: Firehouse 13

Crime Scene Cover-Up

Dead Man District

Target on Her Back

K-9 Protector

A Stranger on Her Doorstep

Also by Amber Leigh Williams

Hunted on the Bay

Fuego, New Mexico

Coldero Ridge Cowboy

Ollero Creek Conspiracy

Married One Night

His Rebel Heart

Wooing the Wedding Planner

Fairhope, Alabama

Navy SEAL Promise

Navy SEAL's Match

SHADOW SURVIVORS

JULIE MILLER

CLOSE RANGE CATTLEMAN

AMBER LEIGH WILLIAMS

MILLS & BOON

First Published in Great Britain 2024
by Mills & Boon, an imprint of HarperCollins*Publishers* Ltd
1 London Bridge Street, London, SE1 9GF

www.harpercollins.co.uk

HarperCollins*Publishers*
Macken House, 39/40 Mayor Street Upper,
Dublin 1, D01 C9W8, Ireland

ISBN: 978-0-263-32226-2

0424

This book contains FSC™ certified paper and other controlled sources to ensure responsible forest management.

For more information visit: www.harpercollins.co.uk/green

Printed and Bound in the UK using 100% Renewable Electricity at
CPI Group (UK) Ltd, Croydon, CR0 4YY

SHADOW SURVIVORS

JULIE MILLER

For Daisy and Teddy—our two doodlebugs. Both blind in one eye. A black Poodle mix, a white Poodle mix. An introvert and an extrovert. One who will never sit in your lap to be petted but who will never turn her nose up at a treat. And the other who can't get enough personal attention and who will take a tummy rub over a treat any day. One who enjoys her solitude, and one who panics when he's left alone. One who was returned to the shelter twice before finding his forever home with us, and the other who was never wanted at all until she was rescued from a horrible situation. You two are so good for each other, and you're good for us. You have to be a special dog to be a Miller dog. Mama loves you both.

Chapter One

Shadow growled.

Tensing, Jessica Bennington looked over at her German shepherd mix with the graying muzzle, who had just risen from his sunny spot in the grass and gone on alert.

Now what? The dogs at her K-9 Ranch rescue and training center had raised a ruckus late last night, too. They had all been locked up in their kennels, the barn, or the house, so she hadn't been worried about one of them getting into trouble. She'd thrown a jacket on over her pajamas and slipped into a pair of sneakers, grabbed a flashlight and Shadow, and gone out to investigate. But by the time she'd checked each and every one of them, the hubbub had died down. One must have seen a fox or a raccoon and barked, then the others would have joined in because no self-respecting dog wanted to be left out of sounding the alarm. Other than a few extroverts who seized the opportunity to get some petting, they'd immediately settled for the night. But since her own K-9 partner hadn't alerted to anything unusual, Jessica had dismissed any threat, walked back to the house, and had fallen into bed.

But Shadow was alerting this morning. His ears flicked

toward the sound that only a dog could hear, his dark eyes riveted to movement in the distance that only a dog could see.

She hated that growl. It was the sound of danger. A threat. Sometimes, even death. It was the sound of salvation and sacrifice.

It was the sound of the nightmare she'd lived with for twelve long years.

She instinctively splayed her fingers over her belly and the scars beneath her jeans. There was nothing to protect there anymore. There never would be.

Barely aware of the younger dog she'd been working with taking his cue from Shadow and turning toward the perceived threat, Jessica felt her blood pressure spike. Both dogs faced the pines and pin oaks that formed a windbreak and offered some much-needed privacy around the small acreage outside of Kansas City, Missouri. She couldn't afford to be paralyzed by the memories that assailed her. She had to push them aside. She had to let Shadow do what she'd trained him to do. She could overcome. She could survive this moment, just like she had so many others.

Jessica forced out a calming breath and stepped up beside the rescue dog that had been her protector, emotional support, and most loyal companion these past ten years. "What is it, boy?"

She sensed the tension vibrating through Shadow but knew he wouldn't charge off to investigate unless she gave him the command to do so. Shadow's black-and-tan coat was longer than a pure-blooded shepherd, thanks to the indefinite parentage of running with a pack until he'd been taken to a shelter in Kansas City and Jessica had picked him to be her first rescue. But that shaggy coat had been a comfort on more than one occasion in the ten years she'd had him. It would be now, too. She slid her fingers from her stomach into the thick fur atop his head, absorbing his heat, finding strength in knowing he was as devoted to her as she was to him.

She would never again be alone and helpless and unable to save the ones she loved.

Not with Shadow by her side.

Jessica finally heard the deep bark of one of her patrol dogs in the distance and relaxed a fraction. Her dogs were doing their jobs. That loud woof was Rex, a big, furry galoot of laziness and curiosity. He was more noise than fight—just the way she'd trained the gentle giant to behave. He wasn't much of a people dog, but he did enjoy roaming the six acres of her Shadow Protectors Ranch. A natural herder and caretaker, the Anatolian had adopted her three goats, a barn cat, and an abandoned litter of possums over the years. Had he found some other critter he wanted to take home to his stall in the barn? While Rex had yet to choose a person he liked well enough to bond with, he made a great deterrent to trespassers who wandered onto her land.

That's when she heard Toby's excited bark joining the chorus. Toby was the opposite of Rex in terms of personality. The black Lab wanted to be friends with everyone, hence he was no kind of guard dog at all. But he was a great noisemaker and loved to be in on the action. Toby and Rex had definitely discovered something near her property line to the west.

Mollie Crane, the client she'd been working with, sidled up beside Jessica, tucking her short dark-brown hair behind her ears. "Is something wrong?"

The younger woman she was helping was one breath away from a panic attack. The man she'd said she needed protection from had really done a number on her. Her fingers brushed against Jessica's elbow instead of reaching for Magnus, the dark faced Belgian Malinois who was training to be her service dog. "Is someone out there? Is it that grumpy old man who works for you? Or his grandson who cleans out the kennels? I'm not sure I like him. He's *too* friendly. Can someone be too friendly? I like his grandfather better. He's not very chatty, but at least he doesn't force me into a conversation or try to flirt with me."

Jessica squeezed her hand over Mollie's fingers to calm her. "Easy, Mollie. Take a breath." She breathed deeply, once, twice, with the woman, who was twenty years her junior. It was easier to control her own fears when she had her dogs or someone else to worry about. "Shadow's on alert because he hears and smells something atypical in his world. The dogs all know Mr. Hauck and his grandson, Soren. This is something different."

"An intruder? Could someone have followed me out here from the city? Wouldn't we have heard them pulling up the driveway?" She was one thought away from hyperventilating. Mollie's fingers were still clenched around Jessica's elbow as she looked down at her dog. "Why isn't Magnus barking? Is it because he's deaf in one ear? Does he not hear the threat? He's not going to be able to protect me, is he?"

Jessica glanced down at the Belgian Malinois who'd washed out of the Army's K-9 Corps because of chronic ear infections and hearing loss. "He's aware. Believe me, he sees more with those eyes than you or I ever will. But he's still in training. We'll get him where you need him to be. Don't worry. For now, let him be a comfort to you—something to focus on besides your fear." She tried to pull away. "I really need to go. If they've trapped a skunk, or there is someone—"

"Okay, um, Magnus?" Mollie picked up the Malinois's leash off the dry grass that hadn't had enough spring rain yet to turn green.

"Not like that." Jessica spared a moment to help her client. "You're the boss. He wants to please you. If you're *not* the boss, he's going to please himself." Jessica demonstrated. "Shadow, sit." She raised her hand. "Down." The shepherd's black nose stayed in the air, even as he eased his creaky joints to the ground. "Stay," she added, although he'd already obeyed her visual cues. She nodded to Mollie. "Now, you tell Magnus."

Mollie dutifully raised her hand. "Magnus. Sit." The young, muscular dog tipped his nose up to her and plopped his haunches on the ground. "He did it!" Mollie's success transformed her wary expression into a shy smile. "Good boy." She scratched the dog around his limp ear. "Now what?"

Although Jessica had spent a fortune to fence in the entire acreage to keep her dogs off the gravel roads and nearby state highway, she knew that a human being could either climb the fence or cut through it if they were agile enough and determined to trespass. "Mollie, I need to go." She needed to check out the hullabaloo as much as Shadow wanted to. "Take Magnus back to the barn and do some bonding with him. You've both had a good training session this morning and need a break."

Mollie's hands fisted around the leash. "By myself?"

"Sweetie, he chose you that first day you came to the ranch. Remember? He came right up to you and sat on your foot? He wants you to give him a chance to be the dog you need." Jessica shrugged, anxious to get to her dogs to make sure they were safe, but equally worried about jeopardizing Mollie's training. Although she earned good money training dogs for several paying clients, she had an affinity for women like Mollie, who *needed* a companion to help her feel safe. Mollie lived on a small budget, working as a waitress at a diner in Kansas City. But because of Jessica's own background with violence, she charged Mollie only a fraction of her regular fee. She would have given the young woman the dog and trained them for free, but she'd discovered she was as much a therapist as a trainer. Jessica understood that Mollie needed to make her own way in the world. She needed to build the confidence that had been stripped away from her by her past, and Jessica would do whatever was necessary to help. "Play a game with Magnus," she advised. "Get on the ground with him and pet him. There are treats and toys in the last cabinet out in the barn." She reached into the pocket of her jeans and pulled out her ring of work keys. She held up a small padlock key. "Here. This will unlock the cabinet."

"Okay. I can do this, right?" Mollie fisted her hand around the keys.

Jessica softened her tone and squeezed the other woman's fist. "Yes, you can. Love Magnus. Earn his trust. Provide his food, leadership, entertainment and comfort, and he will be your best friend—the most loyal friend you will ever have. Answering the specific commands you need will come later." She gave the other woman's shoulder one more squeeze before pulling away. "Please. I need to see what's going on. I need to make sure none of my protectors are getting themselves into trouble."

Mollie nodded, accepting the mission Jessica had given

her. Using a hand signal to get the tan dog's attention focused on her, she spoke in a surprisingly firm voice. "Magnus, heel." Then she tugged on the leash and the dog fell into step beside her.

"Just like that. Good job. You'll be safe in the barn."

Shadow remained at her feet, but his nose and ears indicated he was anxious to check out the disturbance, too. Could the ex-husband Mollie was so afraid of have found her here, eight miles outside the KC city limits? Jessica released her dog from his stay command. "Shadow, seek."

Needing no more encouragement, he took off at a loping run, and Jessica jogged to keep pace with him. She slowed as they reached the trees. Although the oaks were just beginning to bud and posed no obstacle, the evergreens had full, heavy branches she had to push her way through. She worried when Shadow dashed beyond her sight. "Shadow?" The barking tripled as the dog joined Rex and Toby.

Jessica pushed aside the last branch, stopped in her tracks and cursed on a deep sigh. "This isn't good."

Chapter Two

A protective anger pushed aside Jessica's fear and she hurried her stride to approach the trio of dogs barking at the white-haired neighbor swinging the barrel of her shotgun from one dog to the next from her side of the fence. "Miss Eloise? Good morning."

"Don't *good morning* me. Your mutts are a terror, Jessica Bennington! An absolute terror." Eloise Gardner had once been a tall woman. But now she was stooped with age and frail enough that she panted from the exertion of holding up the heavy gun and walking the quarter mile from her house to the fence. She nodded toward the broken railing that butted up against Jessica's chain-link fence. "Look what they did to my fence."

The log fence was little more than faded wood and chipped white paint after years of weather and neglect. The top rail looked as though it had rotted through and splintered in half beneath the weight of someone leaning against it or stepping onto it. Or maybe it had finally surrendered under its own weight to age and decay.

Keeping her demeanor calm so the dogs would obey her, Jessica called them to her side. "Rex! Toby! Shadow! Come."

The three dogs lined up beside her, and with a set of nonverbal commands, they sat and lay down. Jessica kept her arm out at a 45-degree angle from her body to make them stay put. Trying not to panic that the shotgun was pointed in her direction now, as well, Jessica drummed up a smile and a civil tone. “Is that gun really necessary? What seems to be the problem?”

The skinny old woman hiked the butt of the gun onto her hip, but kept it trained on the dogs and Jessica in a distinctly unneighborly fashion. “Your dogs are wild beasts and need to be put down. Not only did a pack of them break down my fence, but one of my chickens is dead. My best layer. Never had problems like this when your grandparents owned the place.”

“I’m sorry about your chicken.” She kept her tone calm, as if she was talking to a nervous dog. “My fence is still intact,” she pointed out. “My dogs didn’t get onto your property. They didn’t break your fence. And they didn’t kill your chicken. Maybe a fox or coyote got inside your chicken coop.”

“Don’t you argue with me. Doris is dead. I already called Deputy Caldwell.”

Jessica’s nostrils flared with a sigh of relief, but for their own safety, she refused to relax or release the dogs from their stay position. “Good. Deputy Caldwell knows my dogs. He’ll straighten this out.” Garrett Caldwell was a captain in the Jackson County Sheriff’s Office, in charge of the patrol division. He was not only in charge of local law enforcement in the county outside of the K C city limits, but he was practically a neighbor, living just off 40 Highway in the nearby town of Lone Jack. He was tough but fair, and the widower had become a friend. “He’ll listen to the facts, assess the evidence. You'll get the answers you need, and my dogs will be safe."

Eloise glanced over her shoulder at the sound of a large vehicle crunching over gravel in the distance. "I expect that'll be him." She wheezed with the effort to keep the gun from pointing to the ground as she faced Jessica again. "You're in trouble now, missy."

Missy? Jessica wanted to laugh. She'd buried a husband and a child and felt as if she'd already lived the best part of her life. But she swallowed the dark humor as she watched the older woman wiggling her nose to work her glasses back up into place without letting go of the shotgun. Eloise Gardner was an octogenarian living a hard, lonely existence, trying to take care of things as best she could without the help, resources, or energy to fully manage on her own. "Miss Eloise, are you all right? Did you take your heart medication this morning?"

"Of course, I did." Eloise touched her age-spotted forehead as if trying to think. "I don't know. I'm not sure."

"Would you let me walk you back to your house?" Jessica offered. "We could check your pill box. I'd be happy to fix you a cup of tea and sit with you for a while." She glanced down at her faithful German shepherd mix. "I'd have to bring Shadow with me, but I promise, the other dogs will stay here."

"I…" For a moment, she looked as though she wanted to say yes to Jessica's offer. "No… Isla's coming today. I gave her money for groceries." Suddenly, Eloise pulled her shoulders back with as much energy as her stooped posture allowed, raising the shotgun once more. "I don't want any of your dogs on my property. And who's fixing the latch on my chicken coop?"

"Miss Eloise?" A deep voice called out.

Jessica watched the tall man in his khaki uniform quietly striding up behind her neighbor. Garrett Caldwell stood a couple inches over six feet, and the protective vest he wore underneath his uniform made his sturdy chest and shoulders seem impossibly broad and imposing.

And then she saw Eloise Gardner swing around and point her shotgun straight at the deputy. "Garrett!"

Her warning proved unnecessary. In one swift, smooth movement, Garrett knocked the barrel of the shotgun aside, tugged it from her hands, and reached out to steady the old woman's arm to keep her from falling. Eloise yelped in surprise and clung to his forearm as he stepped behind her and braced her against his chest. All the while, he held the gun out with one strong arm and kept hold of Eloise until she stopped swaying.

The old woman's breathing fell back into a more normal rhythm, and Garrett released her and stepped back. "You all right, Miss Eloise?" Although she still seemed a little surprised by how quickly she'd been disarmed, she nodded. Then he turned his sharp green eyes across the fence to Jessica. "You okay?"

Jessica nodded, despite the lingering frissons of alarm that hummed through her veins. "Thank you, Deputy."

He touched the brim of his departmental ball cap, then concentrated on the white-haired lady beside him. "I'm not comfortable with you pointing a gun at me or anyone else when I haven't checked it out for myself." Garrett's tone held all the authority of his position, yet was surprisingly gentle with the frightened, angry, and possibly confused woman.

"It's not loaded. I just wanted to scare her. I don't feel safe around her dogs."

"All the same." He opened the shotgun, verified there were no rounds inside, then tucked the disabled weapon in the crook of his arm. "I want to make sure everyone is safe. Including you. This twelve-gauge seems a little too big for you to handle properly."

"It was my Hal's gun." Eloise sounded wistful at the mention of her late husband. "He took down an elk with it."

And she'd pointed that blunderbuss at her dogs? And her? And Garrett?

"I'm sure he did, ma'am. Now, what seems to be the problem?"

Eloise clutched Garrett's muscled forearm that was decorated with a faded black tattoo from his time in the military. "I want you to arrest this woman for siccing her dogs on my chickens."

Now that the imminent threat had been neutralized, he launched into investigator mode. "One of Jessie's dogs went after your chickens?"

"No," Jessica protested.

"Yes." The older woman's breathing was a little ragged. She pressed a gnarled hand against her heart. "During the night. Of course, I didn't hear it, but one of those mutts chewed through the latch on my coop and the hens got out. This morning, there were hardly any eggs when I went to gather them, so I know something upset them. I found Doris dead by the side of the highway. She was my best layer." Even though she was shorter by a few inches, the white-haired woman managed to look down her nose at Jessica. "Your dogs chased her right out into the road."

"My dogs haven't left my property," Jessica insisted. Then she dropped her voice to a whisper she hoped only Garrett could hear. "Although, they did go off about two o'clock this morning. I never saw anything. Maybe she had an intruder, and that's what they heard."

His lips barely moved as he answered in an equally hushed tone. "I think she needs to relax and put her feet up for a bit. She looks pale and sounds winded."

"I asked if she took her medications this morning. She couldn't remember."

"She's upset about her damn chicken."

"Not. My. Dogs."

Garrett arched a brow over one moss-colored eye, silently asking her to give up the argument. Then he smiled at the older woman and spoke in his full, deeply pitched voice. "Are the rest of your chickens okay, ma'am?"

After several moments, Eloise nodded. "They were all inside the fence this morning, but the latch is broken. Someone braced it shut with a rock."

"Well, my dogs didn't do that."

"Jessie." Garrett's eyes narrowed, asking her to be the more magnanimous complainant here. Once she nodded, he turned back to the older woman. "Miss Eloise, you go back to your house. I'll meet you there in a few minutes to take your statement and return the gun. I'll look around to make sure everything is secure."

"Thank you." Once the white-haired woman had taken a few steps toward her house, Garrett crossed to the fence. After a quick inspection of the broken railing, he braced one hand on a sturdier post and swung his legs up over both fences onto her property.

The moment he dropped down onto the grass, Shadow raised his head and growled. Rex yawned, growing bored with staying in one place. Toby's tail was wagging hard enough to kick up a cloud of dirt and dry grass on the ground behind him, but even the friendly Lab who'd greeted Garrett on more than one occasion eyed Jessica's hand and maintained his stay position.

Garrett froze in place, and Eloise hurried back to the fence in a huff. "You see, Deputy? Those dogs are a threat to all of us."

"No, they're not." Jessica was tired of defending herself and the work she was doing here. She latched on to Garrett's gaze and willed him to side with her. "These are three of my best students. None of them are smarter than Shadow. They know the property lines, and that they aren't to cross them without me. They guard *my* land. They don't invade hers. They're all well-fed and have plenty of stimulation. They don't need to be stealing chickens for breakfast or chasing them for entertainment."

Garrett nodded toward Shadow. "If these dogs are so well trained, why is that one growling at me?"

"Because you're holding that gun. You're half a foot taller than me and you look like a threat." She glanced at her outstretched hand, still holding her dogs in place. "But he won't go after you unless I give the command."

"The fence is broken, Jessie." Making the concession to Shadow's watchful eye, Garrett laid Eloise's open shotgun on the ground behind him. He visibly relaxed his posture, although he didn't move any closer. "Your smaller dogs might not be able to get out. But one of these three could."

"Are you going to call them off?" Eloise prodded, seeming more energized now that backup had arrived.

"Are you going to accuse my dogs of something they didn't do?"

"Jessie." Garrett exhaled a weary breath, drawing her attention to the silver-studded beard stubble shading his jaw. Standing closer, she realized the lines beside his mouth were etched more deeply than the last time she'd seen him.

"Garrett?" Something locked up deep inside her fluttered with concern. Maybe the same impulse that had her worried about Eloise's health. Garrett looked exhausted. Had he worked the night shift? Had he even slept? Who looked out for the strong boss man when he had a rough night? Apparently, it wasn't a job he did for himself. "Are you all right?"

He let out his breath on a slow, weary exhale, but didn't answer. Whatever fatigue she'd detected didn't stop him from smiling at her neighbor and speaking in a tone that commanded authority, even as his words offered compassion and reassurance. "Miss Eloise, go back to the house and fix yourself a cup of tea or a shot of whiskey to calm your nerves. I'll be over in a few minutes to return your shotgun and take a closer look at what happened."

"All right. I could do with a few minutes to myself." The older woman smiled. "With Doris's demise, I guess I'll be making fried chicken for dinner. Deputy, if you'd like to join me. Isla will be here. She'd love to see you." The older woman pushed her glasses up on the bridge of her nose and winked.

"Your granddaughter?" Jessica thought she detected a ruddy hue to Garrett's carved cheekbones and held back a smirk at his embarrassment. "She's a mite young for me, ma'am."

"Nonsense. She's thirty. Just broke up with her latest boyfriend. I told her he was no good. Out drinking nearly every night. Probably doing drugs."

"Isla or the boyfriend?"

Eloise bristled at the question. "I'm just telling you she's available."

"I appreciate you thinking of me, ma'am. But I'm not interested. I'm just here to do my job."

Eloise propped her hands on her hips. "You've been widowed for ten years, Garrett Caldwell. It's time you got laid again."

There was definitely a blush now. Jessica curled her lips between her teeth to hide her grin at Eloise's blatant matchmaking attempt. Just because the man had lost his wife to cancer a decade earlier didn't mean he hadn't dated or been with a woman since then. Garrett Caldwell was a catch. If you had a thing for silver foxes with a sense of humor and muscles to spare. She doubted if he needed Eloise Gardner's or anyone's help if he wanted to get laid.

Of course, Jessica hadn't slept with a man since losing Jonathan twelve years ago. Being abstinent for that long, she was practically a dinosaur, or at least an old maid. Dogs, friends, and more often than not, loneliness were her companions. But it was a choice she'd made. Whatever decisions Garrett had made about his love life, it wasn't her business. Nor was it Eloise Gardner's.

But Garrett had the situation well in hand. He pointed to the chicken coop and house beyond. "Go home, Eloise. And don't you be aiming a gun at your neighbor or her dogs again, you hear me?"

"Yes, sir." She turned and headed back to her house, her steps much lighter than a woman in her eighties ought to be.

"Oh, I like a man who gets bossy and says what he means. Just like my Hal used to..."

Once the older woman was out of earshot, Garrett cursed a single word, then faced Jessica again. "I wouldn't put it past Miss Eloise to wring the neck of that chicken herself and call my office as an excuse to get me out here. She's lonesome, her granddaughter's horny, and quite frankly, I feel safer on this side of the property line than I do on hers. Now, please call off your dogs, so we can talk."

"You poor man." Jessica barely masked her grin as she released the dogs. Toby and Rex scampered away to find their next adventure, but Shadow thrust his head into her hand, demanding pats, and remained by her side. "Terrorized by a lonely eighty-five-year-old woman with arthritis and heart issues. Need me to rescue you?"

He scrubbed his palm over the stubble of his jaw, and she was struck once again by how tired he looked. Okay. Not in the mood for teasing.

"I'm sorry, Garrett," she apologized. "Clearly, you're here on business. Thank you for alleviating the threat and not forcing me to lock up my dogs. Looks like it's already been a long morning for you. May I offer you a cup of coffee?"

"It's been a long twenty-four hours," he admitted. "I've already had too much coffee. Besides—" he grinned, and she pretended she didn't find this boyish, charming side of Garrett Caldwell as attractive as she did his scruffy workaholic look "—I've got a caramel macchiato for you out in my truck."

So, they *were* doing the teasing thing, after all. Jessica smiled. Apparently, he'd stopped at the coffee shop in town. Occasionally, she'd met him there when their schedules allowed, and he knew her weakness. "Are you trying to bribe me?"

"If I have to. I'm asking for your help."

"Oh." The seriousness of his tone ended the friendly banter they usually shared before it ever got started. "Did you or one of your team pick up another stray? Is the shelter full?" She'd helped the sheriff's department several times in the past, rounding up strays and housing them for a few days until she found a safe shelter where they could be housed in Kansas City or one of the nearby small towns—if she didn't have the time or space to take on a new project herself. "I've got a client here right now I need to finish with, but I can drive into Lone Jack after that if you need me."

"I've got human problems this time."

Jessica tilted her gaze up to Garrett's, analyzing what had stamped his handsome features with such fatigue. The mask of charm he'd used with Eloise had vanished. "Did you sleep at all last night? Are you working a case?"

Instead of answering her questions, he asked her one. "Are you pressing charges against Eloise? She did threaten you with a gun—even if it wasn't loaded."

"No. I know she's had a hard time of it since her husband died. I knew her daughter, Misty—Isla's mother—from spending summers here with Gran and Papa. But I haven't seen her once in the three years since I moved here and started transforming the property from a working farm into a rescue operation and training center."

"Yeah, Misty followed a man to Montana—or maybe it was Wyoming. Eloise doesn't talk about her. I don't think that was an amicable parting." Garrett shrugged. "Isla's no help. She can't keep a job or a man. And I know for a fact that Isla's ex-husband, and at least one of the men I've seen her hanging with at the bar in town, have rap sheets. Drugs. Drunk and Disorderlies. Burglary and theft."

"Wow." Jessica hadn't realized just how dangerous some of the people in Eloise Gardner's world could be. "No wonder her reaction was to call you and protect herself with a gun. Do you think either of those men, or even Isla, are a threat to her? I know she has some money from her husband's life insurance. She has the spirit of a cantankerous old woman, but she's fragile."

"I know. It worries me, too." Garrett tugged off his ball cap and combed his fingers through the salt-and-pepper spikes of his short hair, leaving a rumpled mess in their wake. Jessica curled her fingers into her palms, surprised by the urge to smooth it back into place. She and Garrett were friends, nothing more. Occasional coworkers who shared a love for caffeine and canines. A widow and a widower who were perfectly content to live out their days without the stress and complications of forging a new relationship. "I was half hoping she was fending off Isla's boyfriend with her shotgun instead of you. I need something to explain the weird things happening around here."

"Weird?" Jessica's hand instinctively moved to Shadow's warm fur. "What do you mean?"

Garrett settled his cap back on top of his head. "The reason I got here so quickly was because I was checking out a vandalism call at the Russells' summer cabin. Someone cut a screen and broke a window. Rifled through the medicine cabinet. Looks like they might have stolen a couple of small items. Didn't touch the TV, though. Probably couldn't get it out through the window."

Jessica drifted half a step closer to Garrett, her body subconsciously responding to the concern she felt for him, even though her brain wouldn't allow her to touch him. "On the other side of the Gardner farm? You think that's related to the dead chicken and broken fence?"

"I don't know. But I don't like a mystery. Too many little incidents like this start adding up, and they become something big. *Something big* is the call I don't want to answer."

Had he been working these *little incidents* all night? She wasn't naive enough to think she'd left serious crime behind her in Kansas City. But Garrett's suspicions made her nervous that something more dangerous than a frightened old woman and a spate of vandalism might be lurking in the hills, forests and farmland around her. "What do you think is going on?"

"Could be vagrants looking for food or a place to sleep. The weather is warming up and we've had a few hitchhikers out on the highway trying to leave the city. Could be bored teenagers entertaining themselves by causing trouble." He shook his head, clearly frustrated by his lack of answers. "My gut tells me it's something bigger. Maybe these petty crimes are a distraction to keep me and my officers busy with calls, so we don't see a bigger threat happening. Someone could be casing the area to plan a bigger score, or they're setting up a drug trafficking route, or they're clearing a path to move stolen goods in or out of Kansas City." He pulled off his cap again and scrubbed his fingers through his short hair. "I just pray there's not something I'm missing because I've lost a few hours of sleep."

This time Jessica did reach for him. She wound her fingers around his wrist and pulled his hand from his hair, stilling the rough outlet for his frustration. His muscles tensed beneath her touch, and she quickly pulled away from the heat of his skin that singed her fingertips. But she didn't back away from her support. "Garrett, you've been with the sheriff's department for twenty-some years. You're captain of your own division." Even without the badge on his chest and the extra bars on his collar, the man exuded wisdom and experience—and the ability to get the job done. "You'll figure it out."

"I don't want anyone taking advantage of that old woman out here by herself. Or you." He glanced back at Mrs. Gardner's place, where he'd parked his truck. "In fact, I brought the coffee as an excuse to get you to sit down and talk to me about Soren Hauck. He and a buddy of his skipped a couple of days of school this week."

"You don't have to bribe me to have a conversation." Jessica considered the teenager who worked for her two evenings a week and on Saturdays. She'd convinced him to pull his long reddish-brown hair back into a ponytail for safety reasons, but wished he'd trade his fancy high-top athletic shoes for a pair of solid work boots. But if he didn't mind getting them dirty, she couldn't really complain. "I don't know if I can tell you anything. I haven't had any issue with Soren not showing up for work. He's good with my dogs. But he's only part-time. I don't see him every day like I do his grandfather." Hugo Hauck had once farmed the land on the other side of Jessica's property. But now that his son—Soren's father—had taken over, the retired farmer had hired on as her part-time handyman, milking her female goat for her each morning and keeping the facilities running smoothly. "Hugo has worked for me since almost the beginning. He's the one who asked if I could take his grandson on part-time when he turned sixteen. Soren got his own car and needs gas money. Plus, whatever else teenage boys need."

Garrett nodded, probably expecting an answer like that. "I wish I could get Miss Eloise to take as much interest in Hugo Hauck as she does in me."

Jessica couldn't help the chuckle that escaped. "Matchmaking, Deputy Caldwell?"

"Trying to get her to focus on any other man besides me. Just because I'm single, it doesn't mean I'm available."

Not available? The most interesting man she'd met since her own husband had died was off the market? Jessica silently cursed the flash of disappointment she felt at his pronouncement. Garrett Caldwell was seasoned like a fine wine. He was fit and masculine, unafraid to take charge and be the boss. She'd learned to be strong and independent since her husband's murder twelve years earlier. And while she was compassionate and patient with clients and neighbors, she didn't suffer fools or cheats or charmers who had no substance to back up their clever words. Garrett Caldwell was all about substance. She might be attracted to a man who could go toe to toe with her, but that didn't mean she wanted to lay claim to one. She needed a friend more than she needed a lover. The county needed a deputy and protector more than she needed a mate. Still, that lonesome kernel of feminine longing that wished for the life she'd lost asked, "Are you seeing someone?"

Garrett held her gaze for several moments. But just when her lips parted to question the intensity of that stare, he answered. "No. But when I do get involved with a woman, it won't be Isla Gardner."

Why did that sound like a promise? And why did all that

unabashed male intensity focused on her make her breath stutter in her chest? Resolutely shaking off the little frissons of interest that made her uncomfortable with the personal turn to their conversation, Jessica brushed a strand of hair off her face and tucked it into the base of her ponytail at the back of her head. "Get things settled with Miss Eloise, while I finish up with my client." She thumbed over her shoulder as she backed toward the trees. "I'll meet you on my front porch in about twenty minutes."

He touched the brim of his cap and turned to the fence to pick up the gun. "It's a date."

His words made her realize that touching him and laughing with him and thinking about his sex life had blurred the line of friendship she wanted to keep between them. She needed to get back to her comfort zone. "Not a date, Garrett. We're two friends of a certain age who like to share a cup of morning coffee."

"A certain age?" He grunted at the terminology. "How old do you think I am?"

"Old enough to turn Miss Eloise's head, apparently," she teased. Because friends teased each other.

"You're only four years younger than me, Jessie. So, you watch who you're calling old," he taunted right back. "I think I've got a lot of good years left, even if you don't."

"You sure know how to flatter a girl."

Something snapped inside her head, and the present blurred into the past.

"You sure know how to flatter a girl." Jessica pouted and tugged her hand from her husband's. "I'm eight months pregnant with the seed you planted there, big fella. Saying

goodbye to me and my 'big baby belly' makes me sound like a beached whale."

John stopped in the foyer and turned, leaning in to press his lips against that pout. He kissed the tension from her mouth and kept kissing her until her fingers were curling into the lapels of his suit and she was stretching up on her toes to drink in the love and passion of his plundering lips.

When he ended the kiss and she sank back onto her heels, they were both slightly breathless. "What I meant to say was goodbye, my love. Have a good day at work. And..." He knelt in front of her, gently cradling her distended belly and pressing a kiss to the visible tremors they could see at the front of her dress where the baby was kicking. "Goodbye to the strong boy my lovely wife is carrying so beautifully for us."

Jessica cradled the back of John's head and smiled in utter contentment as he crooned love words to the infant she carried. "Much better, Counselor."

John was smiling as he picked up his briefcase and reached for the front door. "Remember to stay off your feet as much as you can today. You're in the office all day, right?" When she nodded, he pressed one last kiss to her lips. "I'll pick up some lunch for us when I'm done with this morning's hearings. Noon work for you?"

"Sounds perfect." He pulled the door open, and Jessica followed to catch it. "I'll see you..."

John had stopped. "What are you...?"

He shoved her back inside at the same time she saw the rumpled, wild-eyed man pointing a gun at John's head.

"You took everything from me! You lousy divorce lawyer!"

The explosion of the gunshot jolted through her.

Zeus heard the commotion and charged from the kitchen, barking a vicious warning.

Something warm and sticky splattered on her face. John crumpled to the porch.

Then the wild-eyed man's eyes met hers.

Run.

"Jessie!"

Strong hands clasped her shoulders and she startled, shaking off the unfamiliar touch.

"Easy. I've got you." A man's face swam in front of hers, and she put up her hands to ward him off. Until his green eyes came into focus, and she read the concern there.

John's eyes were blue.

The wild eyes were brown.

"Garrett?" She patted him on the chest, obliquely wondering why it was so hard. She breathed in deeply, silently cursing the cruel tricks her mind could play on her, even after all this time. "I'm okay." She took another breath, then another, pulling herself squarely back into the present. Then she felt a warm paw pressing against her thigh, and she collapsed to the ground to wrap her arms around Shadow's neck and bury her nose in his fur. "I'm okay. Mama's okay. You haven't had to do that for a while, have you, boy. Good Shadow."

"Good boy." Garrett went down on one knee in front of her, running his hand along Shadow's back, comforting the dog when Jessica wouldn't let him comfort her. "Where'd you go? I said your name three times."

"Sorry."

"Don't apologize." Garrett pulled back as she embraced her dog. "The flashbacks suck, don't they?"

"I haven't had one in a long time. But they're still there,

every now and then." She forced her nose out of Shadow's fur and looked at Garrett. "You have post-traumatic stress, too?"

"I wasn't a choirboy in the Army." His face creased with a wry smile that never reached his eyes. "A good ol' country boy like me who grew up hunting? I was a sniper."

Jessica's stomach clenched, imagining the violence he must have dealt with fighting a war. "I'm sorry, Garrett. You must have seen some awful things. Done some things you aren't even allowed to talk about."

"It was a while ago. I've talked to a therapist. The military is getting better about helping their soldiers cope with what we have to deal with." He threaded his fingers into Shadow's fur again, and the dog lay down, now panting contentedly between them. "What about you?"

"Talk to a therapist?" She nodded. "She was the one who recommended I get a dog ten years ago. So, I wouldn't be alone on the nights I couldn't sleep, when the memories tried to take over."

"Shadow's your lifeline," Garrett speculated.

She smiled at her beloved companion. "I didn't initially train him to put his paw on me to wake me up or pull me back to the present. But he was a natural. Dogs are so empathetic. They pick up on emotions—happiness, excitement, anger, distress."

"And your success with Shadow inspired you to start K-9 Ranch—to rescue dogs and help others who need a friend."

Jessica could feel her heart rate slowing down, the nightmare receding and her thoughts clearing. Part of her recovery was due to Shadow's warmth and support, but she suspected part of her ability to breathe more easily was due to Garrett's calm, deep-pitched voice and the quiet conversation they were sharing. "Gave me a purpose. A reason to stop grieving around the clock and get up in the morning."

"Do you know what set it off this time?" he asked.

Uh-uh. Now that she had the nightmare under control, she wasn't dredging it up again. How did she explain the perfect storm of Eloise's gun, the feelings for Garrett she refused to acknowledge, and the innocent phrase that had been some of the last words she'd spoken to her husband, anyway? Jessica pushed to her feet. "You'd better go. I don't want Eloise on my front step like Almira Gulch with a basket trying to take Toto away from Dorothy."

Garrett straightened as well, his shoulders blocking the morning sun, he was standing so close. "Are you all right? Should I call someone?"

"There's no one to call." Shadow stood beside her, leaning against her leg so that she could continue to stroke the warmth of his head "I have everything I need right here."

"You can call *me*. Anytime."

"You're not on duty 24/7."

He reached down to scratch around Shadow's ears, but angled his gaze up to hers. "No. But I am your friend 24/7. Call whenever you need me."

Jessica covered his hand where it rested on Shadow's shoulder. "Only if you promise to do the same. Like when you pull an all-nighter and need a break from interviewing victims and suspects, and analyzing crime scenes." She quickly stepped away the moment she felt her body's desire to move *toward* him. "I need to get back to my client, Mollie. Right now, she's afraid of everything and everybody. Including the dog she wants to adopt."

Garrett inhaled a deep breath, his posture and tone shifting into deputy mode. “Afraid? Anything I need to know about?”

Like he needed to take one more burden onto his broad shoulders this morning. Besides, she truly hadn’t seen any evidence of a threat to Mollie beyond the woman’s own skittish behavior. Jessica shrugged. “She drives out from Kansas City. Divorced from an abusive ex. As far as I know, she dumped him and she’s trying to move on with her life.”

“Does her situation trigger you?”

“No. My husband was never violent with me. John was a good man.”

“She have a restraining order out on him?”

Jessica nodded. “Mollie showed me his picture. But I’ve never seen him in person. If I find out anything that’s concerning, I’ll let you know. Otherwise, I want her to trust in me. And in Magnus.”

“The deaf dog?”

She was much more comfortable talking about work. “Only in one ear. He makes up for it with the other. And killer eyesight. I’m teaching them to rely on hand signals more than verbal commands. But it’s a process.”

Garrett crossed back to the fence to retrieve the empty shotgun. “Maybe I will run prints on this fence and the chicken coop, see if I can get a match to the break-in at the Russells’ cabin. Just to rule out a trespasser who might be following your client. Let me know if whoever is scaring her shows up out here. Lock yourself and Mollie in the house with the dogs if you see her ex. Stay away from the windows and call me.”

“I will.”

He glanced back across the fence. “Wish me luck. If Isla is there already, I may be calling for backup.”

Jessica appreciated that he could make her laugh, especially after her mini meltdown. She suspected the man could handle himself in any situation. But he was too much of a gentleman to be downright cruel to her needy neighbor. “Good luck. Figure out your mystery. Then bring me my caramelly coffee, and we’ll talk more about Soren.”

He paused with one hand on the fence’s top railing. “You’re sure you’re okay?”

“I will be.”

He touched the brim of his cap, then vaulted over the fence again.

Jessica watched him stride away. The man had a nice ass to go along with those broad shoulders. And he always got her coffee order right when he stopped by the ranch.

She could see why the Gardner ladies had the hots for him.

And why she had to keep her guard up around his take-charge strength and surprisingly gentle compassion. She couldn’t do a relationship again. Not even with a good man like Garrett. She’d had love. She’d been growing her family. She’d planned a future. And every last bit of it had been violently taken from her.

She was a survivor.

She could live her life. Be useful. Find joy and a purpose with her dogs.

But she wasn’t strong enough to love and lose again.

Chapter Three

"Come on, Shadow." Jessica patted the rangy dog's flank and headed through the trees back to the house.

She needed to think about why the flashback had hit her in the middle of her conversation with Garrett. She'd been doing so well for such a long time that it was disconcerting to find out how her mind could unexpectedly and painfully snap her back to the past. She was supposed to be fine on her own. She *was* fine on her own. She had coping skills that should have defused the waking nightmare long before it sucked her in. Instead, she'd been blindsided by the memories, and now she felt raw and vulnerable.

And worse, Garrett, a man she called her friend and whom she admired, had seen her lose it.

She needed to clear her head and focus on something else, so that she could look at the situation objectively and come up with a plan to identify the trigger and neutralize its effect on her. She thought she'd gotten past the sight of a gun triggering her PTSD, and certainly, once Garrett confirmed the shotgun wasn't loaded, she hadn't viewed Eloise as a threat. An annoyance, maybe—someone she worried about—but not a threat. And, of course, she'd uttered the same phrase to

Garrett that she had to John all those years ago, just before his client's ex had ended his life. There had to be something more working on her. Was there something pricking at her subconscious? Some detail in her life that her eyes missed, but her mind was subtly aware of? Was there something about her world she wasn't able to control? It had been a few years since she'd had regular sessions with her therapist. Maybe it was time to give her a call to do a follow-up wellness check, just to make sure she wasn't regressing.

With that much of a plan in mind, she crossed the driveway that led up to the house. Walking past the kennels and training corral, Jessica petted the dogs who ran up to her, looking for Mollie and Magnus. "Mollie?"

Soren was at school—at least he should be—and Hugo would have already shooed the goats out into their pasture and was probably running errands since she didn't see his truck parked in its usual spot beside the barn. Maybe she should offer Hugo's services to Eloise. See if her neighbors could distract each other long enough to get them out of Garrett's hair and create a peaceful coexistence for her, as well. She'd offer to pay him to repair Eloise's fence and chicken coop.

"Jessica?" The dark-haired woman hurried out of the barn. Magnus jogged along beside her, a faded red KONG wedged squarely in his jaw. Good. Mollie had taken her advice and had been playing with her dog. "I didn't know whether to come and find you or wait until you got back."

"Why?" Worried that the young woman's flushed cheeks meant something more than running around in the fresh air with her dog, she reached out and squeezed Mollie's hand. "Is something wrong?"

Mollie tugged her into step beside her. "I think you've had a break-in."

"What?" Three properties in a row that had all had some kind of trespasser? What was going on around here? "Show me."

Jessica moved ahead of Mollie into the cooler air of the barn. Other than the goats, who stayed inside each night, and a box secluded in a stall where an Australian shepherd stray had given birth to a litter of mixed-breed puppies a few weeks ago, the barn was used for storage and a sheltered training facility when the weather outside wasn't ideal. Under her direction, Hugo and his grandson had enclosed two of the stalls and added a concrete floor to secure Hugo's tools and have a place to store the donations of food and supplies she often received.

The Australian shepherd raised her head when the women walked past with Shadow and Magnus. "Hey, mama. You okay?" Some of the straw in their stall had been squashed, though that could just have been Hugo taking in fresh food and water for the dog. A quick check showed they were all safe. The pups were either nursing or sleeping. "Good girl."

Walking to the far end of the barn, Jessica could see the damage that had been done. The door to the first storage room was shut tight, with the padlock secured through the latch. But the door to the second storage room stood slightly ajar. The padlock was still secured through its steel loop. But the hinge that secured the latch to the doorframe was bent and hanging by a single screw, and there were gouges in the wood around the lock, as if someone had taken a rock or hammer to it when they couldn't get the padlock open.

"It was like this when you came in?" Jessica asked.

"Not exactly," Mollie answered. "I unlocked this room to get Magnus's toy." She touched the first door. "But as soon as he realized this was where his KONG was stored, he got excited. He jumped up and scratched at the wood. He must have jostled the frame. The latch fell off, and the door drifted open. Then I saw the mess inside."

"It looks as though someone tried to make it look like it hadn't been disturbed. But he lacked either the tools or the time to do so."

"I didn't touch anything. I know the police don't like it when you do. In case you want to report it." Mollie pointed to the barn's open archway. "I took Magnus outside to play so that he wouldn't accidentally do more damage and waited for you to take a look at it."

"Good thinking." Jessica put the dogs into a stay and told Mollie to keep hold of Magnus's leash. Then she pulled her sleeve down over her fingers and nudged the door open.

A creepy sense of violation ran its chilly fingers down her spine as she surveyed the room. Everything was askew on one of the metal shelves inside, as if some critter had run along the back and knocked things out of place. A glass mason jar where she stored treats lay shattered on the floor. And while she was certain it had been full, most of the treats were gone. She spotted a torn bag of dog food with kibble spilling out. Old blankets that had once been neatly stacked were now piled haphazardly on the floor. There was a depression in the middle, as though the careless critter had made a nest there. And one of the blankets—probably the oldest and rattiest one of all—was missing. Who would steal a holey blanket but leave the old radio/CD player on the worktable untouched? She supposed a possum or rat could have gotten in by crawling through a gap in the siding below the barn's outer wall. It wouldn't be the first time a wild animal had helped itself to her supply of dog food. A raccoon would have the dexterity to pad its nest with the blankets, but that explanation didn't quite make sense, either.

Jessica made several quick mental notes of all that was damaged or missing before backing out. She shooed the curious dogs away from the door and reached for the cell phone in her back pocket. She bypassed calling 9-1-1 and pulled up the number of the man she knew was already working the case.

Jessica hated to dump anything more on Garrett Caldwell's plate today. But she had a feeling he'd want to know that her place had been included in his weird crime spree.

First, a busted fence abutting her land, and now a broken hinge and a ransacked storage room? Someone seemed to be making their way through all the properties south of 40 Highway, heading east out of the city. There was definitely a spate of petty crimes moving through the county. Although, unless she counted the chicken, there was no murder, assault or other violent crime. Was Garrett right? Maybe Soren and his truant friend had been messing around last night. Could all these little incidents be indicative of something sinister going on? Were they a prelude to something more threatening about to happen?

"Deputy Caldwell." Even as she felt guilty about reporting yet another incident of vandalism, Jessica warmed to the sound of his voice, and the wary trepidation she felt eased to a manageable level. He must have recognized her number or name on his phone. "Jessie?"

"Are you still coming over?"

"I'm headed to my truck now."

"Good. I have something to show you."

She heard his weary sigh. "Why don't I think that means you baked a batch of your peanut butter cookies to go with our coffee?"

"Sorry. Your mystery just expanded into my barn."

His powerful truck engine roared to life in the background. "I'm on my way."

Jessica tucked her phone back into her pocket. She wanted these break-ins solved, too, now that it had come to her K-9 Ranch. Even without Garrett's instincts and experience to suggest it, she had a feeling there was something bigger and more threatening lurking in the fringes of her world.

Twelve years ago, she hadn't known just how dangerous the world could be. Now she couldn't help but think the worst.

She wanted to believe that whatever had gotten into the storage room and made that little nest wasn't human.

But only a human would need to break the lock to get inside.

GARRETT HAD NEVER been so glad to get a phone call reporting a break-in in his whole career. Jessie's message was the excuse he needed to finally extricate himself from Eloise Gardner's machinations and enlist one of his officers to take over for him at the Gardner farm.

Eloise had indeed forgotten her heart medications that morning, so he'd sat at the kitchen table with her and watched her take the pills and check her blood pressure before jotting down notes about her morning. A quick inspection of her chicken coop revealed that nothing had chewed through anything. Yes, the gate to the yard had been forced open, and there was evidence that the chickens had scattered, then been chased back in—minus Doris, of course.

But the gate had been tied shut with a chunk of faded red yarn. Garrett knew Jessie had trained her dogs to do a number of amazing things. But not one of them had grown opposable thumbs and the ability to tie a knot.

Isla seemed to have forgotten the grocery list Eloise had given her, and when Eloise told him she'd given Isla her debit card to purchase the groceries, Garrett had immediately called to make sure she wasn't spending her grandmother's money on clothes or partying or her latest boyfriend. His instincts had proved to be sadly accurate when he heard a man's voice yelling at Isla to get off the phone and get her butt out of the car to get the cash they needed from the ATM. Not that the conversation he'd overheard was proof enough to stand up in court—maybe they were using cash for the groceries. But it was reason enough to dispatch a second officer to the bank to get a better idea of what might be going on. At least, he could get a possible ID on the shady boyfriend. Taking advantage of an elderly citizen was one of Garrett's pet peeves, and something he was always willing to investigate.

But he had a bigger case he needed to focus on right now. And he could guarantee that Officer Maya Hernandez wouldn't have to fend off Eloise's repeated attempts to get a man to stay for dinner and married off to her granddaughter.

Plus, he was worried by Jessie's news that something odd had happened at her place, too, last night.

Garrett dashed out to his truck and started the engine. He barely resisted turning on the lights and siren. He raised his hand in a quick wave to Officer Hernandez as he barreled past her down Eloise's gravel drive.

Jessie needed him. And, even if it was just the badge she needed right now, that spoke to every protective male instinct in him. That was the problem. Jessie Bennington was stubborn and independent in a way his Hayley had never been. In the years since they'd met over a call to round up a stray that had gotten trapped in a condemned building, he'd learned that Jessie was smart and funny and caring. But the moment things seemed to get too personal, she threw up walls and attitude as if she had something raw and vulnerable inside that she needed to protect.

The hell of it was that, after witnessing her panic attack this morning, he suspected she was protecting herself from something horrific. He wanted in behind those walls so that he could help keep her safe from whatever that horror might be.

Garrett understood that she didn't want to be taken care of. His late wife, Hayley, had been sick with cancer on and off for so long that it had become second nature to be more caretaker and companion than equal partner or certainly lover. It had been his honor and duty to leave the Army and be there for the woman who had owned his heart since they'd been high school sweethearts. But it had also been emotionally exhausting. He'd grieved, thrown himself into his work, first on the department's special teams unit, and then as a senior deputy. Eventually he'd been ready to move on, had given dating a few tries, and run into more Isla Gardners than anyone he'd actually consider diving into a long-term relationship with.

Then Jessica Bennington inherited her grandparents' farm and had become part of his world.

Jessie had shown him how attractive a different kind of woman could be. Mature sensibilities. Strong. Driven. Funny. Sexy without even trying with that long gorgeous silvery-blond hair and trim figure. He wanted to mean something to her. She might not need or want a caretaker, but she could certainly use a partner, couldn't she? Yet, waiting for her to reach the same decision he had already reached required the patience of a saint. Garrett liked to think of himself as one of the good guys, but he was no saint.

Whether or not she ever decided to give him a shot, or clung tightly to her friends-only rule, he'd worry about her anyway. He knew a little about her past—her husband had been killed in a home invasion, and she'd been wounded. Certainly, that was trauma enough to stick with anyone. But he hadn't witnessed her have a flashback before. The sheer terror in her pale features had made him want to wrap her up in his arms and carry her far away from whatever nightmare had seized her.

If whatever she wanted him to see on her property had triggered even an nth of the fear he'd witnessed this morning, he was going to go alpha male on somebody's ass. And probably pay the price when Jessie told him to back off and do his job—that she didn't need or want a protector to rescue her.

Caring about Jessie Bennington was an exercise in patience and frustration.

Deep breaths, Caldwell. He mentally calmed himself the same way he had before making a kill shot or taking down a perp like he had during his years as a sniper. Tamping down his emotions and slipping on the mantle of Deputy Garrett Caldwell, he slowed his truck and rolled up to Jessie's house without spitting up too much gravel.

Jessie waved to him from the barn, and he climbed down from his truck and strode toward her and the woman with curly dark hair standing beside her. The younger woman had a white-knuckled grip around the leash hooked up to the Belgian Malinois sitting beside her.

Garrett shortened his stride and slowed his pace. Jessie's client must have a thing about men in uniform—or men, period. He recognized the nervous look of an abused woman and wondered who had put that wariness in her eyes. She was another rescue project of Jessie's, no doubt. He did what he could to help ease the young woman's anxiety by moving closer to Jessie and taking off his cap to make a polite introduction. He scrubbed his fingers through his spiky hair, suspecting he was making more of a mess rather than straightening his appearance. "Jessie." She nodded in greeting. "You've had a break-in here, too?"

"Mollie discovered it. She volunteered to stay in case you have any questions for her." That had been a big ask, judging by the woman's reluctance to make eye contact with him. "This is Garrett Caldwell. Mollie Crane," she introduced. "He's a friend as well as a captain in the sheriff's department. You can trust him. I do."

Friend. Trust.

He was grateful for Jessie's words and vowed to make sure he lived up to that faith in him. Anything else between them could come later—if she ever gave him the chance. Garrett extended his hand. "Ms. Crane. Nice to meet you. Sorry it's under these circumstances."

Slowly, the woman brought her hand up to lightly grasp his. "Nice to meet you, Deputy Caldwell."

Garrett smiled and quickly released her hand. "You want to show me what you found?"

"Magnus. Heel." Mollie tugged the flop-eared dog to his feet and led them into the barn. Garrett couldn't help but notice that she kept one hand on the dog's short fur, just like he'd often seen Jessie reach for Shadow. The dog was an anchor. A comfort. Something to focus on besides whatever trauma she was dealing with inside her head.

What Mollie Crane lacked in confidence, she more than made up for with impeccable manners and an eye for detail. Thirty minutes later, she and Magnus were driving back to Kansas City, and Garrett had a thorough report from the two women, detailing the mess in the storage room and the suspected items that were missing, including a blanket, kibble, and some dog treats.

Not exactly a million-dollar crime spree. But something weird was going on in his part of Jackson County.

By the time Garrett had snapped a few pictures with his phone, Hugo Hauck had returned, and between the three of them, they got the storage area cleaned up and had reattached the hinge, so that the door would close. While they worked, Garrett asked Hugo a few casual questions about Soren. The old man praised his grandson for his affinity in working with the dogs, but he also complained that the teen had made some new friends, and Hugo caught them drinking beer out in one of the pastures one night. He even went so far as to say that he'd smelled pot on the boy's clothing, and that his parents had laid down the law about taking away his car and other privileges if he went any further down that road.

Garrett wanted to talk to Soren himself, get a feeling if the disciplinary consequences had been enough to scare him away from his experimental behavior—or if he and his friends had simply gone underground and gotten sneakier about their vices. Maybe by breaking into a deserted cabin to party? Or engaging in other criminal mischief while under the influence of drugs or alcohol?

It was after twelve by the time Hugo left to go home and Garrett walked Jessie back to her house. Shadow ambled up the porch steps ahead of them and curled up on the cushions of the teakwood bench near the front door.

"I'm afraid your coffee is another casualty of this morning's events. It's ice-cold by now," he apologized. He stopped on the sidewalk as Jessie climbed the front steps, ostensibly because he needed to get back to the office to type up his reports and check in on his staff—but also because he enjoyed watching Jessie's backside in the worn, fitted jeans that hugged her curves. He was due one good thing today, wasn't he? He'd had a hell of a long shift since reporting for duty yesterday morning and working through the night. He wasn't being pervy about it. Just taking note of something that gave him pleasure, and then he'd be on his way. "I need to get preliminary reports written up on all these incidents. Maybe I'll find a thread that connects them. Then, hopefully, I can take off early and get a decent night's sleep tonight." Possibly feeling ignored that he'd mentioned shut-eye instead of a meal, his stomach grumbled loudly enough that Shadow raised his head at the noise. He chuckled as he patted his flat belly. "And possibly eat."

"Possibly?" Jessie turned on the porch with an inscrutable grin on her face. She crossed her arms and studied him for several moments before she spoke. "Do you have plans for lunch?"

"You doing okay?" He frowned at the unexpected invitation. Was she worried about staying alone at the ranch after her break-in? "Need me to stay?"

She came down two steps to meet him at eye level. "Are *you* doing okay? When was the last time you ate or slept?"

"I grabbed a Danish when I got our coffee."

Garrett wasn't exactly sure what career she had before investing her time and money into K-9 Ranch, but he suspected it was something like corporate raider or drill sergeant, based on the stern look she gave him. "When was the last time you ate anything that had vitamins and nutrients in it?"

"I'm not one of your dogs. You don't have to feed me or pat me on the head. I'm a grown man and can take care of myself."

"Well, you're doing a piss-poor job of it this morning from the look of things. You haven't shaved." She reached out and brushed a fingertip across his jaw, and he nearly flinched as every nerve impulse in his body seemed to wake up and rush to that single point of contact. "Not that the scruffy look doesn't work on you. But I know you take pride in looking professional. You're surviving on caffeine and sugar. And the lines beside your eyes are etched more deeply when you're tired like this. I've got plenty of leftovers I can heat up, or I can fix you soup and a sandwich."

Ignoring his body's disappointment at how abrupt her touch had been, he eyed her skeptically. He was attracted to her, yes, but he cared about her well-being even more. "Does this have anything to do with what happened earlier this morning?"

"You mean my little freak-out?"

He liked that she didn't play dumb by pretending he was talking about anything other than that panic attack she'd had. "Are you trying to show me that nothing's wrong? That you're strong enough to take care of everyone else, from Mollie to

Miss Eloise to me?" He zeroed in on those dove gray eyes. "When you should be taking care of yourself?"

Her chin came up, even as she hugged her arms around herself again. Yep, this woman wore invisible armor the same way he strapped on his flak vest every morning. "I'll admit that staying busy provides a distraction for me. But to quote a certain deputy—I'm *your* friend, too. 24/7. Feeding you lunch on a busy day is something friends do for each other. Besides, if you don't take care of yourself, you won't be any good to anybody. And we need you."

"We?"

"Jackson County. Your officers and staff. The Russells. Miss Eloise." Her arms shifted and tightened. "Me."

Hearing her admit that she needed him, even so reluctantly, sparked a tiny candle of hope inside him. Some of the fatigue in him eased at the idea of spending time doing something that didn't require his badge and his gun for a while. And there was a definite appeal to spending that time with Jessie. "All right. A friendly lunch sounds nice. Talking about something other than work for thirty or forty minutes sounds even nicer." A breeze picked up a wavy tendril of hair that had fallen over her cheek, and he fought the urge to catch it between his fingers and smooth it back behind her ear. When she smiled at his response, she lit up like sunshine and vibrated with an energy that touched something hard and remote inside him and reminded certain parts of his anatomy that he was far from being over the hill. "Let me call in to my staff that I'm off the clock for thirty minutes or so, then I'll come inside and wash up."

"Let yourself in when you're ready. I'll be in the kitchen getting things heated up."

Heated up? Yep. The parts were definitely working. She was talking food, and his hormones kicked in as if she was coming on to him.

Before he could embarrass himself, or her, with the interest stirring behind his zipper, Garrett tapped the radio strapped to his shoulder and called in a Code 7, indicating he was taking a break from service to eat. He got a quick status report from his office manager, made note of a couple of items to follow up on and more tasks that he could delegate to officers on staff. Talking business generally dampened any sex drive and put him in the right frame of mind to share lunch with Jessie without spooking her.

"Jessie?" Shadow greeted him at the door when he stepped inside, seeming much happier to see him now than when he'd been holding Eloise's shotgun.

"Back here. Lock the door behind you, please."

"Will do." Garrett removed his hat and hung it on a peg on the hall tree beside the stairs that led to the rooms on the second floor. Respecting her need for security, he turned the dead bolt in the front door before following Shadow through the front hallway that ran all the way back to the kitchen. He hung back in the archway of her homey gray and white kitchen, which was filled with both antiques and modern stainless steel appliances. He watched her set out bowls and pull a foil-wrapped loaf of something out of the oven. The enticing smells of whatever she was heating in the microwave made his stomach grumble again.

Jessie laughed and nodded toward the refrigerator. "There's sun tea in there. Or you can pour yourself a glass of milk or grab a bottle of water."

"May I get you a drink?"

"Tea, please. Hey, would you refill Shadow's water bowl? Last night, he left my room for a late-night snack, and I guess he knocked his feeding stand over in the dark." She smiled over at the long-haired shepherd mix who was walking in circles to find just the right spot to lie down on what Garrett suspected was one of several beds around the house. "Just toss that wet towel in the laundry room. Then sit and relax."

Jessie sliced corn bread and ladled up bowls of stew while Garrett completed his assignments. He felt himself relaxing at the normalcy of working together to complete domestic tasks. He'd been gone a lot in the early days of his marriage with training and deployments, while Hayley had run the house and taught kindergarten. But once he'd chaptered out of the Army to be with Haley those last two years, one of his favorite things was simply spending time with her—doing small jobs like these around the house while she supervised. Or sharing the work when she was strong enough to help. This felt a little like that, only different because Jessie was less fragile, and certainly more bossy than Haley had been. This felt almost date-like because they were spending some quality time together that had nothing to do with work. She trusted him enough to invite him into her space, to let him get acquainted with her routine. This time meant everything to him because he knew better than to take any moment for granted when it came to being with someone he cared about.

He reached for the faucet on the sink and his shoulder accidentally brushed against hers. When Jessie scuttled away from the unexpected contact, Garrett frowned and purposely moved some space between them.

That subtle revelation of discomfort beneath Jessie's welcoming facade erased his pensive smile and reminded him that this was neither a date nor domestic bliss, and that she seemed almost desperate to keep him at arm's length even though she was the one who'd invited him here. He circled around the kitchen island instead of taking the shorter route to Shadow's bed and feeding stand and set the water bowl on its rack.

He waited while she carried their plates to the antique oak farm table, keeping the width of one of the ladder back chairs between them. "Maybe while we're eating, you could explain a little bit about your flashback this morning."

She swung her gaze up to his. "Garrett—"

"I don't want to be the thing that triggers you. Whether it's the gun or my size or my gender, I want to know so I can avoid making things worse for you."

She reached across the chair to touch his forearm, her fingers sliding against the eagle inked there. So, she wasn't averse to touching him. But she wanted to control how it happened. Her skin warmed his, and his nerve endings woke with eager possibilities again. Still holding his gaze with a wry smile, she pressed her fingertips into the muscle there. "You don't make things worse for me. And I'd never want you to stop being the man you are." With one final squeeze, she released him and pulled out the chair opposite his. "To be honest, I'm not sure what set me off this morning. Probably a combination of things. Or something subconscious that I'm not aware of. If you don't mind, I wouldn't mind talking it through with someone."

"I don't mind." He pushed in her chair for her before taking his seat.

A few minutes later, he was digging into a bowl of fragrant, hearty beef stew and a slice of corn bread slathered in butter and honey. He let her eat a healthy portion of her meal before he pushed her to share some of her story with him. "I know you've been a victim of violence. You told me your husband was shot and killed."

"Wow. When I said I wanted to talk, you jumped right to the heart of the matter."

"We can talk about the weather or the prospects for Royals baseball this year, if you prefer."

"No." Jessie set her spoon on her plate and pushed the rest of her lunch away. "John was killed by the ex-husband of one of his clients. Lee Palmer didn't like the divorce settlement John negotiated. I think he blamed John for the whole divorce going through. When John saw what was happening, he pushed me away, right before Palmer shot him in the head."

Garrett made a mental note to look up Lee Palmer and make sure the man was sitting on death row for murdering an officer of the court. He kept his voice gentle, trying not to sound like a county deputy pushing for answers. "Did something about Miss Eloise or this rash of petty crimes trigger a flashback?"

"I don't think so. I mean, I wasn't thrilled that she was pointing a gun at us." Her gaze drifted over to the bed where Shadow was snoring. "Palmer killed our dog that day, too."

Garrett polished off the last of his corn bread, waiting for her to continue.

"Zeus, our dog at the time, went after that guy with a vengeance after Palmer shot John. He attacked him and held him at bay long enough so I could get away." He hated the clinical way she was reciting the facts, and suspected that was yet another way she coped with the trauma of that day. "I locked myself in the bathroom, called 9-1-1—although neighbors had also reported the shooting and the police were already on their way. That bastard shot him. Zeus gave his life so that I could live."

"That explains your need to rescue all of these dogs. They're like your children. You raise them well. You train them to do what your Zeus did if necessary. Make sure they all have good homes and a purpose. It's a noble way to honor his sacrifice." He leaned back against his chair, keeping the hand that had curled into a fist at her story hidden beneath the table. "Eloise pointed a gun at your dogs."

"I didn't panic when Eloise had the gun."

"You panicked when *I* had it. Shadow growled at me. *I* was a bigger threat."

She shook her head. Then she pushed to her feet and carried their plates and bowls to the sink, obviously needing a break from the heavy topic. "You always carry a gun. I'm not sure that's it, either."

As much as he wanted to believe she wasn't afraid of him, even subconsciously, he had to make sure. "What did the shooter look like?"

"Nothing like you. Shorter. Younger. Beer belly. Desperately needed a shower." He could see her dredge up the memory. She grasped the edge of the sink and squeezed her eyes shut against it. "Wild brown eyes."

Garrett beat back the urge to go to her, to take her in his arms and offer comfort. But she'd asked for a sounding board, someone to talk to, someone to help her figure this out. He was the guy who solved mysteries. That's who she needed right now. And he'd be damned if he'd be anything else but exactly what she needed.

"He was a man." Garrett suggested another possibility. "Any man threatening you could be a trigger."

"No." She came back and sat in the chair right beside him. "The guns don't help. The dogs protecting me could be part of it. But I think…my emotions…" Her eyes lost their focus. "In my head, I was losing everything that mattered all over again."

"What mattered? You lost your husband to violence. Zeus."

She pulled her hands from the tabletop and splayed her fingers over her stomach, as if she was caressing something precious. "I was eight months pregnant when I was shot. I lost the baby, our little boy. He was my last link to John, and… The damage was too severe. The surgeon removed my uterus, tubes, and ovaries. I lost the ability to ever have children."

He bit back his curse at the injustice of this woman being denied the child she clearly had wanted. "I don't remind you of a baby, do I?"

Her gaze snapped up to his. "Of course not."

"Do I look like your husband?" He wasn't doing a very good job of keeping the edge out of his tone. He understood violence and loss. He'd taken lives and buried loved ones. The injustice of all Jessie had suffered ate away his ability to be the impartial sounding board she'd asked for.

"John had dark hair, too. But he had more of a runner's build. Wore a suit and tie to work. You're…beefy. More…" She shook her head. "Not really."

"What was different this morning?" he pressed. "What mattered that you thought you were going to lose?"

Jessie considered his question, studied him intently. He thought he saw a glimmer of understanding darken her eyes. Then shock quickly took its place. Oh, hell. The resolve that was guarded and cautious and willing to wait for this woman crumbled into dust as he processed all she wasn't saying.

Eloise had pointed the gun at *him*, too.

"Me? Did you think you were going to lose *me*?"

She never answered because Shadow's feeding stand slammed into the end of the cabinet. "What the…?" A muffled whimpering noise and clear thumping against the cabinet pushed Jessie to her feet. Garrett followed her to the dog's bed near the back door to discover Shadow lying on his side with his legs stretched out and twitching as if he was trying to swim. "Is he having a dream? Shadow!" Jessie dropped to her knees, her hands hovering above her beloved pet as if she wasn't sure how or if she should touch him. "What's wrong?"

Garrett knelt beside her and took in the dog's drooling and small, but rapid, head movements. "Looks like he's having a seizure." Jessie placed her hand gently on the dog's flank. The fact that he didn't startle and wake to her touch confirmed his suspicion. "Has he seized before?"

"No. Is this what happened last night? I don't understand."

He'd had enough training as a medic to start asking questions. "Who's your vet?"

"Hazel Cooper-Burke."

"In KC?"

Jessie nodded without looking up. She was trying to pet the dog, but he kept jerking beneath her hands. "He's hot to the touch. I don't know what to do."

Garrett clasped her by the shoulders and pulled her to her feet. "Call Dr. Coop." Now that she'd been given a task, she nodded and pulled her phone from her jeans. Meanwhile, Garrett scooped up the shaking dog and carried him out to his truck, bed and all. Jessie grabbed her purse and followed right on his heels. "Jedediah Burke's wife?" he clarified. "I know Sergeant Burke through the KCPD K-9 unit." He nodded toward the crew cab's back door handle and Jessie pulled it open. He gently laid the large dog on the seat and scooted him over to make room for a passenger. "Get in the back. She's in a new building after that bomb took out the old one. I know where I'm going."

"I will. Thanks, Hazel. We're on our way." Jessie ended the call and juggled the items in her hands to put them away. "She says to bring him right in. It could last anywhere from thirty seconds to five minutes. It's been more than thirty seconds, hasn't it? I'm supposed to time it. She asked if he had a head injury? If he'd been hit by a car? Has he eaten anything he shouldn't? Caffeine? Chocolate? He's been with me all morning. I don't know what—"

Garrett tagged her behind the neck to stop her panicking and help her focus. His palm fit perfectly against the nape of her neck. He tunneled his fingers beneath the base of her ponytail and loosened some of the silky waves of hair, willing her to catch her breath. "Get in the back and buckle up. Comfort him. I'll get you there as fast as I can."

Jessie's gaze locked on to his. She wound her fingers around his wrist and squeezed her understanding. "Thank you for being here with me."

He leaned in and pressed a kiss to her forehead. "Nowhere else I'd rather be. Get in."

Once he closed the door behind her, Garrett climbed in behind the wheel, turned on the lights and siren, and raced toward the highway.

Chapter Four

"Idiopathic epilepsy?" Jessica stroked her fingers through Shadow's fur while Dr. Hazel Cooper-Burke finished a routine examination on the dog on the metal exam table between them. "What's that?"

Shadow lay there like the Sphinx, his head up, his tongue out and gently panting, his demeanor as relaxed as any other visit to the vet's office these past ten years. Other than a few pokes of a needle, he liked the staff here and knew there would be a treat for him at the end of the visit. His present behavior seemed so normal that Jessica found it heartbreaking to think how out of it he'd been at the house almost an hour earlier. Despite Garrett leaning against the wall behind her and Hazel being a good friend, she was reluctant to break contact with the dog who meant so much to her.

Dr. Cooper-Burke finished her exam and ruffled the fur around Shadow's ears and muzzle. "Good boy." Shadow ate up the attention before demolishing the treat Hazel rewarded him with. "Basically, it means we don't know what's causing it. With Shadow's age, we know it's not genetic epilepsy—he would have shown the symptoms long before now. I see no signs of a head injury or heat stroke. It could be a brain tumor. Something in his diet. It could be aging and cognitive decline."

Jessica frowned, frustrated that the vet couldn't give her a definitive answer. "Shadow's as smart and alert as he ever was. And nothing has changed in his diet, although, it's possible he could have gotten into something he shouldn't."

Garrett pushed away from the wall and came to stand beside her. "You think someone poisoned him?"

Jessica glanced up, sharing her explanation with both friends. "Not everyone is a fan of my dogs. Even though it's private property, I'm certified, and it's a completely licensed and vetted business."

"I'm guessing if it was intentional poisoning, he'd have vomiting or diarrhea. And he seems perfectly fine now. Plus, you might have other dogs showing symptoms." Hazel reached across Shadow's back to squeeze her hand. "Jessica, it could be as simple and heartbreaking as an end-of-life thing. A dog his size and age..."

"Shadow's dying?" The question came out almost a sob, although she already felt cried out after the fast drive into the city to the vet clinic. She immediately felt Garrett's hand at her back, its warmth seeping into her skin and short-circuiting the impulse to break down again. "There's nothing you can do?"

Hazel hastened to reassure her. "Eleven years old for a dog his size is pretty advanced. And I'm guessing life wasn't kind to him before you took him in. Look at all the gray in his muzzle. Sadly, it's the natural progression of things."

"I know." Understanding the situation logically didn't feel like much of a balm to her psyche. She pressed against Garrett's hand, reining in any pending sense of loss and kept it together so that she could understand all the necessary facts. "What does this mean for Shadow? What should I expect?"

"I can treat the symptoms. Idiopathic epilepsy isn't going to kill him, and he doesn't feel any pain while he's seizing. But it's a neurological disorder that can come with aging. It's all about his quality of life now. As long as he'll take the diazepam pill with a bite of cheese or a dog treat when he starts to seize, we'll go that route. If swallowing becomes an issue, the seizures become frequent or last longer than a few minutes, we'll switch to a larger dose through a suppository." She turned away to get the prescription bottle her vet tech had set on the counter and handed it to Jessica. "You're okay giving him the pill?"

"Of course. I have other dogs who get medications."

Hazel smiled. "I never worry about a Jess Bennington dog because I know you'll take good care of him. Let's follow up to see how things are going in another month, okay? He may not have a seizure between now and then, but if he does, give him the pill and be sure to time the length of it, then give me a call."

"I will."

"Any questions?"

Jessica leaned over to kiss the top of Shadow's head. "If this is an end-of-life thing, how long does Shadow have?"

"He's in good health, otherwise. Possibly a year. Maybe a little more or less."

Jessica wasn't quite ready to process what that meant. Shadow had brought her out of the depths of her grief and anger. He'd given her someone to love, something to trust without fail. He'd inspired the idea of K-9 Ranch, given this new version of her life a purpose. She couldn't picture what life without him would look like. But he'd given her so much over the years, she also knew she'd do whatever was necessary to make his remaining time as rich and comfortable as possible.

"Thanks, Hazel." She tucked the prescription into her shoulder bag and helped Shadow down. Then she circled around the table to hug her friend, silently thanking her for her care and kindness to both her and her patient. When she pulled away, she glanced up at Garrett. "I'm ready to go whenever you are."

He settled his hand on the small of her back again and guided her out the door. He paused to shake hands with the vet. "Thanks, Dr. Coop. Say hi to Burke for me."

"I will."

He held on to the veterinarian's hand and glanced toward the front entrance. "It's getting dark outside. Is Burke coming to pick you up? Or do you want me to wait and walk you out?"

Hazel shook the bangs of her short pixie cut hair. "Careful, Jessica. I think this one is as overprotective as my Burke is. When you've had a day as tough as this one has been, let him do his thing and take care of you. You can be strong again tomorrow."

It was on the tip of Jessica's tongue to correct her friend's perception of her relationship with Garrett. But Hazel's advice sounded pretty good right now. And she couldn't deny how much worse this life-changing news would have been without Garrett at her side. "He has been awfully good to me today."

"I suspected as much." Hazel traded one more hug before pulling away and looking up at Garrett. "Take care of my friend, okay? This is going to be tough for her."

"I'll do my best."

She scooted them toward the front door. "I'll lock up behind you. I'll be fine. Burke and Gunny both should be here in a few minutes."

At the mention of Hazel's husband and his K-9 partner, Garrett nodded and led Jessica out to the parking lot.

She was exhausted from the tension that had been vibrating through her from the moment she realized something was wrong with Shadow. Since the dog was feeling fine now, he wanted to sit up in the back seat and stick his nose out the window of Garrett's truck. She settled into the front passenger seat, tipped her head back against the headrest, and closed her eyes. The moment he climbed in and started the engine, she rolled her head toward him and studied his rugged profile and indomitable strength. That strength had gotten her through today, just as Hazel had said, and she was grateful. "What am I going to do without Shadow? He's my…everything. I can't lose him."

He turned those handsome green eyes to her. "You're not going to find out today. Let me get you two home. We'll drive through someplace and get dinner so you don't have to cook."

When he pulled out of the parking lot, she turned her head back to look out the window. The streetlights were coming on and rush hour traffic was beginning to thin out as they drove out of the city. Hazel had stayed late after closing for her. Too many people had done too much for her today. She needed to be more self-sufficient than this. "I'm not hungry."

"Taking care of a friend goes both ways, Jessie. You have to eat something. You need to keep your strength up so you can take care of Shadow. He'll worry about you if you don't."

The dog would worry? *Smooth, Caldwell.* She almost

smiled, but that required more energy than she had at the moment. And what she *should* do wasn't the same as what she wanted. So, she took Hazel's advice to heart. "Will you stay with me for a while? I mean, eat dinner with me?"

"I have to go inside your place, anyway. Left my hat there. Clever of me, wasn't it? Made sure I had a reason to come by and see you again, whether you invited me or not?"

She knew there was a teasing response to that goofy reasoning, but she didn't seem able to do lighthearted right now. "Never mind. You've already done so much for me today, and that's after pulling an all-nighter. You need to sleep."

Garrett grumbled something in his throat, and the glimpse of humor he'd tried to cajole her with disappeared. "I'm coming to your house for dinner, Jessie. And I'm staying as long as you need me."

"As my friend." She needed to remind herself of the distinction. That she was strong and whole—well, whole enough—and didn't need a man to take care of her. But it had been a blessing to have this one around today.

"As whatever you need."

GARRETT WRAPPED UP the cheeseburger Jessie had barely touched and stuck it in the fridge in case she was hungry later. If nothing else, she could give the meat to Shadow. He had a feeling that dog was going to be spoiled rotten now that she knew he was nearing the end of his life.

He gathered up the rest of the trash from the burger joint where they'd stopped and put it in the trash can under the sink while Jessie loaded their plates into the dishwasher. At least, she'd polished off her fries and a couple of his, along with most of a chocolate milkshake. It wasn't the healthiest of meals, but it was better than trying to go to sleep with a stomach that was empty and a head that was full of worry.

Jessie had a little more color in her face than she'd had earlier. But her movements seemed strained and sluggish, as if she was sleepwalking and simply going through the motions of cleaning up after a late dinner. Not for the first time that night, she wandered over to the edge of the counter to glance down at Shadow lying in his bed. The dog appeared to be as tired as his mistress, but he still raised his head and looked up at her. "It's all right, boy." She reached down to scratch around his ears. "I haven't forgotten. We'll go in a few minutes."

"Go? Go where?" he asked.

"Nightly rounds around the kennels. Make sure the dogs are all okay before we turn in." She propped her elbows on the counter and rested her chin in her hand, still watching Shadow as he settled back down in his bed. "Everything about him feels so normal, like he's the same old Shadow I've always known."

Garrett moved to the edge of the counter beside her and rested his elbows on the granite top. "You need him, don't you."

She nodded, and once more Garrett was struck by the urge to touch the long tendril of silvery-gold hair that hung against her cheek and brush it gently behind her ear. "He's more than a pet. More than a protector. He was my sanity when I couldn't move past losing John and the baby. My security blanket. He rescued me more than I ever rescued him."

No, what he really wanted to do was release her hair from its ponytail and comb his fingers through its long, wavy length—find out if it was as silky and voluminous as it looked once it was freed from its restraints. But he schooled his hormonal impulses and settled for butting his shoulder gently against hers. “He’s a lucky dog.”

She nudged his shoulder right back. “I’m a lucky mama.”

He considered what she’d told him earlier about all she had lost—not just her husband and pet, but the chance to be a mother. No wonder she was gun-shy about starting a new relationship. He and Hayley had never had kids. First, he’d been gone, and then, no matter how hard they tried, they hadn’t been able to get the timing right. Then she’d been sick, and there’d been no time at all. Not having kids was one of his biggest regrets. As a soldier and officer of the law, he might not be the best bet because of the inherent dangers of his job. But Hayley would have made a great mother. She was so patient and energetic with her students, and she’d taught them so much.

He glanced down at Jessie. She’d have made a wonderful mother, too. She’d be a strong role model for any daughter, a caring example for any son, and a staunch supporter for any cause or activity they might be interested in. He supposed that was why Shadow being diagnosed with idiopathic epilepsy was such a blow to her. Her dogs were her children. She raised them, took care of them, trained them, loved them. Then she sent her dogs out into the world to help others. Today she probably felt a lot like she was losing her child all over again.

Garrett reached over and pulled Jessie’s hand from her chin. He splayed his larger hand against hers, then laced their fingers together—drawing her attention up to him and forging a tender connection. “I know you’re exhausted. Why don't you head on up to bed, and I'll check the kennels for you before I go."

"*You're* the one who must be exhausted. The dogs are my responsibility. Besides, it will give Shadow one more time outside to do his business tonight."

He wasn't surprised that she was trying to reset the boundaries between them. But she shouldn't be surprised that he was going to fight to maintain the new closeness that had sprung up between them today. "Then let me grab my jacket from my truck and I'll come with you."

"Garrett—"

"Humor me." When she straightened up and tried to pull away, he tightened his grip and cradled her hand between both of his. "You had a shotgun pointed at you this morning. You had a PTSD episode. You shared some disturbing details about your husband's murder and got bad news about Shadow. Dr. Coop was right. I feel a little overprotective where you're concerned. I'm not going to apologize for wanting to make sure nothing else happens to you."

She did surprise him by reaching up and laying her free hand against his stubbled jaw. Such a sweet, gentle touch. And his body was crazy to absorb as many of those casual caresses as she wanted to give out. "Thank you. I'd appreciate the company. I don't particularly want to run into one of your vandals by myself out there."

Nodding at her agreement, he pulled away and went out to his truck to pull on his uniform jacket. The calendar might say it was spring, but the night air was cool and overcast. The long-range forecast called for rain and warmer temperatures that would green things up. But until the warm front came through, it felt more like autumn than spring.

Although Jessie had some outdoor lighting at the kennels and barn, he grabbed the flashlight from his glove compartment and met her and Shadow around the side of the house. At the reminder of the mini crime spree, he felt better safe than sorry about making sure they had a secure path. The dog trotted on ahead, following where his nose was taking him, yet often looking back to make sure Jessie was still in sight as they walked the length of the outbuilding that housed her rescue dogs. Garrett refilled some water bowls with a hose while she greeted each dog by name and petted them through the fencing as well as checking to make sure each latch was secure.

"You keep them all locked up at night?" he asked, rolling up the long water hose and hanging it at the end of the building.

"Except for Rex and Toby. They're trained to guard the property, and I don't worry about them running off. Although Rex likes to bunk down with the goats in the barn, instead of using his doghouse." Just then, Toby trotted out of his own doghouse and jogged up to them, his whole butt wagging with excitement at the late-night visit. "And Mr. Personality here bunks wherever it suits him. Sometimes, his doghouse. Sometimes, the front porch. Sometimes, in the barn with his big buddy. Who's my good Toby?" She petted the black Lab around his face and ears. Then, when Garrett patted his chest, the energetic dog rose up on his hind legs and braced his front paws against him so that Garrett had full access to rubbing his flanks and tummy. "I think he likes you."

"We had a hunting dog like Toby growing up. Ace was more subdued, though." He pushed the dog down and Toby trotted back to his doghouse, where he picked up a rawhide chew and lay down to enjoy his treat.

"Where'd you get that, boy?" Jessie asked, frowning. "Did you find that treat in the barn?" She turned her attention to the well-maintained red structure. "There was a shattered treat jar in the storage room. I wonder if he got in there once the door was busted open. Or if whoever broke in tossed him a treat to distract him."

Garrett heard the suspicion in her tone, but he had already turned his light toward a sign he found even more worrisome. "How many clients do you usually have out here during the day?"

"Two or three. Unless I'm having a group training session. Then it can be up to ten or twelve." She walked up behind where he had knelt to study the curving driveway and parking area. "Why?"

Shadow came up beside him and dipped his nose to the tire track Garrett was inspecting. "What do you think, buddy? Does this look off to you?"

Shadow sat back on his haunches and raised his dark eyes to him. Garrett interpreted that as a tacit agreement to his suspicions.

"Garrett?"

He stood and pointed out what he was seeing with his flashlight. Several rows of tire tracks were imbedded in the dirt and gravel leading from the main drive to the barn. The tracks crisscrossed each other to the extent it would be hard to determine the exact course of the vehicles that had left them. But he counted at least five different tread marks, including a distinctive asymmetrical tread usually used by souped-up sports cars or off-roaders. Not something the meek Mollie

Crane on a budget or an old farm truck would use. He pulled out his phone and snapped pictures of each distinctive tread. "You had company out here while we were in KC."

Jessie crossed her arms beside him. "I forgot to text Soren and let him know I was gone. He probably stopped by for his shift to feed the dogs. They're all in their kennels, and the goats are in their stall, so someone took care of them. I'll text him in the morning to confirm."

He visually followed the dusty tracks. "If this was Soren, he didn't come alone. These extra tracks weren't here when we went inside for lunch."

"I canceled my afternoon appointments before we left Hazel's office. Do you think whoever broke into the storage room came back for something else?" He could see her visibly shivering in the cool air. "Sometimes, people get lost and turn around in the driveway." She shook her head, dismissing the possible explanation, even as she said it. "But not this many vehicles in one day. And there's room to turn around by the house. They wouldn't come this far onto the property unless they were coming to see me. Or my dogs." She turned back to the kennels. "Do you think the dogs are okay?"

Garrett caught her by the elbow before she could charge back to the kennels. "You've already checked every last one of your charges for yourself. They're fine. Here. I don't know if you're spooked or you're cold. But this will help." He shrugged out of his sheriff's department jacket and wrapped it around her shoulders. "Better?"

"Probably a little of both," she admitted, offering him a weary smile as she shoved her arms into the sleeves and overlapped the front beneath her chin. "You are a furnace, my friend. Thank you."

"You're welcome." Once he was certain she wasn't on the verge of panic over her dogs again, he shined his flashlight up at the device anchored above the barn door. "Is that a security camera?"

She nodded. "I've got one that points down toward the kennels and the training yard, and one at the front gate so I can tell when company is coming."

Cameras were a good thing. Cameras might finally give him the answers he needed. "Do they record? Or are they real-time monitors?"

"They back up the live feed for twenty-four hours at a time on my computer unless I make a copy." She burrowed her fingers into Shadow's fur beside her. "I can go up to the house and pull up the feed. See if I recognize any of the vehicles."

"Mind if I come with you?" The dust had settled in these tracks, indicating whoever had made them was long gone. He could conduct a more thorough search of the grounds, but his gut was telling him he wouldn't find anything.

"Of course, not." She fell into step beside him as they headed back to the house. "You don't need to check the perimeter or follow those tracks to see where they lead?"

"No. Whatever happened out here is over and done. I'll get one of my officers to drive out and look around. Let's get you in the house."

The hairs at the nape of his neck were sticking straight out with a subconscious alert that something was very, very wrong here. He was still waiting for the big event he suspected all these little criminal hiccups were leading up to. His years as a sniper, learning the patience to lie in wait until his target appeared—and all his years of experience with the sheriff's department—kept telling him that something was about to hit the fan big-time. And the fact that several of them were centered around Jessie didn't sit well with him. He needed to stay sharp and figure out what was going on before Jessie or anyone else got hurt.

Several minutes later, they were sipping on fresh cups of decaf coffee—Jessie's doctored up with cream and sugar—and sitting in front of the computer in her office. They'd fast-forwarded through the daylight hours, getting glimpses of Mollie Crane's small car and Hugo's truck, and Garrett's heavy-duty departmental pickup. The images had gotten darker as night set in, and slightly distorted by the light above the camera.

"There's Soren." She stopped the scrolling images and pointed to the screen. The teenager was climbing out of the passenger side of a car. "I recognize his ponytail. Toby runs up to meet him. He recognizes him, so no one sounds an alarm. But that's not Soren's car."

Garrett braced his elbows on his knees and leaned forward to study the grainy image. "Can you print me a copy of that?"

"Sure."

The printer whirred in the background while Garrett squinted at the screen. "Do you recognize the driver?"

"No. Soren's late, too. He's supposed to come at five o'clock, but the sun would still be up then." She still huddled inside his jacket, apparently unable to shake the chill from outside. She took another sip of her hot drink and cradled it between her fingers. It would be so easy to drape his arm around her shoulders and share some of his body heat, or even pick her up and set her on his lap in the same chair and wrap her up against his thighs and chest. More body heat meant a warmer Jessie.

More body heat meant trouble.

"Ready to see more?" Jessie's question startled him from the decadent spiral of his thoughts.

Man, he was tired. He shoved his fingers through his hair. He couldn't even drum up the willpower to keep his lusty thoughts about Jessie buried inside where they couldn't distract him with false hope. "Yeah. I'll run that picture by Hugo, see if he recognizes his grandson's friend."

"Garrett?" He flinched as her warm hand settled on his knee. "Are you okay? We can do this tomorrow. You need your rest."

Garrett covered her hand with his before she could pull it away. Damn those gentle touches of hers. They stirred up his senses and sneaked beneath his skin, giving him a glimpse of how good a relationship between them could be. If only she felt the same connection he did. Correction, if only she'd allow herself to feel the connection they shared.

"There has to be more on this recording. I want to finish it up."

"And find answers to your mystery?"

He squeezed her hand beneath his. "Yeah. It's hard to relax when there are loose ends bugging me like this."

He was more pleased than he should have been when she left her hand clasped in his and set down her coffee to continue scrolling through the recording.

"Stop." Garrett was the one who finally broke the connection when a dark Dodge Charger drove onto the screen. "Who's that?"

"Look at the bling on that," she pointed out unnecessarily. "No teenager can afford that car." Without asking, she was already printing out a picture of the sports car. "I have no idea who that is. Can you make out the license plate?"

He pinched the bridge of his nose and rubbed his eyes. They burned with fatigue, but if he blinked enough, they would clear, and he could study the images more closely.

"A partial. He left the souped-up tire tracks." The glare from the headlights obscured the vehicle identification and passengers inside, and when they made a U-turn and sped away, they kicked up enough dust and gravel to see only a glimpse of the generic Missouri license plate. "Hopefully, it's enough to run." He pulled out his phone and called the sheriff's station. "Caldwell here. I need you to run a partial plate for me on a Dodge Charger. Black or dark blue. Over-the-top trim and underglow lights." The officer covering the night shift took down the info. "I know it's not much. Find out what you can and get back to me. I want a BOLO out on the car. If it shows up anywhere between Kansas City and Lone Jack, I want to know about it."

"Yes, sir."

Jessie slowly scrolled the images forward while Garrett ended the call, then rewound them to the beginning of the clip. "What do they want?"

"Nothing good." Any clear view of the driver was obscured by the headlights, although he was of slighter stature than the guy who got out on the passenger side. The baggy jeans and loose jacket made Garrett think the guy was carrying a weapon. And there was no way to get a description of his face. Even with darkness falling, he wore dark glasses and a cap pulled low over his forehead. "Can you make out any identifying marks on his hat or jacket?"

She shook her head. "A sports logo, maybe. The picture on his hat could be barbells? It's not like when Soren and his friend stopped by. This guy gets out of his car, and Toby and the other dogs raise a ruckus. The moment Rex runs out of the barn to check out who's there, both men get back in and drive away."

He reached down to scratch Shadow around his ears. The dog had settled below the desk at Jessie's feet. "Thank God for your dogs. Or we probably would have had another incident."

"You think these are the same guys who broke into the Russells' cabin and terrorized Miss Eloise's chickens?"

"These guys don't look like vandals to me. And they're clearly not good ol' country boys. There's too much money in their clothes and car."

"Illegal money?"

He couldn't prove it just by studying a grainy image, but his years of experience told him the answer was yes. "Probably drugs or moving stolen goods. Or something to do with your dogs."

"Like dog fighting? I have one pit bull rescue out there, but she's not even a year old." He watched the color drain from her cheeks. "Do you think they were here to steal bait dogs?"

"We don't know anything yet." He squeezed her knee as he pushed himself upright and stretched the kinks in his back and shoulders. "Let's not go there."

She glanced over and caught him yawning behind his hand. "I'll zoom in as much as I can and print a picture for you."

"Would you copy the whole thing to a flash drive for me? I'd like to go over it again tomorrow when my eyes are fresh." He smirked. No sense hiding the truth. "Better yet, I'll have one of my officers whose eyes are twenty years younger than mine take a look at it."

"Garrett, you need to go to bed."

"Pot calling the kettle black, Ms. Bennington. You've been on a long, emotional roller-coaster ride today." He checked his watch. "Good grief. It's two in the morning."

"I don't think I'll be sleeping much tonight." She mimicked his yawn while she waited for the image to print and dug a flash drive out of her desk. "Shadow seems so normal now. Like that seizure never even happened." She inserted the data stick to copy the video file. "But now I know there's this time bomb inside his head, and it could go off at any time."

Garrett pushed to his feet and returned his chair to the kitchen table. "Dr. Cooper-Burke said it could be weeks or months before he seizes again."

"Or it could be days." Her soft gray eyes were watery with unshed tears as she followed him to the kitchen and handed over the evidence he'd requested. He was surprised at how right it felt for her to walk past his outstretched hand and line her body up against his. She curled her fingers into the front of his wrinkled uniform shirt and rested her forehead at the juncture of his neck and shoulder. "I can't lose him, Garrett."

"Honey, you're exhausted." He dropped the photos and flash drive on the table behind her and wrapped his arms around her. He wished he'd taken off his flak vest so he could feel her curves and heat pressed against him. But he wasn't about to push her away to do so. "Why don't you take him upstairs and get ready for bed. You can watch over him until you fall asleep."

She felt the barrier of protective armor between them, too, because she lightly rapped against his vest. "This isn't very conducive to cuddling, Deputy," she teased.

Garrett tightened his arms more securely around her. "Don't worry. I can still keep you warm."

"And keep the demons away?"

He pressed a kiss to her forehead. "I'll try."

Her fingers found the edge of his vest and curled beneath it. "What if Shadow has a seizure in the middle of the night? What if I'm asleep and can't help him?"

"This is going to be your new normal for a while. You'll figure it all out." When she steadied her emotions with a deep breath, he made an offer. "Would you feel better if I stayed? Kept an eye on things while you sleep?"

Strands of her silky hair caught in his beard stubble as she shook her head. "You can't stay awake two nights in a row."

"I'm not going to leave if you need me. I'm a light sleeper. If I hear something, I'll wake up." She pulled back, considering his suggestion for several seconds. When he saw the polite dismissal forming on her lips, he argued his case. "I know you've got guest rooms upstairs, or the couch is fine. I'll sleep better, too, if I'm here. That way I'll know you're safe, that you don't have any trespassers, and the horrible things I can imagine happening during the ten minutes it would take me to get to you won't keep me awake."

She reached up and threaded her fingers through the messy spikes of his hair and tried to smooth them into place. More gentle touches. This woman was so damn addictive. "Then the practical thing would be for you to stay with me tonight. That way, we can both get a good night's sleep."

"I can work with that." She pulled away entirely and wrapped his jacket more tightly around her, in lieu of his arms. He'd take that swap, knowing his jacket was going to retain some of that faint lilac scent that clung to her skin. Soap or lotion, he imagined. "Go on up and get ready for bed. I'm going to walk around the house and check things out one more time."

She motioned for Shadow to come to her side. "I'll set out a new toothbrush for you in the main bathroom upstairs. Need anything else?"

"I'm good."

"Good night, Garrett."

"Good night."

By the time he returned after securing the entire house, inside and out, and after one more call to the C shift to drive by Jessie's ranch a couple of times through the remainder of the night, he crept back upstairs to find her asleep on top of her bed, with Shadow stretched out beside her. Although she'd left a lamp on for him in the guest room across the hall, Garrett lingered a moment in her doorway, taking in the sweetly homey sight.

She'd conked out in her clothes, her hand resting on the dog's shoulder. She'd hung his jacket over the back of a chair where she'd tossed her insulated vest and kicked off her lace-up boots. But she still wore her long-sleeved T-shirt, socks, and jeans. She'd brushed her hair out in silver and gold waves that flared over the pillowcase behind her, and he felt his weary body stirring with the desire to bury his nose in those glorious waves and claim this brave, battered by life—but refusing to be beaten—woman for his own.

Needing to move away from that dream before he did anything to ruin the gentle tension that had been simmering between them all day, Garrett quickly brushed his teeth and took care of business. He stripped down to his T-shirt and pants before coming back to her doorway for one last reassurance that she was safe.

Jessie had rolled over, and in the dim light from across the hall he watched her eyes blink open into slits, then close again. “That’s not sleeping,” she murmured drowsily. “That’s hovering in the doorway and staying awake.” She stretched out her hand without raising it off the bed. “If the guest room is too far away for you to relax, stay with me.”

The tension inside him settled at her invitation. “You’re sure?”

“I have a feeling you won’t sleep if you don’t have eyes on me.” She paused to cover her adorably big yawn. “This isn’t a seduction, Garrett. Nothing’s going to happen. There’s a dog in bed with us.”

“I’d like to hold you,” he confessed.

“I’m okay with that.” Her eyes opened fully to meet his gaze. “I’m having a hard time shaking the chill of the night outside. Or maybe it’s all in my head. But I could use the body heat.”

Body heat. Garrett bit back a groan. But out loud he said, “Happy to be of help.”

He went back to the guest room to turn off the light and grab his gun and holster. When he returned, she’d dozed off again. He set his weapon within reach on the bedside table, then climbed in beside her.

But she wasn’t as asleep as he thought. The moment his head hit the pillow, she scooted closer and snuggled into him, one arm folded between them, the other resting across his waist. She nestled her cheek against his shoulder and buried her nose at the base of his neck. He slipped his arm behind her back and held her loosely against his side. But she pulled her top leg over his thighs and slipped her toes down between his knees, wrapping herself around him as if she was using him for a body pillow. "An absolute furnace." She buried her lips and nose against his neck. "Mmm…you smell good."

"I smell like a forty-eight-hour shift and too much time in dusty barns, vet's offices, and at crime scenes."

"Mmm-hmm."

"Jessie?" This time, there was no answer. She was more asleep than awake now, and they were snuggled up as close as two people still wearing most of their clothes could get. Who knew this prickly, independent woman was such a cuddler? It was another glimpse of vulnerability he'd do his damnedest to protect. He indulged his senses by tangling his fingers through her silky hair and bringing it to his nose to breathe in her flowery scent. Then he pressed a kiss to her forehead. "Sleep, hon. I've got you." He reached across her to rest one hand on her precious Shadow. "I've got you both."

This was the closeness and contentment that was missing from his life. Sure, he wanted to find out what kind of passion was locked up behind Jessie's protective walls. He wanted to kiss her until she couldn't think of any man but him and feel her body come to life beneath his. But he wanted this, too. He needed this.

With the woman he was falling hard and fast for secure in his arms, Garrett finally surrendered to his body's bone-numbing fatigue and fell into a deep sleep.

Chapter Five

Garrett woke up feeling surprisingly refreshed, even after only a few hours of sleep. But the schedule that had been ingrained in him years ago by the military and law enforcement meant he was an early riser. Most mornings he did some kind of workout. On others, he drank his coffee and read his newspaper or reports that needed his attention.

This morning, he wanted nothing more than to linger in bed with the woman still tucked up against his side, breathing evenly in restful sleep. But an eager panting from across the bed made him suspect his morning had already been planned for him.

The moment he began to stir, Shadow raised his head from his spot on the other side of Jessie. The two males acknowledged each other. And, by mutual agreement, neither of them made a sound as Garrett extricated himself from the cheek resting on his chest and the arm curled around his waist. Shadow quietly jumped down while Garrett pulled his jacket from the chair and tucked it around Jessie since they'd slept on top of the covers. He put on his shoes, hit the john, and went downstairs with Shadow following closely on his heels.

Several minutes later, the dog was happily munching on

his breakfast and Garrett was carrying two steaming mugs of coffee back up to Jessie's bedroom. He found her squinting against the sunlight that peeked around the curtains at the window. "You awake?"

Jessie stretched out the kinks in her limbs. But when she breathed in deeply, her eyes popped wide-open. "Is that coffee?"

Garrett chuckled at her hopeful response. "Yes. I thought I'd spoil you a little this morning. Helped myself, too."

"That's fine." She propped the pillows against the headboard and sat up, her cheeks pink with the anticipation flowing through her. Garrett set their mugs on the bedside table and perched on the edge of the bed facing her. Her soft smile was prettier than any sunrise. And her eyes, rested and no longer red with tears, reminded him of the moon on a cold, clear night.

When Garrett reached out to brush her hair off her cheek and tuck it behind her ear, she mimicked the caress. She combed her fingers through his hair in a hopeless attempt to tame the unruly spikes. Another smile. "It never cooperates, does it."

Her gentle touches nourished a hungry spot in his soul that, being a widowed workaholic, had gone without for too many years. "That's one reason I keep it short."

She drew her fingers down to trace his jaw and he dropped his gaze from her eyes to her soft pink lips. Her bottom lip was curved and plump, and the upper was narrow and arched. The asymmetry of her mouth was as intriguing and beautiful as the rest of her. When she scraped her palm across two days' worth of beard stubble, her nostrils flared. And when her fingertips tugged slightly against him, he closed the distance between them and covered her mouth with his.

He lost himself in the feeling of Jessie's lips surrendering beneath his. He leisurely took his fill of her little grasps and nibbles, of her angling her mouth first one way, then another as she got acquainted with his kiss. With his pulse revving up and his desire spinning out of control, he stroked his tongue along the seam of her lips, and she parted for him. Garrett delved in to fully taste her for the first time. Her tongue was still minty from brushing her teeth the night before. Although her responses were gentle, there was no shyness to the rasp of her tongue sliding against his or the tips of her fingers clinging to his face and neck.

At the tiny whimper from her throat, he captured either side of her jaw between his hands and tunneled his fingers into her hair. He tilted her head back against the basket of his hands and leaned in to claim the passion freeing itself from the tight confines of her guarded personality. No nubile, desperate young woman like Isla Gardner could hold a candle to the measured release of Jessie Bennington's passion. The cautious beginning of this embrace only made the gift of opening up and sharing herself with him that much more precious. What she demanded, he gave. What he asked for, she returned to him tenfold.

About the time Garrett became aware of the pressure swelling behind his zipper, he had the idea that patience might be a better course for this newfound closeness than laying her down on the bed and stabbing his palms against the tight points of her breasts that poked to attention through the cotton of her shirt. And about the time that thought made him ease back from her beautiful mouth, Jessie slipped her fingers between their lips and abruptly pushed him away.

"That was a nice *good morning.*" His tone was embarrassingly breathless as he smiled his thanks and pleasure. "I could wake up like this every day."

Oh, hell. This was more than her coming to her senses before he could. That was panic in her eyes. Her pink, kiss-swollen lips spoke of shared passion, but her pale skin and eyes, which seemed to focus everywhere around the room except on him, sent a message of uncertainty and maybe even regret.

He rested his hand on her knee. "Jessie?" She jerked her leg away from him and hugged her knees up to her chest. Maybe she didn't understand what she'd done for him last night, that he wasn't expecting anything more from her right now. "That's the best I've slept in a long time. My body seemed to naturally relax, knowing you were here with me. I could touch you, and I didn't worry or wonder about anything. I felt…safe…with you beside me."

Her nod said she understood, maybe even felt the same way. But her words said something else. "Shadow needs to go outside." She patted the bed beside her, as if she'd just now realized the two of them were alone. "Where's Shadow?"

"He's fine. He got through the night without any issues. I already put him out. He's downstairs eating breakfast now."

"I need to check—"

"No, you don't. We've already walked the perimeter to make sure there are no new tire tracks, and I've talked with my staff. No sightings of a car matching the description of the one you caught on camera—and not enough of a plate number to positively identify the car's owner. You can talk to me for five minutes," he gently chided. "How did you sleep? Are you feeling stronger this morning?" He picked up her mug and handed it to her. "Drink your coffee before it gets cold."

"Fine. Yes." She looked down into the milky brown depths of the coffee. "Did you put cream and sugar in it?"

"Yes." That's right, he paid attention. He knew how ridiculously sweet she liked her coffee.

She set the mug back down without tasting the drink and stood to pace back and forth between the bed and the door. "You shouldn't have kissed me like that."

Garrett stayed where he was, hoping a calm voice and less intimidating silhouette would help her calm herself. "Why not? You seemed to enjoy it. I know I did."

"Of course, I did. I wouldn't have kissed you back if I felt pressured or I didn't like it. But I—"

"You shouldn't have plastered your body against mine all night and made me believe you like me." He caught her hand when she moved past him again. "We needed to hold each other last night. I'm okay with that. That kiss was just the punctuation to the need we shared."

"Garrett—"

"I know you feel the chemistry between us, too."

"No. No chemistry. We're friends. Period." She pulled her hand away and spoke firmly, as if saying it out loud made it so. At least she was making eye contact now. "Last night, I was vulnerable. I haven't been held like that for twelve years, and I needed you. Your strength. Your warmth. Just…solid you to hold on to. You helped me through a tough day, and I'm grateful. But that doesn't mean we're an item now. Just because you spent the night—"

"—in the same bed—"

"—doesn't mean we're dating. You don't even like me that way."

Garrett sprang to his feet. "The hell I don't. You think I sleep with every friend who's having a rough go of things? What do you think that kiss was about? I bring you that fancy coffee I can't stand three or four mornings a week just so I can sit on the front porch and spend time with you. I stayed with you yesterday well beyond my body's limits and the duties of my office because you needed me, and I was worried about you." She tipped her head back to hold his gaze but didn't retreat. "I. Like. You. A lot."

"Garrett—"

"I guess I don't know how you feel about me. I thought I did, but maybe I was wrong. I believed you were keeping me at arm's length to protect yourself, because you were still grieving for your husband, or you felt guilty about caring for another man, or you just don't want to risk getting hurt." Bingo. He felt her flinch like a punch to the gut. He blew out his anger and breathed in sadness, mourning the loss of what could be between them. "But don't tell me how *I* feel. I know exactly what my emotions are. How much I'm attracted to you, how I love to see your smile. How you make me laugh, how much I admire you for all you've accomplished. How much I want to kiss your beautiful mouth again. I can keep my distance for now if that's what you want. If that's what it takes for you to get comfortable with me being in your life. But make no mistake, I *am* in your life. And until you tell me you don't feel anything at all for me, I'm not going anywhere. I will never be dishonest with you. I was hoping you could do the same for me."

"Garrett, I can't… You want honesty? I lost *everything*

once. And it broke me. It has taken me twelve years and a therapy dog to get to where I am now. I can't do that again." She reached out but didn't touch him. "You deserve a woman who can give you her heart and her body and a family and forever. As much as a part of me might want to be that woman—I'm not. I'm damaged goods. And I don't just mean I can't give you children."

"You're not..." But he didn't finish the argument. If that was what she believed, then he wasn't going to change her mind by arguing with her. Instead, he plowed his fingers through his hair and tried to let her know that he understood how hard it was to find and trust a new relationship later in life, especially after surviving a tragedy the way she had. "After Haley, I wasn't sure I could love again, either. My heart felt all used up. Then I met you, chasing down that stupid stray dog, and I wanted to try." She had to understand this wasn't a fling for him, that nothing he felt for her was casual. "I still want to try."

Confusion was stamped on her face as she hugged herself tightly. He wanted to take her in his arms and shield her from the stress she was obviously feeling. But he didn't. She didn't want him to, and he would respect that.

"I don't want to give you false hope. I care about you too much to want to be the woman who hurts you." Her words were painfully sincere.

"What if you're the woman who makes me happy? Hell, Jessie, I'm a patient man. But you've got to give us a chance."

She shook her head. "You're easy to love, Garrett. But that also means you *won't* be easy to lose."

Now he did reach for her. He needed the connection. He

feathered his fingers into her loose waves and brushed her hair behind her ear. "You're not going to lose me."

"You wear a gun and a badge, Garrett. You deal with violence on some level every day of your life. I'm not sure I can live with that."

Now the flashback this morning made sense. Eloise had trained her gun on *him*. Whether or not she realized it, Jessie had reacted because on some level, she already cared for him—and she'd thought she was going to lose him.

"I can't give up my job, Jess."

"I would never ask you to."

"I've got another fifteen years before they force me to retire. It'll end up being more of a desk job by then. But I love doing what I do."

"And you're good at it." She laid her hand over his where it rested against the side of her neck. "I'm not asking you to wait for me to be whole again. I may never be. I'm telling you to move on."

"No." Not an option for him. He was going to fight for them even if she couldn't. "Jessie—honey—you are stronger than you know. Look at all the people you help. Look at the animals you've helped. You run a successful business—and don't think I don't know that some of it's charitable work. Look at how far you've come. On your own."

She let go and moved away to count off perceived shortcomings on her fingers. "Flashbacks? Bawling when my dog gets sick? Screwing up the best kiss I've had in years?"

At least they were on the same page with the physical connection they shared. "You didn't screw up a damn thing. And Shadow is more than your dog. I'd be worried if you didn't lose it a little bit."

"If that's how I reacted to his diagnosis, how do you think I'm going to react if something happens to you?"

Garrett inhaled deeply. She couldn't see what was so clear to him. "You might cry. You might use a friend's shoulder to lean on. But then you'd suck it up and get on with living. You're like me in that respect. You get the job done. Because you have to. It may not be pretty. It may not be easy. But you do it. And hopefully, there's someone kind and caring and supportive around to help you do it."

Her eyes looked hopeful, although he could tell she was trying to come up with another argument to chase him out of her life. Thank goodness he wasn't some impatient young buck who moved on to the next pretty thing when the woman he really wanted proved to be a challenge. Convincing Jessie to take a chance on loving him might not be easy, but she was so worth the fight.

But he had to table the fight for now. His phone rang and her cell dinged with a text on the nightstand just a few seconds later.

He pulled his phone from his pocket and read the number. "Sorry. This is work." He crossed to the relative privacy of the guest room across the hall. "Deputy Caldwell." His morning went from bad to worse as he listened to his officer share the details about a countywide search for two missing children.

By the time he'd hung up, Jessie stood in the doorway, holding up her phone. "I got an Amber Alert." The public notice she'd received would have been brief and to the point. "Two children?"

"Yeah. Runaways from Kansas City." Garrett suited up while he talked, tucking in his black T-shirt and strapping his protective vest over his chest. Then he pulled on his uniform shirt and buttoned it as he returned to her bedroom to retrieve his belt, gun, and badge. "The whole county is on notice. No clue where they went. The father didn't report them missing until this morning."

"How long have they been missing?" Jessie followed, sounding stronger and looking less pale now that the conversation was centered on something other than him and her and the relationship she wasn't ready for. "Does your office know what happened?"

"They haven't shown up at school for three days. They alerted the father."

"Three days? And he just now reported it? Is there a mother in the picture? Did he think the children were with her?"

He shook his head. "Apparently, she died three years ago. Drug overdose. Dad has custody."

"Is there a relative? A sitter?"

He adjusted his belt at his waist and secured his holster at his hip before heading downstairs. "KCPD has checked all known connections with no luck. Official report says they got on the bus to school, but never reported to their classrooms."

"Why would they run away?"

"That's the million-dollar question. They're from a low-income neighborhood and money's tight. They're on the free meal program at school, and teachers reported that they sometimes wear clothes that they've outgrown. But they do well in their classes, and the dad is holding down a job as a delivery driver. They don't have a history of running."

"He must be out of his mind with worry." Her hands settled on her stomach and his heart wept for the baby she had lost. An incident like this was probably a nightmare trigger for her. "Do you think they were taken?"

That was every cop's worst fear. "Two children that young don't just disappear."

"I hope they're okay."

"Me, too. These are always the worst calls. Human trafficking or the death of a child? They're the hardest cases for me to handle." He grabbed his hat off the hall tree and headed to the front door. "I need to help find them."

Jessie hurried down the stairs behind him. "Do you want some breakfast before you go?"

"No."

"But I kept you up so late. You haven't even been home yet."

"I have a clean uniform at the sheriff's station. I'll shower there."

"I'm just trying to help. It's what a friend would do." She sounded a little lost. She was probably replaying every word he'd said to her and trying to figure out where she stood with him now. "I'm guessing that's not what you want from me."

He needed to get to the station to see where they stood on the search, coordinate with KCPD, and call in all available staff to help—and reassure them that even though seventy-two hours missing generally didn't bode well for the victims, they weren't giving up until they were found. The reasons why and gathering evidence as to any foul play would come later. Right now, priority one was locating the two reported runaways.

But then he remembered that as strong and tough as Jessie was on the outside, there was a vulnerable woman underneath who'd desperately needed the warmth of his body and the shelter of his arms last night. He could use a little tenderness and support right now, himself.

Garrett turned to her, snaked his hand around the back of her neck, and kissed her soundly, thoroughly, and far too quickly. He still cupped her nape gently and rested his forehead against hers. Her eyes tilted up to his, and he covered her hand resting against his chest. "I can't turn off how I feel about you, Jessie. You let me in last night, and it's hard for me to step back and pretend it never happened. But I hope you still trust me, that if you need me again, you'll call. About Shadow or Miss Eloise or late-night visitors or anything. I'll try to dial it back a notch so we can still be friends, so I can still see you and be a part of your life."

"You would do that? Even if it's only coffee on the porch in the mornings?"

"Even if it's only that. Look, I admit that I'm a workaholic. But I'm at an age where I've decided I need…want more than that." He released her to touch her hair and smooth the long waves down her back. "You're the most interesting, intriguing thing that's happened to me since Hayley died. I look forward to seeing you, discovering what we might laugh about—or argue about—next. I care about something beyond work now. I'm…*alive* again with you. I don't want to lose that."

"You are a grown, virile man. You need more than I can give you."

He shook his head. "I just need *you*. Maybe one day you'll believe it's safe to risk your heart on me. I'll keep it safe. I promise. I won't cheat. I will never lay a hand on you in anger. I'll do everything in my power to give you what you want, and more importantly, what you need." He pulled her hands from his chest and retreated a step. "But if that never happens, I want you to know that you're still safe with me. I'll still help you keep those mutts safe. I'll still be your friend."

"I don't deserve that kind of promise, Garrett."

"Yeah, you do." He lowered his head to press a quick kiss to her lips. He acknowledged the urge to claim those lips the way he had earlier, to show her exactly how good they could be together, that she was anything but *damaged goods* in his eyes. But this wasn't the right time. She wasn't ready for that. She might never be. So, he pulled away.

He put on his hat and strode out the front door. He had work to do.

GARRETT CROSSED HIS arms over his chest as he stood at the one-way mirror outside the interview room at KCPD's Fourth Precinct office. Since he was coordinating the search for the children listed as missing in this morning's Amber Alert outside the KC city limits, he'd been invited in to observe the most recent interview of the children's father, Zane Swiegert.

The guy looked understandably rough after finding out his son and daughter had disappeared. His clothes were wrinkled and stained, and he needed a shave. He'd been tearing up and his nose was running from the times he'd broken down during the interview. Although he and Hayley hadn't been blessed with children, Garrett knew he'd struggle to deal with it if someone he was responsible for—someone he loved—was harmed or taken. He thought back to yesterday when Jessie had suffered that flashback. He'd wanted to fix it for her, make whatever frightened her so go away. He was desperate to help, to protect, to take care of her. He hated feeling helpless.

Maybe Zane Swiegert felt helpless, too.

But his years in law enforcement left him feeling more suspicion than sympathy for Daddy Swiegert. The man was hiding something. Maybe it was as simple as being a lousy father and feeling guilty for losing track of his own children. Or maybe it was something more sinister.

Someone knew where those children were. Someone knew what had happened to them. Was it Swiegert?

The detectives interviewing Swiegert asked him to retrace his children's steps the morning they'd gone missing. He'd gotten them up for school and walked them out to the bus stop where they'd been picked up for school. They ate breakfast at school. Nate Swiegert was in the third grade; his younger sister, Abby, was in kindergarten. Yes, he knew the name of Nate's teacher, although he couldn't seem to come up with the name of his daughter's teacher. After school, they were supposed to walk over to a friend's apartment and stay with him until Zane got back from driving his delivery route late that night.

But none of those details were what pinged on Garrett's radar as he studied the relatively nondescript, brown-haired, blue-eyed man in his midthirties. Swiegert wore a small, bright white cast on his left hand, indicating he'd broken some fingers. Very recently. Maybe he'd punched a wall out of anger, guilt, or frustration. Or he'd been distracted and overtired and gotten into some kind of accident—shut his hand in a car door or put it through a window. Plus, the guy was sweating. Inside an air-conditioned building on a mild spring day, he was sweating.

Swiegert seemed even hazier recounting his own movements since the last time he'd seen his son and daughter. He'd driven his route that day but didn't show up for work yesterday. He said he'd called in sick with the flu, but his supervisor never got such a call. Why didn't he pick up his children at the friend's home? Because he was sick. How did he injure his fingers? At work. But you didn't go to work, the detectives reminded him. Then he got angry and sobbed again. Why were the cops grilling him and not out combing the streets for Nate and Abby?

A shadow fell over Garrett, and he turned to the tall, lanky man wearing a suit and tie who stepped up beside him. "You think he's faking it?" Detective Conor Wildman looked more like an up-and-coming executive at a Fortune 500 company than a WITSEC agent turned KCPD detective. He had been the one to call Garrett in from the sheriff's office in Lee's Summit. "I know I'd be out of my mind if anything happened to my daughter or wife. But there's something else going on with this guy, if you ask me."

"The tears? The sweat?" Garrett shrugged. "I think he's in legitimate pain. Though it's not all about his kids. Either the painkillers he was given for that hand have worn off… or he's going through withdrawal."

"Then your suspicions are the same as mine. I'm guessing he was off someplace getting high when his children went missing. It took him three days to sober up and realize they were gone." Wildman handed Garrett a file folder to read. "That's Swiegert's rap sheet. Wouldn't be the first time he's used cocaine."

"Or else the drugs are how he's coping with the stress. You do a tox screen?"

"Bad PR to lean too heavily on the parent until the kids are found."

Garrett skimmed the file. Drug possession arrests. Petty

crimes to support his habit. "How did that guy keep custody of his children?"

"He was clean for a while after a mandatory stint in rehab following his wife's overdose. Kept his nose clean long enough to maintain a steady job and get his kids out of the foster system."

"So, this guy is a loser who doesn't deserve those kids. But he loves them, and they love him, and he's trying as hard as he can to stay clean or at least use less. So, the State and KCPD are doing all they can to reunite them?" He handed the file back to Detective Wildman. "Why am I here to listen to his sob story? Either something happened to them three days ago, they were taken and are long gone by now, or they ran away of their own volition. In which case, they've been surviving on the streets or out in the elements. None of that is good."

"I'm not affiliated with the missing persons' case, Deputy." That piqued his interest. "I'm part of a drug task force trying to take down a major player here in KC—Kai Olivera."

Garrett nodded. "I know the name. Second-generation American gangster living the dream in the big city. Human trafficking. Drugs. Small arms smuggling. I've made traffic stops on the highway where we've intercepted a couple of his cross-country shipments. I'm sure some of our locals who like to indulge themselves have bought his product off the streets. Is Zane Swiegert a customer of his?"

"He has been on and off for a few years." Wildman turned away from the interview to face Garrett. "My intel says Swiegert is driving for him now, too. He's using his delivery job to make drops and pick up payments from Olivera's people on the streets."

This scenario just got worse and worse. "So, Daddy Dearest is a scumbag who doesn't deserve those kids when we do find them." He refused to say *if* the children were found. "Why am I here? Arrest him already, and let me get back to work."

"We think Swiegert is key to bringing down Olivera."

"He's not going to testify against his supplier and employer." Although if there was any hint that he might, it could explain the damage done to his fingers—and why he seemed more nervous about the police asking so many questions than he was worried about his kids. "You think Olivera took the kids to leverage Swiegert into keeping his mouth shut?"

"I've got an undercover operative in Olivera's organization. While Olivera isn't above recruiting underage girls into his human trafficking business, my man hasn't seen or heard of anyone as young as elementary-school-age children being lured in with the promise of drugs, family, or money."

"That's a relief. Of sorts. Still doesn't put us any closer to finding those children." Garrett knew there had to be more to this conversation than idle speculation. Conor Wildman wanted something from him. "What is this meeting really about?"

The detective glanced around before ushering Garrett out of the interview watch room and over to the empty meeting room next door. "Zane Swiegert isn't the only witness who could talk to us about Olivera's activities. My inside man has spotted Olivera and one of his lieutenants entering Zane Swiegert's apartment building on more than one occasion. While Nate and Abby were present."

Garrett swore. "The children? You want them to testify against that scumbag?"

The detective nodded. "Our information officer updates the public so they can assist with the search."

"What kind of car does Swiegert drive?"

The detective arched an eyebrow. "That's random."

"Not really."

Conor pulled up his phone and looked it up. "An old-model Ford Bronco." So not the lit-up Dodge Charger that had shown up at Jessie's ranch yesterday evening.

"What about Olivera? Anybody in your investigation drive a shiny new Dodge Charger fitted with underglow lights?"

Conor shook his head. "But this crew gets new vehicles all the time. Part of it is because they modify them to transport their coke and pot. Once we ID one of them, that vehicle is retired and torn apart at a chop shop. And part of it is just because Olivera and his crew have got a ton of money to spend. Are you going to explain that question to me?"

Garrett scrubbed his fingers through his hair. "Just some unexplained traffic in my part of the world. We may not be the only ones looking for those kids."

"Any sign of Kai Olivera?"

"A residential security camera caught a couple of vehicles where they shouldn't be. The images weren't clear enough to make an ID." He purposely left Jessie's name out of the conversation since she valued her privacy so much. "Are you familiar with K-9 Ranch?"

"That lady who trains protection and companion dogs?" Detective Wildman nodded. "She's done some good work for victims of violent crime. Our police psychologist, Dr. Kilpatrick, sent an officer who was struggling with PTSD to her."

"That lady is good friend of mine."

"That's where the car was sighted?"

"If Zane Swiegert thinks they have to—"

"He'd cooperate with KCPD to protect his childr
rett shook his head. Kai Olivera might be the wor
worst and needed to be taken down. But to ask a thirc
or kindergartner to testify against him...? "That's a r
big risk you'd be taking."

"When I say Kai Olivera is bad news, I'm being n
Detective Wildman's flair for sarcasm was obvious. "I n
someone to find those children and put them into protect
custody at a safe house before we move on Olivera." Wil
man pulled out a chair and sat. "A tip from the Amber Aler
Hotline said two children matching Nate and Abby Swiegert's descriptions were spotted the morning they went missing
getting on a public transit bus headed east out 40 Highway.
Into your neck of the woods."

Public transit didn't come out as far as Lone Jack where he lived. But if they took it to the end of the line and got out, they could hike or, God forbid, hitchhike to get farther out of the city. "So KCPD is focusing their search east of the city in Jackson County."

Detective Wildman nodded. "Your jurisdiction."

Garrett pulled his ball cap from his back pocket and
in the chair across from Wildman. "I've had a rash of br
ins and petty thefts the past three days. My money w
teenage vandals. But it could be the kids stealing sup
finding a relatively warm spot to stay for the night

"You looking into those?"

"I was until the Amber Alert took precedence."
string of random crimes did make sense if he
the right context. "Has information from the ti
to the press? Would them heading east be pub

Garrett nodded. "And you believe Swiegert is tied to Olivera?"

"I'm certain of it."

He was already on his feet and pulling out his phone to text Jessie to make sure she was okay, that there hadn't been any other unusual incidents at her place.

"Caldwell." Garrett stopped in the doorway at Detective Wildman's harsh tone. "Are we on the same page here? If you find those kids, I want to be the first person you call. Not the search team, not Family Services. I need to know they're safe and off the playing field so I can put the pressure on Swiegert and nail Olivera."

"You'll be the first call I make."

Chapter Six

Jessica looked up from the A. L. Baines fantasy novel she was reading and wondered what the dogs out in the kennels were going on about now. So much barking. She knew sometimes it was a chain reaction type of thing—one dog saw or smelled or heard something, and all the others chimed in. But after the recent break-ins and mysterious late-night visitors she'd had, she wondered if there could be something more to it.

Although, anyone who tried to break into a place with so many dogs was either stupid or seriously desperate. *Seriously desperate.* That sounded dangerous. She couldn't be amused by her dogs' doglike behavior if there was someone dangerous out there.

After slipping a bookmark between the pages, she set aside her book and woke up her laptop that she'd brought to the coffee table to pay some bills earlier. She pulled up the camera feeds outside. Nothing at the front gate. But since her phone hadn't pinged, she hadn't expected to see anything suspicious there, anyway.

She watched a couple of minutes of the camera feed from the barn. No strange cars. No Soren Hauck. No faceless strangers. But something was out there. Even with the grainy nighttime images of black and white and gray, she could make out several of her charges pawing at their gates at the front of their kennels. Rascal had his little black nose poking through the chain links, and Jasper had his big jowls pressed against his gate to get a closer look at whatever the other dogs had seen. Even her eleven-month-old pit bull, Baby, was at her gate, her whole body bouncing with every bark.

Was that…?

Jessica pulled the computer onto her lap and replayed the last few seconds. There was a ghost of movement, something darker than the rest of the shadows that darted around the corner of the kennel and disappeared into the camera's blind spot at the far end of the building. Whatever she'd seen was low to the ground, small and quick. Skunk? Raccoon? Someone's feet? She shook her head at the fanciful reminder of the witch's feet curling up and disappearing in *The Wizard of Oz*. Her heart rate sped up a notch, but she instantly felt Shadow's head resting atop her thigh.

"I'm okay, buddy," she reassured him, and thanked him with a rub beneath his collar. "That scene in the movie always freaks me out a little bit." She tried to freeze the image, but it was just a blob of shadow among the shadows. "I don't know what that was." She sat back and watched the dogs still barking at the disturbance that seemed to have scuttled out of there, at least from this angle. "If this is going to be a thing out here, maybe I'd better invest in more cameras. I've got too many blind spots."

She was beginning to understand Garrett's frustration with an unsolved mystery. Replaying the image again, she realized that whatever had cast that shadow never appeared on screen. It was as if it had started to come around the end of the kennels, then darted back to its hidey-hole when it saw the reception of twelve dogs waiting for him. Waiting for *it*? She glanced up. Was *it* still out there? She'd locked the front and back doors, hadn't she? Jessica exhaled a deep breath, forcing herself to relax. Of course, she'd locked the doors. She kept them locked whether she was inside the house or out with the dogs, and certainly when she left the ranch. And she'd double-checked them after letting Shadow out that last time after dinner, before she'd picked up her book and laptop and curled up beneath the throw blanket on her couch.

She watched Toby bound through the camera feed and disappear after the blur of movement she'd seen. That wasn't anything much to worry about. Toby had two speeds—fast and playful, and flat on his belly to lounge or sleep. She'd seen him chase after autumn leaves floating through the air, so his pursuit of *it* wasn't necessarily cause for alarm.

But where was Rex? Apparently, whatever had stirred up the others was beneath his interest. That calmed her a little. He was the true guard dog of the ranch, and if he wasn't worried, she wouldn't be, either. Soon enough, the barking outside subsided into the quiet night air, and she saw the dogs settle down into their beds or go back to a late-night snack in their kennels.

Jessica reached over to pet Shadow, who was stretched out on the sofa beside her. She always loved the warmth that came off his body and relished the way he stretched and rolled beneath her hand so she could scratch just the right places to make him feel better, too. "Well, that was a big hullabaloo. But if you think we're okay, then I'll think that, too."

She set the laptop back on the coffee table and checked the time on her phone. She should make herself get up and go to bed, only, she had a feeling sleep would be elusive tonight. Too many fears and memories had been stirred up in the past forty-eight hours for her to trust that she wouldn't have nightmares or that Shadow wouldn't have another seizure. The only time she'd been able to truly stop the worries and feel safe was when she'd plastered herself to the heat and strength of Garrett's body last night. She had a feeling that wasn't going to happen again anytime soon. Not after her panicked reaction this morning. Too much had happened between them too fast for her brain and her trust to keep up. She knew she had feelings for him, but risking the hard-won stability in her life was a mighty big ask. He promised to be patient with her, but was that fair to Garrett? He was a mature, accomplished, sexy man. He deserved a woman who could be his equal—not one he had to *be patient with* and take care of. He'd already gone through that with his late wife and her battle with cancer. Jessica's issues were emotional, not physical, but that didn't mean she wouldn't be a burden rather than a help to him.

Before setting down her phone, Jessica glanced to see if she'd had any more texts from Garrett. He'd checked in with her midmorning, telling her he'd showered and shaved and eaten a breakfast burrito, so she didn't have to worry about him not taking care of himself. She'd sent back a smiley face and assured him she was fine and not to worry about her. She'd worked with two clients today and put all her dogs through some kind of training exercise—as normal a day for her as she could ask for.

Around five o'clock, he'd updated her on the search for the missing children. No leads. No luck. Allegedly, they'd taken a bus east on 40 Highway until the route ended. After that, who knew? There were so many highways crossing through Kansas City, that if someone had picked up the children, they could be several states away in any direction by now. KCPD had some suspicion about the father, since he'd waited so long to report them missing.

She sensed there was something he wasn't telling her. But she assumed it was related to the investigation, and that he couldn't share information about the case. All she knew was that it was all hands on deck in the search for those runaways, and that Garrett would exhaust every skill and connection he had until they were found. When she expressed her sympathy for the father, Garrett had replied with a cryptic response about Mr. Swiegert having trouble of his own to deal with.

Jessica had answered with a brief text saying if there was any mystery to be solved, she was sure he would figure it out. The children were the priority right now, not proving whether or not the father had committed any crime, or if he should at least be reported to Family Services. He'd answered with a single thumbs-up emoji and gone silent for the rest of the evening.

It would be another late night for Garrett, and she felt guilty that she'd misled him and made him so angry this morning. Had he eaten lunch? Dinner? A true friend would fix him a sandwich or grab a to-go meal and take it to him at the sheriff's office.

So why hadn't she done that already?

Probably because she knew deep down inside that there was something more than friendship between them. Garrett might be brave enough to embrace the possibilities, but she was not. It scared the daylights out of her to admit that she'd been falling in love with Garrett Caldwell for some time now.

Maybe she wasn't ready to give her heart to anyone. But she could do better by him than she had this morning. "Do the right thing, woman," she encouraged herself out loud. Shadow flicked his ears as if he agreed. "Bossy."

She pulled up Garrett's number and typed out a text.

Jessica: I'm sorry about this morning. In case it wasn't clear, I'm grateful for everything you did for me yesterday and last night. I'm okay now. Don't worry about me. I don't want my hang-ups to distract you from doing your job or taking care of yourself.

His answer came through almost immediately.

Garrett: Can't promise I won't worry about you.

Jessica: No. Focus on those kids. They need you more than I do.

When he didn't immediately reply, she sent another text.

Jessica: Not to sound like an old nag, but have you eaten anything since that burrito? Put your feet up for ten minutes and rested your eyes?

Garrett: No and no. But it's nice to have someone worry about me.

Jessica: I never promised I wouldn't worry about you, either. ;)

Garrett: Okay if I bring you coffee in the morning?

Jessica: I'd like that. I will consider everything you said. I can't make any promises, though.

Garrett: That gives me hope.

Another text followed moments later.

Garrett: And fair warning... I will be kissing you again. I need that connection.

Jessica: That's your idea of being patient with me?

Garrett: Did you miss the part about me saying I needed you? It's been a tough day.

How could a text convey such exhaustion and frustration? The woman she'd once been before tragedy had irrevocably changed her would have reached out to offer comfort and strength. Hell, the woman she was now wanted to do that for Garrett. She wanted to be what he needed. She wanted to be the woman he could depend on. She wanted to be enough.

Jessica: Okay. One kiss.

She smiled at his answer.

Garrett: I'll take it.

It wasn't fair, but she felt a little lighter at the idea of seeing Garrett tomorrow morning. She was even tamping down anticipation at kissing him again. Would it be one of those quick, branding kisses where he held the back of her neck and made her feel surrounded and cherished by him? Or one of those toe-curling seductions like she'd woken up to this morning, where she'd momentarily forgotten her name as well as all the reasons why she wasn't a good bet for a relationship?

Jessica started to text him good-night and wish him luck on his team's search, but Shadow suddenly hopped up on all four legs and nudged his nose through the curtains to look out over the front porch. "Now what?"

A split second later, she heard Rex's deep woof. She hadn't gotten any notification on her phone that someone had driven onto the property, but she trusted Shadow's and Rex's instincts more than she trusted computer electronics when it came to security.

She pulled up her computer screen in time to see Rex chasing Toby out of the barn. That was weird. The only time she'd seen Rex turn on his patrol buddy was when Toby had been pestering the Anatolian's adopted goats. Jessica tapped Shadow's shoulder to bring his attention back to her. "Do we need to check this out?"

The rangy German shepherd mix jumped down and made a beeline for the back door.

"Give me a minute," Jessica chided, reaching for her lace-up boots. By the time she pulled on her denim barn coat and tucked her keys, phone, and flashlight into its roomy pockets, Shadow was scratching furiously at the door.

For a split second, she wondered if she should call Garrett or even 9-1-1 to report the commotion after so many destructive incidents happening on her and other farms in the area. But if she was tired, he had to be beyond exhausted. She didn't need him to come to her rescue again. Especially if this turned out to be nothing more than a raccoon in the barn or Toby trying to play with the goats again.

Jessica locked the door behind her and texted Garrett.

Jessica: Sorry to cut this short. Dogs are going off. Don't see anything on the cameras. Checking it out.

Garrett: Wait. I'm in the city right now. I can be there in twenty minutes.

Jessica: I have a dozen dogs to back me up. I'll be fine.

She turned on her flashlight, confirmed there were no unfamiliar vehicles in her drive, and nothing big like a deer or bobcat or neighbor with a shotgun wandering too close to her facilities. No, whatever had made Rex cranky enough to scoot Toby out of the barn probably wasn't a threat to her.

But there *was* a threat.

When she heard Shadow growling, she took off at a run to reach him in the barn. Once she got inside, she flipped on the lights and tried to make sense of what she was seeing. Shadow, the old man of the ranch and undisputed leader of the pack, was crouched down in the dirt in front of Penny and her puppies' stall. Oh, no. Had a fox or coyote gotten in and gone after one of the pups? If so, why wasn't Mama Penny going crazy? And what was Rex carrying in his mouth as he trotted back to his home with the goats?

"Shadow?" Jessica slowly approached the dog, knowing when he was tense and on guard like this, it was wise not to startle him. "Shadow." She called out more forcefully. When he looked up at her, she motioned him to her side. She grabbed hold of his collar and inhaled a steadying breath, bracing herself for a predator or carnage or whatever the dogs had cornered in the barn. Flipping her flashlight to arm herself with a club if necessary, she released Shadow, slid open the stall gate, and stared right into the tines of her own pitchfork. She retreated half a step. "Oh, my."

The little boy wielding that pitchfork had blue eyes, dirty, disheveled brown hair and a fist-sized bruise at the corner of his mouth. "Leave us alone!" he warned. "We're not hurtin' anybody."

Us? She raised her hands in the universal sign for surrender as she leaned a little to one side to spot a small, blond-haired girl in the straw, curled up beneath the missing blanket from her storage room. A bobtail Australian shepherd puppy was snugged in her arms. Penny seemed to be okay with these children in the stall with her puppies. She seemed familiar with them, knew they weren't a threat.

Jessica brought her gaze back to the boy who was so staunchly defending the little girl. "Did you break into my storage room last night?" She remembered the indentation in the straw. "Did you sleep here?"

He pulled his narrow shoulders back. "I didn't steal your blanket," he insisted, glancing down at the sleeping girl. "It's right there."

"I don't mind that you borrowed it. You're taking care of her."

"Abby's sick. I was looking for medicine." Some of the defiance leaked out of the boy's tone and posture. "She was so cold, she was shivering." He sounded scared and tired, and had clearly been smacked hard enough to leave that bruise, but the pitchfork never wavered. "I'm sorry I broke your jar.

I gave the treats to your dogs so they wouldn't bark at us all the time."

"That was smart." Jessica's praise seemed to quiet his fear a little bit. "I hope you didn't cut yourself on all that broken glass."

He gave his head a sharp shake.

"Are *you* warm enough?" she asked. The sleeves of his denim jacket didn't reach his wrists, and he wore only a thin T-shirt underneath. "I could get another blanket for you."

"I'm okay," he insisted. "I have to stay awake to protect Abby."

Jessica's heart nearly broke at this boy's staunch defense of the little girl. She suspected there was a whole lot of backstory she was missing here. But the reasons behind their rough condition and hiding out in her barn didn't matter. She needed to get that weapon out of his hands and get them both the help they needed. She just had to keep talking until she could get the boy to relax, sort of the way she'd calm a skittish dog to earn his trust. She pointed her head toward the far end of the barn, where Rex had gone. "Rex is that big dog. He doesn't like a lot of people. But the fact that he took a treat from you means you're good with dogs. He knows you're an okay guy."

"He wouldn't let me pet him."

"Nah. He's not into that. He's happier hanging out with his goat friends." She glanced down at Shadow sitting beside her. "Would you like to pet a dog?"

His blue eyes widened. "He growled at me."

"Because he was protecting me. Just like you're protecting Abby." She stroked the top of Shadow's head. "He won't hurt anyone unless I tell him to, and I would never do that."

This boy was such a thinker, evaluating his options. He looked to be about eight or nine, just a few years younger than her own child would be now if he'd survived. But he seemed old beyond his years. "I wanted to pet the puppies, but I read that you aren't supposed to handle puppies too much when they're still with their mom."

"That's right." She was starting to make some progress. He was carrying on a conversation now. "Do you like to read?" He nodded. "I've got a ton of books in my house. Would you like to see them?"

"Mrs. Furkin said I shouldn't go anywhere with a stranger."

"Who's Mrs. Furkin?" A babysitter who was missing her charges, she hoped.

"My teacher. I'm in the third grade."

He didn't get his advice from a parent? Some other family member? Jessica knew she was about to say and do a few things that most children were taught to ignore to keep them safe from a stranger. "Is Abby your sister?" He nodded. "I'm Jessie. Jessie Bennington." She wasn't quite sure why she'd used the name Garrett called her, but it seemed friendlier, easier to pronounce. "What's your name?"

He hesitated for a moment, as if debating whether or not it was safe to answer. "Nate."

No last name. But she'd work with whatever the boy gave her. Without moving any closer, she risked putting her hands down. "You're not going to poke me with that thing, are you?" He leaned the pitchfork against the wall of the stall but kept his hand on it. That was probably as much of a welcome as he was going to give her right now. Jessica inched closer. "May I check on Abby? See if she's sleeping okay?"

At least, she hoped the girl was just sleeping. Jessica's stomach clenched at the idea of the child suffering out here on the chilly spring night. She'd like to get in there to see just how ill the little girl was. She looked to be about five or six. How long had they been out in the elements like this? Did Abby need to see a doctor?

"Nate, I'm going to show you something." Using her hands and a clear voice, she gave Shadow a series of commands. "Sit. Down. Stay." Shadow's tongue lolled out the side of his mouth and she knew he was relaxing now that the pitchfork had been set aside and she wasn't being threatened. Then she held out a hand to the boy. "Come here, Nate. See how relaxed Shadow's ears are? Curl your fingers into a fist like this." She showed him what she wanted him to do. "Now hold it close to his nose and let him sniff you. He'll realize you're Rex's friend, and that Penny isn't worried about you being around her puppies. Dogs use their noses more than anything to learn about their world. Once he's familiar with your scent, he'll let you pet him. In fact, I bet he'd really like it if you would."

Although he avoided touching her hand, Nate knelt in the straw near Shadow and let the dog sniff his fist. When the dog slurped his tongue over the boy's fingers, Nate jerked back and landed on his butt in the straw. "I thought he was gonna bite me."

Jessica smiled and petted Shadow. "No. That means he likes you."

"He does?"

"Sure. It's a puppy kiss." She curtailed her instinct to reach for Nate and help him move closer. Instead, she demonstrated how Shadow liked to be petted. "Try again. Like this." Nate almost smiled as he petted the top of Shadow's head without incident. "You may smell like the treats you handled. That's a good smell to him."

For the first time, a spark of excitement in Nate's voice made him sound like a true little boy. "Can I give him a treat?"

"You may."

Nate scrambled away to unzip his backpack and pulled out a beefy chew. To his credit, Shadow eagerly took the treat from the boy's hand and lay down to enjoy it while Nate petted him some more.

"Good boy, Shadow." She praised both the boy and the dog for handling this first meeting so well. While Nate was distracted with the dog, Jessica scooted across the straw to check on Abby. Even before she brushed aside her curly blond hair and touched the girl's skin, she could feel the heat radiating off her fragile body. The girl had a fever, and her skin was pale. She murmured her brother's name at Jessica's touch and rolled toward her, but didn't completely wake up. "How long has Abby been sick?"

"Since last night. She threw up the dog food I gave her."

Jessica thought *she* might be sick. They were eating the dog food? "When was the last time you ate? People food?"

"We tried to eat the eggs next door, but they were gross. I like 'em scrambled."

"I do, too. With some cinnamon toast and bacon. I've got all that in the house. I could make you some."

Nate remembered his charge and came over to kneel on the other side of his sister. "I'm not leaving Abby."

"I have food for her, too. What does she like to eat?"

"Cereal with marshmallows in it."

"Well, I don't have any of that. But maybe I have something else she'd like." She picked up the spotted puppy and set him back in his box with Mama Penny.

When she came back to smooth Abby's hair off her warm forehead, the little girl opened her eyes. "I like your puppies. I named that one Charlie. My best friend at school is named Charlie."

"That's a good name." She smiled down at the little girl, who seemed to be more trusting than her big brother. "My name is Jessie, and I'm here to help you. Is your tummy upset?"

Abby glanced over to her brother, then nodded. "I frowed up."

"That's okay. That's just your tummy trying to feel better."

Jessica felt she'd won them over enough to take charge a little more. She looked at Nate. "Has she had anything to drink today?"

"We drank some water from your hose. I put it in the water bottles we brought from home."

Between hose water and raw eggs, she had to wonder if the girl had picked up some kind of intestinal parasite. She mentally crossed her fingers that this was just a touch of the flu, or the manifestation of the girl's exhaustion and their sketchy diet. And as much as she wanted to ask them where *home* was, Jessica had a feeling she already knew the answer. Besides, getting these children fed and taken care of had just become priority one. "I'd like to take you both inside my house, where you can sleep in a real bed and eat some real food." She pulled out her cell phone and showed it to them. "I have a friend in the sheriff's department. He's the police outside of the city. May I call him? He could help you."

"No!" Nate slapped her hand and knocked the phone into the straw. "I don't want to go back to Kansas City. He'll hurt Abby."

"My friend Garrett won't hurt your sister."

His eyes widened with fear, and he moved between Jessie and his sister. "The bald man will."

"Who's the bald man?" Jessica shook her head and focused on priority one. The details as to why Nate was protecting Abby didn't matter right now. These children were frightened and needed food and help. "I don't know any bald man. He isn't here. My dogs wouldn't let him hurt you."

"If you make us go back, we'll run away again."

"I don't want you to go anywhere except inside my house, where I can help Abby and get you both someplace where it's warm and safe."

Abby whimpered between them. "Natey, I don't feel good. My tummy's empty."

"Can you make her better?"

"I can try." Jessica picked up her phone. "But I need to call my friend. I won't let him take you anywhere. I need his help to take care of you."

"Natey, I want to sleep in a bed. It's itchy here." Abby reached out for her brother. "Can't the dog lady help us? She's not like Daddy's friend. She's nice."

So many questions to ask about what these two had been through. But Jessica held her tongue and waited for big brother to make his decision.

"It'll be okay, Abs." Nate squeezed his little sister's hand. "Jessie knows all about dogs and medicine. She's gonna take care of you."

"Thank you." Jessica wasn't about to correct the boy's mistaken assumption about her skill set, not if it got him to cooperate with her. Abby wore a sparkly pink tracksuit, but had no coat, so Jessica tucked the ratty blanket around her small form and scooped her up into her arms.

Abby curled into Jessica's chest. "You smell like flowers."

"Can you put your arms around my neck?" With a weak nod, the little girl slipped her grubby hands around the collar of Jessica's coat. She weighed less than some of the dogs she manhandled for baths or trips to the vet. "Nate, will you grab her book bag and bring it with us? Yours, too."

He dutifully picked up both their backpacks but hung back. "Can Shadow come with us?"

"He goes everywhere I go." Although Shadow was looking to her for his next command, she gave Nate the job instead. "Say his name, then 'Heel,' and tap your thigh. He'll fall into step beside you."

Jessica hurried out of the barn, ignoring the barking from the kenneled dogs. Behind her she heard a small voice, "Shadow. Heel. He did it!"

"Good man." She let her praise get both boy and dog moving. "Let's go."

Jessica carried Abby into the house and up the stairs to lay the girl on the bed in one of the guest rooms. Nate and Shadow trotted up the stairs right behind them. The boys stayed in the room with Abby as Jessica hurried into the main bathroom to retrieve a cool, damp washcloth and a thermometer. Nate hovered at the end of the bed, watching her every move as she tended to the girl. Abby's fever wasn't dangerously high, but she needed to cool down and get some fluids in her. And brave little Nate needed to eat.

She gave the girl a sponge bath of all her extremities, then removed her tennis shoes and tucked her beneath the covers. "Will you sit here and hold your sister's hand while I talk to my friend? Make sure she keeps the washcloth on her forehead. We need to get her fever down."

Nate took her place sitting beside his sister on the bed while she stepped away and pulled out her phone again. When she looked at her screen, she saw several messages from Garrett.

Garrett: Jess? Still there?

Garrett: You okay?

Garrett: I'm on my way.

Garrett: Jess?

She pulled up her keyboard and started to text him.

She looked into a pair of distrustful blue eyes and decided to call Garrett instead. Nate needed to hear what she was saying and not think she might be telling her deputy friend something other than what she'd promised.

"Jess?" He answered on the first ring. "Why didn't you answer me? There's been a development in the investigation. The kids' father may have some criminal ties. I need to you stay inside and keep things locked up."

"There's been a development here, too. Before you get

here, stop and get me some children's acetaminophen and lemon-lime soda."

"What? Why?"

"I found your runaways."

Chapter Seven

"They doing okay?"

Jessica felt Garrett lean against the doorframe behind her as she watched Nate and Abby sleep in the guest bedroom across the hall from her own room. Abby was curled up in a ball around the doll she'd pulled from her backpack. It was missing a hunk of red yarn from one of its yellow ponytails. But she could tell it was well loved and had been played with and cuddled often. Nate, on the other hand, was spread out like a starfish on a pile of blankets and a sleeping bag on the floor. Her ever-faithful Shadow was stretched out on the pallet beside him. A night-light beside the bed and the light she'd left on in the hallway bathroom cast the only illumination on the second floor.

"For now. He ate everything I fixed for him. Man-sized portions. He's a starving growing boy." She glanced up at the real man beside her and found him staring at the children as intently as she had. "Abby ate the applesauce and some of the toast I gave her so the acetaminophen wouldn't upset her stomach. Thank you for bringing that. Her temperature's down below three digits already."

"Glad to do it." His voice was a low whisper against her

ear. "Did they tell you anything more about what they've been through?"

She shook her head. "Abby doesn't say much, and Nate is pretty guarded. I think they've been in survival mode for so long, it'll be hard to earn their trust." She rubbed her hands up and down her arms, warding off an inner chill. "I'm half afraid they're going to bolt if I stop watching them."

His hand settled at the small of her back, sharing some of his warmth and reassurance. "I think they're taking their cues from the dogs. If Shadow and the others trust you, then maybe they can, too. At least a little bit. Any trouble getting them settled down?"

"I had them both take a bath. Then I started reading *The Phantom Tollbooth* to them. All Abby cared about was the picture of the dog with a clock in his belly. She dozed off in my lap. But Nate made it through two chapters before he admitted he was sleepy."

"He's a tough kid."

"Tougher than he needs to be at his age." Garrett made a soft sound of agreement in his throat. "I wanted to give them each their own room. She wouldn't even get in bed until Nate came in. I made him a pallet on the floor. He pulled it between the door and the bed. She didn't fall into a deep sleep until he lay down beside her and held her hand. He didn't give up until Shadow came in and lay down beside him."

"I can only think of one reason why he'd want to position himself between his sister and the door," Garrett grumbled.

"To protect her?" Garrett was practically vibrating when she nudged her shoulder against his. "Let's take the conversation downstairs." When Shadow raised his head to silently ask if he needed to go with her, she smiled and made it clear he was off duty for now. "Stay here, good boy. Relax." The dog laid his head back down on Nate's outstretched arm. It was probably the pallet he was enjoying, although she didn't think either the dog or the boy minded the company and warm body beside him.

Downstairs, Garrett peeked through the windows and checked the locks while she went to the kitchen to brew them a fresh pot of decaf coffee. He pulled out a stool at the island counter, braced his elbows on top, and scrubbed his fingers through his hair in that habit of his that indicated fatigue or frustration. Jessica's heart squeezed at the rumpled mess he left in its wake. As much as she wanted to go to him and straighten those sexy spikes of hair, she kept her fingers busy pouring their coffee. She set a steaming mug in front of him and doctored up her own drink before pulling out the stool beside him to sit.

She waited for him to sip some of the reviving brew before she voiced her own concerns. "What happened to those children? Nate said the 'bald man' wanted to hurt Abby. What scared them so badly that running away was their only option?"

"The 'bald man'?" Garrett glanced up from the drink he'd been studying. "Did they give you a name?"

"No."

"But you think they've seen him? Had contact with him?"

"Enough that they're deathly afraid of him. Were they talking about their father?"

Garrett set down his mug and pulled out his cell phone. "This is their father, Zane Swiegert."

She leaned over to look at the candid shot that had been taken through a window at a police station. Zane Swiegert looked like a taller, grown-up version of Nate with brown hair and blue eyes. But he also looked…wild.

Wild brown eyes.

Jessica squeezed her eyes shut and shook off the memory of her husband's murderer before a flashback could take hold. When she opened her eyes, she discovered that she'd latched on to Garrett's forearm, much the same way she reached for Shadow whenever she needed to anchor herself to reality.

"Jessie?" Garrett's hand closed gently over her own, warming it against the ink of his military tattoo. "What's wrong?"

She drummed up a wry smile but didn't pull away. "I'm okay. He just…" She inhaled a steadying breath. "With that unwashed, uncombed hair and the circles under his eyes, he reminds me of Lee Palmer."

"The man who killed your husband and shot you?"

She nodded. "Palmer was high on something when he came to our house that morning. Probably had to be to make sense of doing something so desperate. As if killing John and trying to kill me would get his wife or his children or his money back." She shifted her gaze from the picture up to Garrett's concerned expression. Although he'd shaved at some point during the day, she could see the dark, silver-studded stubble shading his jaw again. "Nate and Abby's father is using, isn't he. He has the same look."

"Yeah. Cocaine seems to be his drug of choice. I snapped that picture when he was in KCPD for questioning today. He sounded like he genuinely wants his kids. But there's something more going on there." After swiping the image off his phone, he leaned over to press a gentle kiss to her temple. "Sorry for dredging up bad memories. Do you need Shadow?"

"No, I need to be strong enough to face this." She squeezed his arm before pulling away. "I want to do whatever I can to help those children."

"I think you've been amazing with them tonight."

She chuckled. "I was trying to remember all the books I read when I was pregnant. They're probably out of date now. Ultimately, though, I'm winging it. I confess, too, that I'm drawing on some of my experience as a dog trainer. Gentle when I can be, firm when I need to be. I want them to know I'm the boss, but I care, and I'll be fair with them. Mostly, I'm crossing my fingers and praying I don't screw anything up."

"Well, it seems to be working."

She wrapped her fingers around her mug to keep them warm. "I know you have to call Family Services and KCPD, but can't we at least wait until morning? They've had a hard three days and Abby still has a slight fever. They need their rest."

"I'm not calling Family Services."

"You're not turning them over to their father, are you? He can't take care of himself, much less two children."

Garrett set down his mug, snagged her hand, and pulled her out into the living room. "I have to call my contact at KCPD to let them know the children have been found. But we won't notify the father yet. There are some things you and I need to discuss."

"I bet. Did you see the bruise on Nate's face? Someone hit him."

"I saw." Garrett halted, his hand suddenly tight around hers. "What about Abby?"

"I didn't see any marks on her," she reassured him. "As protective as he is of her, I can see Nate standing between her and any kind of threat. But they're both suffering from neglect. Their clothes don't fit. They aren't being fed. I'd like to do some shopping for them tomorrow." She tugged him along behind her and sat on the sofa. "Do you know who the bald man is Nate talked about?"

"I think so." Garrett settled onto the cushion beside her and pulled up another picture on his phone. This one was a mugshot of a beefy, brutal-looking man with bushy dark eyebrows and a shaved head. To cap off his arrogant, intimidating look, he had a black skull tattooed on either side of his scalp. "This is Kai Olivera. He's the reason you and the children are staying hidden here tonight instead of going back to KC. He's bad news. Drugs. Human trafficking. Illegal arms sales. He started off as a gangbanger and worked his way up to being king of his own criminal empire."

"I think I'm scared of him, too." She shuddered and looked away from the image. "How would Nate and Abby meet someone like him?" When Garrett hesitated, she pushed. "You need to tell me everything. If they're staying here and we have to protect them, I need to know what we're up against."

His rugged face softened with a smile that didn't quite reach his eyes. "I like how you say 'we.' That you see us as a team."

"You aren't going to leave us here alone, in case one of these guys shows up, are you?"

"No."

"Then, yes, we're a team."

His shoulders lifted with a deep breath, and then he got down to the business of explaining just what kind of threat

Nate and Abby were facing. "Swiegert works for Olivera. Started off as a customer, now he helps him move product."

"Product? Their dad's a drug dealer, too?"

He nodded. "And he's still using, based on what I saw this afternoon. I don't know if Zane Swiegert sent his kids away to protect them from Olivera, or if they figured out for themselves that they were in a dangerous situation. I need to talk to them ASAP and find out what they know."

"They need their sleep first," Jessica insisted. "And another good meal."

"Agreed. I'm going to hang around and keep an eye on the place tonight. I'd like to talk to Nate in the morning after breakfast." He angled himself toward her, then pulled her hands between his, chuffing them to warm them up. "I'm also going to introduce you to the detective who's running the KCPD task force to bring down Olivera. Conor Wildman. He and his team will help us protect the kids, but I want you to be familiar with their faces. You see anyone around here you don't know, you lock yourself and the kids in the house, and you call me or Conor."

"I will. I was thinking of installing some more security cameras, too."

"You're a woman after my own heart."

She turned her hands to still his massage and let them settle atop his thigh. "I thought the way to a man's heart was through his stomach," she teased.

"Not mine. I've been at this too long and have seen too much. Knowing the things I care about are well guarded and secure? That's what makes me happy." He grinned. "Although I wouldn't turn my nose up at a homemade pie."

"Duly noted." Jessica looked toward the kitchen. "I think

I still have a bag of cherries I pitted and froze last summer after picking them off of Gran's trees out back."

"Wait. You bake?" He sank into the back of the sofa and raked his fingers through his hair. "Ah, hell. How am I ever going to keep my hands off you now?"

She laughed out loud at that, appreciating that they could lighten the mood between them after sharing such a heavy discussion about druggies and dealers and task forces that were all interested in the two children sleeping upstairs.

But this was a serious discussion, and she'd asked to know everything Garrett did. "So, what happens now? How long can the children stay with me? And are we far enough away from Kansas City that there's not an imminent threat from Kai Olivera or their father?"

"Let me make my phone calls." Garrett pushed to his feet and headed for the hall tree to retrieve his hat. "Sit tight for tonight. I'll be back to interview Nate in the morning."

"You're not staying the night?" After that talk about security protocols and safeguarding things he cared about, she was surprised that he was leaving.

"Not that I didn't enjoy wearing you like a blanket last night..." Her face heated at the memory of just how needy she'd been. "But it's probably for the best, so the kids don't stumble in and find a man they only met a couple of hours ago asleep in your bed. I'd rather they build trust in you, so they have at least one adult they'll turn to before they decide running away again is their best option, rather than have me scare them off. Abby didn't say a word to me, so she might be afraid of men. Nate? He's still sizing me up. I'm not sure if he trusts the badge or not. I'm guessing he expected a cop to help them somewhere along the way, and they let him down. I'll be fine in my truck."

His reasoning made sense. Although, she believed if Nate and Abby got to know him, they'd learn he was another adult they could trust. "You don't think that will look suspicious that you're sleeping in your truck if anyone is watching the place? What if you stay in one of the other guest rooms? Or on the couch?"

He considered her invitation for a moment, then hooked his ball cap back on the hall tree, a sure sign he was staying. "The couch. That will put me between the door and you three upstairs." She nodded, feeling relieved to know he'd be there with them. "I've already called in one of my officers to keep an eye on the outside tonight. Plainclothes. I don't want to draw any attention to your place in case Swiegert or Olivera or someone else who works for him is looking for the kids out this way. Since I'm a regular visitor, my departmental truck shouldn't look too out of place."

"Should I cancel my training sessions tomorrow?" she asked. "Call Hugo and Soren and tell them to stay away?"

Garrett shook his head. "I think you should keep your routine as normal as possible. The neighbors will talk if you start making calls like that. Olivera is going to have his people out trying to find information on those kids. An abrupt change in routine or building this place up like a fortress will get the gossips' tongues wagging, That's the kind of intel Olivera will want to check out."

"Will we be safe with just you and your friend Conor? You know I don't keep any guns in the house. After John..."

"I understand. With the kids here, I don't want them to have access to firearms, either. I'll keep my rifle locked in my truck, but I'd like to keep my sidearm with me. Conor will be armed, too."

She nodded. "You had your gun last night, and I was mostly okay with it."

Garrett reached out and caught a loose tendril of her hair. He rubbed it between his thumb and fingers before tucking it behind her ear. He feathered his fingers into the hair at her nape and cupped the side of her neck and jaw. "I'm sorry I can't do better than *mostly okay.* But I'm not going to leave you or Nate and Abby unprotected."

"I know you won't. But it's not all on your shoulders, Garrett." She looked toward the front door. "A dozen dogs on the property, remember? We'll know someone's here long before they get to the house."

"You're sure about me staying here? I would like to be close by."

"I'm sure." She wrapped her fingers around his wrist and tilted her cheek into his touch. "I'll bring down a pillow and some blankets for you."

He nodded his thanks. "Why don't you go on up to bed. I'll get my go-bag from my truck so I can change out of my uniform, then I'll lock everything up behind me. Keep Shadow upstairs with you. He'll sound the alarm if anything gets past me."

She didn't like the sound of that. "Don't get dead protecting us, okay? I wouldn't deal very well with that."

"I won't. Good night, Jessie."

She stood there, still holding on to his wrist, not moving away. "Aren't you going to kiss me good-night?" She wasn't sure if she sounded seductive or pathetic. It had been a long time since she'd felt enough for a man that the difference mattered. "You said you were going to kiss me again."

"Maybe you should kiss me, instead," he teased. But his smile quickly faded, and he pulled away at her wide-eyed response to his dare. "Sorry. I said I wouldn't push."

"No, I..." She grabbed a handful of his shirt to keep him from retreating. She willed those handsome green eyes to understand that she was trying, but that none of this flirty, intimate banter came easily for her. "You understand I'm the queen of slow movers when it comes to relationships. It has been a long time since I even wanted to try. Not since John."

"Ah, honey. I don't know what to say to that. I've cared about you for so long. I want more, but I don't want to screw anything up."

Releasing the front of his shirt, she wound her arms around his waist and hugged him. She hated that his protective vest created a barrier between them, but she found the gap between the bottom of the vest and the top of his utility belt and clung to the warmth emanating from the man underneath. His strong arms folded around her, and she nestled her forehead against the base of his throat. "I'm just glad you're here. You're warm and strong and...you ground me. You keep me out of the dark places in my head and keep me moving forward. I'm used to handling everything on my own—well, with Shadow's help. But I feel stronger when you're with me—like, I can handle whatever I have to because you're here to back me up if I need it."

"Just like Shadow. I'm your support man."

She shifted her hold on him, leaning back against his arms and framing his rugged, wonderfully tactile face between her hands, then tipped his face down to hers. "Not like Shadow. I would never kiss him on the lips."

Feeling brave, Jessica pushed up on tiptoe and pressed a sweet kiss to his mouth. His response was infinitely patient, his lips resting pliantly as she explored his mouth and learned the different textures of his beard and lips and tongue. Then he captured her bottom lip between his, to taste, to suckle. The tips of her breasts grew hard and strained against the itchy lace of her bra. Her pulse thundered in her ears and the long-forgotten weight of molten desire pooled between her legs. There was no plunging, no claiming, just a tender exploration that went on and on until she frightened herself with how much more she wanted from this man.

When she pulled away with a stuttering breath and buried her head against his neck once more, Garrett tightened his arms around her. His lips pressed against her hair. "I could live on that kiss for days." His voice was a grumbly, deep-pitched whisper. "Thank you for pushing yourself out of your comfort zone."

"Thank you for being so patient with me."

"We'll get there." He pressed another kiss to her hair and closed his hands around her shoulders and pushed her away to arm's length. "I'm beat. I need to get some sleep, too. Go on." He turned her toward the stairs and playfully swatted her butt.

She whipped around, surprised by the touch.

"Too much?"

With a blush warming her face, she smiled. "My forty-six-year-old body appreciates that you like a little of what you see."

He leaned in, bracing his hands on the wall on either side

of her and practically growled. "I like a lot of what I see. I liked a lot of what I felt smushed against me last night, too."

Resting her hand at the center of his chest, she tilted her eyes to his. "The feeling is mutual."

He pushed ever so gently against her hand, moving in as if he was going to kiss her again. But at the last moment, he turned his head, shoving his fingers through his rumpled hair and backing away. "Slow mover. I can respect that. It may drive me crazy, but you are totally worth the wait." He reached behind her to capture her braid and pulled it over her shoulder. He dragged his fingers along its entire length before resting it atop the swell of her breast. "I want you all-in with this relationship when it happens."

"*If* it happens."

He shook his head. "*When.* Tomorrow. A week from now. Two years down the road. You and me? We're gonna happen."

She shivered at the certainty of his promise. "Good night, Garrett. I'll see you in the morning."

She hurried up the steps to the linen closet to retrieve a pillow and cover for him. From the bottom of the stairs she heard, "*When.*"

Chapter Eight

Garrett ignored the twinge in his back from sleeping on Jessie's couch and poured his second cup of coffee, biding his time until Nate polished off his stack of silver dollar pancakes, scrambled eggs, and bacon at the kitchen counter. It was a perfectly good couch. It was almost long enough for his body, and he'd been plenty warm. But he'd been half on alert against any noises inside or outside the house; he'd been half-hard after that incredibly sweet, mind-blowing kiss Jessie had initiated; he had a fifty-year-old back, and it was the couch.

Sleep seemed to be in short supply hanging around Jessie and K-9 Ranch, but he wouldn't trade his time here for anything in the world. This feeling of chaotic domestic bliss, this sense of home, had eluded him his entire adult life. But this morning, being a part of Jessie's world, he felt like this was where he belonged. This was what his life was supposed to be like. Although he wore his gun and badge on his belt, he was dressed down in jeans and a navy-blue T-shirt, enjoying what was, for him, a leisurely morning. And a twinge of back pain wasn't going to dampen the pleasure of sharing this morning with Jessie, Nate, and Abby one little bit.

He leaned his hips against the counter and watched Jessie help Abby up onto a stepstool beside her to show the little girl how to make pancakes on the griddle pan. Jessie had carefully braided Abby's hair back into a pigtail that matched her own. And she was being very careful about keeping little fingers away from the hot griddle and the stove's gas burners. Garrett enjoyed the view on so many levels, watching the females work side by side. Jessie's backside in a pair of worn jeans was a thing of beauty. He had yet to hear the little girl speak to anyone except her brother, but she enthusiastically emulated Jessie and drank in everything she wanted to teach her. Abby was a beautiful child, sweet and delicate—but he suspected there was a lot of tomboy and modern woman inside her wanting to get out. He couldn't think of a better role model than Jessie Bennington, who'd overcome adversity, launched her second career, and made a living rescuing and helping dogs, children, clients in need, and even the occasional lonely workaholic deputy.

Even Toby and Shadow were circling the deck outside the French doors that led out back, leaving nose prints on the glass. He couldn't blame them for wanting to be a part of breakfast at Jessie's house, too.

He'd already gotten up to meet Hugo out in the barn to help with the dogs, goats, and morning chores—and to fill him in on the situation inside the house. Not that he expected the older man with a hearing aid and arthritic fingers to put himself in the line of fire should anything go down here at the ranch. But another set of eyes keeping watch on things and reporting anything unusual couldn't hurt. He intended to have a similar conversation with Hugo's grandson when he showed up for work this evening.

"Can I have more milk?" Nate slapped his empty glass down on top of the island.

"*May* I have more milk?" Jessie corrected without missing a beat. She turned and smiled at the boy. "And a *please* would be nice at the end of that sentence."

Nate rolled his eyes and huffed out an annoyed breath. But he did what was asked of him. "May I have more milk, please?"

Garrett set his mug down and reached for the glass. "I've got it." He opened the fridge and refilled the glass, then set it on the counter. "And now you would say…?"

Nate's blue eyes met his. "Thanks."

"You're welcome." He nodded over his shoulder toward the woman at the stove. "And who made your breakfast?"

"Thanks, Jessie."

"Thank you, Jessie." Garrett added his own gratitude, showing Nate that he wasn't singling out the boy and asking him to do anything he wouldn't do himself. "Home cooking beats a microwaved burrito at the station house."

She turned and shared a pretty smile. "You're both welcome."

Nate didn't pick up the glass until Garrett released it completely. But then the boy drank half of it in a few big gulps. The milk mustache left behind on his top lip reminded Garrett that Nate Swiegert was still a little boy, despite his very grown-up efforts to protect his sister and get them both to safety.

Garrett checked his watch. Detective Wildman would be here soon, and then the busy normalcy of this morning would be erased by some serious police work and outlining the rules of protective custody for Nate and Abby.

"Are you sure we won't get into trouble if we don't go to school today?" Nate asked. He glanced at Garrett but directed the question to Jessie.

"Nope. Think of this like your spring break. Although, I did print off some math facts you can practice to keep your skills sharp. Plus, I want you to do some reading on your own. Then I'm going to give you another lesson on how to work with the dogs."

"Sweet." Nate was clearly excited about a chance to be with the dogs again.

Abby turned on her stool. "Natey, can I come look at the dogs with you?"

Jessie answered. "I want you to take it easy today, Miss Abby. Your fever may be gone this morning, but I don't want you to do too much and get sick again." She smoothed the little girl's braid behind her back, an affectionate gesture meant to ease the sting of denying her dog-time. "I want you to take a nap if you feel sleepy. Otherwise, I'd like you to show me all the letters and numbers you know how to write, and we'll practice writing your name." Jessie tapped the end of Abby's nose. "And if you're still feeling good this afternoon, we'll go out to the barn to visit Penny and her pups. I'm sure Charlie misses you."

Abby clapped her hands in little girl excitement. She glanced back at her brother, as if checking to see if her enthusiasm was warranted, and when he nodded, she beamed a smile up at Jessie.

Jessie smiled right back, looking as light and unencumbered by the past as Garrett had ever seen her. "See all the holes in the pancake where the bubbles have popped?" Abby nodded. Jessie slipped the spatula into the girl's hand and curled her own fingers around it. "That means it's time to flip your pancakes. They're almost done."

Abby might not have spoken to anyone besides her brother, but that didn't mean she wasn't interacting with Jessie. Or Garrett. The little girl celebrated her first successful-ish pancake by scooping it onto the spatula and holding it out to him. Her smile was the best invitation Garrett could have. "Hey. You did a great job." When she continued to hold out the small, misshapen pancake, Garrett realized it was a gift. "Oh. You want me to eat it? You don't want to eat your first one?"

Apparently, eye-rolling ran in the family.

Garrett grinned and reached for the offering. "Thank you, Abby." The pancake was freshly made, and still hot to the touch, but he picked it off the spatula, rolled it up and stuffed the whole thing into his mouth. "That's really yummy." He wasn't lying when he smiled and praised her. "Good job."

Her answering smile was worth the heat that singed the roof of his mouth.

Garrett poured himself some cold milk and drank it down. As he cooled his mouth, he looked over the rim of the glass and caught Nate watching his reaction to Abby's overture of friendship—possibly to make sure he didn't say or do anything that would upset his sister. Every choice Nate made, from running away to sleeping arrangements to keeping his eye on Garrett reaffirmed his suspicions that Nate was protecting Abby from something horrendous. His blood boiled with the possibilities of what that could mean and made him more anxious to interview Nate to get the answers he and the KCPD task force needed. And, it doubled his determination to keep this little family of circumstance safe from the evil that had chased them out of Kansas City.

Needing to keep his hands busy and his demeanor calm so he wouldn't become the thing that frightened these children, Garrett opened the dishwasher and started loading the dishes, glasses, and utensils they'd used. His movements must have been a little too sharp because when he straightened to rinse out the mixing bowl and whisk Jessie had used, he found her watching him over the top of Abby's head. The look of concern stamped on her face told him he wasn't fooling anybody with his just-another-morning-on-the-ranch routine.

"You okay?" She mouthed the words.

Garrett exhaled his anger on a heavy breath and raked his fingers through his hair. She turned off the stove and pushed the griddle to the back while he went back to the dishes.

A knock at the front door made him pause. "That'll be Conor." Garrett had already warned the children that an adult should always answer the door. But when Jessie automatically headed out of the kitchen, he grabbed her by the elbow and pulled her behind him. "Just in case it's not someone we know, let me go first."

She nodded, then reached up to straighten his short hair. The caring gesture eased some of the anger that was still scalding like acid through his veins. "Once I meet your friend, you can talk to Nate in the living room. I'll keep Abby busy in the kitchen or upstairs."

"Thanks."

"Of course. Remember, you're the adult, even though Nate plays like he is. Be gentle with him. He's a little boy who's been scared out of his mind, not a hardened criminal."

Garrett mimicked the same caress, gently brushing a loose strand of silvery-gold hair off her forehead. "I won't make things any worse, I promise."

WORSE FOR NATE, NO.

Worse for Garrett…?

He was vibrating with the kind of anger he hadn't felt since he'd seen a terrorist strap a bomb to his own child and send him out to greet the convoy of soldiers while Garrett and his spotter watched and provided cover from higher ground. He'd warned his team over their radios about the shifting makeup of the crowd. In a matter of seconds, the friendly greeting had morphed into an attack. With his teammates trapped among supposed friendlies who had suddenly become their enemy, Garrett had been forced to pick off the insurgents in the crowd targeting the soldiers—including the boy with the bomb—so that his team could rescue their wounded and escape.

With his hand clenched into a fist behind his back, he listened to Nate tell his story to Conor Wildman. To Conor's credit, the detective kept the conversation going with a few calmly voiced questions. But Garrett could tell by the tight clench of the detective's jaw that the boy's story was getting to him, too.

"And that's the night when the bald man and his friends hurt your father?" Conor asked.

Nate nodded. He'd already identified a picture of Kai Olivera as the *bald man*. He'd never actually been introduced to the drug dealer, so he didn't recognize his name, but called him by the apt descriptor. He'd forced his way into their apartment one night to have a *conversation* with his father. He'd also shared the creep's fascination with Abby after another visit where he'd held his sister on his lap the entire meeting.

"Dad didn't have his money." Because he'd been snorting

the coke himself with his girlfriend du jour and had passed out instead of making deliveries and picking up payments from the dealers on his route. It was bad enough that Nate had witnessed his father getting high in their apartment and had had to make peanut butter and jelly sandwiches for dinner for himself and Abby. But the fact that he'd seen Olivera and two of his enforcers punishing Zane left a foul taste in Garrett's mouth. But Nate continued on matter-of-factly recounting his experience as if he was telling them about his day at school. "I hid Abby under her bed when they started fighting. I told her to stop crying and be as quiet as her doll, so no one knew she was there. But Dad stopped when they dropped the end of the sofa on his hand. My dad cried, too. Real men aren't supposed to cry."

"They do if they're hurting as much as I suspect your father was," Conor said, trying to show a little sympathy for a man who'd blown his responsibilities to his family in so many ways. Zane Swiegert was still Nate's father, and the boy probably had a lot of mixed feelings about the man. "Did you try to help him?"

Nate nodded, his gaze darting from Conor to Garrett and back. "The bald man knocked me down. He called me a little baby and said I was in the way. He told me to go back to my room and let the men settle things."

Settling things between Kai Olivera and Zane was when the most heinous bargain of all had been made.

Olivera would cancel Zane's debt and let him live in exchange for Abby.

Garrett's nails cut crescent-shaped divots in the palm of his hand as he replayed those words over and over in his head. A sweet little girl as payment for a drug debt?

No wonder Zane Swiegert was so desperate to find his children. But was he trying to save them? Or his own skin? Either way, Kai Olivera wasn't putting another hand on Nate, and he wasn't taking Abby.

No. Never. Not gonna happen.

Not while there was still breath in Garrett's body.

He could see that Conor was having trouble dealing with the information Nate was sharing, too. He paused long enough that Nate squirmed uncomfortably in his chair. The detective held up a hand, asking Nate to be patient a few minutes longer. Conor's nostrils flared with a deep breath. "You're certain that's what the bald man said? He'd let your father live if he *gave* him your sister?"

"I locked the door to our bedroom, and I laid down on the floor. I could hear the men talking through the gap underneath my door."

"And your dad agreed to the deal?" Conor asked.

For the first time, Nate hesitated to answer. "Abby was scared. She didn't want to go with the bald man. He said he'd give Dad twenty-four hours to pay him back, one way or the other."

"Did your dad help you run away? Or did he agree to the deal?"

For the first time, Garrett saw a sheen of tears in Nate's blue eyes. But the moment he remembered his assertion that crying was a weakness, he angrily swiped the tears away. "Dad said we could never be a family again, that he didn't want us anymore. He said I had to take Abby away and keep her safe. He gave me twenty dollars he'd stashed in the freezer and said we weren't ever to come home again."

Conor closed his notebook and tucked it back inside the

pocket of his suit jacket. "He gave you the responsibility of being the parent instead of doing the job himself?"

Nate's legs swung like pistons beneath his chair. He clearly was done sitting still and answering questions. "I want to go check on Abby. Okay?"

Garrett never wanted to hug a child as badly as he wanted to hold Nate. But that wasn't what Nate needed right now. In addition to some serious professional counseling, what this brave boy needed right now was contact with the one family member he could rely on. He needed to know that his sacrifice to protect his sister hadn't been in vain. Learning to trust another adult would come with time. He hoped.

Garrett stood abruptly, ending the interview, allowing all three of them to catch their breaths and ease some of the tension from the room. "Thank you for talking to us, Nate. You've helped a lot. We'll be able to find the men who hurt you and your dad, and the information will help us do a better job of keeping you and Abby safe." He laid his hand on Nate's shoulder, and though the nine-year-old didn't jerk away, he didn't exactly warm to Garrett's touch, either. "Although, you might have to tell your story again someday."

"To a judge?"

Garrett nodded.

"Will you help my dad, too?"

Not high on his list of priorities, but it was important to Nate. Garrett squeezed his shoulder before releasing him. "You and your sister are my first priority. But if I can do anything for your dad, I'll try. You understand that he's broken the law? That if I see him, I'll have to arrest him?"

Nate nodded. "But the bald man will kill him if he can't find Abby."

Also true. "Yeah, bud." Garrett hooked his thumbs into his belt beside his gun and badge. "Between you, me, Jessie and Detective Wildman, we'll keep Abby safe." He glanced back to see that Conor was standing, too. "If Detective Wildman will help me, we'll do what we can to protect your dad, too."

"You bet." Conor pulled back the front of his jacket and tucked his hands into the pockets of his slacks. "Thank you for your help this morning."

Nate considered the grown men's response to his request, no doubt weighing his conflicted loyalty to his father who'd created this dangerous situation against his desire to simply be a normal kid without life-or-death concerns.

Garrett tried to give him some of the latter. "You did good, Nate. Abby and Jessie are on the back deck. If you want, you can go out with them and play with Toby. But stay where we can see you. I need to talk to Detective Wildman for a few minutes."

He ran all the way through the house to the back door before he stopped and turned. "You're not gonna ask Abby any of these questions, are you?" Even drawn up to his full height, Nate stood two feet shorter than Garrett, but he heard the man-to-man tone in the boy's voice. "She won't talk to you. Talking about the bald man makes her cry."

"You aren't the only one protecting her now, Nate. I'll do everything in my power to keep you and your sister safe."

Nate evaluated Garrett's promise, shrugged, then pulled open the back door. "Okay." He charged across the deck to the railing overlooking the back yard. "Toby!"

The black Lab loped up the steps to accept the bacon the boy had stashed in his pocket. Then the two were chasing and wrestling across the back deck.

Conor stepped up beside Garrett. "If he's this good a witness in a courtroom deposition, Kai Olivera will go away forever."

"If Nate makes it to a courtroom." Garrett glanced at the younger man and shook his head. "This isn't just about your damn task force. He's nine years old, for God's sake. He shouldn't have to testify. He shouldn't even know about drugs and enforcers and protecting his sister from a deviant like Olivera."

"You think Olivera wants to sell her or keep her?"

"Does it matter?" Garrett shoved his fingers through his hair. He'd kept his cool for about as long as he could manage. "He doesn't get to touch her again. Ever."

"Agreed. One hundred percent. But it could decide whether I cut off his head or his private parts when I arrest him." Right. He'd forgotten that Wildman used wicked sarcasm to dispel the tension he felt.

Garrett needed something more physical. He started pacing. "That's why he waited so long to report them missing. He was giving them a head start."

"And now Olivera is probably putting the screws to him pretty hard to find his payment for the missing drugs and money."

Garrett eyed the younger man. "You need someone from your task force to pick up Swiegert and put him in protective custody."

"It's on my to-do list. But Swiegert's gone to ground since our interview yesterday. He probably realized how much trouble he's in."

"Or he's somewhere getting high again. Drowning his sorrows. Easing his pain. Forgetting he even has kids."

Conor pulled out his phone to check his messages. “There’s nothing new from any of my team. You don’t think Olivera took him out already, do you?”

Garrett paced across the living room. “What’s it going to do to those children if he gets killed?”

“My question is, why wouldn’t he take the children and run away with them?”

He paced back to the kitchen. “An addict with only twenty dollars, a broken hand, and a lowlife like Olivera after him is a lot harder to hide than two small children.”

“Take my pocket change and run?” Conor shook his head. “It’s not much of a plan.”

“He’s not much of a father.”

“Sounds like you’ve gotten pretty attached to those kids already,” the detective speculated.

“They’re important to Jessie, and that makes them important to me.” He raked his fingers through his hair. That wasn’t the whole truth. “Kids in danger is a real trigger for me. Goes back to my time in the Army. Innocent bystanders getting killed? Children brainwashed by a parent or elder to sacrifice themselves for the cause? I just want them to be safe and not have to worry about the kind of crap you and I take care of every day.”

Conor’s grim expression indicated he understood where he was coming from.

Conor punched in a number on his phone and put it up to his ear. “I’ll see if I can call in reinforcements to help track down Swiegert.”

“What if he’s complicit in all this?” Garrett felt his blood pressure rising. “What if Swiegert doesn’t give a damn about those kids, and he wants to find Abby and make the payment as badly as Olivera does? Use his daughter to get back in his boss's good graces?"

He stopped midstride and braced his hands at his waist and stared out the back door windows. Jessie was working with a small terrier mix and showing Abby the hand signals to get the dog to sit and stay. Although Abby was more about rewarding the dog with treats and exchanging pets for licks than in learning the actual skills, she was talking—to the dog. Nate had found a Frisbee and sent it flying from the edge of the deck. Toby was off like a big black bullet, chasing it down and leaping at the last moment to catch the disk squarely in his mouth. Then Jessie showed him how to call the dog to return to him. Nate's narrow shoulders puffed up when the Lab did exactly as he asked, trotting up the stairs and dropping the disk at his feet for a reward of more petting and a treat. Nate threw the disk again and Toby was off to the races.

It was a normal scene. They were having fun. They were being kids.

The inside of Garrett's stomach burned with the goodness of it all, and just how quickly these moments of happiness could be destroyed.

He sensed the distant contact and shifted his gaze to find Jessie staring back at him, frowning with questions and concern.

Garrett blinked and quickly turned away. He ran into Conor Wildman's watchful blue eyes. "You okay?" the detective asked.

"I need a minute." He didn't bother trying to gloss over his dark mood. The detective was too perceptive for that. He heard Abby squeal in delight and Jessie laughing through the back door behind him. He was jealous that they could find any happiness in all of this. And he didn't intend to spoil that for them. He pointed a commanding finger at the detective. "You got eyes on them for now?"

"I got this." He nodded toward the front door. "Go. Burn off your steam. I need you to have your head in the game. I don't want to traumatize these kids any more than you do."

Garrett slammed the door behind him and hurried down the porch steps. His first thought was to get in his truck and drive fast to somewhere, anywhere. But the rational voice in his head reminded him that he was the protection detail. He might not be a sniper staking down a rooftop or a mountain ridge. But he was the backup he'd promised KCPD he'd provide. He was the last line of defense who would keep Jessie, Nate, and Abby, and this whole damn county safe from Swiegert, Olivera, and his crew. He wouldn't abandon his post.

He stalked past his truck and headed to the barn. The dogs raised a cacophony of alert and excited barks as he passed their kennels. Rex came around the side of the barn, identified him, then loped away to whatever corner of the property he was patrolling today.

The cooler air of the barn tempered his anger for a moment. But then the images of everything Nate had told him filled his head. He hadn't been there, but he'd fought in a war, he'd worked a SWAT team, he'd led his patrol division to every kind of call imaginable. His imagination was as vividly clear as if he'd witnessed all Nate Swiegert had for himself.

An overmuscled, tattooed thug cradling sweet, quiet Abby on his lap and not giving a damn that the little girl was crying.

Nate finding his dad passed out on the living room floor and dragging the grown man's body over to the couch.

A nine-year-old boy wearing clothes that no longer fit him staring into empty kitchen cabinets and finally making a dinner of peanut butter and jelly sandwiches for him and his five-year-old sister. Again.

A desperate, broken man sending his young children out into the world with a twenty-dollar bill, as if that alone would protect them from the evils pursuing them.

Kai Olivera smiling with a devilish expression that matched the skulls on his temples telling Zane Swiegert he could pay his debt with his little girl.

With a feral roar, Garrett swung around and punched his fist against the post beside one of the stalls.

He heard Mama Penny's yelp of surprise a second before he felt the hands closing over his forearm and pulling his arm down to his side.

"Garrett." Jessie's firm voice called him from the depths of his mind. Every muscle in his forearm was tense beneath her grip. "You're bleeding." Then one hand was cupping the side of his jaw and angling his face down to hers. He was drowning in the turbulent gray waters of her beautiful eyes tilted up to his. "You keep it together, Garrett Caldwell. Those kids don't need anyone else scaring them."

He breathed in deeply, once, twice, willing the anger to leave him. But it only morphed into a sense of helplessness. "Are they safe?"

"Yes. I left them with Detective Wildman and Shadow. You're the one I'm worried about. I could see you were upset. When you stormed out of the house—"

Upset? Hell yeah, he was upset. There were so many good people in this world who'd been denied children. Like this woman right here. Like Hayley. Like him. While Zane Swiegert had those two brave, beautiful children to call his own. His hand curled into a fist again. "Who does that? It's bad enough that he forced that boy to be the adult in the family. That he let Olivera hit him. But he'll leave him alone if he hands Abby over to him? Who sells his own child?"

"A monster. Not a man." Her steady voice calmed him. He focused on where she touched him—his face, his forearm. He couldn't even feel the pain where the skin over his knuckles had split. "What those children need right now is a good man. Nate, especially, needs to talk to and spend time with someone who shows him how a real man acts. That's you, Garrett. He needs *you*."

But all he could see was that little Afghan boy again, his father guilting him or brainwashing him or tricking him into sacrificing himself to take out a few American soldiers. The memory of how he'd had to line him up in the crosshairs of his rifle scope and pull the trigger before the boy could detonate the bomb was as vivid as the bruise on Nate's face. Using a child. Throwing away a child. "Zane Swiegert doesn't deserve to be a father."

"Maybe not. But you can't think about that right now. You have to think about the children. You have to let go of your anger and focus on what they need."

"What about what I need? What about what you need?"

"What do you mean—?"

Garrett captured Jessie's sweet face between his hands and crashed his mouth down over hers. Anger morphed into passion. Desire morphed into need. Her lips parted beneath his and he thrust his tongue inside to taste the essence of coffee and bacon and Jessie herself. When her arms came around his neck, he skimmed his hands down her back, pulling her body flush with his. But it wasn't enough. It wasn't nearly enough.

The frantic need he felt wasn't all one-sided, either, and Jessie's eagerness fueled his own. Her fingertips pawed at the nape of his neck. And then with a moan deep in her throat, she grabbed a fistful of his T-shirt in one hand while the other swept against the grain of his hair, exciting him with hundreds of tiny caresses before she palmed the back of his head and turned him to an angle that allowed her to nip at his chin, press a kiss to the corner of his mouth, then allow some mutual plundering of each other's lips again.

His blood caught fire, burning the anger from his system and leaving him aware of her lush mouth and womanly curves plastered against his harder angles. Needing more, wanting everything, he palmed her butt with both hands and lifted her into his heat. Her breasts flattened beneath his chest as he pushed her back against the post and trapped her there. He finally tore his mouth from hers and trailed his lips along her jaw until he captured her earlobe and pulled it between his teeth. She shivered against him and breathed his name.

He'd gone so long without this. So long without her. So long without love.

"Garrett." She wrapped one leg behind his knee, giving him the access to thrust himself helplessly against her heat. Her lips brushed against the throbbing pulse in his neck. "Garrett, we have to—" he claimed her mouth again and poured everything he was feeling in one last kiss "—need to stop."

"I know."

His body was going to hate him for this. But as her fingers eased their tight grip on his hair and neck, he pulled his mouth from hers, pressing one light kiss, then two, to her warm, swollen lips before he let her feet slide to the ground and he rested his forehead against hers. He was hard as a rock inside his jeans, not bad for a man his age, but he felt lighter, saner, more grounded now that he and Jessie had taken their fill of each other.

It took a little longer to even out his breathing. A few moments more before he could fully lose himself in the stormy gray eyes looking up at him.

"I'm sorry." He gently rubbed his hands up and down her arms. "I'm sorr—"

"Don't." Her fingers came up to sweep across his mouth, reminding him just how sensitized they were after that kiss on steroids. "Don't you dare apologize for losing it a little with me. After twelve years, I sometimes forget what passion feels like. How…heady it is to be needed like that."

"I didn't give you much choice."

"If I had said no, you would have stopped."

"You've got that much faith in me?"

"Yes. I know you have demons, too, Garrett. And the story Nate shared with you and Conor triggered them. But I also know you are a protector down to your core. If you weren't, you wouldn't have gotten so upset." She ran her hands across his chest and shoulders, as if smoothing out the wrinkles she might have left there. Then she leaned back and took a stab at straightening his hair. He treasured the gentle caresses as much as he did every kiss they shared. "Are you better?"

He was. He'd needed a physical outlet for his emotions, and she'd somehow known and been there for him. Such a strong woman, yet so caring and feminine. "Feeling a little raw," he confessed. "But better."

"Good." She pulled his hand from her arm and turned so she could put even more space between them. "Now let me see your injury."

She cradled his bigger hand gently between hers to inspect how his knuckles had fared against the post. She clicked her tongue, then grabbed his wrist and tugged him into step behind her.

She paused at the first storage room door, inserted a key into the lock, and opened it. Larger than the room that had been broken into, this one had a huge stainless steel sink where she could wash the dogs. She turned on the water and pulled his hand beneath the warm stream to clean the debris out of his wound while she opened a cabinet and pulled out a first aid kit and a bottle of hydrogen peroxide. She hooked her foot around a tall stool and pulled it out from beside the sink. "Have a seat."

He turned off the water and dutifully sat in front of her while she used a clean towel to dry his skin and gently dab at the blood seeping from his split knuckles. "Did I hear you correctly? Zane Swiegert plans to use Abby to pay off his debt to Olivera?"

Garrett nodded. "Nate overheard his dad talking to Olivera. That makes him a witness. Swiegert and Olivera are going to want to shut him up so he can't talk to the cops or testify against them."

"His own father?"

"Supposedly, it was his idea for the kids to run away, but…" Garrett swore under breath. "Drugs change a man. I'm sure Swiegert didn't mean to endanger his children, but a desperate man does desperate things. And the main thing an addict is thinking about is his next fix. Not his job, not his family, not even his own health. I think they're both a threat."

He raised an eyebrow at Jessie's answering curse. "I will not lose another child, Garrett. Not to the kind of violence you're talking about. I can't."

He stilled her hand beneath his. "We won't let that happen. Between KCPD and my team, we'll keep round-the-clock watch on your house." She nodded and went back to work. "And I'm moving in until this is over. *I* am going to watch over you and the kids. I want to talk escape strategies and survival protocol with you and them, too."

"I'm okay with that." She soaked a cotton ball with the disinfectant. "Do you want to talk about it?"

"When I think about what Olivera wants to do with Abby. How he hit and belittled Nate…it takes me back to some places I don't want to go." He winced at the sting of peroxide on his open wound. The foolish mistake of punching the barn post was certainly bringing him back to reality. "My wife dying wasn't the only reason I had to leave the Army. They could have put me behind a desk or in a training camp. But I couldn't guarantee that I could take the shot anymore."

"Those flashbacks are a bitch, right?" Although he was at first taken aback by the vehemence of her words, he looked up to see a smug smile on her face. She beat back her demons every damn day. He would do the same. "Want me to train a therapy dog for you?"

He chuckled. "Nah. I've got *you*."

"I'm your therapy *woman*?"

He stopped her doctoring and reached up to tag her behind the neck to meet her eyes and make sure she understood just how serious he was about the two of them. "You said I ground you. That I'm the solid, reliable man you can depend on. I feel the same way about you. I've seen and lost too much in my life. But with you, all that becomes the past. You make me want to stay in the present and look forward, not back. I see what the future looks like when I'm with you. I see everything that's missing in my life. I want that future. I like how I feel when I'm with you. Please give me the chance to love you, Jessie. I feel like you're the reward for surviving everything I've lost."

She shook her head with a wry smile and concentrated on wrapping the self-stick tape to keep the gauze in place around his hand. "I've got too many hang-ups to be anybody's reward."

"I don't want perfect. I want perfect for me." He touched two fingers to the point of her chin and tilted her face up to his. "That's you. I want you. I need you."

"Garrett…"

"I know, I know. I'm too intense and you're a slow mover. Let's get through this mess with Olivera and Swiegert first. Make sure those children are safe and in a loving home. Then maybe I can woo you at your pace." He released her when he could feel the apprehension vibrating through her. "This may feel sudden to you, but it's not to me. I love you, Jessie Bennington. I know it in every bone of my body. I just hope that one day you'll take a chance on loving me, too."

"I want that, too, Garrett." *But…* That unspoken word echoed through the small room. She turned away to drop the soiled items into the trash. "I don't know if I can convey just how scared…"

Her voice trailed away when his phone buzzed in his pocket. As a lawman, he couldn't ignore a potential emergency. He read the number. "It's Conor." He rose to his feet. "Caldwell here."

"You need to get in here." It wasn't the five-alarm emergency of intruders on the premises, but it was an emergency nonetheless. "There's something wrong with Ms. Bennington's dog. The kids are freaking out."

Garrett hung up and grabbed Jessie's hand in his injured one. "It's Shadow. He's having a seizure."

Chapter Nine

Jessica stood in the shadows of her living room watching Garrett stretched across her couch in a T-shirt and sweat-pants. His bandaged hand was thrown up and resting on the pillow above his head. He'd kicked off the blanket and his feet were propped on the armrest. She wondered if he really could compartmentalize the stress and responsibility he took so seriously and relax his mind enough to sleep. Of course, he'd been burning the candle at both ends so much recently that maybe his body was exhausted enough that it wasn't giving him any choice but to sleep.

Hugging her arms around her waist, she leaned against the archway near the foot of the stairs and studied him from the top of his mussed salt-and-pepper hair down to the mascu-line length of his toes. Maybe this was enough, simply reas-suring herself that he was here. Knowing he could be right beside her in a heartbeat if she needed him.

She admired the flat of his stomach and the narrow ver-tical strip of dark hair exposed between the hem of his shirt and the waistband of his pants. Even that was sprinkled with shards of silver hair, and she was curious to discover if all the hair on his chest was peppered like a silver fox. She'd loved

John dearly, but it had been a long time since she'd felt so viscerally attracted to another man. She might not have all the lady parts she'd once had, but there were still other parts of her that stirred with unmistakable interest in all the things that made Garrett so distinctly male. Beard stubble. Firm lips. Deep voice. Broad shoulders. Muscled chest.

She was visually making her way down his sturdy thighs when one green eye blinked open.

"Jessie? You okay?"

She swung her gaze back up to his. "I can't sleep."

Both eyes were watching her now. "The kids?"

"Dead to the world."

"Shadow?"

"Fine. He responded to the pill as quickly as Hazel said he would and has been taking it easy ever since. I fear his loyalty has switched to Nate." She sighed, feeling both a little lost and happy she'd trained Shadow so well. "That dog is intuitive. He probably senses that Nate needs some unconditional love and support from a furry friend right now."

He held out his hand. "Do you want to cuddle?"

"Not exactly."

He swung his legs over the front of the sofa and sat up, looking wide-awake and a little worried now. "Talk to me."

Jessica straightened and crossed the room on silent feet. "I've been thinking about something you said today. In the barn."

"You mean when I was losing my—"

"No. After that."

"I'm sure it was pithy and life altering. What did I say?"

"You said I was your reward for surviving everything you've lost." She circled the coffee table and sat—close enough to feel his heat, but not close enough to touch. "I feel the same way. You're my reward for surviving. I'm so grateful you're part of my life. I'm grateful you're here with us now." She ducked her head, letting her loose waves fall around her face. She was uncertain until that very moment what she wanted to say to him. She tucked her hair behind her ears and raised her gaze to his again. "But I don't want gratitude to be the only thing between us."

"It's not."

"My *pace* is all about self-protection. I want to be braver than that. I want to live like you do. I want to love again. I'm falling in love with those children. And you know how I am with my dogs." He nodded, listening carefully, just one more thing that made it easy to open up to him. "You taking care of the things that are precious to me makes it awfully hard not to fall in love with you."

He reached over and tucked a wayward tendril of hair behind her ear. "I'm not doing it to impress you. Those things matter to me, too, because you matter." He arched an eyebrow. "But I am making progress with you?"

Very definitely. She stood, holding out her hand in invitation. "Come to bed with me."

"I'm comfortable with sleeping down here."

"I'm not."

Nodding his understanding of her sincerity, he pulled his gun and holster from the drawer of her coffee table and stood. Once he'd pocketed his phone, he took her hand and followed her up the stairs.

They paused to look in on the children and dog. All safe. All fast asleep.

"Is Conor or one of his men outside?" Jessica whispered.

Garrett pulled the door to, leaving an opening just wide enough for Shadow to step out if he needed to. "One of my officers, Levi Fox, is parked at the end of your driveway until his shift ends in the morning. Maya Hernandez will replace him until KCPD sends one of their unmarked cars out to take over."

She probably should be embarrassed by the state of her rumpled bed. But she'd tossed and turned, rethinking everything that had happened over the past few days and remembering the only time she'd truly relaxed was when Garrett had held her that first night here. Releasing his hand, she quickly straightened and fluffed the sheet and quilt, then sat on the edge of the bed and patted the mattress beside her. "I'm pretty rusty at this, but I want you."

He tucked his gun in the bedside table and set his phone on top. "To sleep? To hold you? Or something more?"

"Yes. All of that." Could she sound any more inexperienced, like she'd forgotten every sexual encounter she'd had? "Maybe in reverse order?"

He chuckled, and she tumbled into him as he sat on the mattress beside her. He draped his arm around her shoulders and tangled his fingers in her long hair. The man was a furnace, and she instantly felt better being held against him. "Just to be clear, we're talking about making love? Then cuddling in the happy afterglow and falling asleep?"

Jessica pulled her knees up and let them fall over his thighs as she turned to wrap her arms around his waist. "Sounds like heaven to me. If you're up for it."

"Trust me. Around you, I always seem to be up for it." He pressed a kiss to the crown of her hair. "I just want you to be sure."

She laughed and remembered how much she loved a man who could make her laugh. Jessica cupped the side of his jaw, tickling her palm against the stubble of his beard, and angled his mouth down as she stretched up to meet him. "Let's start with a kiss. We can start where we were last night and end up where we were in the barn this afternoon."

"Sounds like a plan." He laughed as he closed the distance between them and covered her mouth in a gentle kiss.

Then he fell back across the bed, dragging her with him until she was lying on top of him. Just as she'd requested, the tender embrace soon became needy grabs and tongues melding together. Her thighs fell open on either side of his hips, giving her a clear indication that he was as into this mutual exploration as she was. His hands swept down her body, then back up, taking her shirt with it. He squeezed her bottom and pulled her up along his body until he latched on to the breast dangling above his mouth. He laved the tip with his tongue as he plumped the other in his hand.

Jessica groaned at the stinging heat that tightened her nipples into stiff beads and shot straight down between her legs. By the time he was done feasting on her other breast, she had pushed his shirt out of the way and found his own turgid male nipple to tease to attention among the crisp curls of silver and sable hair that dusted his chest. Her hair cascaded around their busy mouths and hands as she leaned over him, and it seemed to drive Garrett's urgency. He alternately tangled his fingers in the long, silky strands, murmuring words like, "Silky…soft…beauty…" before tugging just hard enough to bring her mouth back to his.

Then his arms banded around her, and he flipped them so that he was on top. He brushed her hair out in a halo around her head as she pushed his sweatpants down over his hips to reveal the erection she'd felt pressing against her. "Garrett…please."

In the next few seconds, her sleep shorts were gone and he was naked, kissing his way from her mouth down over her belly. It was her only moment of hesitation, and she grabbed his chin and turned his face up to hers. "I have scars," she gasped, her words breathy and uneven with desire for this man.

Garrett pushed himself up over her and dipped his head to reclaim her lips in a tender kiss. "So do I. Want to see them?"

"Not right now. Not really." She valiantly tried to remind him that she was forty-six, had been pregnant once, and bore the scars of both the bullet and her surgeries.

But he wasn't having any second thoughts. "Me, neither." He splayed his hand over her belly, touching it as if it was precious to him. "I mean, I care about what they mean. I care so much about you." He planted a quick kiss to her lips, then resumed his path down her body. "But seriously, Jessie. I'm a man. I've got it bad for you. And if I don't get inside you in the next few minutes, I'm going to embarrass myself and finish this off without you." His hand slid down to cup her, and she bucked against his grip. "Every inch of you is beautiful to me. Please. Let me do this."

All she could do was nod. And when he asked about protection, she kissed him again, thanking him for treating her like a normal, desirable woman. "I can't get pregnant, remember? And I haven't had sex since John died, so I'm clean."

"Me, too. Thank you for this gift."

"Thank you for making me feel safe enough to want this." He settled his hips over hers, nudging at her entrance, and the pressure building inside felt as exciting as it was unfamiliar. She wasn't some born-again spinster who'd gone too long since she'd been with a man. She understood now that she'd just been waiting for the one she wanted to be with. "Now, Garrett."

There was a little discomfort when he first pushed inside her. But with his thumb strumming her back to that wild readiness, they quickly fell into a timeless rhythm that neither age nor abstinence nor tragedy could ever completely erase. Jessica wound her legs around his hips and welcomed him with the sense that she was finally where she wanted to be. There were no acrobatics or fancy words, just a man and a woman and the love that had grown slowly and perfectly between them, finally reaching the light and blossoming into a feeling so right, she gasped with the pleasure of it.

She shattered into a million pieces and rode the shock waves as Garrett groaned with satisfaction and completed himself inside her.

Several minutes later, after bringing her a warm washcloth to clean and soothe her tender flesh, Garrett lay back and pulled her into his arms. She draped herself against him, deciding this closeness was much more enjoyable with no clothes between them. "Feeling okay, hon?"

Jessica would have laughed if she had the energy. She murmured, "Uh-hmm. You?"

"If I was any more okay, I'd be dead."

She was drifting off to a contented sleep as he covered them both and set the alarm on his phone. "I'll sneak out later before the kids wake in the morning. You can put a T-shirt back on then, too."

She kissed his chest, thanking him for his consideration.

Then he closed his eyes. Embracing the knowledge that this was what happiness felt like, Jessica snuggled in and fell asleep.

SPENDING FIVE DAYS with Nate and Abby, and five nights with Garrett in her bed—not always making love, but always holding each other close—made Jessica feel like a young woman with a good life ahead of her again.

She was a little sore, a little tired, a little scared. But her life was filled with so much purpose now. She had more to look forward to than work. She basically homeschooled the children in the morning while Garrett went to work so that no one watching the house would think anything unusual about a sudden change in his schedule, while another officer either from the sheriff's office or KCPD watched over the house. She scheduled training sessions in the afternoon for her clients, while the children stayed indoors and out of sight.

And though she hadn't said the *love* word out loud, she felt it ready to burst from her heart. She felt it from Garrett, too. With each chaste kiss, every laugh, every smile. She felt it in the eager way he touched her body, and in the firm yet patiently paternal way he worked with Nate and Abby.

They had finally reported Nate and Abby being found to Family Services and, under strict orders from a judge, promised to keep their whereabouts secret until the danger had passed. The social worker who'd driven out to check on the welfare of the children had even agreed to expedite a temporary foster care placement with Jessica that wouldn't be processed through the system until they were sure Zane Swiegert couldn't track them as the custodial parent. Paperwork was also being drawn up to terminate Swiegert's parental rights.

But again, nothing official was going forward as long as Nate and Abby were in protective custody.

Conor Wildman and his wife, Laura, were good people. Laura had taken the initiative and gotten some new clothes in the right sizes for Nate and Abby, and had picked up a couple of age-appropriate toys and games for them. Their daughter, Marie, was just a year younger than Abby, and when the family came over for dinner, the little girls played together and seemed to become fast friends.

Shadow hadn't had another seizure since the morning of Conor's interview with Nate, and she hadn't had another flashback since Garrett and the children had moved in.

It wasn't perfect. Abby communicated in her own way, but still wasn't talking to any adults. And Nate seemed to be waiting for the other shoe to drop. He'd gotten him and his sister away from Kansas City, but he rarely dropped his guard, except with the dogs. He reminded Jessica of the way she'd been even a couple of weeks ago. Happy but afraid. Confident but worried. Wanting to be free of the violence that haunted him, yet always expecting it would one day return. Jessica and Garrett had discussed their concerns with the social worker, and she promised to have a child psychologist lined up to talk with Nate and Abby as soon as it was safe to do so.

If she was being completely honest with herself, Jessica was still waiting for the other shoe to drop, too.

This morning Jessica was on the back deck, sipping an iced tea and watching Nate play the flying disk game with Toby out in the yard while Abby finished up her schoolwork at the table across from her. The little girl had lit up when Hugo brought over one of Penny's puppies as a reward for doing her schoolwork. With the promise that she'd return the puppy to the barn after lunch, Hugo had patted Abby's head and traded a salute with Nate before he climbed into his truck and headed home for the day.

The hair at the nape of her neck prickled to attention when Shadow growled from the deck beside her. One second, he was lounging in the relatively warm sunshine. The next, his hackles were up, and he'd jumped to his feet.

"Shadow?" Setting her drink down, she checked her watch. Nothing had pinged on the camera alert, indicating they had visitors. She skimmed the backyard and peered as much as she could into the trees lining the property. The puppy whimpered with concern as Shadow looked toward where Miss Eloise had shown up with her shotgun last week and growled again.

Today, she only hoped it was a lonely old woman with a shotgun.

Then she heard Rex's booming bark. Toby alerted to the sound like a call to battle and raced off into the trees. To her horror, she watched Nate take off right after him.

"Nate, stop!" Jessica was on her feet, hurrying down the steps with Shadow loping beside her. The little boy reluctantly stopped and came trudging toward her. She combed her fingers through his sweaty hair and brushed it off his face in a tender gesture he jerked away from. But there was fear trembling in his bottom lip, despite his defiance. "I'll check it out with the dogs. Get your sister in the house. You know what to do."

He glanced up at Abby, who cradled the puppy in her arms at the top of the steps. Her blues eyes darted between Jessica and her brother. Nate nodded and raced up the stairs to grab her hand. "I know."

Jessica waited until Nate had locked the back door behind them. Then she brushed her fingers across Shadow's head and issued the command. "Shadow, seek."

The dog raced into the trees, and she jogged after him.

But when she cleared the low-hanging evergreen branches, she pulled up short at the sight that greeted her. Not Miss Eloise complaining about her dogs and a dead chicken.

Parked just on the other side of her fence was Isla Gardner and a heavy-duty pickup pimped out with red and orange flames painted across the sides and tailgate. And yeah, there was some kind of short rifle on a rack in the back window of the truck. Isla looked a little pimped out herself with her bleached blond hair pulled up in a bouncy high ponytail, her painted fingernails bedazzled with sparkly jewels, and her white tank top pulled tight enough to look uncomfortable over her unnaturally perky breasts.

But the scariest thing about Isla was the tall, muscular man beside her, wearing a denim cut over a sleeveless white T-shirt. He had a sleeve of tats up and down his left arm and wore dark glasses that completely masked his eyes. He sported a brown crewcut, a long beard that would rival any '80s rock band guitarist, and he had a black skull tattooed on the side of his neck. More alarming yet, he had both hands on the top railing of Miss Eloise's fence as if he'd been about to leap over it onto Jessica's property.

"Jessica, hi." Isla greeted her with a friendly smile and reached for the bruiser's hand. "I'm showing my boyfriend around the place."

"Hey, Isla." She noted that while Isla held tight to her new man's hand, he didn't care enough to fold his around hers, as well. While that was a pitying observation compared to the way Garrett treated *her*, Jessica's focus was on the dangerous-looking man and the neighbor who'd never been this neighborly before. "What is it with your family and my animals?"

"Grandma told me she'd had a run-in with you and your dogs and Deputy Caldwell. Are you dating him?" she boldly asked.

Thinking of where Garrett had spent the last five nights, she'd have to say yes. But something told her to get this get-together over with as quickly as possible without raising any suspicion. "How's your grandmother doing?" she countered. "Taking her meds?"

"I guess." She eyed the big Anatolian shepherd, who was eyeing her. "Are you going to call your dogs off?"

"They're on my land, so no, I don't need to."

Rex paced back and forth along the fence line, barking an occasional woof when he got too close to the visitors on the other side. Toby trotted eagerly beside him, still carrying the Frisbee Nate had thrown in his mouth. Jessica could have easily called them over and ordered them to sit. But she liked the idea of having a couple of big dogs between her and her unexpected guests. She kept Shadow beside her, curling her fingers into his fur to keep herself from panicking.

After a glance from the man beside her, Isla giggled. "Well, I figured since we were neighbors, we could come over and visit this way."

"Not unless you want Rex to take a bite out of you. He doesn't like surprises."

Isla's smile faded and she propped her hands on her hips.

"Well, that's not very neighborly. What if I came over to borrow a cup of sugar for Grandma?"

"Did you?"

Finally, the behemoth spoke. "I heard about this place. You rescue dogs and turn them into attack dogs." Despite his size, he had a raspy, oddly pitched voice.

"Service dogs," she corrected. "Medical alert dogs, companion animals, sometimes a guard dog."

He turned his head, following Toby's bouncy movements. "What's that one got in his mouth?"

"Toby, come." The black Lab trotted up to her and sat. Jessica tapped the top of his muzzle. "Drop it."

She quickly scooped up the warped plastic disk and tucked it into the back of her jeans before petting the Lab and sending him back to trail after Rex. "It's a dog toy."

"Looks like a child's toy to me," he argued.

"Not if one of my dogs decides it's his to chew up." She squinted up at him, wishing she could see his eyes so that she could give Garrett and Conor a better description. "Who are you?"

"I'm with Isla."

Not an answer. But that wasn't any more suspicious than the tattoos and lack of eye contact.

"Kevie, don't be mean. I said I'd show you around Grandma's place and introduce you to the strange neighbor lady. Told you she prefers dogs to people."

She'd trade the *strange* insult for a little more information on the new boyfriend.

"How long have you two known each other?" Jessica asked, trying to keep her tone politely serious. With the matching tat, this guy had to be working with Kai Olivera.

But did Isla know what was going on? Was she aiding and abetting a criminal or being taken advantage of?

"I met Kevie about a week ago at a bar up in Lone Jack." She walked her fingers up over his bulky shoulder. "I don't think I've hit it off with a guy as fast as I did with you."

The moment she touched her long nail to his lips, he grabbed her wrist and twisted it roughly down to her side. "I told you not to do that." When Isla rubbed her wrist as if his grip had hurt her, he tapped the end of her nose and flashed a quick smile. "Baby."

Isla smiled as though the endearment made everything better. "What can I say? He gets me."

Or he's using you. To get to me and the children.

Speaking of children… Suddenly, Kevie wanted to talk. "Hey, I've got a friend in the city. His kids have gone missing. Have you seen a little blonde girl about yea high?" He spread his thick fingers down by his thigh. Then raised it a few inches. "Or a boy about this big?"

With her worst fears confirmed—that this guy was looking for Nate and Abby for his pal, Olivera—she carefully schooled her voice into a friendly, yet casual tone. "We're kind of in the middle of nowhere here. Children don't just wander by. Unless they're farmers' kids. And I know most of the locals. They stop by the house to sell things for school fundraisers, that sort of thing. I've got one young man who works for me a couple times a week. But he'd be taller than what you're looking for."

"Show them the picture, Kev—baby," Isla suggested, finally grasping that he didn't want her blabbing his name to Jessica.

"Yeah." Kevie pulled a folded piece of paper from the back

pocket of his jeans. He shook it open and handed it over the fence. It was a photocopy of a flyer with Nate's and Abby's school pictures Zane Swiegert must have made and distributed around the city. "That's them. You seen them around here?"

Jessica shook her head and handed it back. But the moment Kevie's hand came over the fence, Shadow growled and Rex gave him a warning bark.

The big man snatched his hand back, his cheeks growing ruddy with anger. "I'm not afraid of your dogs," he insisted.

"You don't have to be afraid of anything, unless you're up to something you shouldn't be."

He turned his face to the side and spit. Jessica was quite certain that was his opinion of a strong woman who challenged his authority. "You got a mouth on you, don't you?"

Again, she ignored the insult in favor of gaining more information. "They're beautiful children. How did they get lost?"

"They're not lost. The little cowards ran away." He pointed a stubby finger at her, and when Toby propped his front paws up on the fence, thinking he was about to make a new friend, the man shoved him away. "You see those kids, give me a call at the number on the back of that paper."

"Or call me," Isla offered, backing away as Kevie stalked back to his truck and climbed inside. "I can get a hold of him."

Isla barely had the door open and her foot on the running board before he stomped on the accelerator and sped away. She fell into the passenger seat and closed the door as gravel, grass, and other debris flew out behind the fishtailing truck.

Jessica quickly shielded her eyes and spun away. She felt

the sting of debris hitting the back of her legs, and heard a yelp of pain. She was grateful for a good pair of jeans and thick boots to protect herself, but knew instantly one of the dogs had been hurt. She should feel guilty for checking Shadow first, but when he seemed fine enough to bark at the truck speeding away, she turned to the other two. With the threat gone, Rex was loping away. But Toby was limping.

"Toby! Here!" Grateful that he was still mobile, she gave him a quick once-over, then scratched him around the ears and urged him to follow her to the house. "Come on, boys. It's for your own safety as well as mine."

Jessica pulled her phone from her pocket and chased after the dogs who were already racing back to the house. She tapped the familiar number and put the phone to her ear, pushing past the trees and hurrying up to the deck.

Garrett answered after the first ring. "Jessie?"

"I need you."

From the sound of his breathing she could tell he was moving. "What's wrong?"

"A man was here. Kevie Something. Said he was Isla Gardner's new boyfriend, but I think he was just using her to get access to the property. He had a tattoo on his neck like the picture you showed me of Kai Olivera."

"Did he hurt you?"

"No, but…"

"But what?"

She stomped up the stairs to the deck, trying to catch her breath so she could talk. "He acted like he knew I was lying about the children. He spooked me. He drove away way too fast. Kicked up gravel. He nicked Toby."

Garrett swore. "I'm leaving the office right now. Get to the kids, then call Hernandez. She's on duty at the gate."

"Are you coming?" She pulled out her keys and unlocked the door.

"I'm on my way. Get inside the house. Lock the doors. Take Shadow and Toby with you. You can doctor him up inside."

"I got the guy's license plate."

"Give it to me." She rattled off the letters and numbers. "All right. I'll run this. See if we can get an ID. I'm guessing he's a known associate of Olivera's. Are the kids okay?"

"I'm not inside yet." Setting aside her fears and focusing on the lock, she got it open and shooed the dogs in ahead of her. "Nate? Abby?" She didn't immediately see them. "You don't think one of his friends got in while he was distracting me?"

"Not with Hernandez there." She hoped. She locked the door behind her and ran up the stairs to their bedroom. She worked outdoors and wasn't afraid of physical labor. But her lungs were about to burst with all this running. "Get eyes on the kids. I'm almost there. Call me right back if something's wrong."

The siren blared in the background before he ended the call. Jessica tucked her phone in her jeans and searched the bedroom. Closet. Under the bed. Behind the door. Shadow followed right on her heels, searching for the children. She dashed across the hall and shoved open the bathroom door. They'd strategized about places in the house where they could hide. This room had a door with a lock and an older tub made of porcelain-coated steel. But there was no Nate. No Abby. Her heart pounded inside her chest. She looked in the tub, in the cabinet under the sink.

"Where are you?" she muttered, looking under other beds and inside other closets. Oh, God. Had someone gotten into the house and taken the children?

She could feel the snaky tendrils of a panic attack sneaking into her head. "Shadow?"

He was at her side in an instant, leaning against her leg. She listened to him panting. She focused on his warmth. She curled her fingers into his coarse long fur and believed that she was safe. "Nate? Abby?"

She realized she was also armed with a powerful weapon. A dog's nose. "Of course." Jessica raced back into the bedroom where they'd been sleeping and scooped up Nate's pillow and pallet, holding them to Shadow's nose. She hadn't specifically trained him to do search and rescue, but she hoped he'd catch on. "Shadow, seek. Find Nate."

Understanding her meaning if not her words, Shadow trotted back down the stairs and went through the living room and ended up in the kitchen. They moved past Toby, who was curled up on Shadow's bed, licking what was no doubt a cut on his leg.

When Shadow sat down in front of the pantry door, Jessica cursed. She'd run right past it looking for the children. But when she heard a puppy whimpering from the other side of the door, she knew she'd found them. "Good boy, Shadow."

She pulled open the door. "Oh, thank God." Abby was crying, holding the puppy in her arms as she hid behind her brother. Almost dizzy with relief, Jessica reached for them. "You're safe. The man is gone."

But Nate had armed himself with the fireplace poker. "We're not going back! You can't make us!"

Jessica retreated a step and Shadow tilted his head, questioning why his new friend was threatening her. "It's okay, Shadow. Good boy." While she petted the shepherd mix, she spoke softly to the kids. "It's okay, Nate. I got rid of him. Do you know another man with a tattoo on his neck like the bald man has?"

He lowered the poker a fraction. But his eyes were wide with fear. "Did he have a long, dirty brown beard?" She nodded. "He works with the bald man. He was at the apartment when they hurt Dad." He lifted the poker and thrust it at her like a broadsword. "He can't have her, either."

For once, she ignored Shadow growling beside her. "No one is giving either of you up. The lady from Family Services said you're with me for the whole month, remember? Longer than that, if I have anything to say about it."

"If you're lying, we'll run away again. You have to at least keep Abby here."

Jessica's overtaxed heart nearly broke. "I'm not lying. I want *both* of you to stay with me."

Abby sniffed back her tears and tugged at the sleeve of her brother's shirt. "Natey, Charlie and I want out of here."

But Nate blocked her with his arm, always the protector.

Jessica reassured Shadow that she wasn't afraid and knelt in front of Nate. "Will you let Abby out? You know I won't hurt her."

All three of them startled at the sound of pounding at the door. "Jessie! It's Garrett. Let me in."

Nate relented his protective stance. He lowered the weapon as if having the other man around meant he could drop his guard a bit. "Deputy Caldwell is here?"

"I called him. He came right away when I told him about the man. He's here to help."

Abby seemed relieved to hear Garrett's voice, too. "Natey..." She slipped around her brother and ran into Jessie's arms.

"Jessie!"

She picked up the crying girl, puppy and all, and hurried to the door. "I'm coming!"

The moment she unlatched the door, Garrett pushed it open and locked it behind him. He cupped Abby's cheek and stroked Jessica's hair. "Is everyone all right?" He quickly surveyed the main floor. "Where's Nate?"

The boy came out of the pantry, still holding the poker. Garrett moved past Jessica. "Did you protect your sister the way I told you?"

Nate's eyes were glued on Garrett's. "Yes, sir. I hid us in the kitchen closet until Jessie found us."

"Good man."

"You can't give us back to our dad. The bald man will hurt her."

"That's not the plan, son." He held out his hand for the poker, and Nate reluctantly handed it over. Jessica wished Nate would let someone comfort him and allow him to be a child again, but unlike his sister, he was a touch-me-not. He seemed to appreciate and respond to Garrett's businesslike directives, though. "Jessie told me Toby got hurt. Will you help her take care of him?"

That made the boy react. "Toby got hurt?" He raced across the kitchen to kneel in front of the black Lab. "Tobes?" He probed the spot where the dog had been licking and found blood in his fur. "He's bleeding."

"Will you help Jessie doctor him up?"

The boy nodded.

Jessica carried Abby into the kitchen, drawn to Garrett's calm, strong presence, just like the children were. He petted the scruff of Charlie's neck, then held out his hands to Abby. "Will you let me hold you while Jessie helps Nate with Toby?" Instead of answering, the little girl stretched out one arm to him, keeping the other secured around her pup. Garrett easily took them both into his arms, nestling her on the hip opposite his firearm. Then he spoke to Jessica. "Go. See if you can calm him down. I've got her. I'll need some details when you're done. I've already called the incursion in to Conor. He's sending backup, and I've got Hernandez walking the property line between here and the Gardner farm. I'll have her do a wellness check on Miss Eloise, as well."

Jessica nodded but paused to pull off Garrett's official ballcap and smooth down his hair. If the cap was off, he was staying. "Thank you for coming so quickly."

He dropped a quick kiss to her forehead. "Nobody's hurting these kids. Or you. Go." He turned away with Abby, carrying her into the living room. "Did I ever tell you the story about the puppy I had when I was little?"

"When were you little?" Abby's shy question were her first words to an adult, and Jessica fought to stem the tears that suddenly blurred her vision.

"A long time ago, sweetie. His name was Ace…"

Chapter Ten

Conor Wildman's suit collar was turned up and his jacket was drenched when Garrett opened the front door to let him into the house two nights later.

The spring rains had finally come. And while the budding trees would leaf out and the grass would turn green once it soaked up enough sun, and the farmers cheered that their crops would start growing, all Garrett could think of was that the dark, overcast sky and wall of rain gave Swiegert, Olivera, and his crew more places to hide.

The security cameras had alerted him to the detective's arrival, but it was too dark to make out who the driver was. If Officer Fox hadn't texted him to tell him Conor was pulling up to the house, Garrett would have met him at the door with his gun in his hand.

He still wore his Glock tucked into the back of his jeans. One of Olivera's men had gotten close enough to touch one of Jessie's dogs. And although Toby's injury had turned out to be no more severe than his own healing knuckles, the danger had come too close to Jessie for his comfort. So, he was armed. He was pissed. And he was deadly. The enemy wasn't getting past him on his watch.

Conor was an ally, not an enemy, though. He folded down his collar and shook the raindrops off his suit coat before stepping inside. He toed off his wet shoes on the mat beside the door and was facing Garrett by the time he'd checked as far as he could see beyond the edge of the front porch and locked the door again.

Conor's collar was unbuttoned, and his tie was missing. The man had had a long day. "We found Zane Swiegert dead. Massive overdose. Don't know if it was accidental, suicide, or murder yet. His body's at the ME's office now."

Garrett appreciated that the detective wasn't a man who minced words. But he wasn't sure how to process the news. His gut reaction was a silent cheer that there was one less lowlife he had to worry about out there in the world. But just as quickly came the thought that somebody was going to have to tell those children, who'd already lost so much, that their father was gone. Zane Swiegert might not win any father-of-the-year awards, but he was someone whom Nate and Abby had loved. And, if Nate's account was correct, he'd done what little he'd been able to in order to help them escape his deal with Kai Olivera. It also occurred to him that their yet-to-be official foster home here with Jessie could continue for real once Olivera was behind bars and the threat to them was over.

He ended up muttering a curse and scrubbing his fingers through his hair. "Those poor kids."

He tilted his head up to where they were sleeping and saw Jessie coming down the stairs. After baths and toothbrushing, she'd been reading them to sleep each night. He sat in on one session and had gotten caught up in the story himself. But mostly, his heart had been aching for that to be his real life—a quiet bedroom, two beautiful children snuggling up on either side of the woman he loved, tucking them in and kissing them good-night—Nate only after he'd fallen asleep and couldn't protest the mushy sign of affection. Then walking across the hall and falling into bed with said woman. They'd make out a little. Or talk. Sometimes, they'd make love. But always, the night ended with Jessie clinging to him like a second skin and him falling asleep, needing her touch like he needed his next breath.

But that wasn't his life. He was a man with a gun and a badge. Danger surrounded them; Olivera wanted to steal away Abby and kill the boy who would testify against him. And though they clearly had some type of relationship, he'd yet to hear Jessie say the three words he most needed to hear. Not *I love you*. Although, she'd already hinted at her feelings for him.

Let's do this.

Or something to the effect that she was done being cautious and ready to go all in on a relationship with him. To give him not just her body, but her heart. To trust him not just during this crisis, but for the rest of their lives.

He didn't need her to give him children. He couldn't promise that he'd never get hurt on the job. He couldn't promise that someone else who felt wronged wouldn't come after him or the people he loved again.

But he could promise to love her with everything he had until the end of his days.

He could have this life.

Tonight, she wore sweats and a hoodie, socks, and wool slippers that had lambs embroidered on them, in deference to the dampness and cooler temperature. Her hair was pulled back in a neat braid, her face was scrubbed clean, and she looked the picture of tomboyish domestic bliss he longed for.

She smiled up at Conor and shook his hand in greeting. "You look like a man who could use a hot drink. I brewed some fresh decaf."

"Actually, I'm a man who could use a beer. If you have one."

"The news is that bad, huh?" She turned into the kitchen and gestured to the table. "Have a seat and make yourself comfortable. I'll get your beer."

She popped open a bottle and set it on the place mat in front of Conor while Garrett poured them both a cup of coffee. He added cream and sugar to hers and carried them to the table, where he pulled out a chair and sat beside her.

He let her take a few sips of the hot drink to warm her up before he reached over to squeeze her hand. "Honey, Zane Swiegert OD'd. He's in the morgue."

Her fingers grew cold within his. "What about Nate and Abby? How are we going to tell them?"

He liked that she'd said *we*, and he loved that the kids' welfare was foremost in her thoughts right now. "We'll talk about it tonight." He glanced over at Conor to make sure he wasn't speaking out of turn. "We can sit them down after breakfast and tell them tomorrow."

She nodded. "Nate will be angry. Abby will cry. I wish we could get that psychologist out here to talk to them sooner rather than later."

"I know," he sympathized. "But we can't draw that kind of attention to the house. Not yet."

Conor downed a long swallow of the tangy drink and nodded. "And in more bad news, there's a chance he wasn't a willing victim. Our medical examiner will have an answer sometime tomorrow morning."

Garrett didn't like the pale cast to her skin. She was clearly upset by the news. But he wasn't surprised to see the color flood back into her cheeks again or hear her get down to business. This woman was made of steel. "Olivera? Do you think he's responsible?"

Conor nodded. "If it turns out to be murder, he's at the top of my list. Swiegert reneged on their deal. A man in Olivera's position can't maintain his power if he allows the people who work for him to cheat him out of what he considers rightfully his."

"You're talking about a little girl."

"And drugs and money." The detective leaned forward in his chair. "This isn't a man with a conscience we're talking about. I'm building a great case against him. Now my team just has to find him and make the arrest."

"And keep anyone else who can testify against him alive," Jessie added.

Conor scrubbed his hand down his stubbled jaw and sat back. "Yeah. That, too."

Garrett kept her hand snugged in his and continued the difficult conversation. "There's no sign of Olivera or his sidekick, Kevie?" None of them laughed at the juvenile nickname for a man who was undoubtedly an enforcer for Olivera.

"Kevin Coltrane." The man had done his research. "He and Kai are cousins. He runs a custom auto shop. That could explain the light-up car you caught on tape out here, and why we're having trouble pinning Olivera to any one vehicle. He and his crew keep changing them. Coltrane and Olivera grew up in the same neighborhood, and they went into the same line of business."

"Dealing drugs?" Jessie asked.

"Kai's the brain, and Kevie's the muscle." Conor took another drink and flashed her a wry smile. "Did his girlfriend really call him that?"

"'Fraid so. He didn't like it."

"I bet not. Women are property to men like that. Not people. The only reason he'd tolerate a nickname he didn't like was if he had to put up with her for some reason."

Garrett could guess the reason. "Like he was using her to get to Jessie. He gets a general location of where the kids were last seen, then he picks up a local and uses her to find out what the people around here know."

Jessie frowned. "You think he figured out that the children are here? Do we need to move them?"

Conor answered for him. "I don't think so. If they are watching the place, then any sudden change, like you and Jessie leaving, would only put them on alert."

Garrett agreed.

"I just wanted to come out and tell you about Swiegert in person. Let you two decide how to break the news to Nate and Abby."

"Thanks, Conor." Jessie stared down into her coffee, deep in thought about something.

The detective polished off his beer and stood. "I wish you were on my team for real, Caldwell. I appreciate your experience and wisdom. Your patience, too, for the most part," he teased, referring to the day Garrett had punched the barn. "I'm not worried about you running the protection detail here."

"Just keep me in the loop on anything else you find out."

"Will do."

The two men shook hands before Garrett walked Detective Wildman to the door and watched him dash out into the rain to slide inside his car. He drove off with a friendly wave and Garrett locked the door behind him.

When he turned, Jessie slid her arms around his waist and walked into his chest. He folded his arms around her and hugged her tight. "Talk to me, hon."

She rested her head against his neck where it met his shoulder. "I don't know how much more of this I can take. With John's death, it was a shock. Unexpected. It was scary and tragic, but I never suspected it was coming. This time I know Olivera is after Nate and Abby—sneaking onto my property, sending his goons to spy on us and intimidate me. I feel like death is coming, and all I can do is wait for it to arrive. Kai Olivera and his greed and vengeance are hunting us, circling closer. I know he's out there somewhere, watching, waiting to attack. But dreading that moment is wearing me down. What if I get careless or fall asleep at the wrong time? What if I don't see him until it's too late? Someone I care about is still going to be hurt or die." She shrugged and burrowed closer. "It's still going to be violent and tragic. Only I'm living with that knowledge for days on end. The stress is wearing a hole in my stomach. What if I fail those children?"

"Not going to happen."

"How do you know that?"

"Because I know you." He leaned back against her arms to frame her face between his hands. "You are strong and resourceful, and more devoted to the things you care about than anyone I've ever met." Her concerns reminded him a little bit of his time as a sniper. The waiting and watching for his target to appear was always the hardest part of an assignment. "You never knew Lee Palmer was coming to shoot your husband and you. But you know Kai Olivera is coming. Don't let that knowledge get stuck in your head and paralyze you. Use it to your advantage. Prepare. Have a plan of attack. You know the layout of this place better than anyone. You know what weapons you can improvise. And you have me."

She reached up to wind her fingers around his wrists. "I don't want you to get hurt, either. I think about that every day, too."

"I'm doing everything I can to be prepared, too," he assured her. "I'm training the kids to do the same. This time you won't be caught off guard. Try to see the hope in that. This time you'll be able to fight back."

She shook her head. "What if I'm not strong enough?"

"You, fierce Mama Dog, are stronger than you know. This is your fortress to command. You have a twelve-dog alarm system. Security cameras. Me. Heaven help Olivera if he puts his hands on you or those children."

"MISS ELOISE?"

Jessica didn't like the concern she heard in Garrett's voice that evening as he answered a frantic phone call from her elderly neighbor.

She looked up from where she was setting up a dredging station to make fried chicken for dinner to meet Garrett's worried gaze. "Have you called an ambulance yet?" He interrupted whatever argument the old woman was giving. "Then you need to hang up and call 9-1-1. I think it'd be for the best. It's better to get her checked out now than to have to drive her to the emergency room later." He got up from the table where he was helping Nate with some math work and strode out of the kitchen. "No, ma'am. I'm working another job. I'm not here for your beck and call. I'll send one of my officers to your place."

"Nate. Go ahead and put away your schoolwork. Get your sister and clean up. She can help you set the table." Jessica washed her hands and grabbed a dish towel to follow Garrett into the living room.

"Is everything okay?" Nate asked solemnly, following her. He'd taken the news of his father's death better than she'd expected. There had been a few tears, but no angry outburst. But he'd been unusually subdued throughout the rest of the day. Abby, on the other hand, had been nearly inconsolable in her grief. Pretty much the only family she'd ever known, other than Nate, was gone. It had taken a visit with Penny's puppies and an exhausted nap in her arms for the little girl to be able to function again.

Jessica wouldn't lie to the boy, but she could ease any concerns he had. "It sounds like Garrett has a call about work. He may have to go take care of someone else who needs him for a while. But he'll be back. In the meantime, Officer Fox is here with us."

"Down by the end of the driveway," Nate pointed out. "It could take forever for him to get here if we need help."

"It's not that far. You'll be okay, bud." Garrett ended the call and ruffled his fingers through Nate's hair. "Go do what Jessie asked you to. I need to talk to her for a minute."

"You'll come back, right?" Nate seemed reluctant to let Garrett go.

Garrett reached out to grip Nate's shoulder. "I'm not leaving you unprotected. Jessie can handle things here for a few minutes, and I'll be right next door. Do you remember us talking about the grandma lady who lives there?" The boy nodded. "She had…an accident at her house, and I need to go over there and make sure she's okay. I'll come back just as soon as I know she's got the help she needs. I need you to stay inside the house and do whatever Jessie tells you to do."

"Wash your hands and set the table with your sister," she reminded him.

Nate turned his sad blue eyes up to her. "You won't leave us?"

Her heart twisting at the anxious request, Jessica borrowed the surprisingly apt and lovely compliment Garrett had paid her last night. "I'm the Mama Dog around this place, aren't I? Of course, I'm staying."

It was reassurance enough for Nate. He nodded, then charged up the stairs. "Ab-by!"

"Inside voice," Garrett called after him. He stuck his finger in his ear and smirked at Jessica. "I swear that boy has no volume control."

Right. Loud, rambunctious boy. Small problem in the grand scheme of things.

"Miss Eloise had an accident?" She followed Garrett to the hall tree, where he grabbed his hat. "Is she all right?"

The night sky lit up through the windows. A loud boom of thunder rattled the panes soon after. Shadow woofed from his bed by the back door. Dr. Cooper-Burke had warned that he might be more sensitive to storms since developing his idiopathic epilepsy. Jessica felt the hair on her arms stand on end in response to the electricity in the air.

"Easy." She felt Garrett's hand on her shoulder and automatically took a calming breath. She watched his chest expand and contract beneath the protective vest he wore and took two more breaths along with him. "You afraid of storms?"

"No." She reached up to clasp his wrist, to feel his warmth and strength and know that she was okay. "Things just seem a little tense around here tonight."

"Do I need to reassure you that I'm coming back, too?"

She shook her head. "I'm not nine years old. I know duty calls. What happened to Miss Eloise?"

His face turned grim. "Actually, she was calling about Isla. Apparently, the new boyfriend assaulted her and stole the money she had in her purse."

"*Kevie* hit her? What a surprise." Jessica felt sorry for the young woman who seemed so desperate to have a man in her life that she'd settle for one who abused her. "Probably his way of breaking up with her now that he doesn't need her help to spy on the neighbors."

"I'm going to call in an officer to take over the call, but I want to head over there to make sure the premises are clear and that Kevin Coltrane isn't in the area again."

Thunder rattled the windows again as the rain poured down. "Are you sure you want to go out in this? Do you have a jacket you can put on?"

He chuckled. "Out in my truck."

"That won't do you much good. You'll get soaked."

"Hey, you survived a trip outside to batten down the kennels and close up the barn to make sure the dogs were all okay."

"That was in daylight. It's dark as pitch out there." She

shivered as another bolt of lightning streaked across the sky. "Except when it does that."

He brushed his fingers over the edge of her hair and cupped the side of her jaw and neck. "I'll be fine. You'll be fine." He leaned in to claim her mouth in a quick kiss. "Besides, if I get soaked to the skin, you'll have to strip off all my clothes and dry me off with a towel."

"You're incorrigible, old man." She mimicked his hold on her face and cupped the side of his jaw to exchange another kiss. "Go. Let me know how Isla's doing, and don't let Miss Eloise set the two of you up."

He plunked his cap on top of his head and adjusted it into place. "Not gonna happen. I'm already taken."

She caught the door when he opened it, and even with the depth of the porch, she felt the cold rain splashing against her face. "What if this is some kind of ploy to get you away from the house so we're vulnerable here?"

Garrett turned at the edge of the porch and came back to her, grasping her face between his hands and tilting her gaze up to his. "You got this, Mama Dog. You've shown me that you can handle anything." He leaned in to kiss her again, quickly, but much more thoroughly. Then he was backing away. "Plus, I'll be back. Believe that. I will always come back to you."

She caught a brief flash of light as he opened the door to his truck. Then his headlights came on and he turned in her driveway to disappear into the night.

"He's coming back," she whispered. Then she felt Shadow's warm body pressed against her side. He must have sensed her anxiety all the way out here. "Right, boy?" She stroked her fingers through his dampening hair. "He's coming back really soon?"

Maybe it was the storm. Maybe his sharp ears had heard something that she could not. Maybe it was only something a dog could sense. But for the first time since she'd begun to train him, Shadow whimpered beside her.

Chapter Eleven

Jessica knew the exact moment her world changed again.

Her phone pinged in her pocket.

She pulled it out and waited for a few seconds for Officer Fox or Garrett himself to call and let her know that someone she knew had turned into her driveway.

She waited.

And waited.

Her pulse rate kicked up a notch.

No one was calling.

"Shadow?" She called the dog to her side, and he answered immediately. She scratched her fingers around his ears, thinking, thinking.

Oh, hell. Her instincts screamed at her that something was wrong. If she was a dog, she would have barked.

She whirled around to the children who were debating about where to put the silverware around the plates on the table.

"Nate! Abby!" Abby startled and dropped a fork on the floor as she grabbed them both by the hand and pulled them into the living room. "Get upstairs. Run. Lock yourself in the bathroom and get down inside the tub. Don't peek out. Don't go anywhere else."

Okay. Not helping. Calm down.

She inhaled a deep breath and bent so she was closer to their heights, even as she tugged them along to the stairs. "Nate, you are in charge of your sister. Make sure she stays quiet. Make sure she stays hidden." Before Abby's protesting whine fully formed, she gave the little girl an order, too. "You are in charge of your brother. Make sure he does everything I say."

Nate stopped and squeezed her hand. "The bald man's here, isn't he."

"Yes, Nate. I think so. We don't have much time."

"Where's Deputy Caldwell?" he asked, latching on to Abby with his other hand.

"He's coming. He's on his way."

"Can Shadow—?"

"No." She answered a little too harshly. "I need him with me."

"He'll keep you safe, Jessie," the little boy whispered.

Jessica pressed a kiss to both their foreheads whether they liked it or not and pushed them toward the stairs. "Lock yourself in the bathroom. Now."

Abby tugged on her brother's hand. "She said we have to go, Natey. It's my job to make you go. Come on."

Good girl. "Stay completely quiet so no one knows you're there. Don't come out for anyone except Garrett or me. Nate, wait." She pushed her phone into the boy's hand. "Text Garrett and tell him we need him. No talking. Just text."

"I thought you said he was coming."

"He is." She hoped. "Tell him to hurry."

She glanced through the windows beside the front door and saw a weird, rectangular light floating up her driveway. What was that? It was hard to make sense of what she was seeing through all the rain.

"Come with us." Nate tugged on her arm, begging her to hide, too.

"No, sweetie." She pulled him to her in a brief hug. "Mama Dog has to take care of business. Lock the door. Hide. Text Garrett. Go!"

The children ran up the stairs. She waited for the sound of the bathroom door closing. Locking.

She ran past the front windows and her stomach dropped down to her toes. "Oh, no. God no."

The weird lights made sense now. They were the underglow lights of the souped-up car she'd captured on her video camera that first night they'd rushed Shadow to the vet and Garrett had stayed with her. She'd bet anything that the two bulky figures she'd seen on camera were Kai Olivera and his big bruiser buddy, Kevin Coltrane.

They were here.

They were here to take Abby and kill Nate. Probably Jessica, too.

Sparing a thought for Officer Fox, she wondered if he'd been called away or if the skull cousins had disabled him somehow. Or something worse.

No time. No time.

Garrett had reminded her that she had time to prep for their arrival, time to formulate a plan of attack. She'd lost a family once before to unspeakable violence.

But she wouldn't lose this odd little family of survivors.

She ran back to the kitchen, searched for those improvised

weapons Garrett had mentioned. There were two prime candidates sitting right there on top of the stove. She cranked the heat beneath the cast iron skillet where she was heating up the oil for the fried chicken.

Then she picked up the chopping knife and went back to work cutting the chicken into even smaller pieces.

GARRETT PLACED THE bag of frozen peas over the bruise swelling on Isla Gardner's cheek and called for an ambulance himself.

With both women talking at once, it was hard to make sense of all the details about what had happened. But he could get the gist of their story.

Isla had indeed been smacked around a bit. Besides the mark on her face, she had bruises that fit the span of a large man's hand around her wrist. Even though she tried to defend Kevin Coltrane, Eloise informed him that Olivera's hulking sidekick had been to the house and robbed her, as well. Most interestingly, he'd threatened to hit the octogenarian if she didn't allow him to park his stupid truck at her place.

And Isla said her boyfriend had been insistent that her grandmother call Garrett for help, that it would make *Kevie* happy if the old guy next door answered their call for help. The old guy wouldn't be as big a threat as a younger officer, so she'd agreed. And she really wanted to make *Kevie* happy so he'd come back to her. It was just a ploy to get Garrett away from the house, a plan to leave Jessie and the children unprotected. He seriously doubted Coltrane ever planned to see Isla again, and she should be thanking her lucky stars that he was getting out of her life.

Once Maya Hernandez had arrived to take the official report from the Gardner women, and the EMTs were checking Eloise's blood pressure and Isla's injuries, Garrett drove his truck along the bumpy gravel of Eloise's driveway and turned to follow the rail fence that bordered Jessie's property.

His suspicions paid off when he found the white truck decorated with flames she had described parked to make a quick getaway with its tailgate facing the fence. A quick check of the plate number on his truck's laptop confirmed that it was Kevin Coltrane's truck. He hadn't been interested in Isla Gardner at all, maybe not even in the money he'd stolen from the two women. This was about finding the children and gaining access to the house while bypassing the security camera and guard at the front gate. It might also have something to do with approaching the house from the side where no dogs would detect an intruder. Even Big Rex wouldn't be able to stop them, because he was locked up in the barn due to the storm.

A bolt of lightning lit up the area well enough for Garrett to confirm that the truck was empty.

So, where were Coltrane and Olivera?

Pulling his cap low over his forehead and snapping his jacket all the way up to the neck, Garrett opened his truck door and stepped out into the deluge. He was soaked to the skin almost immediately and gave a brief thought to the teasing remark he'd given Jessie about drying him off. But he was more focused on finding the answer to the mystery of Coltrane's truck. A broken window on a summer cabin, a broken latch on a chicken coop or storage room—those could be attributed to two runaways looking for food to eat and a warm place to sleep at night.

But a truck parked in the back acres of a woman's land

she didn't even farm anymore hinted at something much more sinister.

He discovered it when he reached the back of the pickup truck. The newly replaced railing had been torn down again, and the chain links had been cut through on Jessie's side of the fence. The hair on the back of Garrett's neck pricked to attention like it had that day in Afghanistan when he'd spotted the kid with the bomb. Things were about to go really bad very, very quickly.

He pulled out his phone and called Levi Fox.

No answer.

He jogged back to his truck and called the young officer again.

No answer.

"Damn it, Fox, where are you?"

Garrett's next call was to Dispatch, warning them of a possible officer down and requesting backup at K-9 Ranch. He told them to notify Conor Wildman at KCPD, as well.

He debated for about two seconds whether to take the long drive back to the highway, then go next door and turn in the long drive up to Jessie's house—or he could take the same shortcut across her land the way he suspected Coltrane had.

He grabbed his rifle off the rack in the back of his truck cab, leaped the fence, and ran.

"DROP THE KNIFE."

With the fury of the storm subsiding to a steady fall of rain, Jessica had no problem hearing that the house was quiet. The children had done exactly as she asked and weren't making a sound.

Stay hidden. Stay safe.

She'd also heard the shatter of breaking glass at her back door, even the lock turning as the intruder reached inside to unlock the door. Shadow barked and raced to the door, but she called him back to her side. Thankfully, he obeyed.

She was down to diced chicken bites now, and still she kept cutting.

Jessica glanced over to see a gun pointed at her. Shadow growled and snapped at the armed man, desperately fighting his basic instinct to go after the intruder. But she was too good, Shadow was too smart, and Kevin Coltrane would never know what hit him by the time they were done with him.

"I said, put down the knife, lady."

She eyed the oil shimmering, rippling in the heavy skillet. "Hello, *Kevie.*"

"I don't like to be called that."

Shadow snarled and she knew he was moving closer. "Why not? Are you going to manhandle me the way you did Isla? What do you want with me?"

"The knife."

The gun barrel pressed against the side of her neck was wet with rain and felt ice cold.

Her breath hitched in her chest. Shadow's ears lay down flat on his head.

She felt her pulse beat against the cold steel of that gun.

"I ain't playin', lady."

"Okay. Okay." Not wanting to test the limits of the Olivera enforcer too hard, she dutifully set the knife down on top of the counter, right next to a pair of oven mitts. "There. I'm not armed anymore. Who brings a knife to a gunfight, anyway, right?"

Her laugh sounded as forced as it felt.

"Shut up, already."

He smacked the butt of the gun against her temple and she tumbled on top of the raw chicken on the counter, her skull throbbing and her vision spinning. The blow must have split her skin because blood was dripping into her right eye.

"You idiot. I need her conscious. I'll make her tell me where they are if they're not here."

"She wouldn't drop the knife," the big man protested. "You want her to stab me with it?"

"Find those kids. Now!"

How had she missed the second man walking in behind Kevie? Jessica pushed herself upright, feeling nauseous as a pair of skull tattoos swam through her vision. Olivera himself. Kai Olivera.

But the other man, Kevin Coltrane, was walking away, doing the boss's bidding.

No, no, no! He was leaving the kitchen. Moving closer to Nate and Abby.

The time was now or never.

"Shadow, now!" The dog lunged at the second man's outstretched hand, clamping down with enough force to break the skin and force the gun he held from his hand.

"Damn mutt! Kevin!"

A gunshot rang out and Shadow yelped. "Shadow!" She foolishly charged after Olivera as he shook himself free of the dog's bite and kicked him toward the door. The second yelp tore through her heart. "Don't you hurt my dog!"

"I got the door." *Kevie* had circled around the island. Good. Forget the kids upstairs.

The two men wrestled the snarling, whining dog out into

the rain and slammed the door shut behind him. While she mourned whatever had been done to Shadow, she sent up a prayer of thanks that he'd been able to defend her.

Two weapons gone. Two to go.

She hoped Nate had gotten hold of Garrett. She'd defend those children to her last breath, but she wouldn't last long against two armed men.

With her aim severely hampered by her spinning equilibrium, she picked up the hot mitts and grabbed the skillet.

"What is wrong with you, lady? Siccing your dog on Kai?" The big man grabbed a towel off the counter and tossed it to Olivera to stanch the wounds on his hand.

When he turned back to her, she hurled the hot oil at his face.

He screamed and wiped at the oil dripping down the front of him, burning his hands and losing his gun in the process. With his skin literally burning and peeling off his cheeks, he collapsed to his knees. Jessie swung the skillet again, this time cracking its heavy weight over the top of his head. He dropped like a stone, unconscious.

Shadow barked outside and scratched at the door. She heard the other dogs answering the alarm in the distance.

One down.

She raised her improvised weapon to strike again, but Olivera had disappeared. Then something hot and sharp and distinctly unsanitary sliced across her arm. Blood seeped up and pooled across her skin. She cried out in pain and let the pan clatter to the floor.

A heavy hand gripped her upper arm and spun her around. "I'm tired of playing these games." He shoved her against the island and bent her back partway across it. Spittle sprayed across her face as he held her own carving knife to her throat. She felt the edge of the blade prick her skin and knew she was bleeding again. "The Swiegerts are here someplace. Tell me where to find them."

"I don't know what you're talking about. You broke into my home. I'm defending myself."

Another cut. She flinched away from the burning pain. "You're not a dumb broad. Don't play dumb with me."

Fine. "I won't tell you."

"Talk, lady. Nate and Abby are mine."

Her back screamed at the angle he forced her into at the edge of the granite counter. "They don't belong to you. Their father is dead."

"Yeah. Because I pumped him so full of prime product—at my own expense—that his head damn near exploded."

Was she about to pass out? Had she heard him right? "You killed him?"

"Don't pump me for information, lady. I'm gonna cut your tongue out, and you won't be able to tell anybody anything." He pressed his forearm against her windpipe. If she didn't die of blood loss, he could strangle her to death. "Where are they?"

"I don't know."

"That's a load of crap. You got about fifteen seconds, and your boyfriend will be coming home to a dead body."

She was getting light-headed. Losing blood. Not breathing right.

She needed more time for backup to arrive. Garrett would save them. He'd promised. "They're not here."

"Where!"

Jessica saw the red laser dot spotting Kai Olivera's temple. But he did not.

"Tell me!"

Jessica turned her head and glass shattered as Olivera's brain splattered across her new kitchen cabinet.

With one last burst of strength, she shoved him off her and collapsed. She was crawling between bodies, blood and an oil slick when the door swung open again and Shadow burst in, with Garrett right behind him.

"Jessie? Jessie!"

Shadow came straight to her and licked her face. Jessica plopped back on her bottom and pulled the sopping wet dog onto her lap. "Did he shoot you, baby? Where are you hurt? You saved Mama. Good boy. Good boy."

"Jessie?" Garrett pointed the barrel of his sniper rifle at Olivera, then kicked his body away from her. "You're bleeding. How bad are you hurt?" Next, he trained the rifle on *Kevie's* prone body. When there was no reaction, he knelt beside the bearded bully and felt for a pulse. Apparently, he could still detect one because he sat back to pull out his handcuffs and locked them around the big man's wrists. Then he turned off the burner on the stove and crouched in front of her. His hand gently caressed her cheek. "Jessie, honey, you need to talk to me." He snatched a towel from the countertop and pressed it against the wound at her temple.

She winced at the pressure on the open wound, then wrapped her fingers around his wrist to stop his frantic movements. "I'm okay. Garrett, I'm okay. Probably need to see an ER. Shadow, too. But I'm okay." She found those loving green eyes narrowed with concern. Her sweet, brave, warrior man. Oh, how she loved him. She cupped his cold, wet cheek. "Get the kids. Upstairs bathroom. They were good as gold, did exactly what I asked." He hesitated. "Go. I told them not to come out for anyone but you or me. And I can't… I can't do that right now."

"Jessie, you're scaring me."

"Go. Make sure they're all right. I need to rest a minute. Shadow will stay with me. Right, boy?"

He scrubbed his hand over the dog's head. "Take good care of her, pal. I need her."

Then he was on his feet. He slipped the rifle over his shoulder and charged the stairs. "Nate! Abby!"

She heard a scramble of footsteps and shouts of "Garrett!"

When she saw them again, he carried a child in each arm and turned toward the kitchen.

"No!" she shouted, stopping him in his tracks. She glanced at the blood and death around her and knew some of it was on her. "Don't let them back here. I don't want them to see any of this."

"Jessie?" Abby called to her.

"I'm okay, baby," she answered, praying her shaky voice didn't worry the little girl. "Go with Garrett."

Lights were flashing through the windows now. Backup was here. The cavalry had arrived.

The front door closed. Jessie leaned back against the counter and closed her eyes, inhaling the pungent, normal, wonderful scent of wet dog and thanking God, the spirits of John and her baby, and any other powers that be that she was alive. Nate and Abby were alive. The threat was over.

When she opened her eyes again, Garrett was kneeling beside her. He picked her up in his arms, dog and all, and carried her out to the front porch and down the steps to the waiting ambulance. He set her on the gurney and the EMTs quickly moved to load her inside to get her out of the rain.

Abby was there, bundled in a silver reflective blanket. She climbed onto the gurney and snuggled beneath Jessie's unblemished arm to rest her head against Jessie's breast. Nate eyed her shyly, then climbed up on the other side, his hand immediately going to Shadow's head to pet him.

The EMTs were already tearing open sterile bandages and pressing them against the cuts on her arm and neck. One shined a flashlight in her face, checking for pupil reaction, then asked her to follow his finger with her eyes. "Slight concussion. She'll need some stitches."

Garrett was the last one to climb on board the crowded ambulance several minutes later. "Conor's here. He'll handle the crime scene. We can answer questions and fill out reports later. Officer Fox had his head bashed in, but he's going to make it. He's on another ambulance. I talked to Hugo. He and Soren will come over and check on all the dogs. I called Hazel Cooper-Burke. She'll meet us at the hospital to take care of Shadow." He reached back to pull the doors shut. "Let's go."

"Sir, that dog can't come—"

"That dog is part of this family," Garrett snapped. "We all go."

Surrendering to his stubborn determination to keep them all together—if not to the badge of authority he wore—the EMT passed the word up that they were ready to leave.

As the ambulance headed down her long driveway, Garrett took a seat on the other side of Abby, holding the little girl between them, reaching over to tag his hand at the nape of Jessica's neck and feather his fingers into her hair at the root of her braid. When the EMTs took a break in tending to her injuries, he leaned in and captured her lips in a sweet, lingering kiss. She cupped the side of his jaw and held on, absorbing every bit of love he had to give her. Garrett Caldwell was warmth. He was strength. He was her future.

"I thought I was going to lose you." He carefully found a spot to rest his forehead against hers.

"You're not going to lose me, Garrett," she vowed. "Ever."

In the crowded ambulance, there was only the two of them. She was injured. She was exhausted. But she was surrounded by love, and she was happy. Finally. Fully. Happy.

He pulled away slightly, a shade of doubt clouding his eyes. "What are you saying?"

"It hurts to love again, to take that risk. But it doesn't hurt to love you."

Abby got squished between them and the EMTs politely looked away as Jessie leaned over to kiss the man she loved.

A small throat cleared behind her, and she looked down into Nate's sweet blue eyes. They were smiling—almost. "Are you two going to be kissing every time we leave the room?"

Garrett chuckled. "Possibly. I might kiss Jessie in front of you, too. Are you okay with that?"

Nate gave the proposition some considerable thought. "Yeah. But not all the time, okay? It's kind of gross."

Garrett extended his arm and shook the boy's hand. "I can work with that."

Garrett shifted so that his arm slipped around her back and his hand rested on Nate's shoulder. He dropped a kiss to the top of Abby's head, tying them all together as a family.

The attack had come.

And she'd survived.

Again.

Only this time, with this man, there would be a happily-ever-after.

* * * * *

CLOSE RANGE CATTLEMAN

AMBER LEIGH WILLIAMS

As this is my tenth Mills & Boon romance and the
ten-year anniversary of my Mills & Boon debut,
I dedicate this book to you, reader.

Thank you for turning the page.

Chapter One

"Hell's bells," Everett Eaton groaned as he crouched in the sagebrush.

Over his shoulder, his newest ranch hand, Lucas, bounced on the heels of his roughed-up Ariats and cursed vividly. "Jesus, boss," he hissed. "Jesus Christ."

"Calm your britches," Everett said as he examined the blood trail in the red dirt of his high desert country homeland. Among the signs of struggle, he saw the telltale teardrop-shaped prints with no discernible claw marks. He lifted his fingers, tilted his head and squinted, following the drag lines in the soil. "He went off thataway."

"Taking Number 23's calf with him," Javier Rivera, Everett's lead wrangler, added.

Everett swapped the wad of gum from one side of his mouth to the other. Standing, he shifted his feet and placed his hands on his hips. The trail disappeared over the next ridge, into the thicket of trees that surrounded Wapusa River, the lifeblood of his family's fourteen-hundred-acre cattle ranch, Eaton Edge and the sandstone cliffs that served as its natural border to the north. He nodded toward the mountain that straddled the river. "I reckon 23 dropped the calf during the night and the damn thing was lying in wait."

"Or smelled the afterbirth and came running," Javier guessed.

"He could have been out stalking and got lucky," Everett weighed. "Either way, he took it up Ol' Whalebones, ate what he wanted and covered up the rest."

"How do you know he's up there?" Lucas asked. His bronze cheeks contrasted with the paleness around the area of his mouth. His head swiveled in all directions as he tried looking everywhere at once. "He could be anywhere."

Everett eyed the back side of the mountain. It curved toward the bright blue sky. "You can hear him in winter. He's most active then. He doesn't go into torpor, like the bear. When Ellis and I rode out to check fences once the snow cleared after Christmas, we could hear his screams echoing off everything and nothing."

"Ah, hell," Lucas moaned. He gave an involuntary shudder.

Javier clapped him on the back. "You stay sharp."

"Watch your mount when you're up in these parts," Everett told him. "And make sure you're strapped. Got it?"

Lucas nodded jerkily. "Geez. Shouldn't the bastard have died like five, ten years ago or something? Ellis figures Tombs is eighteen. Mountain lions aren't supposed to live that long. Are they?"

"Not in the wild," Javier considered. He swapped his rifle from his left hand to his right, following the river with dark eyes. "Twelve years is a long life for a cougar. Could be another cat, moving into Tombstone's territory. Right, boss?"

"Maybe." Everett scanned the sagebrush, the canyons and

the sandstone and couldn't chase the eerie sensation creeping along his spine.

Someone…or something was watching. "Mount up. I told the sheriff we'd meet near the falls."

Lucas sighed as they approached the three horses knotted together near the river's edge. "Sure wish we were riding in the other direction."

Everett laid his hand on his red mare's flank. Crazy Alice had been restless approaching Ol' Whalebones, tossing her head and the reins. She'd sensed that something was off long before he had. He patted her, then seated his rifle into the sleeve on the saddle and swung up into position with the ease of someone who'd spent a lifetime there. As he waited for the others to do the same, he knuckled his ten-gallon hat up an inch on his brow to get a better look at the canyon.

Tombstone was a legend and had been for as long as he could remember. Everett had first seen the mountain lion while camping with his brother, Ellis. Tombstone had watched them around their fire for the better part of the night. No one had slept. Everett remembered how the cat's eyes had tossed the firelight back at them. It was then he'd first seen what distinguished Tombstone from other cats—a missing eye.

His behavior, too, set him apart. Mountain lions shied away from human activity. It was why so little was known about them. In the last hundred years, only twenty-seven fatal cougar attacks had been reported. It was the rattlesnake they had to worry about most on the high desert plain.

But Everett had known that night what it was to be prey. He hadn't cared for it.

He'd seen Tombstone again off and on through the years.

Males were territorial and Tombs ruled Eaton Edge's northern quarter and the surrounding hunting grounds.

Everett didn't believe in omens, but even he had to admit that it was strange how every time he or Ellis or their father, Hammond, had spotted Tombs high in the hills, trouble had followed. Hammond's first heart attack, the deaths of Everett's mother, Josephine Coldero, and his half sister, Angel, his sister Eveline's car accident…

Over the last year, Everett had convinced himself the animal was dead…until his father's death over the summer and a ride into the high country where he had seen Tombs take down a small elk.

Everett may be chief of operations at Eaton Edge, but it was Tombs who was king in these parts—and Everett reluctantly gave him his due.

He clicked his tongue at Crazy Alice, urging her to walk on.

"What's the sheriff and deputies think they're going to find up here?" Lucas asked as his neck mimicked a barred owl, rotating at an impressive angle so he could scan the shadows cast by boulders.

"Hiker," Everett grunted.

"Just one?" Javier asked.

"Yep. Kid thought he'd livestream his ascent," Everett said.

"He didn't make it?" Lucas asked. "Seems easy enough."

"The climb's intermediate," Javier noted.

"The broadcast cut off before he reached the top," Everett said. "No one's seen or heard from him in three days. Parents in San Gabriel are worried."

"How old?" Javier asked.

"Sixteen," Everett noted.

Javier made a pitying noise. “Same age as my Armand.”

“Shouldn’t he be in school?” Lucas asked.

Everett raised a brow. “Shouldn’t you?”

“I got kicked out,” Lucas informed him. “Didn’t my mom tell you?”

Everett pursed his lips. “Your mama told me you were too much to handle and thought I could do something about it.”

“How’s that coming, *amigo*?” Javier asked, with a sly grin under the shade of his hat.

Everett shook his head. “I have a habit of inheriting problems of monumental proportions.”

“Sure wish you had your dogs with you,” Lucas told Everett as they crossed a stream. “They’d be able to smell a lion. They’d warn us, wouldn’t they?”

Everett scowled, thinking of the three cattle dogs he’d raised from pups. “I’m not keen on putting any of them on Tombs’ menu.”

“He wouldn’t attack them. Any animal would run from their baying. Even a predator.”

Everett couldn’t predict what Tombs would do, but he had trained the dogs for protection as much as herding. If they scented danger, they’d go looking for it. Everett couldn’t think of any circumstance where Bones, Boomer and Boaz meeting Tombs wouldn’t end in at least one of them maimed or killed.

“You’ve got a hot date tonight,” Lucas recalled.

“What do you know about it?” Everett barked.

Lucas scrambled. “I heard it.”

“From?”

“Mateo. Spencer told him. Spencer heard it from the house. Nobody knows who you’re going out with.”

Lucas was baiting him, and Everett wasn’t willing to share

any of his plans for the evening. He gnawed at the wad of gum in his mouth. “What’ve my plans got to do with anything?”

“We won’t make it back to headquarters by sundown,” Lucas considered. “I figure you’d have sent Ellis in your place to find the guy.”

“Kid went missing,” Everett reminded him. “If he’s camped out somewhere on the Edge, I aim to find him.”

The horses climbed to the mouth of a natural arch where the river sluiced and gurgled busily from the mouth of a cave. Water flowed freely now that the snow had melted in the Sangre de Cristo Mountains.

This was the lifeblood of Eaton Edge. The river fed the grass that made cattle ranching in the high desert of New Mexico possible.

As they neared the falls, Everett tugged on Crazy Alice’s reins. A smile transformed the grim set of his mouth. The loss of 23’s calf had unsettled him. But the sight ahead made the trouble slink back to the corners of his mind. “Howdy, Sheriff,” he called. He took off his hat.

The Jicarilla-Apache Native American woman was five feet three inches at the crest of her uniformed hat. Under the two-toned, neutral threads that suited her position, she was built solid. Everett couldn’t help but let his gaze travel over the hips under her weapons belt or the swell of her breast underneath her gold badge and name plate.

Sheriff Kaya Altaha’s black-lensed aviators hid eyes as dark as unexplored canyons. If she’d take them off, he’d see the usual assemblage of amusement and exasperation that greeted him under most circumstances. She addressed him. “You’re late, cattle baron.”

"We set out at dawn, like I promised," he assured her, dismounting. He flicked the reins over Alice's ears and led the horse the rest of the way. "Ran into a snag a quarter of a mile south of here."

Her frown quickened. "Trouble?"

"Heifer dropped a calf before dawn," he said, fitting the hat back to his crown. "Something carried it off."

Kaya's frown deepened. "Did you find any remains?"

"Other than a blood trail..." He shook his head. "Cat took off in this direction."

"You think it was lion."

"I know it was. Normally, we don't keep the heifers this far north when the mountain's waking up for spring, especially not during calving season. 23's a wily one—makes a habit of slipping through fences. The big cats are more likely to carry off pronghorn, small deer, rabbit..." He wished she'd take her hair down for once. She kept it knotted in a thick braid at the nape of her neck.

Everett would love to see it free. He'd bet money it was as dense as plateau nights and as soft as the Wapusa between his fingers when it ran down from the mountain.

Something tugged just beneath his navel—a long, low pull that snagged his breath for a second or two.

That wasn't new, either.

Everett had had to come to terms with the fact that he had the hots for the new sheriff of Fuego County. He'd been wallowing in that understanding for some time—since the shoot-out at Eaton Edge over Christmas that had led to her being shot in the leg and, after some recovery, promoted to the high office she held now.

Everett knew what he wanted, always, and he chased it

relentlessly. But the last eight months of his life had changed him. He'd been shot, too, in a standoff between a cutthroat backwoodsman and his family. He'd nearly died. Recovery had been a long mental process with PTSD playing cat and mouse with him. He'd found himself in therapy at the behest of Ellis and their housekeeper turned adoptive mother, Paloma Coldero. He'd set aside his chief of operations duties until doctors had given him the go-ahead to continue.

He had hated the hiatus. He'd worked since he was a boy—to the bone. He'd quit high school his senior year to help his father manage the Edge. Everett had never *not* worked.

After Hammond had died in July, work had felt vital. If he wasn't working, he was thinking about the state of his family and the grief he still hardly knew how to handle, even after all his months sitting across from a head doctor in San Gabriel.

Kaya Altaha had been a bright spot. The then-deputy had saved his life in the box canyon last July. Not only that—she'd checked in on him regularly. She'd worked to clear the name of Ellis's soon-to-be wife, Luella Decker.

The first time he'd smiled during his recovery, it'd been with her.

He hadn't known there were feelings attached…until Christmastime, when he'd seen her blood in the hay of his barn. He'd smelled it over the stench of cattle and gunpowder. To say he'd been worried was a damned lie—he'd gone over the flippin' edge.

She tucked her full lower lip underneath the white edge of her teeth, nibbling as she looked beyond him into the hills that tumbled off south. "Anyone get a look at the predator?" she asked.

He had to school himself to keep from rubbing his lips together. "Happened before dawn, as I said. Blood was dry."

"I'm sorry to hear about the calf," she said sincerely.

He could feel her eyes through the shades. He felt them from tip to tail. "I'm not looking forward to telling my nieces. They love the little ones come spring."

She studied him a moment before the professional line of her mouth fell away and a slow smile took over.

He darted a look at the two deputies roving around the space between the falls and the arch walls before he brought himself a touch closer, the toes of his thick-skinned boots nearly overlapping hers. He lowered his voice. "You can't be doing that."

"What am I doing?" Her jaw flared wide from its stubborn point when she smiled.

He'd thought about kissing that point…and a good many things south of it. "Flashing secret smiles at me and pretending I'm not going to do anything about it."

"I don't play games."

"You know what that mess does to me," he said, "and you're betting on me not doing anything about it."

"You wouldn't," she said.

"Why d'you figure that, Sheriff Sweetheart?" he asked with a laugh.

The smile turned smug. "Because I know the only things Everett Eaton fears in this life are bullets and bars. Not the honky-tonk kind—the ones that hem him in and keep him away from…all this." She gestured widely. "Despite how much we both know you like a challenge." She tossed him back a step with the brunt of her hand and raised her voice to be heard by the others. "Hiker's name is Miller Higgins.

He's sixteen years of age. Five-eight. Roughly one hundred and fifty pounds. His last known contact was three days ago at approximately 10:23 a.m. The family reported him missing yesterday when they couldn't get in touch with him via cell."

"Cell service is low here," Javier noted. "How good was the quality of the livestream video?"

"Not great, but good enough to establish where he was and what he was doing," Kaya replied. "If he fell during the hike and injured himself, he might have lost his cell phone or damaged it. That's the working theory. He left his car on the access road to the northeast. Deputy Root will fly the surveillance drone once we get to the top. I plan on combing every inch of this mountain and the surrounding area until we find Higgins. If we need to bring in more search and rescue people, we'll do so."

"Nobody knows Ol' Whalebones as well as me and Ellis," Everett explained. "He'll join us tomorrow, if need be. We'll find Higgins. I'd like Lucas to wait here with the horses since there've been signs of predators about."

She inclined her head. "Fine. Let's split into groups and hit the trail."

Chapter Two

"Ol' Whalebones wasn't always yours," Kaya told the cowboy. It was better than telling him to hold up and slow the eff down. Bastard was like a cat as they hiked toward the summit. She could hold her own athletically. But his legs were nearly the length of her body.

Everett took a glance back. He stopped, planting both feet in the rocky hillside. He extended a hand.

He wasn't even winded. She gritted her teeth as her bad leg shouted in protest and she took the offering. His touch was rough, taking her back to the day she'd been shot.

My hands are only good for cattle branding...

It was hard to reconcile the hard face of Everett Eaton with the pale shell he'd been in his cattle barn that day. He'd been using those hands to stop the bleeding in her leg—or trying. She liked his hands, and she was afraid she'd told him as much as she'd faded in and out of consciousness.

She had saved his life once, too. Hard to believe things had come full circle.

He pulled until she was even with him. She let go of his hand to take hold of the branch of the shrub tree to her left. "Thanks," she said.

"Take a minute," he ordered.

"No," she said. "We'll be losing the light before we know it."

"You can't climb if you can't breathe," he told her. "Here."

He unclipped the water bottle from his belt. She took it when he unscrewed the lid.

He watched her drink. She was aware of him enough to know it. She wondered if he counted the number of times her throat moved around her swallows. It made her hot.

Stop it, Kaya. She was sheriff now. There were those who thought she'd earned the position, and those who didn't. The latter had a strong sense she'd been voted in out of sympathy when she was shot by the former sheriff, Wendell Jones.

She might wear the badge, but she had a lot to prove. There was no time to lust after a long, tall cowboy with issues of his own. She handed the bottle back to him.

He took a sip, too. Then he lowered the bottle back to his belt and fastened it. "I know Whalebones didn't always belong to us. It was Apache."

"It didn't belong to anyone," she argued. "It was a sacred place. The Jicarilla called it Mountain That Breathes Water. Water is sacred to our people."

He grabbed the wrist of the hand she had wrapped around the branch. "Don't use trees for leverage. They've got shallow roots. A branch can snap. If you need to grab onto something, you grab onto me. I'm not going anywhere."

She pushed off the tree. Instead of grabbing him, she clambered her way up the mountain. It was best just to keep going—ignore the low simmer and smooth timbre of his words and what they did to her. "Do you get hikers out here often?"

"Sure. Ol' Whalebones was once the place to go for camping in Fuego. Ellis and I led a few expeditions ourselves. That all changed when Tombstone established his territory."

"I looked into it," she admitted. She could hear Everett coming at the same easy pace behind her. She wanted the lead. His Wrangler-clad buns were too distracting. "There've never been reports of hikers at Eaton Edge. Not officially."

"When they do it the right way—knock on the door at headquarters and ask for permission—we normally give them the go-ahead. They can't leave any trash, must be out by a certain date and time and are responsible for any injuries or loss of gear that happens on the mountain."

"That's big of you."

"It was Ellis's idea. Dad went for it. I had to go along."

"Should've known it was your brother's idea." The brothers Eaton didn't have much in common other than height, horsemanship, ranching and the web of laugh lines they carried around their eyes even when they weren't amused. While Ellis was easygoing by nature, Everett had a well-earned reputation for being difficult to deal with. He was loyal as hell to anybody he thought of as his—family, hands and the few friends he counted as his own… Anybody else was practically the enemy.

Ellis was a frickin' marshmallow by comparison.

Kaya may have been an officer of the law for a decade, but she was also a single, red-blooded woman who liked the look of cowboys. She'd been wondering for a while why her glands had danced toward prickly over princely. She liked things that lined up. Puzzle pieces that fit neatly together. Her clear-cut certainty came from years of honed gut instinct.

Everett Eaton was a gray area.

She'd been toeing that gray area for a while.

There was nothing certain about him. She hadn't yet had the nerve to cross the line in the sand she'd drawn between herself and Fuego's most storied cattleman.

"Did Higgins contact anyone at Eaton Edge about climbing Ol' Whalebones?" she asked.

"I checked with Ellis and Paloma. Requests normally go through them. Nobody'd heard of him before yesterday."

She climbed to an embankment and stopped to look around. As he climbed to her position, she bent over double, planting both hands on her left thigh. It sang an ugly operetta that made her molars grind. She heard him closing and straightened. "No sign of a hiker."

He stopped, too, and scanned. "No tracks, either."

She took the radio off her hip. "Root."

"Yeah, Sheriff?"

"Status report," she requested, cutting into the hissing static. As she waited for a reply, she took the bottle Everett offered her again and sipped. The breeze was high, cooling the perspiration on her face and neck.

"Javy and I made it around to the east side. We're making our way up to the top."

"Any sign of Higgins?" she asked, passing the bottle back to Everett.

"Not even an empty Doritos bag."

"I want updates every ten minutes," she told him. "Higgins had to climb either the east or south side, and it hasn't rained. Signs should still be there."

"Ten-four. We'll check in soon."

"Thanks." She clipped the radio into its holding on her belt. "Damn."

"What about the live broadcast?" Everett asked. "Didn't the kid say which approach he took?"

She shook her head, shifting her weight to her right leg. "He kept going on about climate change, cultural landmarks… His profile took up much of the frame so there aren't any discernible background features. And the livestream was cut off just before the summit."

Everett assessed her. "You're hurting."

"I'm not," she lied through her teeth. "We need to keep moving."

"Does your leg bug you like this all the time?" he asked as she established the lead again.

She dismissed his worry. "It doesn't bug me anymore. Period."

"Should've left you with Lucas and the horses."

She rounded on him, happy when her feet didn't slide down the slope. "If I'd known you were going to nag this much, I'd have thought better before calling you out to help."

He tilted his head. "My land, my call."

She scowled. It would be so easy to dislike him, as most people did. Why had she never disliked him? She sniffed and caught a strong enough whiff of something foul to distract her. "Didn't you shower this morning?"

The blade of his nose sharpened, and his nostrils narrowed as he took in a long breath, scenting the air. "It's not me." His eyes narrowed, too, as recognition hit his cobalt blue eyes. The pupils grew larger. "That's something dead."

Her head snapped in the direction of the wind. "That way." There was a clutch of trees clinging to the cliffside. She picked her way in that direction, crossing from the trail into the shrubby undergrowth.

"Let me go first," he said, taking her arm.

"Hi, I'm the sheriff. Nice to meet ya," she drawled, refusing to give up the lead once more. "Stay behind me or I'll make you wait here."

Her stomach tightened as she made steady progress sideways across the mountain. Automatically, her hand went to her hip, fingertips brushing the sidearm on her belt. She squinted, trying to see into the shadows of the trees. She recognized the smell. Death, a scent ingrained in the walls of her memory. "Goddamn it," she said under her breath as she narrowed the distance to the grove. "Stay back," she told him firmly, holding up a hand.

"Like hell," came the response at her back. He was coming, too.

She cut the urge to roll her eyes, tilting her chin as she peered into the stand. She took a step into the stubble of thicket that grew at the base of the trees.

It would have taken her longer to find it if not for the flies. Near the center of the stand, a small pile of dead leaves and natural debris gathered. She crouched, narrowing her eyes. Holding her breath, she brushed away the detritus. She hissed at what she found, sitting back on her heels.

Over her head, Everett cursed. "That's a body," he said.

"What's left of one," she confirmed. She pressed her lips together, careful not to breathe too deeply.

"It ain't human."

"No," she agreed. She tried to recognize something of the small animal. "This is something's prey. And it's fresh, so that means—"

Everett cursed again, filthily. He yanked her to her feet. "Get up now!"

"What?" She saw the pallor of his face. It was achingly familiar. "Everett, what—?"

"Look at the trees," he said, bringing the rifle he'd strapped to his back around to his front.

She saw the markings on the trunks. Claw marks. She lifted her Glock from its sheath as her pulse clambered into high gear. "You think…"

"Hell yeah," he confirmed, all but herding her back the way they'd come. "He knows we're here."

"He who?" When Everett continued to push her out of the trees, she raised her voice. "Everett!"

"Move!" he ordered.

Underneath his pallor, she recognized fear. Her response was visceral. It urged her into a sprint. Everett followed close on her heels. Her heart beat in her ears when his hand clamped on her shoulder, keeping her within arm's length.

They made it back to the trail. Everett kept his rifle up. "Look for the ears in the underbrush," he said, pivoting. "You see them first."

Kaya scanned. With everything waving in the breeze, she couldn't detect anything. She shook her head. "Who do you think is out there?"

"Christ, woman. Don't you know this is Tombstone's territory?"

Tombstone. Stories of the one-eyed cat had seemed mythical. "Tombstone's…real?"

"*Hell yeah,* he's real!"

She saw the sweat on his neck and blinked. "You've seen him."

"Saw him hunting in the summer and heard his screams just three months back."

Kaya released a breath before she raised the barrel of the gun to the sky and squeezed off a round. She did it twice, then again. Birds scattered and the thunder of the shots echoed off everything.

Nothing sprang from the grass except a fluffle of rabbits.

She lowered the gun. "He's not here. They run at the slightest sign of humans."

Everett was still tense as a board. "You don't know Tombs. Not like I do."

She observed the tight line of his mouth, the successive lift of his shoulders as his lungs cycled through quick, quiet breaths. She opened her mouth, but the radio on her hip crackled. "Altaha. You read?" came the brisk sound of one of her deputies.

She took the radio out of its holding and raised it to her mouth. "All clear."

"You fired?"

"Three shots. Affirmative. We came across a cougar den. Had to make sure we weren't being stalked."

"Ten-four. You want us to keep going for the summit?"

"Yes," she agreed. "Be watchful and keep checking in. Over." She clipped the radio back in place. "Relax. We're not getting carried off like your calf."

"Yeah," Everett bit off, watching the boulders in the near distance as if one of them would pounce at them if he let his guard down.

Kaya laid her hand flat against the warm line of his back. "You're really spooked."

"I'm not spooked," he said with a deep frown as he lowered the weapon a fraction. He didn't stop scanning the hillside. "I'm ready."

She noted the half step he took toward her, until her front buffered his arm. "You'll have to tell me what that's about."

"You ever seen a cat that size take down an animal?"

"Haven't had the pleasure, no."

"You don't see it coming," he said. "Its prey doesn't see it coming. Hell, the devil doesn't see it coming. It'll wait an hour if it must for its prey to feel secure—for it to get close enough. And it moves like a wraith. It goes for the throat, mostly. Tears out the guts. It feeds. Then it buries the rest for later."

She fought a shudder. "It's an animal, cattle baron. Flesh and blood. Not the bogeyman."

"Let's keep moving. We'll have better visibility from the top."

She pursed her lips when he took the lead this time. Keeping her hand on her sidearm, she followed no less than a few feet behind, her eyes trained to the periphery.

EVERETT PROPPED THE rifle muzzle on his shoulder as he watched Kaya assess the day's findings.

No hiker. No body, either, other than Number 23's calf, or what was left of the spindly little thing. Everett didn't figure Tombs had gotten much of a meal off it. Calves weren't particularly meaty.

As Kaya's gloved hands handled the tennis shoe Deputy Root had found near the top of the east trail, Everett noted the line buried like a hatchet between her eyes. She turned the shoe, checking the bottom, then pulled back the tongue to peer inside. "Men's size nine," she reported to Root as the man took notes. "The tread's new. Very little wear. No tear. Make a note to question the family. See if any of them know if he recently bought a brown pair of Merrell Moabs. Have them check for receipts." She lifted the shoe's opening to her nose. Her studious frown deepened as she lowered it. "Definitely fresh." She placed the shoe gingerly in an evidence bag and sealed it. "This needs to be labeled."

"Yes, sir," her other deputy, Wyatt, said as he took the bag from her.

She pulled off her gloves as she scanned the other evidence bags. They'd found one half-full canteen, one selfie stick, two crinkled foil gum wrappers and one bullet casing. She lifted the bag with the casing and walked to Everett's position. Holding it up for him to see, she asked, "You do any shooting on the mountain?"

"Not in ten years," he replied. She allowed him to take the bag. He laid the plastic-wrapped casing across his palm. "This is newer. Maybe not from the last week, but recent."

She nodded, taking it back. "You know anybody else who shoots on the mountain?"

"No," he said. "We haven't had hikers since last spring, and we make it clear—no shooting unless it's necessary to defend against wildlife." When she continued to measure him, he sighed. "I can track down the waiver the last campers signed. It'll have contact information. I'll have Ellis pass it on to your department."

"I'd appreciate it," she whispered.

He wanted to smooth the line between her eyes away with the rough pad of his thumb. "You got that same funny feeling in the pit of your stomach that I do?"

She blinked, the thoughtful glimmer disappearing as she lowered her gaze to his chest. "I've got questions."

"Like why we found one shoe and no kid."

She nodded. Her lips disappeared as she pressed them inward.

"Sun's going down," he said when her attention turned again to the mountain. "There's no use searching after dark. Cougar's most active between last and first light. We'll hit it again in the morning."

"I know."

Everett shifted his feet when she didn't look any less discomfited. He spoke in an undertone he knew she didn't want to hear. "You know if that kid's alive, he'd have said something, called for help, after you took those three shots."

"Maybe," she muttered. "Doesn't make leaving for the night easier." She looked back at the shoe Wyatt carefully labeled. "My gut tells me Miller Higgins never left Ol' Whalebones. I can't face his family until I have more."

It'd weigh on her. It'd weigh her down hard. It took everything in him to stand his ground and keep his hands to himself.

Lucas called to him from the horses gathered near the river. "Boss, we should head south for home. Don't you have that hot date?"

Kaya's eyes widened as she looked in the boy's direction. "Who with?" she called.

Lucas fumbled at the sheriff's attention. "Ah…he never said. I just know he was real jazzed about it."

Kaya turned a stunned look back at Everett. "What's that look like?"

Lucas filled in the blanks. "Oh, you know, he's not much a grinnin' man. But once he got word that the date was on, he's been slaphappy."

"I'd like to see that," she mused, scrutinizing every inch of Everett's face. She might've looked amused to anyone else, but he saw the gleam in her eye and his heartbeat skipped. That look was damn near predatory. He cleared his throat and looked long in Lucas's direction.

The boy's smile subsided. "Sorry, boss. Ready when you are," he said before turning away to busy himself with Crazy Alice's bridle.

"Hot date, huh?" Kaya said, refusing to take her attention elsewhere.

"I think so," Everett mused.

"Hmm."

"Sheriff," Deputy Root said. "I put the evidence in your saddlebags."

"Good work," she said. "Mount up. I'm coming."

Everett gave Lucas and Javier the signal to do the same but walked Kaya to her leopard Appaloosa. "Nice horse," he commented, touching its nose. The horse breathed on him, its nostrils filling his palm and warming it with a searching snuff.

"Name's Ghost," she said, adjusting the stirrups. "She likes sweets."

The deputies walked their horses at a safe distance. They were far enough away. Everett felt free to touch her finally, turning her to him. With Ghost's long form between them and the deputies and his own men, Everett filled the space between them. "Are you okay to ride?"

Her smile came slowly. It didn't stretch to fill the ridges of her cheekbones as he'd seen it do at its height, but it warmed. "I was born on the rez. I can ride with the best of them."

"You can find the access road okay?" he asked. "Dark's coming on quick."

"We'll find it," she assured him. She paused, her gaze tracking the line of his throat. Her voice lowered a fraction. "You better get along. Wouldn't want you to miss that date."

"You're not backing out?"

She lifted her eyes to the passing clouds. With the sun low to the west, they burned. "I'll let you know."

"Don't back out," he said.

A laugh sounded in her throat. "Careful. You sound a little slaphappy."

"Lucas doesn't know what he's talking about."

"No?" she said, and she ran a hand down the length of his shirtfront, making the skin underneath the buttons judder. "Pity."

He caught her wrist before she could feel his muscles quiver under her fingertips. "Eight o'clock, right?"

"Better make it nine, at this rate."

He grinned. "Sure, Sheriff. Sweetheart."

She brought both hands to his lapels and pulled him down to her height. Dropping her voice to a whisper, she cautioned, "Easy on the endearments. I have a reputation to establish."

"I'm aware of your reputation." All he saw…all he wanted…was her mouth under his. "Just as I'm aware it took me three months, thirteen days and nine hours to talk you into going out with me. I'll be damned if I screw this up now." He bent his head to hers and took her mouth.

She made an involuntary "*Mmm.*" He released her, stepping away just as fast as he'd swooped, lest he take more than he should with his men and hers within shouting distance. His blood had quickened at the taste, the promise of her. “Don’t back out,” he whispered.

She pressed a hand to her horse’s saddle, touching her mouth. She dropped her hand when she saw him watching. “Ride on. Isn’t that what cowboys are supposed to do?”

He tipped his hat to her. “Ladies first.”

Chapter Three

Kaya was more tired than she would have liked. And she was worried. She'd expected to find more of Miller Higgins on Ol' Whalebones than his right shoe.

The shell casing bothered her long after she left the station house. She'd stayed long enough to stable Ghost and update the mayor on the hiker's whereabouts—or lack thereof. Then she fielded the phone call from Higgins's mother and arranged for the next search party to meet at the base of the mountain the following morning.

Her house was near downtown Fuego. It was small. She liked to think of it as cozy—cozy enough for one…and that was stretching it. Its one redeeming aspect was the little windowed alcove off the kitchen she used for her round bistro table and as many potted plants as she could squeeze in along the walls. She set her bag down there, taking out the file on Higgins.

She opened it. His smiling photograph stared back at her.

"What happened to you on the mountain?" She wanted to know. He was just a kid—one with strong convictions… But a kid just the same.

She closed the file and told herself to end the questions

for the night. If she continued, questions would spring into more before she had a hydra-like situation on her hands. She wouldn't be able to concentrate on anything if she didn't let the inquiries lie.

She checked the time on the stove display and cursed. It was a quarter past eight. She unbuckled her weapons belt and slid it off as she veered toward the bedroom.

As she showered, the questions didn't stop coming.

If it was an accident, what happened? Did he fall down the mountain? Was that why there was only one shoe, the new selfie stick and his half-drunk canteen? Where was Higgins's pack? Every hiker carries a pack. Where was his camera and cell phone? What caused him to stumble? Was it the cougar?

No, Kaya thought. *No*. If it had been the cat, there would have been evidence of that…

Everett's visual came back to her, accompanied by his grim baritone.

...it goes for the throat, mostly. Tears out the guts. It feeds. Then it buries the rest...

There had been no tracks on the summit. No blood they'd been able to see. No remains of any kind…except for the shoe. There weren't drag marks through the brush.

Which brought Kaya's questions around to…

Foul play? Did someone else beat Higgins to the top of Whalebones? Had the perpetrator been waiting? Was their meeting coincidental? If so, why did the perpetrator attack? Was the shoe left behind when the perpetrator carried the body off?

She remembered the absence of blood or drag marks.

Was the perpetrator smart enough to cover his tracks?

Dogs, she thought. They needed search dogs on the summit tomorrow. She needed to call Root, set it up…

She pulled back the shower curtain and checked the watch she had left on the counter. *Eight-thirty.*

She quickly washed the shampoo out of her hair and shut off the tap. She towel dried her hair before she remembered to shave.

It had been so long since she'd dated, she was out of her routine. Placing one leg on the closed commode, she lathered one part of her leg after the other before dragging her razor over it, as carefully as she could manage in a hurry. She nicked herself only once on the knee before she finished. She bounced on the toes of her left leg a bit as she lowered the right back down to the ground. It ached in the center of her thigh. Telling herself to remember to take a pain pill before she left, she went into the bedroom to find something to wear.

The little black dress wasn't new. She shimmied into it, grunting a bit to fit it over the wide points of her chest and hips. She was more muscular than she'd been when she bought it. She tried not to think about her mannish shoulders as she turned to look in the full-length mirror she'd mounted to her closet door.

The dress hit her midthigh. She didn't remember it being that short.

"Hmm," she said as she turned to the side, examining. It was hardly appropriate for someone of her rank.

She thought about her former boss, Sheriff Jones, in something this short and snorted in reaction.

She trailed her fingertips over the gunshot wound he'd put in her. It was completely visible below the hem.

She sighed. That wouldn't do. Nothing halted revelry like a solid reminder that she'd almost lost her life in her date's hands.

She decided on a maxi dress that exposed her shoulder line and one leg up to the knee in a slit. Seeing that another ten minutes had passed, she rummaged through shoes until she found a pair of wedge heels that matched, then went into the bathroom to find her makeup bag.

"You're sheriff now," she said out loud as she applied mascara, wary of messing it up and having to start over. "Men should take you seriously, Kaya, with or without mascara… whether you're cuffing them…dating them…" Still, the thought of going on this date without mascara… "Nuh-uh," she decided as she switched eyes.

She felt the minutes tick by as she pulled the towel down from her hair. The strands fell to her waist, wet as a drowned rat. "Be late, cattle baron."

The doorbell rang promptly at nine o'clock, causing her to groan at the state of things. Her hair still wasn't dry. There would be no fancying it. "Hold on a minute," she said with bobby pins between her teeth as she knotted her hair on top of her head and hastily pinned flyaways.

By the time she threw open the door, he'd taken to pounding on it with his fist. "Yes," she said, exasperated. "I can…" She trailed off, noting the sport coat over his clean-white button down. His hat was in his hand. His tousled black hair was thick and clean. His dark beard had a nice sheen. He'd trimmed it. "…hear you," she finished, lamely. "Wow. You look…decent."

She'd never seen Everett Eaton look so shiny. Not outside

of a wedding or a funeral. And he always looked like his family dragged him to those kinds of things.

"I should hope so," he said. "Paloma threatened to hold me down and shave me." His smile came slowly as he lowered his gaze from her made-up face to her bare shoulders, over the pattern of the dress, down the long slit. "You look fine, Sheriff. Damn fine." And he made a noise in his throat that shot straight through her.

She gripped the door, feeling his eyes everywhere. *Here we go again.* What was it about this cowboy? She made the mistake of shifting onto her left leg in a casual stance. She ruined it by moving to the other leg quickly. Hissing at the pain, she closed her eyes for a moment and touched her brow to the cool wood underneath her hand.

"Hey," he said, stepping over the threshold. "You doing all right?"

"Mmm." She mashed her lips together and offered a nod. He wouldn't get the best of her tonight. If they were going to do this…if she was going to take this leap with him—ill-fated or otherwise—she wanted to be at her best. He'd saved her life, after all. The least she could do was wait for a night when she wasn't worn down. "Listen. I hate to do this. But it's late and there's a lot on my leg… I mean, *my mind.* Maybe we should do this another—"

"Nope."

She jerked her head back. "I'm sorry. 'Nope'?"

"That's right," he said with a decisive bob of his head. "Nope."

He made the *p* come to a point at the end. She narrowed her eyes. "You don't want me tonight, Everett."

He didn't miss a beat. "I beg to differ, sweetheart."

"I'm distracted," she said, ticking the excuses off on her fingers. "I'm tired. I'm a little cranky. I'm more than a little sore…"

"I'll take you any way I can get you. Distracted, tired, cranky… If you're hurting, I'll carry you," he revealed.

"Oh," she said, not at all swept off her feet. "That's nice."

"As for the sore part, I plan to buy a large bottle of wine for our table when we get to the restaurant for our reservation in…" He checked his big, silver watch. "…a half hour. And I'm not waiting another three months for you to decide that this is right again, so get your bag because otherwise I'm hauling you over my shoulder and we're leaving without it."

She blew out a hard breath. "I'd like a word with whichever barnyard animal raised you."

"Can't," he said. "We sold it for beef a while ago."

When she only stood staring at him, he made a move toward her.

"All right!" she shrieked, dancing out of his reach. She muttered as she went back into her bedroom. "I am the sheriff," she reasoned as she shoved her Glock down into her beaded bag with her wallet and phone, then yanked a sweater off a hanger and stalked back to the door.

"WHY WASN'T THERE MORE?" Kaya questioned. "Why weren't there signs of a struggle? If he fell on the trail, we should have found his body near the trail. Unless something or someone dragged him off…"

Everett bobbed his head in a nod as she went on about the day's search and all the questions that had arisen from it. He poured her another tall glass of wine. At least she was drinking it. He wondered how many glasses it would take for her to forget about work. She was well into two.

He raised the label of the wine toward the light, squinting to read the alcohol ratio. He raised a brow and set it back down on the table.

Kaya Altaha was far from a cheap date.

She'd ordered a steak, like him, and wasn't that just a turn-on? She looked good in candlelight, so good he wondered why he'd taken her out in public and not back to the Edge where he could kick everybody out of Eaton House and distract her with something other than red meat and wine…

Because clearly those two things weren't doing the job. Neither was the fancy restaurant with its crystal chandeliers, fine china, white tablecloths and overdressed servers. He picked his whiskey glass up off the table, tossed back the contents and savored the burn of top-shelf liquor. Setting the glass down, he leaned forward and asked, "You wanna dance?"

She fumbled in the middle of another question. Her mouth hung open, red as a poppy and glistening, like she'd coated it in gloss. She looked around, as if noting the chandeliers and other well-dressed patrons for the first time. "Yeah, there's no dancing here," she pointed out.

"There could be," he considered. He reached across the table and laid his hand next to hers on the tablecloth.

"No," she decided.

"You're a fine dancer, as I recall." And he smiled at the memory of spinning her around the kitchen at Eaton House.

A glimmer of that memory lit her eyes and shined.

He nudged his hand toward hers so that his first finger grazed hers.

The glimmer faded and her hand retreated. She looked away. “I haven’t danced. Not since then. My leg…”

“It’s hurting you,” he knew. “It hurts a sight more than you let on.”

“I get through it,” she said, clutching the stem of her wineglass without lifting it.

“Do you take something for it?”

She thought about it. “Not tonight. Damn. I forgot.”

He could see a web of pain floating translucent over the powerful line of her brow. He remembered the pain in his chest waking him up in the middle of the night for weeks after Whip Decker shot him and all the mixed-up nightmares that had made it impossible for him to sleep through the night during that time. “Here,” he said.

Her eyes widened as he scooted his chair around the table, making enough noise with the legs screeching across the marble floor that the restaurant patrons swiveled toward the commotion. “What are you doing?”

“Gimme,” he said, reaching underneath the tablecloth to wrap his hand around the smooth slope of her calf. He pulled it into his lap, edging closer still. Her perfume was heady, and he got lost, so lost he almost didn’t see her grimace. “Easy,” he murmured, keeping his eyes on hers as he followed the trail of satin skin up the slit of her dress to her thigh. Digging his fingers in, he urged himself to be gentle as he massaged.

He heard the quick, almost inaudible catch of her breath. “You know,” she said, “this is more of a third date kind of thing.”

He chuckled, then gentled the kneading when he saw the line of her mouth tense. “Are my hands too rough for you?”

"Your hands," she murmured. She closed her eyes. "No. Not for me."

He fought a curse. He was afraid she'd have him panting like a cartoon character by the night's end. "You see some-one about the pain?" he asked, diverting his mind elsewhere as his fingers continued to work.

"I'm told it's normal," she said, tipping her head back slightly. Her eyes rolled once before she closed them. "I'm still going through physical therapy."

"Hmm," he said, biting the inside of his lip when she made an agreeable noise. "I'm not a fan of doctors on the whole, but PT helped me." Almost as much as talk therapy, but he didn't mention that. He still had his qualms about telling people he saw a psychiatrist.

"You need to stop," she said, placing her hands over his.

"Why?"

"Because people will think you're doing something else under the table."

"I am doing something."

"You *know* what I mean."

"I don't give a hot damn what people think," he reminded her. He grinned because he could see the touch of pink at the crests of her cheeks. "And as much I like where your head's at, sweetheart, that's not a first date kind of thing, either."

"No?" she asked as he pulled his hands away. She sat up straight, her leg easing off his lap. "Most cowboys expect that sort of thing."

"I'm a bit more refined than your average cowboy," he revealed, lifting a finger to a passing server. He raised his empty glass.

She snorted. "You? Refined?"

He slid her a long look, rattling the ice in the glass.

She licked her lips. Her gaze touched on his wrist. “Sorry.”

He saw those dark eyes dart elsewhere and frowned down at his wrist with the expensive watch. Wondering why it made her uncomfortable, he fit his shoulders to the back of the dining chair and tried to read her. Hammond had bequeathed the watch to him…one of the few nice things his father had collected through the years for himself. Like Hammond, Everett was a simple man. He didn’t like fuss. But the occasion had called for a bit of shine. He felt the sting of his father’s loss as he watched the low light dance across the band.

“Tell me the truth,” she asked, carefully. “When was the last time you took someone to bed?”

He tried not to be thrown by the question. “It’s been a minute,” he mused.

“Not since Decker shot you?” she asked.

“Hell no.” He’d been in no place to think in terms of sex or what led to it.

“How long then?” she asked.

“Is this a first date conversation?” he teased as the server brought another glass of whiskey. “Thanks.”

“I don’t care,” Kaya replied.

He raised his hand in an empty gesture. “I don’t know. Two…maybe three years?”

Her brows hitched. “Why that long?”

He lifted a shoulder. “Haven’t found anyone worth courting. ’Til now, that is.”

“You need to court a woman to sleep with her?” she said in amusement.

“Well, yeah.”

"Is that why you're here with me—because you're courting me?" she asked, picking through the words carefully.

He bobbed his head and kept her locked in his sights as he raised the glass to his mouth again. "I'd say that's a fair assessment."

She narrowed her eyes as he tossed the whiskey back. "At least he's honest, ladies and gentlemen," she murmured and took a long drink from her wineglass.

"What's wrong with me courting you, Sheriff?"

"It's not the courting I'm worried about," she said with a shake of her head. Dangling the glass with her thumb and two fingers on the rim, she studied him with her cop eyes. "Why me?"

"Why *not* you?"

"That's not really your answer, is it?"

He shifted in his chair. "Cards on the table?"

"I'd like that."

"Fine." He cleared his throat. "I want to find out what this is."

"What?"

He gestured from him to her and back quickly. "This. You know what I'm talking about." When she eyed him uncertainly, he groaned. She was going to make him spell it out in this fancy schmancy restaurant over candlelight and frickin' canapes. "I want to figure out whatever it is I feel—for you."

She stiffened. Her eyes bounced between his in quick succession, but she stayed quiet, waiting for him to elaborate.

He gripped the whiskey glass hard. "During my recovery—" he continued, carefully "—the one person I looked forward to seeing, or even really wanted to see, was you. The one person who never failed to make me grin like an idiot was you. And when the sheriff took a shot at you, I nearly lost that. It scared me more than I thought it could."

"Everett..."

"You wanted to hear," he reminded her.

She settled back, a line digging deep between her eyes as it had earlier that evening.

"I've done a lot over the last several months to eliminate my fear," he revealed. "I've lost people and I'm still dealing with it. It hasn't been easy. It helps, whatever this is. You help...just having you here...lookin' at you. I'm drawn to you, and I want to know why. I want to know you better. I need it."

Her throat clicked on a swallow. "What if..." She stopped, thought about it, then continued, perturbed. "What if I'm a disappointment? You've put me on a pedestal, from the sound of it. That's a tough way to begin a relationship. Expectation's already through the roof where you're concerned."

"The hell with expectation," he dismissed. "My question is, what took you so long to say yes?"

She measured the width of his shoulders. "You're a complicated man, Everett. Some would even say you're a hard man. I'm the sheriff, and you don't have much regard for the law when it comes to your own."

"Who does?" he asked, raising the glass for another drink.

"Me," she replied pointedly. "I do."

"So...you don't want me because you assume I'm not an easy person to live with," he weighed.

"I *know* you're not an easy person to live with," she retorted. "I have it on high authority you're a verifiable pain in the ass." She hesitated, looking down at her lap to fiddle with the cloth napkin she'd laid there. "And I never said I didn't want you," she added quietly.

Why did she have to look away? He wanted those dark eyes on him, always. "Damn, but I'd like to see you with your hair down. Just once."

She closed her eyes. "Don't change the subject. This is serious."

"How long?"

"How long what?"

"How long have you been living with the fact that you want me and keeping me at arm's length?" he asked.

She chose not to answer.

He went a step further, urgency driving him. "I nearly died last summer. I had to watch you bleed. I'm no longer in the business of waiting around to see what life's going to hit me with. I'm tired of getting hit. I see something I want…something I need… I chase it. It'd be nice if you'd let me know how much longer I'm going to be chasing you—because I'm too deep in this to stop."

She propped her elbow on the edge of the table and cradled her temple. After a minute of watching him watching her, she sighed. "All right."

"All right what?" His heart banged in anticipation.

"We do this," she considered. "We see where it goes. But on my terms."

"Name 'em," he said.

She leveled an accusing finger at his chest. "If you brush up against the wrong side of the law while we're together, I'm out."

He offered a crooked smile. "Okay."

"Let's keep this between us. I'm new as sheriff. I'm still

trying to gain the respect of certain parts of the community. I don't need talk interfering with that."

"You know how hard it is to keep a secret in Fuego."

"I do," she told him. "Which is why I assume you made reservations out of town."

"I'm banned from Grady's Saloon," he reminded her. "Hickley's BBQ doesn't exactly scream 'date night.' And the steak at Mimi's isn't much to write home about. Third?" he prompted.

"I won't sleep with you," she decided.

He hissed. "That hurts a little."

She held up a hand. "No matter where the courting, as you say, leads… Until I know what we're about…until I'm sure, we keep it PG. Okay?"

He let his eyes rest on her exposed collarbone. Her skin was the color of wheat before harvest and the hollow at the base of her throat fluttered with her pulse. "Can I still think about you naked?" he asked, low.

It shocked a laugh out of her. Smiling widely, she gave an affirmative nod. "Yes," she granted. Then she groaned. "It won't be easy."

"I'm a hard man," he replied, "as you say. I don't do things easy."

"I'm aware of that," she mused. "I'll give it a month. If this doesn't burn out or fizzle and we don't disappoint one another, we'll see if it's worth staying the course."

He raised his glass. "You drive a hard bargain. But I'll take what I can get."

She raised her glass, too. They tipped them together, clinked. "You're worth it," he said as he lifted his glass and drank.

She sipped and muttered, "You'd better be."

As Everett pulled up in front of her house, Kaya unbuckled her seat belt. "Well, this was…something."

He cranked the gearshift into Park. "I'll walk you in."

She grabbed his arm to stop him from turning off the ignition. "No."

"But we're courtin'," he reminded her. "I should walk you to your door like a gentleman."

She leaned into his warmth. "You're not a gentleman and I'm not a lady. We've got something warm and yummy here. You walk me to my door, I'll be tempted to invite you in, despite what I agreed to in that classy restaurant. You'd best stay put."

He raised his hands from the steering wheel. "Hey, you're the sheriff."

"That's right." Grappling for his shoulders, she brought him closer and dropped her voice to a whisper. "Now, I order you to kiss me good night—like you did earlier—so I can go in and think about what I've done."

His quiet laugh blew across her mouth. "You might be a woman after my own heart. Isn't that something?" He gripped the back of her neck, long fingers splaying up into the taut nest of her bun as he tipped his head to the side and took the kiss further, his tongue sliding over her lips to part them.

She caught herself moaning. He made her feel soft, pliant, female. She was so stunned that her mouth parted, and she felt the quick, hot flick of his tongue against hers.

She was practically panting, she found, as his hand firmed against the dip of her waist. She pushed her arms through the parting of his sport coat, all but bowing her torso to his to gather his heat for her own. Her head dipped back on her neck as he took what he wanted, and her hands splayed across the long, firm line of his back.

The big, tough cattle baron had been pining for her—Kaya. Wasn't that a trip?

She was tripping, all right—high on his earthy scent and the sound of his breath clashing with hers in the quiet.

She felt his hand scale her ribs, cruising toward her breast.

She twined her fingers through his before sliding it away. She broke away from his mouth in a faint protest she'd have to chide herself for later. Pressing her lips together, she edged away, toward the passenger door where she'd have stayed to begin with if she'd known what was good for her.

She lived off her mind and her gut and the cool voice of reason. One drink of Everett Eaton and it all turned to ash.

He knocked his head back against his headrest and groaned. "And here I was thinking you didn't want to get all hot and bothered," he said between his teeth. "That'll linger."

"You just hold that thought," she suggested, making herself turn the handle and open the door. She hopped out of the cab.

"I'll see you tomorrow, Sheriff Sweetheart," he called in his distinctive baritone. "Bright and early, like I promised you."

Her legs weren't steady. She blamed it on the wine he'd bought her. "Good night, trouble," she volleyed back and closed the door between them.

Chapter Four

"We've covered most every inch of the east and south sides of the mountain, and we've swept most of the north side as well. It's been two days and we've found nothing else but an old hair scrunchie, two empty beer bottles and some rusty tent stakes," Kaya said. She was back on the summit of Ol' Whalebones for the third morning in a row with her deputies and a ragtag team of professionals and volunteers.

Word of Miller Higgins's disappearance had spread. They'd found a news van from Taos at the end of the access road where they unloaded their horses for the ride to the mountain at dawn. Kaya had forbidden them from coming farther than the eastern trailhead. "If we don't find anything today, we're going to have to bring in a chopper."

Deputy Root's attention was on the screen of his mini-laptop. His reconnaissance drone was in the air, searching the rocky west side of the ridge. "You're comfortable having members of his family come out to help?" he asked.

Kaya shook her head. "Not in the least. If we find remains… And with cameras waiting at the base of the hill… It's hard for people to keep their heads when shock and grief are taking a sucker punch at them."

"The father's a decent tracker," Deputy Root reported. "With him and Wolfe Coldero, the drone and dogs you had the handlers haul out here, chances are good we'll find something."

Kaya hoped she wouldn't regret involving the Higgins family in the search for Miller. "I put Wyatt and Ellis Eaton with the father and son team. If they find anything first, those two are the most calm and compassionate. I warned the handlers about the cougar den. That's probably going to occupy most of the dogs' attention."

"Is it true about Tombstone?"

Kaya narrowed her eyes at Root. "I never saw him. But I'm told this is his territory. If he's still alive. Seems a bit of a stretch. Stories of Tombstone are older than my niece, Nova, and she's driving now. Still, every team has protection and is on the lookout."

Root paused, handling the drone's joystick. "Is it possible Higgins isn't on the mountain?"

It had crossed her mind. Higgins's mother had searched his room at their home in San Gabriel and found an empty Merrell shoe box with a receipt dated a week prior to the boy's livestream. Size nine. Brown. Moabs. They had one shoe and no Miller. The information fed the deep pit in Kaya's stomach.

Everett had sent men out to the four quarters of Eaton Edge. If Higgins had run in that direction, she could only hope they'd find him alive. It had now been five days since Higgins's last contact. "We can't assume anything until we've searched every inch of the mountain. Is there a clear path to the western part of the ridge?"

He panned and zoomed on his screen. "It'll be a lot more challenging than other parts. You up for it?"

She hated the question but understood it. Three days of hiking had given her a noticeable limp. She'd had to skip this week's physical therapy session, too. "Call a handler and Wolfe Coldero's team. Tell them I want him and half the dogs with us."

LIKE EVERETT, WOLFE COLDERO was a polarizing figure in Fuego. The tall, dark cowboy was mute, his origins a mystery. He had come to Eaton Edge as a boy, lost and broken, and he'd served time as an adult. It didn't matter that he'd been exonerated of the crime Wendell Jones had sent him up for. Some people still talked of him only in whispers.

Kaya knew him to be a man of exemplary character, if mysterious. He was also one of the best trackers she'd ever worked with. As the dogs yanked their handler onward over the tumble of rocks and boulders that pitted the northern portion of the mountain, Wolfe followed at his own pace, stopping to crouch on and off the path.

When he stopped again, Kaya let the others go ahead. She chugged water from her canteen. While no was looking, she choked down some Advil.

The sun was high so she could discern little of Wolfe's face under his worn, black felt hat other than a contemplative frown and sharp-bladed jaw. His finger had dug a circle in the dirt. He shoved aside a small rock, another, then he raised his head, finally, and whistled in her direction.

She moved to him, kneeling with a short wince. "What'd you find?" she asked.

He pointed to a small object in the soil.

Kaya lowered her head further. "It's metal." She reached into her pocket for her gloves. After pulling them on, she took further precaution by prying the metal object out of its dirt bed with a pair of tweezers. She lifted it to the light so they could both examine it. "An earring," she said. "Gold. The real thing. It's not tarnished or corroded. I'd say it's been here awhile if you had to dig it up like that."

Wolfe nodded his agreement.

"I doubt it's to Miller's taste," she went on. "But I can't see a situation where a camper would wear something this nice out in the elements." Reaching into her back pocket, she pulled out a small evidence bag. "God, your eyes are good."

He rolled his shoulder in a shrug and stood. When she shifted from one foot to the other to do the same, he grabbed her under the shoulder to help. "Thanks," she said as she put the bag and the tweezers away and pulled off her gloves. "I should catch up."

He walked on with her, scanning the ground.

"How're wedding plans coming?" she asked. "It's only a month from now, isn't it?"

He nodded and sent her a small, sideways smile to show her that plans were going well.

"You and Everett getting along?" she wondered.

Wolfe made a so-so motion with his hand. Kaya made a noise in answer. Everett's long-running feud with Wolfe had only just cooled in the last year when Wolfe and Everett's sister, Eveline, fell in love. Kaya had never known what Everett and Wolfe had fallen out about when they were teens living on the Edge, but it had divided the house, with Wolfe going to live with the operation's foreman, Santiago Coldero. Not long after, Everett's mother, Josephine, had left her husband and three children to join Santiago and Wolfe at Coldero Ridge on the other side of town.

The resulting scandal had lit the touch paper for town gossips and was still the subject of their tongue wagging at times. It was exacerbated by the fact that the events over the last summer had stirred the mystery surrounding Josephine's and her youngest child Angel's deaths seven years ago.

The sound of a dog's baying carried on the wind, followed by a second and a third. Kaya quickened her pace. She had to climb over a rocky ledge to get to the handler's position. "Did they find something?"

The dogs were straining against the handler's lead. "They won't get away from the edge," he informed her. "Something must be down there."

Kaya tested the ground, looking for cracks. The outcropping hung lengthways over a sharp drop. This side of the mountain more closely resembled the buttes that littered the high desert landscape. "Get them back," she advised, edging closer to the cliff. The wind came up to meet her, teasing the flyaway strands that had come loose from her bun. Holding on to her hat, she turned her gaze down below the outcropping.

"There's another ledge down there," she noted. "I can just see it. Other than that, there's nothing for thirty feet or more."

"There's no way for us to get down there safely," the handler said.

As Wolfe came forward, she asked, "Ever done any abseiling?" At his frown, she course-corrected. "Rappelling?" At the shake of his head, she pursed her lips.

"Could be the dogs smell that mountain lion again," the

handler explained. “Though that’s a long drop…even for a cat.”

Her thoughts exactly. She unseated the radio from its holding on her belt and brought it to her mouth. “Root, do you copy?”

“Ten-four.”

“We made it to the north ridge,” she relayed. “And we need your drone. Tell Wyatt to bring climbing equipment. Does anybody have experience with cliff descent?”

Static hissed momentarily, then the familiar timbre of Everett’s voice called back. “Affirmative.”

She frowned. Of course it would be him. “I need you, too.”

A pause hovered before Everett’s message came back. “On the way.”

“ARE YOU SURE you know what you’re doing?”

Everett glanced up from the climbing harness Ellis secured around his middle. Kaya’s gaze was on Root’s drone as it sailed over the cliff edge, scanning. But he knew she meant the question for him. “Ellis and I used to do this every weekend,” he told her. “Didn’t we?”

Ellis gave a jerky nod. “During the misspent years of our youth, yes.”

“Did you do it here?” she asked.

Ellis shook his head. “There’re some canyons and cliffs at the state park we liked to hit.”

Kaya held her elbows and leaned back slightly—to keep the weight off her bad leg, Everett knew. She met Ellis’s stare, probing. “Is he any good?”

Ellis’s mouth moved in a small grin. “He’s a risk-taker. But he knows what he’s about.”

"Why does the first part not surprise me?" she said, looking to Everett with an ounce of accusation.

He smiled broadly, feeding the rope through his hands. "You worried about me, Sheriff?"

Root yelped.

Kaya leaned over his laptop screen. "Do you see something?"

"Directly below," he said, making minute adjustments with the joystick. "Do you…see that?"

Kaya's hand came to the deputy's shoulder. "Can you zoom in?"

Everett watched the hand flex. He heard Kaya's breath stutter and moved forward. "What's wrong?"

She held up a hand. "Stay back."

"Why?" Everett asked. "What's down there?"

She raised herself to her full height. His lips parted when he saw that all the blood had drained from her face. "We may have found him."

KAYA HAD EVERYONE pulled back from the north ridge and a perimeter established. She ordered Wyatt to get Higgins's father and brother to the base of the mountain with a reminder to keep them clear of reporters.

She called in crime scene technicians. It took most of the afternoon for Miller Higgins's body to be recovered from its unlikely resting place.

Along with others.

"Jesus God Almighty." Deputy Wyatt, normally a stickler for professional lingo, swallowed hard as the bag containing the final unidentified victim came into view via a complex system of ropes and pulleys. "That's *four*."

Kaya had seen the bones underneath Higgins's in the drone footage. But she hadn't counted on four, either… "Three unidentifieds."

Root had been reticent since seeing the images on his computer screen. He was several shades beyond pale underneath his freckles. "Where were the birds?"

Kaya narrowed her eyes. "What?"

"The birds," Root said again. His voice sounded dull and his eyes tracked the movement of the techs as they carried the body away. "They should've been here—for Miller, if not the others. He was…fresh."

Kaya lifted her chin, understanding.

It was the medical examiner, Damon Walther, who answered. "The birds have already been here, deputy. They'd finished their job before your search began."

Wyatt blew out a full-length curse, shifting his feet on the uneven ground.

"That'll make determining cause of death more difficult." Kaya knew. "I want this to be priority when you get these bodies back to the morgue. I don't have to tell you what kind of case we might have on our hands here."

Root's lips parted. They were the same color as his skin. "I… I think I'm going to…"

She gave him a light push. "Take a minute. Get yourself together. Miller Higgins's relatives are waiting below. We all need a handle on this before we meet them." She'd be lying if she said that grim feeling she'd had in the pit of her stomach throughout the day hadn't grown. On the back of her tongue, she could taste something bitter and acidic that didn't make it easier to negotiate what was happening in her stomach. She took her hat off as the techs passed by and felt more than saw her deputies do the same.

When the techs had carried the body some distance away, she settled her hat back on her head and scowled at the view from the top. "What the hell happened on this mountain?"

Chapter Five

Everett waited his turn. There was no getting to Kaya through the snarl of people at the trailhead. He waited with Crazy Alice, holding her reins and those for Ghost, who'd been busily munching sweets Everett had stashed in his saddle bag.

He wasn't sure exactly what condition Miller Higgins had been in when Kaya and the others had found him. He'd known by the grim set of her mouth and the appearance of crime scene technicians on the scene that it wasn't good. She'd sent Everett back behind the police perimeter, despite his insistence to stay.

I need you to do this, Everett, she'd told him. *Don't argue with me.*

The words hadn't wavered, but he'd seen what was in her eyes.

She'd seen death. They'd been too late to save the kid.

The choppers had come and gone—not one, but three, which had given everyone at the bottom of the mountain more to talk about. The Fuego police had thankfully separated the kid's father and brother from the small herd of journalists.

He saw Kaya come off the mountain, cutting a swath through the reporters and cameras. She'd gone straight to where police had ensconced Higgins's family and stayed there for half an hour.

By the time she came back to the horses for Ghost, the circles under her eyes were as dark as bruises.

"You okay?" he asked.

She didn't meet his gaze. "I need to return to the station. I'm meeting the rest of the family there. And I need to make a statement to the press. It won't wait until morning. Dispatch called. Apparently, there are more reporters gathered there outside."

"You're tired," he told her.

"I know what I am," she snapped. Then she paused, taking the reins from him. "Sorry. It was rough up there."

"He's dead," Everett said quietly.

She pressed her lips together, unable to confirm or deny. "Listen, if reporters show up at the Edge—"

"No comment," he said and nodded. "I know."

She searched his face, then lowered her voice. "This could be trouble for you. Your family."

"Whatever happened, happened on our land," he stated. "Yeah. I expect there'll be a fair few questions."

Her scanning eyes fell on the buttons on his front. "I can't discuss it any further—with you or anyone. Don't push me."

"No," he replied. "So long as you promise me you're going to eat something when you get back to the station house. You need energy."

She shook her head. "No, I..." For a moment, her lips trembled. She cast a look in the direction of Ellis and Wolfe who were close by. "No."

Everett felt the lines dig into his brow. "Christ. Must've been bad up there."

Silently, she motioned for him to step back so she could mount her horse.

He stood by for a few seconds before reaching out, just enough to brush his knuckles across the tense muscles of her jaw. “Get back safe. You hear me?”

She jerked a nod, placed her foot in the stirrup and boosted herself up, swinging her other leg over Ghost’s back. She settled into the saddle, let the Appaloosa shift underneath her, then clicked her tongue. The horse walked on.

Everett watched as Root and Wyatt joined her on their mounts. They broke into a trot, then a gallop.

Ellis’s mount, Shy, nickered close behind him as his brother crossed to Everett. “She thinks there’s trouble in it for the family?”

“Mmm,” Everett responded. He saw Wolfe come to stand on Ellis’s far side. His hands moved to communicate in sign language. “What’s he saying?” Everett demanded.

Ellis watched his friend’s motions. He and Wolfe had bonded soon after the latter had found a home at the Edge. Their friendship had lasted through the twisted forays of their family histories. “He says whatever happened to the kid wasn’t an accident.”

Everett frowned at the man in the black hat. He didn’t feel a lot of warmth for Eveline’s fiancé. But Wolfe’s instincts tended to be better than others’. “How do you figure?”

Wolfe signaled. Ellis translated, “She didn’t talk to the press. Neither did either of the deputies. And why would there be three choppers for one body?” Ellis braced his hands on his hips. “She did tell us, didn’t she, that this was going to bring trouble to the Edge?”

Everett picked through Kaya’s words. “And here I thought

we'd put trouble to rest with Whip Decker's death and Sheriff Jones's arrest."

"We need to know what happened up there," Ellis countered. "Preferably before reporters come to call. We need to know how to respond."

"Simple," Everett said. "No comment."

"Everett—"

"You heard me." He intervened before his brother could voice any more cautions. "Whatever happened on Ol' Whalebones, I aim for us to pass well below the radar. We've been through enough trouble to last us a lifetime—and Eatons tend not to live as long as others."

"Don't remind me," Ellis muttered. "And you won't be saying that around my fiancée."

Wolfe gestured in agreement.

"It's a bad legacy," Everett acknowledged. "But we don't have a choice other than to live with it." He patted Crazy Alice's muzzle when she nosed his elbow. "If I don't get you home to your women, I'm going to be persona non grata. Let's ride."

KAYA COULD DEAL with the press. She could deal with the curious bystanders who'd come to her office, expecting a definitive word on the situation. She could even deal with the questions inside her head and the sick feeling that wouldn't leave her alone.

Sitting down with Miller Higgins's mother, father, brother and sister, however, was something else altogether. This part of the job wasn't easy for anyone in law enforcement. Her emotions played close to the surface. When handling family of the deceased, she struggled even under the best of circumstances.

This was far from the best situation. She had four bodies in the morgue.

When she saw the mayor stride past the press pack and into the station, she allowed herself a lengthy sigh.

True Claymore was all swagger, even on bad news days like today.

His smile didn't quite meet his eyes, as it normally did. He was classed up, as always, in his embroidered black Western coat that was open over a pressed, white shirt complete with all the sterling accoutrements he felt necessary to reinforce his white-collar status—bolo tie with its prominent, engraved *C*, and an enlarged belt buckle with its crossed pistols and the words "GOD, FAMILY, COUNTRY" displayed underneath—up to the buckle of his hat band.

Kaya steeled herself. For all his charm, the good mayor did nothing to whet her appetite for his regular visits. He liked his finger in every pie if they smelled well enough of power and influence, which he'd enjoyed in this town for too long.

Her becoming sheriff hadn't pleased him. He'd done what he could to sway the election a different way.

Chiefly because he knew, unlike her predecessor, that she could not and would not be bought.

He tipped his hat to her. "Hell of a day, Sheriff Altaha. Hell of a day."

"I didn't see you on the mountain, mayor," she stated, "though I'm assuming you know as much as those people outside, which is next to nothing at this point."

"Come now, Kaya, honey," he said, sinking his hands into his pockets. "You know I've got my sources. You didn't find just one person dead on Ol' Whalebones."

Kaya caught the gasp from her assistant, Sherry, at her

desk. Irritated, she jerked her head toward the door of her office.

"Sherry," Claymore said in greeting as he passed her by. "How's the baby?"

"He's doing great, Mr. Claymore, sir," Sherry stuttered.

"Ah, that's fine, real fine," he schmoozed.

Kaya spread the door open. "We're all on the clock here."

As an invitation, it was poor. But the thought of having to deal with this clown inside the enclosed space of her office made her already upset stomach clutch. Claymore's cologne all but strangled her as he moved into her office. She shut the door and went behind the desk to put space between them. "The details of this case are being kept under wraps until we know more. In fact, they're on a need-to-know basis."

He messed with his tie. "That's just the thing, honey." Spreading his hands, he raised his brows. "In order to handle the press and questions from my constituents, I need to know. The bodies were found on Eaton Edge. There's been quite a lot of trouble out that way over the past year. I'd say you should start your investigation there."

"I never said there was foul play involved," she noted. "I won't know that until I speak with the medical examiner."

He rolled his eyes. "Come on, Kaya—"

Her restraint snapped. "It's *Sheriff*, actually. When I held the position of deputy, you never addressed me as anything but that. I don't recall the two of us getting any more familiar with each other over the past three months nor do I anticipate that happening anytime in the future. So you will address me as Sheriff Altaha and when I tell you the details of this case or any other are need-to-know you will take that as my word. Do I make myself clear, Mr. Claymore?"

His good-natured smile slipped. He was too smooth a man to let aggravation take hold, as she had. She knew, though, as the playful light in his eyes dimmed and a muscle in his cheek flexed, that she'd hit the mark. "We'll see about that, Sheriff. Yes, we will see. Have you dealt with the family of the hiker?"

She curbed the urge to club him over the head. "Have I *spoken* with Miller Higgins's father, mother and siblings? Yes. At length. They should be left alone. Instead of focusing on the press and the curious gaggle of townspeople outside, why don't you utilize your mayoral powers to inform people that the Higginses should be left alone? I'm sure they'd appreciate it."

Claymore took in a long breath. "Very well. You will keep me apprised of the nature of this case. It'd be best—for all involved."

He strolled out. Sinking into her chair, she pressed her hands to her temples. She was distressed when they shook. Pressing them between her knees, she willed herself to get it together.

She hated how much True Claymore still rattled her.

Unable to dwell on the reasons why, she opened the top desk drawer and found the Advil she kept there. There was a half-drunk Pepsi can on her desk from the day before. Claymore had left the door open so she called through it. "Sherry?"

"Yes, ma'am… I mean, sir." The woman, who wasn't but a few years younger than Kaya, bustled in. "What can I do?"

"Could you get me a bottle of water?" she asked. "And maybe something small to eat. Nothing heavy. I'd appreciate it."

"I can run down the street and see if the deli's still open," Sherry offered.

"Thanks," Kaya said. "And you know not a word to those outside..."

Sherry bobbed her head quickly. "Mum's the word."

Kaya tried to fix a smile in place. Sherry had been hired by Jones, so Kaya had inherited her as an assistant. Knowing she had a baby at home, Kaya hadn't contemplated firing her, though she'd been cautious with her, unsure whether she still felt allegiance to her former boss.

Sherry hesitated on the threshold, worrying the pad of sticky notes and pen she carried with her. "Did you really find more than one body?"

Kaya closed her eyes briefly. The images were still fresh in her mind. And after her visit to the morgue, there'd likely be more to contend with. "It's late," she countered. "Once you come back from the deli, you need to go home and see your family."

Sherry handled her disappointment well. "Thank you, ma'am. Sir. I'll be back shortly."

Kaya found herself alone in the station house. Root was dealing with reporters. Wyatt had escorted the Higgins family home to San Gabriel for the night.

She'd seen her share of the dead. She'd been a rookie cop on the streets of Taos where the crime rate was anything but low. Her two years in uniform there might have made her, but they'd also exposed her to victims of overdose, homicide, accidental death and suicide.

She'd learned early that she could either compartmentalize it all, funnel it away or get overwhelmed so she'd done the former—to survive. To keep going because being a cop was the only ambition she'd had that mattered. Failure was not an option.

It still wasn't. She hadn't come back to Fuego County and joined the sheriff's department so that she could take over Wendell Jones's position. She'd had no ambitions there whatsoever. Nor could she turn her back on the people who'd thought she was best suited to the position.

She'd wanted to find Miller Higgins alive. She had needed to find him and return him to his folks.

She flicked open the report on her desk and stared at his photograph, as she had so often over the last few days.

There hadn't been a homicide in Fuego County in well over a year. But she had little doubt that Higgins had been murdered…along with the other three people they'd found with his body on Ol' Whalebones.

Murder had come to Fuego four times, which meant her department wasn't just dealing with a dangerous perpetrator. They were dealing with a serial killer.

KAYA PUSHED THROUGH the doors of the morgue. There was no one at the reception desk. Dr. Walther had volunteered to stay in after hours to see that the bodies were well cared for. Half the fluorescent lights in the lobby had been switched off.

As she turned toward the swinging doors of the examination room, she came up short. Her hand nearly jumped to her sidearm before she stopped it. "Damn," she said as the man just before the doors turned and she was able to see his face in the small amount of light from the lobby. She swallowed the curse because the mystery man was Reverend Huck Claymore. "Sorry. My nerves are on a hair trigger."

"It's understandable," he said in his level voice. The only

place she'd ever heard him raise it was during passionate sermons from the pulpit of the local church.

Kaya had always felt conflicted about him. He was True Claymore's older brother. He'd grown up at The RC Resort, same as the mayor. Neither man had wanted for much. Huck's suit might not be as flashy as his brother's, but even she could see that it was tailored. His tie was silk, and his boots weren't the least bit scuffed. He rarely smiled. She'd never heard him crack so much as a meager joke. He was a sober, weary-eyed man whose presence was a comfort to the citizens of Fuego.

He studied her closely with his unchanging expression. "How are you, Sheriff Altaha?"

She wasn't looking for comfort any more than she'd ever sought any of his preaching. Still, it was a kind, even question she'd be rude to rebuff. "I'm all right," she lied. When he lowered his chin, she sighed. "I've been better. May I ask what you're doing here, reverend?"

He didn't so much as blink. "To pray for the poor souls you took off the mountain this afternoon."

"Right," she said, feeling like an idiot. "That's kind of you, reverend. But we can't allow you beyond this point."

"I understand," he said with a passive nod. "Will the Higginses be returning tomorrow morning to identify their son?"

Kaya nodded. "Ten o'clock."

"I'd like to be here," he requested. "They might need some comfort during this time."

"Of course," she granted.

His lips curved but his eyes didn't track. "Thank you, Sheriff. I hope my brother hasn't been giving you any trouble over your investigation so far. He tends to overstep in these matters."

"I can handle the mayor."

As he regarded her, his eyes followed the path of his smile for the first time in Kaya's memory. Something gleamed to life there that he quickly shuttered. "I have no doubt you can." He reached up and pinched the edge of his white Stetson. "God be with you, Sheriff Altaha."

"And with you." The words didn't come as easily to her as they did him. She waited until she heard the entry doors swing shut behind him before she pushed through the doors into the exam room. "Sorry. I'm behind schedule."

Dr. Walther peered at her through his protective eyewear. He used a scalpel to point to the wall. "Gown. Gloves. Hairnet."

She grabbed what he told her to and donned each, carefully. There was one body on the table. The other victims were likely locked up in the cooler already. The ME's office was small and understaffed. The complete results of each autopsy were weeks out. But she'd wanted to gather any early impressions Walther had as well as view what had been collected with the remains.

The drone had been far enough away to give her only a vague impression of the damage done to Higgins over the last three days. It had given her more than enough, however, to tell her that he was no longer part of the living world. And yet she still felt sucker punched when she leaned over the table and viewed him close-up.

"The wildlife did their work," Walther acknowledged.

"Will you still be able to determine cause of death?" she asked as her stomach flipped the deli sandwich Sherry had brought her.

"After a proper examination," Walther granted. "There are tears and lacerations to the face, arms and torso."

"His family's coming tomorrow," she cautioned. "They can't see him like this."

"His wallet was still in his pocket," Walther revealed.

"Identification and cash?"

"Both," he said, pointing to a tray. "He had upwards of two hundred dollars on his person. Technicians also found a pocketknife with his name carved into the handle."

"What about his phone?" she asked. "He was livestreaming with it or a camera at the time of his disappearance."

"No phone, no camera," Walther answered.

"His pack?" she asked. "Hikers always have packs."

"Yes. Its contents have been catalogued. Would you like to see the full list?"

"I would," she said. "Have you found any other wounds on the body other than tears and lacerations on the front?"

Silently, he instructed her to help him turn Higgins's body onto its right side so the back of his head was facing her. "There's a large wound on the back of his head—a result of the fall, but it also could be consistent with—"

"A killing blow or gunshot wound," she observed. "You'll have him tested for gunshot residue?"

"Samples have already been taken. They'll be sent to the lab first thing in the morning. We'll also be sending DNA from the other victims."

"Maybe we'll get one or more matches with Missing Persons," she hoped. "I hate that we couldn't bring him home to his family alive."

"He was the same age as my oldest, Libby," he mused,

nursing his scalpel. He rocked back on his heels, viewing the dead with more compassion than clinical interest.

"Take all the time you need for results. I want the killer found as much as the next person, but you won't get any pressure from my department if it means a thorough report."

"The mayor's going to have something else to say about how fast things should be done."

"I'll take care of True Claymore and anybody else who tries to interfere so you can focus on the dead. I'd like to see the rest of what was found at the scene. Personal belongings of other victims…anything the killer might have left behind…"

"The first tray is what we found on the boy," Walther reported. "The second contains everything else taken from the scene."

"Thank you," she said, veering around the exam table. Miller Higgins's clothes had been bagged and tagged, as had his personal belongings. His library card lay alongside his driver's license. Something about that tugged at her heart. His pack had contained three calorie bars, a half-full hydration pack, a compass, waterproof matches, a minitorch, a machete and its sheath that looked unmarked as if he'd yet to have had a chance to use it, a stick of deodorant, dissolvable wipes and a first aid kit that had never been opened.

The name carved in the handle of the jackknife hadn't been engraved by a professional. It looked like something he might have done himself.

Kaya frowned deeply when she saw the lone shoe among the clothes removed from his person and moved to the second tray.

Her eyes skimmed over one belt buckle, several more

boots—these dirty and weathered—a slender wristwatch that was feminine in appearance, one hoop earring that could have been a match to the one Wolfe Coldero had found and then landed on a bracelet. It was a C-shaped cuff that wouldn't have gone all the way around the wrist. It was lined with silver.

She reached for it, turning the face of the piece toward her.

Her heart stuttered.

The cuff was inlaid with turquoise. In its center was the letter *S*.

Her focus narrowed on the simple inscription. She went numb. Her ears filled with distracted buzzing.

She must've made a noise because Walther's gloved hand came to rest on hers.

She jerked. "I…" She was breathing through her teeth. Her pulse was high and the buzzing was incessant. "This piece," she stammered. "I know this. I know who this belongs to!"

Chapter Six

Everett hadn't heard from Kaya in two days—unless listening to her press conference on the local news counted.

...recovered the remains of a sixteen-year-old male. He has been identified as Miller Higgins of San Gabriel. While searching the area, three other unidentified bodies were found...

She'd sent her deputies to the Edge to interview everyone on the premises. They asked questions about the comings and goings in the northern quarter over the last week—casual, routine questions that shouldn't have put his dander up.

But they did. Everett couldn't believe the police thought anyone at the Edge was responsible for Higgins's death. Rumors were rampant in town. Ol' Whalebones had been cordoned off. He and his men had been asked to leave it alone, pending further investigation.

Kaya hadn't said it on the news or otherwise, but everyone from Fuego to San Gabriel had. There was a killer on the loose.

That wasn't the only thing putting Everett on edge. Because the four bodies had been found on his family's mountain, the name Eaton was firmly entrenched in rumor and suspicion. With Eveline's wedding coming around the bend, people were pointing fingers.

There was nothing he disliked more than gossip. Unfortunately, Fuego was the gossip capital of the civilized world.

Even the church on Sunday stank of tittle-tattle.

Paloma always insisted he, Ellis and Eveline attend church with her. She'd somehow won the trifecta this week, roping all three of them into the front pew alongside Luella, Wolfe and Ellis's girls, Isla and Ingrid. Everett passed much of the service ignoring the whispers exchanged behind hands at their backs, swapping folded notes back and forth with his youngest niece, Ingrid, instead. She had a head for mischief and an intolerance for sitting still for more than five minutes at a time—two traits she shared with her uncle.

They had to be sneakier than sneaky to not draw the attention of Paloma who wouldn't hesitate to put a stop to it. Eveline caught his eye once, then subsided when Ingrid placed her finger over her mouth. His sister had smiled and looked the other way.

Ellis was distracted with Luella. She was tense amongst the other townies and with good reason. As Whip Decker's daughter, she'd been branded as troublesome the moment she was born. Whether she deserved the moniker or not, she'd long been branded "Devil's Daughter" by the people of Fuego County.

Everett saw Ellis place his hand on her bouncing knee where he drew circles with his thumb. If anyone could ease Luella's troubles, it was Ellis. He had a way with the woman he'd claimed as his own in high school. She'd slipped through his fingers, and he'd gone on to marry Liberty Ferris. But after the divorce and a fateful winter, Ellis and Luella had come together once more and it didn't look like they would be parting again.

"Psst!"

Everett glanced at Ingrid on his left. He took the note she slid across the surface of the hard bench. Making sure Paloma was still listening to Reverend Claymore, he unfolded the small scrap of paper to find another sketch of a horse.

Ingrid was turning out to be quite the artist.

Everett played along, knowing she was looking for his insight as much as his praises. He picked up the pencil without an eraser he'd found next to the Bible underneath the seat and scribbled, *Nice one. Pass it to LuLu.* He folded the square, then held out his hand as if to shake. She squeezed his fingers, taking the little note as she did. She opened it and read it while he did his best to look uninvolved. Then she folded it again and reached over her father's lap to tap Luella on the wrist.

Both Ellis and Luella looked. Silently, Ingrid did the same faux-shake with Luella she had with Everett, leaving Luella with the folded scrap. She unfolded it with hands that shook only slightly…

A smile bloomed across her face. She swept red curls from her cheek and greeted Ingrid with a soft look. *Thank you*, she mouthed.

Ellis reached his arm around Ingrid's shoulders and drew her close against his side. The child went willingly, casting a grin back at Everett as she did so. He gave her a thumbs-up but stopped when Ellis caught his eye. Shrugging, Everett tried to tune back into the reverend's spiel about sin and damnation and stopping the devil's wicked work in their good community.

Everett glanced over his shoulder, restless. The sanctuary was packed. The question was which of these sinners had been on his mountain. The killer hadn't been on the back of Ol' Whalebones just once. They'd returned over and over and over again. Everett figured it was someone from the county, likely Fuego itself, though he'd thought they'd combed out a fair good many wrongdoers over recent months—Jace "Whip" Decker, Wendell Jones…hell, even lewd Rowdy Conway had been flushed out.

He aimed to do any amount of legwork possible to catch whoever had brought death to Eaton Edge and stop them from killing anyone else there.

His gaze roved over those assembled, searching each face. He knew them all by name. He'd gone to school with some of them. He'd been on the rodeo circuit with others. Hell, he'd raced cars with a few. There were friends and there were rivals.

When his eyes hit the back of the church and Kaya standing near the door, arms crossed over her sheriff's uniform, he felt his heart give a lurch.

She'd been avoiding him. He had no doubt about that. The question was why? Why had she sent Root and Wyatt to question him, his family, his men? Why hadn't she told him about the bodies herself?

Was it because—deep down—like the rest of them, she was distancing herself from everyone at Eaton Edge because she thought somebody there might be involved in the body count?

He turned back around, rolling his shoulders. She hadn't met his stare, but he could feel it like an itch between his shoulder blades. Restless from having sat too long and the strong ache in his chest that he would not name because he knew what was good for him, no matter what had passed between him and the good sheriff of Fuego County, he leaned over his knees, wishing Huck Claymore would just shut up already so he and his family could escape with their dignity intact.

A movement out of the corner of his eye caught his attention. It was a wave from the left of the pulpit where the organist Christa McMurtry sat, watching him.

She was always watching him. She beamed, curling her fingers his way.

"Hellfire." His mutter fell into one of Reverend Claymore's pauses. Heads turned, Paloma leaning clear out in the open to scowl at him. He looked away, up at the pulpit, and saw the elder Claymore eyeing him with strong disapproval.

Join the party, reverend, he thought bitterly.

EVERETT FOUGHT HIS way to the back of the church once the service was over. He fought so hard, he elbowed several people out of the way and nearly knocked down Turk Monday, the former manager of Fuego's bank. Once he found sunlight and fresh air again, he nearly stumbled down the length of the church steps…

…and found that Kaya had escaped already.

"Ah… Mr. Eaton?"

"What do you want?" He settled down when he saw that it was Nova, a waitress at Hickley's BBQ. She had long raven locks that were straight as an arrow, wide dark eyes narrowed against the angle of the midmorning sun and prominent cheekbones that marked her as Kaya's niece. Kaya's sister, Naleen Gaines, was Nova's mother. "Sorry," he said when he saw her take a half step back in retreat. He sank his hands into his pockets, hoping for a less menacing impression. "Church makes me mean as a woke bear."

The lines of her mouth wavered, and he wondered if that wasn't amusement lurking beneath. "I've been meaning to speak to you, Mr. Eaton."

"Call me Everett, Nova. I've known you since you were in diapers. And nobody calls me Mr. Eaton," he told her.

"Everett," she said, treading lightly. "I was wondering if you'd consider taking on a new hand at Eaton Edge this summer."

He made a thoughtful noise. "Depends on if they're any good at the kind of work I need them for. I'm already apprenticing one man. Not that he's much of a man…"

"Are you talking about Lucas?" she asked. "Lucas Barnes?"

He groaned. "The pain in my ass." When he heard the last word slip out, he sighed. Now he was going to have to apologize.

She surprised him by laughing. Catching his stunned gaze, she lifted her hand, subsiding. "Sorry. It's just… I know him—from when he was still in school. He gave the teaching staff fits."

"I'll bet he did." He inclined his head. "You know somebody I can take on?"

"Yeah," she said, standing a little taller. "Me."

"You?"

She narrowed her eyes. "Just because I'm a girl doesn't mean I don't know how to herd. Don't you have a sister? Doesn't she ride out with the men?"

"Occasionally," he said. "And it's got less to do with you being a female and more to do with the work itself. We don't just herd. We feed, wrangle, fix fencing, pipes, brand, tag, sort, vaccinate… No matter the season or the weather—hot, cold, rain, high desert sun, snow—we ride. It's tough on a grown man. Much less a teenage girl."

"My stepfather, Terrence Gaines, has been showing me the ropes at his ranch," she said. "It's a small operation, but we do all those things there, too. And my father…well, my biological father—Ryan MacKay?"

"I know him. He's my stable manager Griff's son."

"He's been teaching me to rope since I was a toddler," she revealed. "And my aunt, Kaya, she taught me to ride with the best of 'em."

"Did she now?" he asked.

"Yeah. She did a lot of trick riding back in the day."

"You don't say." He considered. The girl hadn't wavered when he'd spoken about the work or the elements. "Wouldn't you rather spend your summer raising hell?" When she shook her head, he had to think harder. "Or…at the mall?"

"You don't know much about teenage girls, do you?"

"No. Look… I'm not going to say no to more help. But I'll need to speak to your mother first. I'm not aiming to get on anyone's mother's list, if you know what I'm saying."

"Sure," she said.

"I can't pay you much of a wage," he said. "At least not at first, while you're still learning the ropes."

"I learn fast," she assured him.

"And there's no way in hell you're sleeping in the bunkhouse with the men," he warned.

"Fine by me," she said. "Spring break's coming up. If you'd like, I could use that time to show you my skills. That way, you'll know what you're getting in the summertime."

"Why not?"

The beginnings of a cautious smile touched her mouth. "You're really saying yes?"

He found himself nodding. "I'm really saying yes."

"Wow. My mom said I didn't have a shot in hell." She beamed. "I love proving her wrong. Thank you!"

He was so shocked when she threw both arms around him, the hug sent him back a step. "Whoa." He caught himself, laughing. "There'll be none of that around the men. And you said your aunt was a trick rider?"

She bounced anxiously on her toes. "Uh-huh."

"You'll need to tell me more about that," he advised.

"Why? Are you interested?"

"In your aunt?" He bobbed his head. "Guilty."

"I didn't know the two of you were—"

"We've been keeping it quiet," he said.

"Oh," she said, lowering her voice and darting a look around. "Right. Okay. Well, what do you want to know?"

"How she's doing, for one?" he asked, feeling lame.

Her expression morphed quickly from playful to troubled.

The mob was beginning to file out of the church en masse. He stepped closer. "What's wrong?"

"I shouldn't say. Mom told me it's a family matter."

Everett tensed. "Does it have anything to do with what they found on the mountain?"

"It has everything to do with that."

He nodded. "I don't want to get you in trouble. Just do me one favor."

KAYA PUT THE phone back into its cradle. She called Root and Wyatt into her office. She closed her file drawer with a thud and folded her hands on the desk. “That was the FBI. They’re sending a man here.”

“They’ll shut us out of the case,” Wyatt complained.

“We’ll have to turn over all the evidence,” Root said. “All those bodies…”

She nudged the file on the desk with her hands. “I’ve been speaking with Walther, off and on. I’ve also been coordinating with the Fuego, San Gabriel and other county police departments and Missing Persons from each bureau.”

“That’s a heck of a thing,” Wyatt muttered. People tended to go missing in the desert quite a bit.

“Together, we may have turned over some results,” Kaya revealed, “but we’ll have to wait for DNA to confirm.” She picked up the folder and thrust it at them.

Wyatt took it. He flipped it open. “Mescal, Sawni. Missing since… Geez, boss. This woman’s been missing for eighteen years.”

Kaya nodded. She threaded her hands together to stop them from fidgeting. “She was seventeen when she disappeared. She wasn’t native to Fuego. She grew up on the rez.”

“Like you,” Root said, innocently enough.

Kaya felt it like a blow. “Like me.”

“Did you know her?”

Full disclosure. There had to be full disclosure if there was going to be trust. “There’s a personal connection,” she admitted. “I’m not willing to elaborate much further.”

They both exchanged a glance, then let it lie. “Last known whereabouts were—”

“Here, in Fuego,” she continued. “After three months, local police and sheriff’s departments stopped looking for her. Though her family and others on the rez never have.”

"Without DNA confirmation, why do you think it was her?" Wyatt asked.

"It's not wishful thinking, if that's what you're implying. A piece of jewelry was found at the site. It matches one I know she owned and wore often." *I had one to match—with a* K. Kaya had had her mother bring it over from their old house where she'd left it when she joined the police academy in Taos. Her piece and the one at the lab were a dead match. "Her grandfather made it for her and one other that I have in my possession."

"Maybe somebody duplicated it," Root noted.

"Maybe she pawned it before she went missing…or somebody could've stolen it," Wyatt said.

"All good thoughts," she acknowledged. "But the pieces line up…a little too neatly now that there are four bodies in the morgue…one of which could very well be hers."

"If one of the bodies does belong to Mescal and the FBI comes in here and says we're off the case, are you going to allow that?" Wyatt wondered.

She weighed the question and all the implications. "I'm not sure," she said truthfully. She flipped open the next file on her desk. "The other possible is Merchant, Bethany. You probably remember her name from the papers. She disappeared a year before Mescal while she was in her senior year at Fuego High School."

"I do remember this one," Root said. "I was a freshman when she was a senior. Head cheerleader, Miss Rodeo like three straight years in a row… She dated all the high-profile rodeo kids. Terrence Gaines. True Claymore. Sullivan Walker. Everett Eaton…"

Kaya pretended her breath didn't snag on the last. "Eaton."

Root nodded. "Oh, yeah. Real hot and heavy, that relationship. 'Course, then his mom up and left his dad for Santiago Coldero. Everett dropped out of school… Things cooled real fast between him and Bethany."

"Her last known whereabouts were at the Lone Star Motel," Kaya noted from the file. "They found an overnight bag, her wallet, keys, even her shoes in Room 10. The bed was still made, however, and it was between her check-in that evening, which she paid for in cash, and her checkout time the following morning that she disappeared."

"How do we know it's her in the morgue, too?" Wyatt asked, his brows low.

"Something that was not found among her possessions in the motel was a wristwatch, one her mother claimed she never left the house without. It was an heirloom that belonged to Bethany's grandmother and was given to her when the woman passed." Kaya sat back. The chair squeaked beneath her. She closed the file on Bethany's picture-perfect smile. "A watch of the same description was found at the crime scene. The family supplied samples as well as dental X-rays. If it's her, we'll know in due time."

"Which would leave one unidentified person," Root said.

"Did Walther say whether or not he's determined cause of death for any of them?" Wyatt asked.

"Just one for certain," she said, grim. "Our hiker, Miller Higgins. Gunshot wound. His skull was tested for gunpowder residue and the wound there is consistent with a gunshot to the back of the head fired at close range."

Root winced a little. "Sounds mercenary. The others must have contusions on the back of the skull as well. That's why the FBI's coming. If a pattern's been established, they must think we've got a serial killer on the loose."

"I don't have to tell you not to pass on any of this information," she reminded them. "The press is on us as it is, not to mention the public. I've had four separate families in my office over the last few days requesting to know whether or not one of the bodies belongs to their son or daughter. One of them was the Merchants. We must keep as many of the details under wraps as we can so that we can build a solid case."

"And then hand it all over to the FBI," Wyatt said dismally.

Kaya frowned. "We'll see."

IT WAS RAINING cats and dogs before she left the sheriff's department and drove home. She thought about stopping by one of the takeout places in town and grabbing something, knowing she was going home to an empty fridge. She hadn't had it in her to face the supermarket or its patrons—not yet, anyway.

She wasn't avoiding people, she told herself. She just wasn't hungry.

Messages had been left on her voice mail at her personal number. There, she'd heard the voices of her mother, her sister, the Mescals…and that was hard to swallow.

And Everett. He'd called, twice—once to leave a message.

That was three days ago. Maybe he'd given up by now.

Just as well, she thought, escaping the rain for the comfort of her home. She'd likely be called back in before daybreak to deal with the arroyos that resulted from these spring cloudbursts. She took off her weapons belt and shrugged off her sheriff's button-down so that her shoulders were bare in her black tank top and she could breathe somewhat easier. She put her official phone on charge as well as her radio, ignored the pit in her stomach by avoiding the pantry and poured herself a cup of coffee.

She was watching the steam rise from the surface as it sat, untouched, on the counter when the doorbell rang.

Wary, she didn't move from the space over the brick cobbles of the kitchen. Fuego was small so it was only natural that some of its residents knew exactly where to find her during her off-duty hours. There had been a few who'd knocked on her door during the week, fishing for more on the case. She'd stopped answering.

She picked up her mug when the doorbell sounded again and then again in quick succession. Thoughtfully, she raised it to her mouth and blew across the surface, letting the coffee's scent curl up her nostrils. Maybe it would help settle her, as nothing else had since she'd recognized the turquoise and silver cuff.

Her mind wouldn't leave it alone. She set the coffee back down, tired and heartbroken all over again.

Had she really thought she'd find Sawni alive? After all this time?

She'd been a fool.

The doorbell was replaced by the sound of a hard knock. A voice followed, terse and familiar. "Hey! Sheriff Sweetheart! Open up!"

Kaya found her feet moving toward the door, abandoning her coffee. She crossed the living space. He was pounding on the door so hard, it was rattling on its hinges. She unlocked the dead bolt, undid the chain and turned the knob, then yanked the door open before he could break it down. "What are you doing?"

The porch light spilled over him. He was standing on her stoop under his hat in the rain. The drops hit the raised concrete platform beneath his boots and splatted noisily, breaking apart and coming in the house. He squinted at her. "What's the matter with you?"

Her jaw dropped. "What's the matter with *me*? You're the one about to break my door down!"

"How else was I supposed to get you to answer?" he asked. "Your family thinks you've done well to isolate yourself. You won't return their calls or mine—"

"How do you know what my family—"

He took a step closer to the threshold, crowding it and her out of the doorway. "What'd you find on the mountain that's made you shut down?"

Her teeth were gnashed and anger ground between them. It felt good, feeling something other than the bone-chilling fear she'd been walking around with. "Get off my porch before my neighbors see you lurking."

"You're going to have to arrest me," he challenged. He scanned her. "Christ. Have you slept since I saw you last?"

Had she expected him to be charming? Women who counted on Everett Eaton turning on the charm would be severely disappointed. She convinced herself she wasn't one of them. "Of course I've—"

"Don't lie to me," he said, grim around the mouth. He planted his hands on either side of the jamb. "I'll bet you're not eating much, either. You look like you're about to drop."

"Why are you here?" she asked him, exasperated.

"You're trying to back out," he decided. "You don't want any part of our agreement anymore."

"I've got more important things to worry about."

"At least call your sister and your niece. They're worried sick."

"Why do think I'm going to take orders from you?" she countered.

"Because you're alone and you're trying to keep it that way—however much you might need somebody right now," Everett stated. "Maybe that person isn't me. I can live with that. But the least you can do is tell me—not dodge my calls."

"You're right."

He opened his mouth to argue further, stopped midword and screwed up his face. "I am?"

Kaya closed her eyes. They wanted to stay closed. "I haven't slept. I'll cop to that. The situation on the mountain…it's far more complex than I thought it could be. There's more I can't tell you. It's personal and it's eating at me. I won't even have the authority to finish it or bring closure to the families. The Feds are on their way. They'll be taking over the investigation as early as Wednesday."

"Why the Feds?" he asked. "Your department's small, but you're capable. You won't stop until you've caught this son of a bitch."

He was going to have so many questions, none of which she could answer. "I want that," she said. "More than you know."

He straightened. "Are you hungry, sweetheart?"

She blinked. "I should eat. I haven't been hungry."

He picked up something off the stoop. A to-go container. "This is from Rocko's."

"Rocko's… Pizza?" she asked, bemused. "That's two towns over. Why—"

"Don't ask me to give away my sources," he said, holding the box out to her, "but I was told it was your favorite restaurant."

She felt the warmth of the cardboard box. "You brought me pizza from Rocko's."

"I want you to be okay. I aim to see to it that you are. You take care of the community, everybody in it. But if you need someone to take care of you, you know where to find me. Are we clear?"

She only stared at him, the scent of Rocko's thick crust supreme curling up her nostrils. Suddenly, she was awake, and she was ravenous. "I don't know what to say."

"Say yes."

There was no refusing him. She pressed her lips together.

He didn't waver. "Is there anything else you need?"

You. In my house. In this space. With me. Her face burned as the thoughts hit home. She settled for shaking her head in response.

"Let me know if that changes," he demanded. "And answer the phone."

"Anything else?" she asked, wryly.

"I'd be inside the house if I didn't think you'd tase me for muddying your floors," he said. "The next time I leave the Edge and track you down, I'm coming in."

She didn't think it'd be wise to tell him she didn't care about her floors. She liked the idea of stripping him down layer by layer just so she'd know warmth again.

This man burned hotter than anyone she'd ever known. It was wiser to keep him out—keep him at arm's length, like she'd planned. But his eyes glinted and the longer she looked at him, the more she wondered just how hot his core was.

"Eat," he said in no uncertain terms. "And get some sleep. I'll say good night."

"Good night," she said. He turned away, walked off the stoop. She shut the door. It took her several seconds to move her feet. She walked back to the kitchen, set the box on the stovetop. She opened the lid. Saliva filled her mouth.

Before she could reach for a slice, one of her phones rang on the counter. She glanced over to see the screen of her personal device lit up. Everett's name was splashed across her caller ID.

This time, she didn't hesitate. She picked it up, swiped, then raised it to her ear. "Hello?"

"Just checking," came the sound of his baritone.

A small smile tugged at her mouth. It kept tugging and she gave in to it. "I thought we said good night."

"We're going to say a lot more good nights before this is all over. You know that, right?"

"Yes," she whispered.

"I'm looking forward to the night I don't have to say good night. I'm livin' for that night, baby."

"I can't handle you when you talk like that," she informed him.

"Good. Maybe it'll make you impatient."

"Good night, Everett."

He cursed but said it anyway. "Think of me, sweetheart." Then he hung up, leaving her with an appetite and need that were suddenly and magnificently awake.

Chapter Seven

Everett stalked into the hacienda-style ranch house ahead of his dogs after a long day of tagging calves and counting cattle. He wanted to drink a beer, put up his feet and leave the paperwork he knew was sitting at his desk for later. The house smelled damn fine, and his stomach rumbled, needing whatever Paloma had thrown together in the kitchen.

No sooner had he taken off his hat than the dark-eyed housekeeper his father had hired over thirty years ago rounded the corner and snapped her apron at him. "Take off those boots. You're tracking in dirt. Don't you have any sense, or has it all vanished with the altitude?"

Everett hung his hat on the nearest peg and stretched his arms from one side of the mudroom to the other. "I was awake with the cock this morning. I don't need you pestering me when we both know I wiped my feet a dozen times before entering."

"You got witnesses to that?" she asked, eyeing him beadily.

Everett growled low in his throat before he turned, opened the door and stepped out onto the welcome mat. He scraped the bottom of his boots on the coarse fibers in exaggerated motions like a mama cow stamping the ground while he tagged her calf. When he was done, he came back in and slapped the door shut with a resounding thud after letting the dogs in, too. "Satisfied?"

"Turn them up for me, one after the other."

"No," he drawled and stomped around her in the direction of the kitchen. The clickity-clack of the dogs' nails followed him across the hardwood.

Paloma pulled him up short with an urgent hand on his arm. "Don't go in there looking like that!"

"Why not?" He loved her. She was more mother to him than the woman who had made him and run away. But he was hot and drained and all he'd thought about for the last hour was settling down with a beer and his dogs.

"There's a man," she hissed, down to a whisper.

Everett raised a brow. "You got a man in here?" He shook her loose. "Does he know he'll never be good enough for you? Never mind. I'll tell him."

She grabbed him again before he could turn the corner. "Not that kind of man, you lout. And haven't I got enough problems keeping you decent without some good-for-nothing boyfriend hanging around?"

"That's the spirit," he muttered, still trying to get a look around the corner. "Who's the guy?"

"He says he's from the FBI."

Everett stopped straining away. "Say again."

"You heard me," she said, lowering her brow. "Everett Templeton Eaton, don't you go all Clint Eastwood on this one. He's no Sheriff Altaha, or Jones for that matter."

"I'll thank you never to mention the good sheriff and her predecessor in the same breath again," he warned.

"You misunderstand," she snapped, pinning him with an expression he'd come to know well over the misspent days of his youth. "An outside agent of the law isn't likely to give you the sort of understanding or leniency that local law enforcement has. Keep that tongue of yours civil. I don't have the wherewithal to bail you out of federal prison."

It wasn't exasperation that gripped her. Not entirely. She was worried about him—more than usual. He felt himself soften. So few people filed away his rough edges, but she could do it in a look. Without answering, he bent to her level and pecked a kiss on her round cheek. Then he ducked into the kitchen to face the man sitting across the room at the table.

Built like a boxer in a flat gray suit that strained around the points of his shoulders, the fella didn't fool Everett into thinking he was as refined as either his clothing or rigid posture suggested. When he stood to greet Everett, opening his mouth to do so, Everett pivoted for the fridge and opened it. He took out his beer, twisted the top off the bottle and tipped it for a long pull as his dogs Bones, Boomer and Boaz drank from their water bowl under the picture window.

The FBI man cleared his throat. "Mr. Eaton, I presume."

Everett drank until the contents of the bottle were half-gone before coming up for air. He checked what was on the stove. Enchiladas. *This better be quick, secret agent man*, he mused before shutting the fridge and turning to face his latest opponent. "If she invited you to dinner, she's overruled. I'm not in the mood for strangers at my table."

The FBI man looked amused. "The sheriff said you're a real mean cattle king. I was half expecting John Wayne to walk through the door."

"Altaha sent you?" Everett asked.

"She asked me to wait until she could smooth the introduction," the stranger said, talking fast with hints of Boston around his consonants, particularly the *R*s. "But I was keen to form my own impression of Fuego's newly minted cattle baron. This is quite a spread," he added. "I understand you're second-generation. Quite an inheritance for a man still shy of forty."

FBI man would have done better to bring the sheriff with him. Everett lifted the beer for another drink. "Just."

The FBI man took that as his cue to introduce himself, stepping forward. He pulled aside his coat to show the badge strapped to his belt. "I'm Agent Watt Rutland."

"The hell kind of name is Watt?" Everett asked.

"Birth name's Walter," Rutland explained. "Father raised six boys on his own, had monosyllabic names for all of us."

"Now, that's fascinating," Everett muttered, kicking out a chair for himself. He turned it and sat down backward, leaning on the ladder-back rail. After another drink, he hung his arms over it to pet Boaz who came looking for a scratch. "What can I do for you, Watt?"

"I think I prefer Agent Rutland for now," he said thoughtfully, pulling a small pad of paper from the lining of his sport coat.

Everett heard someone clearing their throat from the direction of the door. He turned his head only slightly, knowing Paloma was just out of view. He remembered her warning, the plea in her eyes, and rolled his. Gripping the bottle in both hands, he asked, "Will you be taking some of the caseload off the sheriff?"

"What do you know about the case, Mr. Eaton?" Rutland

asked, shifting on his chair. He clicked the button on the top of his pen, ready to scribble on the pad he'd spread open on the tabletop. "Or can I call you Everett?"

"Eaton's fine," Everett admitted. "Just leave out the mister. I'm not my father."

"He passed recently, didn't he?"

"Nine months ago," Everett said. Long time to go without the leathery sound of the old man's voice or the sight of his time-and work-worn boots crossed on top of the office desk. Covering up his grief the way his therapist had told him to stop doing a long time ago, Everett sipped his beer again, then swallowed hard. "I know there were several bodies pulled off our mountain. Three unidentified females and one boy. The kid, Higgins, that went missing recently from San Gabriel. Foul play's involved though nobody's saying how, specifically." He frowned at the stranger across from him. "If the FBI's here, I'd say foul play's been chalked up to murder and it's serious business."

"Is murder ever not serious business?" Rutland asked conversationally.

The casual tone wasn't fooling Everett one bit. Rutland had come to Eaton Edge to study Everett and study him hard. *I'm not going to squirm for you, secret agent man*, he determined. "You've got to look in my direction because you see it as my land."

"Well, isn't it?" Rutland asked.

"It belongs to the family," Everett told him. "So does the business. And there's not a thing going on here that we don't know about."

"If that tracks," Rutland considered, "then one of you knows what happened on Ol' Whalebones. Don't you?"

Everett didn't answer, nor did he lower his stare from the FBI man's. He finished off the beer.

Rutland unclicked the pen and placed it and the notebook back in the lining of his coat. "How's about this? You clean up. Get your story straight. Then you come by the sheriff's department tomorrow morning where my team and I can interview you formally."

As Rutland rose from his seat, Everett raised a brow. "Do I need to bring a lawyer with me?"

Rutland paused. "Representation isn't necessary. But if you've got reason to believe you need counsel, you're well within your rights."

"As a suspect," Everett assumed.

"As a person of interest," Rutland said evenly. Then he stuck out his hand.

Everett didn't bother to stand or shake it.

Rutland dropped it. "I'll note that in my report."

Everett waited until the sound of his high-priced brogues faded before he gave in to a long exhale, trying to release the tension from his shoulders.

Another bottle of beer dropped to the table in front of him. Paloma's hand touched his shoulder. "We got trouble?" she asked, taking the empty bottle from his hand.

"Why would we when I didn't kill Higgins or any of the others?" he asked.

Paloma dropped to the seat Rutland had abandoned. Everett was shocked to see a full beer in her fist, too. To his knowledge, he rarely saw Paloma drink more than champagne at New Year's or wine at Christmas dinner. He recalled the time he'd had to pick her, Eveline and Luella up at the police station where they'd been detained on a trumped-up drunk and disorderly charge after Margarita Night. It nearly teased a smile out of him. She choked the bottle top, twisted off the cap and tipped it to her mouth for a delicate sip.

When he and Ellis were troublemaking youngsters, she'd known how and when to put the fear of God into the two of them. A ranching woman to the core, she could boast as many callouses and scars as either of them.

But Everett had never had any doubt that Paloma was a lady. She'd tried her best to breed him, Ellis and Eveline to be polite and well mannered.

He'd given her hell. There were times he felt sorry for it. She was the only woman who'd ever loved him for who he was without condition.

"If he's got nothing on you," Paloma considered, "why'd he come all this way to make introductions?"

"To his mind, it's my mountain. He and his team are going to be crawling over this place like ants." It was going to annoy him. Everett opened the new beer. It hissed and the cap clinked when he tossed it onto the table. He crossed his arms over the top of the chair and peered at the view of the barn and corrals from the window over Paloma's shoulder. "They better not do anything to stall operations."

"You don't think he's already looked into you and everybody else here?" Paloma asked. "You don't think he may not like something about your past and was trying to shake something loose?"

The concerned light in her eyes hadn't ceased. Rutland was causing Paloma to worry, and that angered Everett. "He won't find anything, will he?"

"What's this formal interview about tomorrow at the sheriff's then?" Paloma asked.

Everett thought about that. "Hell if I know."

Paloma watched him drink. "You need to call Ellis, Eveline and the others."

The others being Luella and Wolfe, as they were family all but in name as far as Paloma was concerned. "No use getting them worked up, too, over assumptions."

"My assumptions come straight from my intuition," Paloma informed him, "which is rarely wrong where the lot of you is concerned. I'd have thought by now you'd have learned to pay attention."

As she picked her bottle up off the table and got up to leave, Everett waited until she brushed by his chair to reach up and take her by the wrist. He waited until her dark eyes swung down to meet his. "I wouldn't lie to you. You know that."

He saw her lips firm but not before he saw the heavy lower one tremble. "Everett, I know you would kill to protect your own. I've never doubted that. But what happened on that mountain was nothing less than evil. That isn't you. I know it wasn't you. I will not abandon you to this scrutiny. I just wish the sheriff's boys and the FBI would leave us well enough alone. Hasn't this family been through enough?"

He held her for another moment, long after he dropped his eyes. The sight of her unshed tears gutted him. "They won't be looking our way for long," he pledged. "I'll make sure of it."

"Don't do anything stupid, *mijo*," she muttered. She *tsk*ed as she passed a rough hand through his hair. "Get a haircut while you're in town tomorrow or I'll take the scissors to you myself."

"You'll have to catch me first," he warned her.

"Hmph."

As she passed into the kitchen to put plates together for the both of them, the tension jammed taut between his shoulder blades and his thoughts didn't stray far from the meeting with Rutland tomorrow morning.

KAYA TRIED TO gauge Everett's face from the corner of the room. She'd been invited to observe Rutland's interview with him—but not to participate.

He'd had his hair trimmed. The tips had been cut far enough back that she could see the pale stripe the sun hadn't touched at the peak of his brow. There were fine notes of gray there, mixed with black. His hat was hooked over one knee of his Wranglers and his plaid shirt was open over a gray T-shirt that fit him well enough she could see hints of definition underneath.

She steadied herself. She'd known the FBI agent would investigate Everett, his family and his employees. She'd had her deputies do the same. She'd wanted him clear. She hadn't wanted his name anywhere near the list of possible suspects. When Root confirmed that his alibi for the window of Higgins's disappearance had checked out, she'd shut herself in her office to breathe a long, hard sigh.

If she was going to go to bed with the man—and after that pizza business at her house, it felt inevitable—he couldn't be involved in this.

Kaya knew Rutland had to go through the same motions and come to the same conclusion about Everett's involvement. It didn't make her any less wary of what Rutland had hidden in the bland file folder on the desk in front of him.

He'd been working Everett for over half an hour with all

the routine questions that Root and Wyatt had already asked. But with the latest news from the forensics lab and Walther's office, there were more questions to be asked.

Rutland reached into the folder and pulled out a photograph of a blonde girl. It was over a decade old. "Do you recognize this woman?"

Everett raised one thick eyebrow. "Her name's Bethany Merchant. She went missing after I left school."

Rutland nodded. "What was your relationship with Miss Merchant?"

"We were involved," Everett informed him.

"Intimately?"

Everett peered at Rutland. "Are you asking if we had sex?"

"I'm just trying to get a more detailed understanding of what happened between you and Miss Merchant before her disappearance."

Everett stared Rutland down. Finally, his shoulders lifted. "We were together. We drank, kissed, partied and yeah, we had sex. Multiple times. You want a list of the places or are you more interested in the positions?"

"There's no need to get testy, *Mr.* Eaton," Rutland said evenly.

Everett tilted his head just slightly and Kaya came to attention when she saw the ready light in his eyes. It meant there was a fight ahead and not a pretty one. "You're the one prying into my personal business. *Watt.*"

She sucked in a breath.

Why was he using Rutland's first name when she hadn't heard him say hers since he'd started asking her to consider him more than a friend?

The hitch of pain came as a surprise. She didn't want it.

She wanted nothing but to focus on the remainder of the interview and get back to the county's and the town's needs.

The hurt persisted, nonetheless. And that set her as ill at ease as the realization in the restaurant that he had put her on some kind of pedestal.

It made no sense. Why would he have all these expectations of her and who they could be together…if he couldn't say her name?

Rutland placed another photograph on the table. "Do you recognize this individual?"

Everett frowned. After a moment, he leaned forward.

Kaya's heart was in her throat as he studied Sawni's picture. *Why?* she thought helplessly as she watched her past and present collide.

Everett shook her head. "No," he answered. "Though she does look familiar. Who is she?"

"Sawni Mescal," Rutland revealed. "She worked in Fuego, not long after Bethany disappeared."

Everett watched Rutland as he shuffled the photos back into the folder. "She went missing, too, I assume." He glanced at the wall. His eyes locked with Kaya's. She felt the impact in her knees. "That's who you found on the mountain?" he asked her.

Rutland cleared his throat. "We can neither confirm nor deny at this time—"

"That's where Bethany's been?" Everett asked, undeterred. "All this time? Her body's been at the Edge…"

The awareness came. Kaya saw it dawn on him. As he trailed off, his chin lifted in understanding. To Rutland, he said, "That's why you think I'm involved. Beyond the fact that Ol' Whalebones is part of the Edge, you think I…

what—killed Bethany weeks after I ended things with her and dumped her on the mountain?"

"Mr. Eaton—"

"No," Everett said. He climbed to his feet. "They looked into me. There are files, records that'll show I was cleared after her disappearance." Again, he looked to Kaya. "You still got those files, sheriff?"

"We do," she answered. "Missing Persons cleared you..."

Everett sensed more. "But?"

Kaya stepped forward. "There were rumors that you and her fought at the rodeo the day before she went missing..."

His gaze circled her face. "So?"

"You may not have killed her," Rutland said. "But you were a man of means, even then. You had enough money and privilege to hire someone to—"

"That's bull," Everett dismissed. "You're talking about my trust fund. If you'd followed through, you'd know that money didn't come into my possession until I was twenty-one. I was barely eighteen when Bethany disappeared. And that wasn't a fight at the rodeo. She came after me, hankering for a dispute for ending things with her after I quit school. I walked away from it. I'd already made my position clear."

"Which was..." Rutland prompted.

"She always talked about going east after graduation," Everett explained. "She wanted to go to college and live there, get out of New Mexico. She had the grades to do it, too. She could've gone to any school, Ivy League or otherwise, and her daddy had the money to pay for anything her scholarships didn't. She wanted me to tag along and start a life with her, wherever she went. But I knew I'd never leave Fuego. I never wanted to. She resented that just like she resented me leaving school because my father needed me at the Edge. I ended things between us because she got her acceptance letter from Princeton, and she needed to know there wasn't anything holding her back."

"If there wasn't anything holding her back, why did she argue with you the day before she went missing?" Rutland asked.

"She was mad because I didn't want to go," Everett explained, "and because I'd told her I didn't love her."

"Did you love her?"

Everett set his jaw. "I don't see how that's relevant."

"Everything's relevant," Rutland explained. "Her parents deserve an answer as to why she was murdered and left on that mountain—a mountain that belongs to your family, Mr. Eaton. Answer the question."

"No," Everett snapped.

"No, you won't answer the question? Or no, you didn't love her?"

"I didn't love her," Everett shot back. "Not enough to follow her across the continental US. Is that the answer her parents want? That I didn't love their daughter the way she wanted me to love her? Is that going to comfort them in their grief?"

Rutland chose not to answer these questions. He'd opened the file again, splaying it wide. Turning it, he revealed the discovery photos and the photos Walther's technicians had taken of the dead in the lab. They scattered under Everett's nose.

Kaya stepped forward, wanting to shuffle them back into the folder where they belonged.

Everett saw them before she could round the table. His

hands lifted. The skin of his face seemed too thin. He released a rough breath and stepped back.

He wavered and she dove.

Before he could stagger or fall, she grabbed him by the shoulders. "Sit down," she murmured. Looking around for his chair, she hooked her toe around its leg and slid it closer. "Just sit, okay?"

"Why would you…?" he groaned as she pushed him into the seat. "You think…"

"Quiet." Kneeling, she framed his face with her hands. The skin around his mouth was white. His lips themselves had turned a shade paler than his skin. She cursed, hooking her hand around the back of his neck. "Put your head between your knees and breathe."

"You think I…" he said again even as he did what he was told.

She didn't like how small he sounded. "Put those away," she snapped at Rutland. "He's had enough."

IT TOOK EVERETT longer than he would have liked to pull himself together. It was bad enough that he'd nearly passed out in the interrogation room.

When he closed his eyes, he could still see the photographs of Higgins, Bethany, the Mescal girl…and whoever the fourth person was.

Higgins's brain cavity had been exposed. Bethany's blond hair had still been visible but her skin had faded away from bone—same with the Mescal girl, only her hair had been dark. Nothing remained of the fourth person except skeletal remains…

The images would live rent free in his mind for the rest of his life.

Everett splashed water across his face again in the men's room. The back of his throat was raw. He'd lost the fine breakfast Paloma had made for the two of them that morning before seeing him off with a reminder about getting his hair trimmed...

He felt older, more burdened. He was far angrier than he had been after Rutland's visit the night before and the reasons weren't settling well.

He'd grown up on a ranch. He knew what became of animals left out to die.

But those bodies in the photographs were human.

The image of Higgins's skull floated back to him. Everett ducked his head to the sink and drank water from the faucet. He swished it around his mouth, trying to rid himself of the bitter taste, then spat it out and shut off the water, finally. He ripped brown paper towels from the dispenser to the right of the mirror, wadded them up and dried his face.

His reflection was clear now, but his eyes weren't. They were bloodshot. Pulling the aviator sunglasses from the neckline of his T-shirt, he took his time cleaning the lenses with the open corner of his plaid button-down before he covered his eyes. He tossed the wad of paper towels in the overfull trash can and opened the door.

Kaya was waiting.

He lowered his head and beelined for the door.

"We'll speak again, Mr. Eaton," Rutland called from the open door of the interrogation room.

Everett ignored him. He could see the outdoors through

the glass. He pushed through the door, letting the sun hit him in the face.

Before the door could swing shut at his back, Kaya exited, too. “Everett,” she said when it closed behind her.

“Nope,” he said, shaking his head as he pivoted in the direction of the parking lot. His voice was raspy and weaker than he needed it to be.

Her hands closed around the bend of his elbow.

“You don’t want to do this right now,” he warned.

She scanned him. “You shouldn’t drive.”

“I’m fine,” he bit off. He felt naked under the glide of her black, knowing gaze and he didn’t need her to know it. “I’m walking, aren’t I? Now let me go. I’m not feeling peaceable, and I know you don’t want to do this dance in town, seeing as you’re determined to keep our relationship a secret from everyone.”

She didn’t loosen her grip. “I’m sorry about what Rutland did in there. It was dirty.”

He made a noise in his throat. He extricated himself and took long, retreating strides to the door of his truck.

“I didn’t know what he was going to do,” she told him. “I wouldn’t have agreed to it if I had.”

“That’s nice,” he drawled, opening the driver’s door. “I’ll see you around, sweetheart.”

Before he could boost himself into the seat, she grabbed him again. “Everett.”

“I can’t do this right now,” he growled. “Step away.”

She pushed herself farther into his space, taking a handful of his shirt. “I can’t let you leave ’til I know you’re okay.”

“I’m okay.”

“You’re not.”

"Just tell me one thing," he said. "I need to know if any part of you believes any of it."

"Believes what?"

He pointed at the building and what had happened inside. "That I did *that*. That I'm *capable* of that."

"Would I be here if I did?" she asked.

"I don't know anything right now," he replied. "You want me to be okay? Turn me loose."

She hesitated, her eyes doing circles around his face. Finally, her hand released his shirt and she shifted onto her heels.

Everett placed one foot on the running board and settled into the driver's seat. He shut the door. He cranked the truck and gripped the wheel.

He saw Kaya walking back to the door. He thought about rolling the window down and saying something but stopped himself. She'd been in that room. Even if she didn't think he was capable of killing Higgins, Bethany and those other people, she'd stood back while others who did questioned him.

He put the truck in gear and pulled out of the parking lot, unable to deal with what was under the surface.

What had he expected? He was someone who notoriously surrendered to nothing in life. So why had he begun to surrender his heart, of all things, to the goddamn sheriff of Fuego County?

Chapter Eight

Kaya didn't want much to do with Agent Rutland, despite their departments working together on the case. She'd spent the majority of time over the last week out of office seeing to her sheriff duties. At some point, she had even stopped checking her personal cell phone. Everett hadn't called or texted once since the debacle at the station.

She patrolled with Root and Wyatt, answering a trespassing call outside of Fuego, which turned out to be a landlord and tenant dispute. That led to a destruction of property charge for the tenant.

A drifter was spotted outside Fuego. When his location was called in to dispatch, Kaya took it. The man turned out to be dehydrated. His shoes were falling apart. When she led him into the sheriff's station to see to his care, she ran headlong into Annette Claymore, the mayor's wife, who had plenty to say about his kind being invited into town. Kaya enjoyed putting her in her place, much like she had put True Claymore in his the day the bodies were found.

"You better be careful," Annette warned her. "If the citizens of this town don't like the way you do your job, they can remove you just as quickly as they appointed you."

"Have a nice day," Kaya said as she led the man into the air conditioning.

There was a medical emergency down the street at the barber shop. When Kaya arrived, Root was performing CPR on one of the cosmetologists, sixty-year-old Mattie Finedale. Paramedics arrived and Kaya helped keep people back so that they could do their job.

Even as Mattie was being loaded into the van, Turk Monday tugged on Kaya's elbow. "When are you going to release the names and cause of death of those poor people on the mountain?" he asked.

It brought attention from others. Soon more questions were hurled at her.

"The Merchants say it was their daughter. Is that true, Sheriff?"

"Was it a serial killer?"

"How close are you to nabbing the killer?"

"Settle down!" Kaya shouted over the ruckus. She heard the doors of the ambulance close at her back as she held up her hands. The siren started up and tires rolled. As its screech wailed into the distance, she shook her head. "People, Ms. Finedale just had a stroke. How would she feel if she knew that before she could be driven off to the hospital, you were causing a scene about a closed investigation that has nothing to do with her? I know you want answers. But there's a reason the investigative team is keeping the details under wraps."

"Do those FBI people think it was aliens?" When others turned to stare openly at Turk, he lifted his shoulders. "What? We're not that far from the rez and Dulce. Y'all know what happened there."

Kaya rolled her eyes as the shouts started back up again. "Quiet!" she yelled.

It worked but for a level voice from the back of the crowd. Annette Claymore spoke up, asking, "Sheriff, is it true you knew one of the people who died on the mountain?"

Kaya frowned at her. If she wasn't mistaken, there was something smug hidden beneath Annette's careful expression.

"The rumors say one set of remains belongs to a girl named Sawni Mescal," she went on. "Wasn't she a friend of yours? You know, back when you were little rez girls."

...little rez girls...

The words struck Kaya. Her head snapped back as if she'd been lashed. The sharp, cold shock washed over her.

The boss wants you to remember what happens to little rez girls when they don't learn to leave well enough alone!

The shouting that echoed from long ago was loud in her ears, as was the sound of her own screaming.

She'd screamed. She'd thought she'd been so tough, so formidable in her own right. But that day she'd screamed loud into the quiet desert void, and no one had heard—except the man who had hurt her and the other who had held her in place.

She drifted back to the present and realized she was facing almost the entire town in the middle of the street, breathing unsteadily. Sobs...or memories of sobs...she couldn't tell... were packed against her throat. She was drenched in cold sweat and all she could see was the satisfied glimmer in Annette Claymore's eyes.

Does she know? Did Annette know what those men had done to Kaya that day on the road to Fuego?

How could she? That was before she married into the Claymore family.

Back when Kaya was a little rez girl, running after something far bigger and more sinister than herself.

"Well, Sheriff?" Annette piped up again.

Kaya's hands were wrapped around the front of her belt too tight. She loosened them and moved to speak.

"Nobody asked you!"

As heads swiveled to the sidewalk, Kaya spotted her teenaged niece standing tall and defiant there. "I've seen cows with more manners than all of you," Nova added. She looked to Kaya, her stubborn chin high, before fitting a pair of trendy sunglasses to her eyes and cutting through the swath of people between her and the door to the ice cream parlor. The kid, Lucas Barnes, who Everett had hired months before, followed her.

That had once been her, Kaya thought. She saw so much of herself in Nova, or who she had been before that day on the side of the road…before she'd had to work to reclaim her power.

The radio on her hip squawked and she took the opportunity to turn away from the crowd. She walked until their restless murmur was no longer a hindrance and unclipped it, raising it to her mouth. "Say again, dispatch?"

"Two-eleven in progress at Highway 8 and Miflin Road. Officer needs assistance."

"Show sheriff responding, code three," Kaya instructed as she stalked to her vehicle. She engaged lights and sirens, dispersing what was left of the rubbernecking hecklers downtown.

"DO YOU THINK people respect you, Sheriff?"

Kaya ground her teeth. Rutland rode shotgun in her truck.

She'd left her service vehicle behind at the station. Her business on the Jicarilla-Apache reservation was personal.

Why had she agreed to let him tag along?

Stupidity, she thought. *Complete and utter stupidity.* "Is this really the conversation you want to have right now?" she asked him.

"The mayor stopped me outside the steakhouse yesterday evening," Rutland revealed, running a hand down his tie. The sun was low, and his brows came to a *V* as he squinted against its rays. "He has some doubt as to your ability to handle this job."

The mayor can bite me. Kaya wanted to say it. She was raw. Sawni's memorial was to take place in half an hour and Kaya was going to have to face her friend's parents. "I never heard him complain about the last sheriff, and he was corrupt."

"Might Claymore and Jones have been involved in corruption together?" Rutland asked curiously.

"It's never been proven," Kaya replied. "But Jones was swayed by Claymore. Jones wouldn't admit to anything under interrogation."

"Do you think Jones meant to kill you when he shot you in December?" Rutland asked. "From what I gather, he wasn't very supportive of his female deputy. It's why you never advanced within the department."

"He argued before the jury that he didn't want me dead," Kaya said evenly.

"He shot you when your back was turned."

She steered the truck over a rise. Jicarilla-Apache land spread out before her. The view was enough to back the breath up in her lungs. But that notion of *home* was as hurtful as it was sweet. Gripping the wheel a bit harder, she noticed the clouds throwing shadows to the west. "He did."

"It's clear to me, whether he stated it for the record or not, that he had something against you. The question is whether the mayor still does."

"It's not my job to find out whether the man likes me," Kaya told him. "The people in Fuego County wanted me to take this job. So I did. If True Claymore has a problem with that, or me, he's welcome to vote for someone else when my term ends."

"Small-town politics," Agent Rutland muttered. He shook his head. "They're just as messy as they are in DC."

"I won't argue that," she stated. "The way you handled the interview with Everett Eaton." She shook her head. "It wasn't right."

"I got what we needed," Rutland said, unfazed.

"Which was?"

"The truth about whether he murdered his ex-girlfriend," Rutland said. "The victims all had close-range gunshot wounds to the back of the head. My guess is their killer forced them to kneel at the edge of the cliff. He shot them and gravity took them over the edge to the ledge below. He knew their bodies would be hidden there. Any animal other than the birds would have a hard time getting to them, even the mountain lion. As long as no one knew the ledge was there, those bodies would never be discovered."

Kaya pushed the air from her lungs. She didn't want to picture Sawni kneeling on the edge of the cliff, but Rutland had painted too clear a picture. "This is what your profiler says?"

"Some of it," Rutland admitted. "They all died execution-style. It was cold. Mercenary. Nobody who could do that over and over again over time would have fainted or tossed their cookies the way Mr. Eaton did when he saw those photographs." He eyed Kaya's clenched hands over the wheel. "I'm sorry," he said. For the first time, he softened from the dogged, hard-edged investigator she'd come to know. "I asked you to bring me with you to your friend's memorial and I'm walking you through the details of her murder. My ex-wife complains I'm insensitive. Apparently, she's right."

"Why did you ask to come with me?" Kaya wanted to know.

"I haven't been formally introduced to her family and friends, other than you and your sister."

Kaya slowed for the speed limit signs. "You think this is the time and place for that?"

"Grief can be revealing," Rutland explained.

"Or maybe you're just being insensitive," she suggested, turning off the main road as he chuckled. The memorial was being held well out of town. Sawni had loved the outdoors, particularly the small cabin near the river. Her parents had chosen that spot to formally say good-bye. Kaya knew they'd chosen it to curtail any media attention, too. Nothing made saying good-bye harder than a nosy press pack.

"You seem nervous."

Kaya swallowed. "I'm fine."

"I spoke to your sister, Naleen. She said you and Sawni were very close. Like sisters in your own right. After she'd been gone for three months, investigators seemed to give up on finding her. You took up the mantle. She thinks that's why you became a cop—to find Sawni or those who made her disappear. Is that true?"

Kaya didn't want to answer. "It was a long time ago."

"Did you ever find anything?" he asked.

Nothing she'd been able to prove. She'd had to live with that, hadn't she? All these years, she'd lived with it. And facing Sawni's family again was so difficult because of it. She'd sworn to them she would find out what happened. They were still waiting for her to deliver.

Finding Sawni's body on Ol' Whalebones wasn't an answer. It'd only brought forth a whole new set of questions.

Yet Kaya wouldn't stop until she had an explanation. Knowing Sawni had been murdered made her more determined than ever to bring closure to the Mescals…and herself.

AT THE MEMORIAL, the Mescals looked at Kaya like they had for over a decade—with warmth, yes. But with those not-quite-hidden hints of regret. Their mouths said *thank you for coming* and *we hope you are well.*

But the eyes. The eyes said, *Why was it our daughter... and not you?*

No amount of time or reflection could make Kaya believe it meant something different. She was here, and Sawni wasn't. *Why*? Sawni's mother's soft, lined face had seemed to question her as she smiled without meaning.

Kaya was only too glad to drop Rutland off at the bed-and-breakfast on Sixth Avenue when they got back to Fuego in the late afternoon. At least he hadn't felt the need for probing questions or small talk on the way home. She couldn't stomach either. She was drained. She'd been holding her thoughts and emotions together with rubber bands.

Those rubber bands had stretched too far. They'd grown wear lines and fissures and were ready to rupture.

Kaya frowned when she pulled up in front of her house

behind an Eaton Edge truck. Putting hers in Park, she spotted no one at the wheel.

Glancing at the house, she groaned.

Everett raised his hand in greeting from his position on the front stoop.

After a week of noncommunication, his timing couldn't be worse.

She didn't see another pizza box. Just a cowboy with a long face and even longer legs taking up space where she'd wanted him, thought about him, practically moped over him since he'd skirted tires pulling away from the sheriff's department days ago.

Bracing herself, she got out of the vehicle and stepped down to the ground. She reached across the seat to the console where the flowers the Mescals had given her, leftover from the service, were tied with a silver ribbon—Sawni's favorite color. She shut the door and crossed the small yard to the house where he was sitting on the stoop. It was so low to the ground that his knees were nearly drawn to his shoulders.

She stopped before him, shaking her keys so they jangled. "You look ridiculous."

"Fine, thanks," he replied. "How're you?"

She found the right key and held it in her hand. "Shouldn't you be castrating something right now?"

"Not until summer," he informed her. He knuckled his hat farther up his brow, gauging her expression. "It'd be rude to castrate a calf just after it's born."

"Kind of rude anyway, don't you think?" she asked.

"You come to the Edge when it's time for business," he advised. "Your perspective might change."

"Maybe." She shook her head. "You want me to ask you in?"

"I've been sitting here for half an hour," he said.

"Why?"

"You drive slow. Nova said the memorial was supposed to end at one o'clock. It's near sundown."

She looked at her front door. He was between it and her. "Are you going to get up so I can pass?"

He made a doubtful noise. "Pretty sure I'm stuck."

She cleared her throat because the urge to laugh filled her—great bursts of it. The grief pushed it, making it more forceful. She didn't give in because she was very much afraid there were tears close behind it.

Her feelings needed to stay in the bottle. There was no collecting them once they broke loose. "I'd make you my new lawn ornament, but people would have too many questions."

"Questions make you uncomfortable," he muttered, reaching out to grab her hand when she extended it.

She went back on her heels to pull him to his feet. He unfolded like an accordion. Ignoring what he said, she unlocked the door, then left it open as she pushed into the house. Laying the flowers on the kitchen counter, she dropped her keys next to them and heard his boots approaching. Trying not to feel insecure about the used sofa or the uneven brick kitchen floor, she watched him come.

The little house felt smaller with him in it.

"Coffee?" she asked, desperate to fill the void as he looked around, trying to get a read on what she surrounded herself with.

"Coffee's fine," he replied.

She snatched the pot from its holding in the coffeemaker and turned to the sink to fill it. "You like it black?"

"As your eyes."

The fine drawl drew the space between her shoulder blades up tight. “Don’t do that,” she urged quietly.

“Why shouldn’t I?” he asked from the other side of the counter.

“I’ve already told you I won’t sleep with you.” But she knew exactly how many steps there were between them and the bedroom to the left.

“I’m not always trying to get into your pants, Sheriff.”

The pot was full. She shut off the water. It was still dripping but she turned with it to face him anyway. “Why do you do that?”

“Do what?” he asked.

“Why do you call me Sheriff?” she asked. “Or sweetheart? Or Sheriff Sweetheart? But never my own name?”

He paused, frowning deeply. “I’ve called you by your name before.”

“Before it was Sheriff or Sheriff Sweetheart, it was deputy or deputy sweetheart. You *don’t* call me by my name, Everett. Why?”

He stared at her and the vehemence on her face. She was breathing hard between them. His gaze skimmed her shoulders, her chest, then lifted up to circle her face again. Dropping his head altogether so his hat hid whatever he was thinking or feeling, he shifted his feet.

She took the opportunity to reel it in—the ready urge to yell at him. The hurt behind the accusations. She did well, normally, to hide these things. She’d had to learn to separate her feelings on the job. She’d done it early and often.

But Sawni’s memorial had scattered all that to the wind. And for the past several weeks, Everett had made her feel…

well, just *feel*. There was no hiding things. She'd known that from the beginning with him and yet she'd reached…

Stupid, she thought again. *You're so stupid, Kaya.* What a surefire way to get hurt.

Everett lifted his head, finally. His jaw was tight, but he met her gaze and held it. "I never call you by name because…"

She waited. "Because…?"

He licked his lips quickly, then spoke carefully. "…because the people who I love tend to get away from me. They leave. Or they die. So…the ones that matter… I tend to push them away somehow or other."

She made a frustrated noise. "Everett, you wanted this. You told me you'd be damned if you'd mess it up—"

"I know what I said," he acknowledged. "Doesn't mean some part of me isn't terrified you're not going to want this in the long run or something's going to put you so far out of my reach, there's nothing I can do to bring you back. Whatever it is that I want or need, it's hard to move past all that when the people who matter to me don't stay."

Love. In the long run. People who matter. The words dropped into the gulf between them and caused her heart to hammer. She didn't know what to say in response.

She placed the dripping pot back in its holding and turned on the coffeemaker. She should invite him to sit. She thought about going into the conservatory, but he'd look just as ridiculous folded into one of those tiny chairs as he had on her stoop. The used shaggy couch was not an option. So she simply waited for the water to boil and the machine to start glugging.

What felt like an eternity passed before the coffee was

ready. She poured it, steaming, into two mugs and passed one over the counter to him.

He lifted it in acknowledgement.

"Don't drink," she warned quickly before he could bring it to his lips. "You'll scald your mouth. Nova told you about the memorial."

"She did," he said with a nod. "She's working at the Edge."

"She told me," Kaya said. "Thank you for giving her a chance. She's wanted this for a long time."

The corner of his mouth lifted. "Girl could be anything. Firefighter. Engineer. Rocket scientist. And she wants to be a cowboy. Your niece wants to ride cattle from sunup to sundown, and she may do it better than half the hands I have on payroll."

Kaya smiled. There was some pride there. Buckets of it. "Naleen wishes she'd move past it, but she's too much like me."

"Then why aren't you a cowboy?" he asked.

"I was," she revealed. "But this isn't about me."

"You're going to have to tell me more, anyway," he told her. "Starting with why finding this Mescal girl's body hurt you so badly you started pushing people away, same as I do."

Kaya nearly denied it. Then she saw the understanding beneath everything. He understood.

"I get what it is to grieve," he explained. "I get shutting everyone else out to do it. Everyone."

"That's not why I didn't tell you about Sawni." Lifting the coffee for a testing sip, she weighed whether she was ready to do this. The liquid was hot, but it didn't burn. She swallowed carefully and leaned over so her elbows rested on the countertop. "This is more than grief."

"Yeah?"

She tilted her head. "Look, if you're not great at listening, then this isn't a conversation you want to sit through."

"I'll sit through anything you've got."

Why did the man who regularly put his foot in his mouth know just what to say to bring her back to him? "Even if it means starting from the beginning?"

"Hey, if I start falling asleep, just kick me."

She snorted a laugh. The bastard. Backing up to the sink, she set the coffee aside and braced both hands on the counter. "Sawni and I grew up together on the rez. We weren't friends—not at first. She was quiet. She let herself pass under the radar in a lot of ways. I think she was afraid of confrontation, even if it was positive."

"And you?" he asked.

"Mmm." Kaya lifted her coffee and found her lips curving over the edge of the rim. She sipped again. "I wasn't quiet, and I definitely wasn't afraid of confrontation. I wasn't an easy child."

"You were a hellion," he guessed.

"That's one way to put it, yes."

Everett stepped around the counter to the other side, raising his mug in toast—one hellion to another. "That's my girl."

Her smile grew to the point she could no longer suppress it. She'd known the telling would be hard. She hadn't known he could make her smile through it. "You and I would have gotten along famously, I think. Sawni was treated as something of a doormat by the other kids. I started standing up for her. She needed someone big and loud and assertive to stand beside. Once she started talking to me, we decided we would be friends, always. It didn't make sense to others that we became so close. I was kind of mean. I could be a bully. She carried around a doll forever. She did everything she was told. I didn't understand why she wanted to be my friend until later. Sometimes the quiet ones will seek out someone stronger than themselves…for protection or…"

"Did you protect her?"

The smile tapered off, slowly. *Not well enough*, she thought. Not when it had really mattered, in the end. "In small ways, I guess," she replied. "Everything was great until we got to high school. Her parents blamed any trouble she got into on me, naturally. And they were right. But then we both started looking outside the rez. We set our sights there. We started going to the rodeo here in Fuego."

"You were half-pint buckle bunnies?" he asked, amused.

"We were spectators," she contradicted.

"I was on the junior circuit for a time," he revealed. "I don't remember you."

"Eaton, your head was so far up your ass you couldn't see past your own nose."

He laughed. Lifting his chin, he scrubbed the line of his neck with a rough, wide-palmed hand. "God, you're right. How'd you know that?"

"Lucky guess."

His grin turned sly. "You knew me. Or you knew who I was."

She raised a shoulder. "Never mind that. It became my single greatest desire in life to ride."

"Did you?" he asked.

"I worked with a trainer on the rez," she said. "Worked my butt off to raise enough money for lessons. Eventually, I joined the junior circuit, too, as a trick rider."

"Apache Annie," he suddenly blurted out, snapping his fingers. He pointed at her. "You were Apache Annie—with war paint and feathers in your hair."

"Yes," she said reluctantly.

"You were the real deal," he breathed. "The other boys and I… We used to watch you. *Everyone* used to watch you. You were mesmerizing."

She blinked at the praise. "I thought the whole lifestyle was mesmerizing. The circuitous nature of things. We traveled around, never stayed in one place. I wanted that—badly enough that I started lying to my mother. She found out and threatened to send me to Santa Fe if I didn't straighten out. She tried getting me several good jobs in Dulce so I'd settle down or stay busy enough to keep me out of trouble. I quit every one of them, or never showed up to begin with. The trail riding job at RC Resort was my mother's last stand. It was either that or move in with my dad in the city, which felt like a fate worse than death. She threatened to sell my horse, too. So I started working for the Claymores…"

Everett's mouth worked itself into a scowl. "It didn't work, I take it."

"It worked okay," she said. "But I couldn't stop thinking about riding. So I asked Sawni to take over for me so that I could go train more and compete. As long as the position was filled, the Claymores had no reason to call my house looking for me. The crazy part was that the Claymores are so blind and idiotic that they thought Sawni was me, just because we have the same color skin. They called her Kaya and instead of asserting herself she went along with it."

Kaya lifted the coffee for a long drink. The next part was going to be most difficult. She hadn't talked about any of it for so long. It had lived inside her head. She'd picked through it over the years, combing through every minute detail, trying to find the point where things had changed, where Sawni's disappearance became inevitable. Was it the rodeo? Was it Fuego itself? Was it the resort? Where had it gone wrong? Who was responsible, other than Kaya herself? "She stopped communicating with me."

"Why would she do that?"

"I've never been sure," Kaya said. "For the longest time, I thought it might be resentment or anger. I was at the rodeo. She wasn't. Or the job sucked, and I was responsible for her being there. But over the years, I started to wonder if it might have been something else. She was seeing someone at the time. She never would tell me who. She didn't want to be teased. She stopped sharing little things at first and then… the communication became less and less frequent. No more phone calls. No more meeting after work or school. She just kind of started to slip away. Then her parents reported her missing. At first, the authorities dismissed it. You know how it is. 'She's out partying.' 'She's at a friend's house.' It was three days after that they began to take it seriously. The first forty-eight hours after someone goes missing are the most crucial. By the time they started searching, she was gone."

"You say you were responsible for her being at the RC," Everett recalled. "Sounds like survivor's guilt."

Kaya nodded. "I am responsible. I'm the reason she's gone. Her parents know it. My mother knows it. My sister. Most people on the rez do, too. Her disappearance was a huge story. The entire community came to Fuego to search for her because that was the last place she was seen. There's security cam footage of her walking into the corner store downtown shortly after her shift. The Claymores said she worked the whole day, even though it was a school day. From the store, there's nothing. She didn't have a car. She took the bus, but there's no record of her getting on the bus that afternoon. The bus driver was subbing for the regular one and he couldn't say whether she got on or not. She never made it to the bus stop in Dulce. Somewhere between the corner store in Fuego and Dulce, she was abducted."

"You never bought that she ran away," Everett assumed. "They would have said she did. They said the same thing when Bethany went missing."

"She wouldn't have done something like that. She wouldn't have put her parents through it. She loved them, respected them. She stopped going to the rodeo because they asked her to. Even when I kept going, she stopped. She was the good one."

"Stop," he said firmly.

"Every time her parents look at me, they think 'It should've been you,'" she said.

"Do they say that?" he asked.

"No. But I know that's what they're thinking."

"No, you don't," he argued. "You've been punishing yourself for this way too long, Kaya."

She sucked in a breath. *Kaya.*

When she stared at him, thunderstruck, he closed the small space between them. His hands closed over the counter on either side of her waist. He leaned in, smelling of leather and horses. She could smell his soap, just a hint of it, and wanted to spread kisses up the chords of his neck.

Everything about Everett was long and rough and certain.

She wanted every piece, she realized—every little piece of him. Even if it ruined her.

"Tell me I'm wrong," he drawled. "Tell me you haven't been destroying yourself over this for years because you think you put her in the hands of her kidnapper."

"Her killer," she said unevenly. "He killed her. I have to live with that now."

"I don't want you to," he said. "That's not a life. She would've wanted you to do better for yourself. That's why she took the job to begin with—so that you could follow the rodeo and your dream. But you didn't. And it's about time you stopped torturing yourself."

"I haven't told you the rest of it," she said. She hadn't planned to. Oh God, could she? She'd never told anyone… Not her mother, not Naleen, not the police or the men she'd shared a bed with through the years… No one. When he dropped his hand from her face and stepped away so she could gather her thoughts, she realized she could at least make the first steps. "I became obsessed with her case. I led search parties. I knocked on doors. I annoyed the police and sheriff's departments to the point where they'd lock their door when they saw me coming. I hung posters, rallied the community to spread the word. I made websites. It went on for a year or more, long after everyone else had given up on her."

"Did you ever find anything else?" he asked. "Any trace?"

"Nothing solid," she said. "I practically stalked the Claymores. I was convinced they had something to do with it. But I could never shake anything loose, exactly."

"Exactly." He latched onto the word. "What does that mean?"

She felt panic tearing at her insides. It trapped the rest of the story in. She closed her eyes. *Not yet*, she thought. She'd come so far already with him. She couldn't go on.

She inhaled, trying to control the fear. The terror. It was ridiculous. She'd been on the job for so long. But she was still scared, and that was the hardest thing of all to live with.

It made her angry. So angry she could scream. "I became a police officer because I wanted to find her. When the police gave up on her and let the case go cold, I felt like the only one who cared about her or any other rez girl who went missing, for that matter. So I joined the academy in Taos and became a beat cop there. Eventually, I got the job as deputy in Fuego County. I gained access to the case files. I fell back down the rabbit hole again and couldn't stop. I nearly lost myself to it."

Everett ran his hand over her braid, soothing. He did it over and over in a silent caress that salved something inside her.

He spoke low and soft. "You didn't give yourself over to it. You wouldn't be who you are today if you had."

"It was my mother, mostly," she admitted. "She deals well in hard truths. She said even if I was any closer to finding Sawni, I was far too close to losing myself in the process. I had to stop, or Sawni and I both would have been gone."

"I'm glad you're not," he murmured. "I've told you, haven't I—that I'd have been lost without you last summer?"

It didn't hurt to hear it again. "Where would your family be if you had been? They need you, Everett. Everyone at the Edge needs you."

He made a thoughtful noise. "I like your hair this way. Even if it's not loose like I want."

"Thank you," she muttered.

"If you never let it loose, why don't you cut it?" He

wrapped his hand around the width of the braid, measuring. "There's so much of it."

"It's part of me," she explained. "It's a part of my story. I don't expect you to get it—"

"I get it."

He did get her, she thought. It was stunning.

"Kaya."

She shivered. It was involuntary and thorough, skating the length of her spine and spreading tingles at the base of her head where his hand came to rest. "Yes?"

"Will you let me take your hair down? I want to feel it in my hands. I want to see it shine."

She placed her hand in the bend of his elbow and followed it up, circling his wrist. "I don't think I can handle that. Not after today."

"Eventually?"

She sighed. "If I've learned anything about the two of us together, it's that it's inevitable."

"What?"

For a second, she couldn't say it. Then she thought about all the other things she couldn't say and pushed it out on a whisper. "Everything."

He sucked in a breath and straightened. "Damn."

She smiled softly. "You were the one who spoke about the long-term."

"I did," he acknowledged.

"You know, I told myself I wouldn't go out with you until I heard you say my name."

"So why did you?"

"You've got nice eyes," she told him. "And a tight butt. And you make me laugh. You're sexy and annoying and you know how to wear a woman down with your big mouth. I may be a cop, but I'm a woman, too. I have needs and feelings and for some inexplicable reason they've both been pointed in your direction for a while."

He removed his hat and tossed it on the counter. His lips moved to hers. He kissed her firmly, cupping the back of her neck as her head fell back and his toes came to rest between hers, the hard line of his body flush against her. She spread her palms against his back and pressed, bringing him closer. She wasn't sure what close enough was anymore. He was beyond that point, wasn't he? But she wanted him closer.

A whoosh of air escaped her when his hands ran down her shoulders and back, over her rear before splaying over the backs of her thighs. He lifted and set her on the sink's edge so they were closer to eye-to-eye.

She wrapped her hands around the counter for balance as his head tilted and his mouth came back to hers for more. She groaned because he was good at this part. His last kisses had lingered for so long. How long would these stay with her?

When he broke away, she started to protest. "I'm sorry," he said on a wash of breath.

"Sorry?" she asked, off balance.

"The other day at the station house," he reminded her. "I was bruised. When I'm hurt or raw, I lash out. It's been that way as long as I can remember, and I'm getting help for it—same as I was getting help for the PTSD last fall. Some habits die hard, and when you stayed silent during Rutland's questioning, some part of me thought it was because your thoughts were in-line with his." When she began to shake her head, he nodded. "I know they're not. You were trying to stay objective. That's your job, whether or not my name's called into question. But I'm sorry."

"It's okay," she said, holding him. "We're okay."

"Yeah?" he asked, tipping his brow to hers.

"Yeah," she answered. She smiled. "Am I still worth the wait, cowboy?"

"Hell yes," he asserted. "I'm not a quitter."

So many men had quit on relationships with her, unwilling to wait for her to give all of herself. Everett was in this, and she couldn't decide if she was terrified or thrilled. "I think I like the idea of being Everett Eaton's woman."

"My woman." He scooped her off the counter and held her so her toes dangled off the floor. His hum of satisfaction vibrated across her lips as his mouth dappled lightly across hers. "You're going to have to come to the Edge. I want to see you ride."

She raised a brow. "Is that so?"

"A horse, sweetheart," he said, but his wicked grin said something else entirely. When her fingers tangled around a hunk of his hair, he hissed and dropped his head back to belt a laugh at the ceiling. "I swear. I meant a horse."

She made a doubtful noise but loosened her hold regardless.

"Your niece hinted at your past life as a trick rider before you did, and I can't get it out of my head—you bareback on that Appaloosa, your hair streaming like a black flag behind you…"

"What is this obsession you have with my hair?" she wondered.

"I'll let you know when I figure it out." He kissed her again, thoroughly.

"Hmm." Her brows came together, and her arms tightened around him. If a swarm of butterflies really was called a kaleidoscope, that was the only way she knew how to describe what happened to her insides when Everett kissed her. "I'll come to the Edge," she agreed. "But only if Paloma cooks us something."

"I might talk her into that," he weighed. "Groveling might be involved."

"Tell her we'll do the dishes."

"She's going to like you so much better than she likes me," he murmured.

She had never understood Paloma Coldero's unconditional love for the eldest Eaton brother…until now. Everett might prove to be as hard to love as others had found in the past, but Kaya liked a challenge. She'd once reveled in them.

She was going to find out what this man was made of. And if those butterflies in her stomach were any indication, she was already too far gone in this particular game of risk.

Chapter Nine

The Spring Festival was a chance for Fuego County residents to mix and mingle. It was a boost to small businesses, and it was considered good medicine for all.

Everett thought it was more headache-inducing than watching Lucas and Nova stack hay bales. He'd rather haul manure or square off with a randy bull than talk to Mrs. Whiting from the bank.

He'd rather pay bills, spray weeds or grind feed than talk to Huck Claymore about Our Lord and Savior, Jesus Christ.

He'd clear brush or even sit across from the family's long-time accountant, J.P. Dearing, discussing taxes before chatting up Christa McMurtry, the organist, who for some reason had moon eyes only for him.

"Poor girl," Eveline muttered, seeing Christa's gaze shining in Everett's direction, too. "If she's looking your way, she's a glutton for punishment."

Everett couldn't fight a sneer. "Her father's going to kill me because she looks my way."

"Can I watch?" Eveline asked in a low drawl that nearly made his lips twitch in approval. She took a loud, crunchy bite of her ice cream cone.

He had to admit, Eveline had come back into her own, co-managing the stable at the Edge with Griff MacKay and recently opening an equine rescue with Luella at Ollero Creek across town.

His sister had come home. She and Wolfe Coldero had found each other, for better or worse. Everett may want to argue with what she was fast building with the man who had once been Everett's biggest rival, but he couldn't argue with Eveline finding herself again—any more than he could quibble over her happiness. "I can't wait until you're Coldero's problem. Not mine."

She wiped a drop of sticky vanilla from her chin. "I'm only leaving long enough to drink daiquiries on the beach and swim naked in the surf with my new husband."

"Washing cats."

"What's that?" she asked.

"I'd rather be bathing Luella's cat than having this conversation," he said.

She hit him in the arm. "You're not getting rid of me. After a week, we'll be back. Then you're going to hire Wolfe for that salary job you've been trying to fill since after Dad died."

He laughed. "I may have agreed to the bastard being my brother-in-law..." He winced, just for form's sake, and had the pleasure of watching Eveline cross her arms and spread her feet in a ready stance. "But that doesn't mean I have to coexist with him any more than necessary."

"Dad gave him a percentage of Edge shares," she reminded him, polishing off the cone and wiping her hands on a thin paper napkin.

"Coldero gave them up. Traded them all for a half-dead horse, as I recall."

"What's mine is his," she added. "And before that trouble with Whip Decker seven years ago, Dad talked about making him foreman."

"Don't remind me," Everett groaned.

"He loved Wolfe," Eveline murmured, "every bit as much as he loved each of us. You know that. You have to know that. He would have wanted you to give Wolfe that job."

"I'm done with this conversation," he replied.

"Fine," she said and rolled her eyes. "Shouldn't we be talking to people like Ellis is?"

"Why?" he asked.

"Public relations," she pointed out. At the sound of his growl, she gestured. "Look. Even Luella's speaking to people."

"She shouldn't have to," he stated. "None of us should have to. Every one of these people whisper about us in church every Sunday. They're the same people who shunned Luella after what happened with her father last summer. They're the same ones who haven't stopped calling our mother a whore though she's been dead for seven years. They made Ellis and Luella's lives hell, circulating rumors about an affair they never had when he was still married. They're the ones who sided with Liberty in the divorce. They wouldn't stop their gabbing after you and Coldero were caught together at Naleen and Terrence's wedding…"

"Of course they gabbed," she said. "We were both in an indecent state."

"That's putting it mildly." He studiously turned his thoughts away from finding Eveline and Wolfe together in the tack room at The RC Resort with their unmentionables down around their ankles. *Changing the tractor's oil. Dig-*

ging ditches in an ice storm. Falling in a cow patty... All things he'd rather do than have this talk. "The point is, we don't owe the people of this town anything, least of all small talk. As far as I'm concerned, Fuego's one big dumpster fire."

"Now you've gone and hurt my feelings."

Everett whirled, bracing himself for what was at his back. Next to him, he felt Eveline tense in tandem with him.

True Claymore beamed from the shadow of his large black hat. His belt buckle caught the sheen of the light and shot sunbeams. The thing was nearly as big around as a tricycle tire. He threaded his thumbs through his belt loops, keeping his wife, Annette's, arm looped through his. "Ms. Eaton," True said, bowing his head to Eveline. "Annette here was just telling me we aren't invited to your wedding next week."

"It's a small ceremony," Eveline informed him. "Family only."

"Word is Javier Rivera and his family warranted invitations," True said thoughtfully.

"He's foreman at the Edge and has been for years," Everett put in. "If that's not family, it's as good as."

"And Rosalie Quetzal is invited," Annette rattled off, counting the names on her fingers. "*And* the Gaines family *and* Ms. Breslin from the real estate office...even a sprinkling of people from your modeling days in New York, Eveline. But not us. You didn't even ask our sweet Huck to officiate."

"Griff MacKay is ordained," Eveline explained.

"You would rather have a grizzly old stable boy conduct your ceremony than a man of the cloth?" Annette asked, round-eyed.

"He's family," Everett said. "It doesn't hurt that his name isn't Claymore."

Annette's mouth puckered, making her look waspish. True's fingers closed over hers, soothing. "Now, Eaton," the man said, shifting his weight. "You've gone and hurt my wife's feelings."

"Didn't know she had those," Everett said philosophically. He didn't back down from Annette's glare. He knew who had started the rumors about his mother, Ellis and Luella, and Eveline and Wolfe and who stoked them tirelessly. He knew what lawyer had put her weight behind the lawsuits and legal claims the Claymores had aimed at Everett and his father through the years, even after he died.

Everett knew who had tried to lure Paloma into leaving Eaton Edge and joining the staff at The RC Resort at his father's wake.

The Claymores had been poaching ranch hands and staff from the Edge since True and Annette had laid claim to it, throwing untold piles of money to transition it from working cattle ranch to luxurious resort and spa. They'd tried to take a piece of the Edge for themselves, crying foul at the informal way their fathers had drawn the narrow margins that existed between Claymore acreage and Edge lands…

Something niggled at the edge of Everett's train of thought. He tried to dismiss it.

The land claim… It had verged on the mountains and the trails. Everett had thought when studying the map that the Claymore's grab for the territory hadn't been about heritage. It had been about hiking. Their spread was flat like Ollero Creek. They wanted to make money off what the Eatons gave hikers free claim to as long as the rules on the mountain were obeyed.

Mountain.

Everett's chin firmed as he looked at True once more. "You son of a bitch."

"Excuse me?" Annette blustered.

True's good ol' boy smile had gone bye-bye. "Better to be the product of a straight bitch than a flaming whore."

Eveline made a disconcerted noise in her throat and stepped forward. Everett grabbed her. "Hold up," he said.

She whirled on him, fury writhing over her fair features. "You cut your knuckles on his real teeth last July for a lot less. You'll let me knock the rest of them out so he has to replace them, too. He won't be able to look in the mirror again without thinking of our family. I call that justice."

"The sheriff'd be a better judge of that," True estimated. Everett saw his nerves in his shifting stance and Annette's readiness in her hard face. "You'll wind up behind bars. There won't be a wedding."

"And won't that be a shame?" Annette chimed.

"Sure would," Everett considered, watching Eveline closely. Goading had always done its job where she was concerned.

Eveline shrugged, bristling his hand off her shoulder. She backed down.

That's right, Manhattan, he thought. *Eyes on the prize.* Whether she married Wolfe or Wile E. Coyote, there would be a wedding at Eaton Edge next week, if only to spite Buffalo Bill and Calamity Jane here. He tipped his hat and said, "Have a nice day, folks."

As he pulled her away, Eveline muttered, "Have you lost the rest of your mind?"

"Everyone's always on me about my mouth and my manners," he said. "I act right, and you still take me to task."

"Do what you want with those two," she invited. "Or better yet, let me."

"You're too skinny to take either one of them," he informed her. He milled through the crowd, dodging plates of BBQ and funnel cakes and pointy metal sculptures from one of the arts and crafts booths. He scanned the crowd, moving on until he neared the sheriff's department. Outside it, under a blue booth, he spotted the two-toned uniform. Picking up his pace, he ignored Eveline's cursing and all but charged.

Kaya crouched in front of a young boy in cowboy boots, smiling as she pinned a plastic sheriff's star to his shirtfront. "You're the real deal now, Officer Lawson," she said as she settled back on her heels and straightened his hat. "Now the first order of business as junior sheriff is to hunt up all the best grub on Food Truck Row. Think you can do that?"

The bespectacled youngster nodded eagerly.

"Report back to me with any signs of doughnuts," she advised. "And make sure to treat yourself to a snow cone. Morale is very important."

"Yes, ma'am," he said, grinning at her toothily before wandering off, parents in tow.

Kaya's smile didn't waver when she found Everett and Eveline. "Well, if it isn't my favorite brother and sister team. I've got some stars leftover. Let me pin one on you."

"Take a break," Everett advised, letting go of Eveline to take Kaya's hand.

She picked up on his urgency. Her smile fled. "Is something happening?"

"Come inside and I'll explain," he said.

She looked to Eveline who shrugged and said, "Don't look at me. He dragged me here."

"I'm on duty," Kaya replied to Everett.

"Handing out buttons?" he asked pointedly.

She let go of his hand to cross her arms over her chest. "It's called public relations, cattle baron. You should try it sometime."

He dismissed her. "I've got no time for that and neither do you. Do you have maps of the mountains north of the Edge inside?"

She nodded. "We have one pinned on the board in the conference room. But you can't—"

"Good," he cut in, starting for the door. "Bring your ass."

"Rude," she said at his back.

He opened the door. Cool air spilled out of the building. "Bring your fine ass," he amended and held the door open for her and Eveline who slapped him in the stomach as she passed.

He merely grunted and moved on. He saw Rutland through the glass in a large room toward the back of the department and rushed the door.

"Everett!" Kaya called. "Don't!"

He ignored her, flying into the conference room. Rutland jumped to his feet. "What are you doing here?"

Everett came to a halt. There were two boards, one nailed to the wall and another that had been rolled in for the FBI agent's use. The grisly images from the crime scene met his eyes. Before Eveline could step inside, he yanked the sport coat Rutland had hung on the back of his empty chair and draped it over the worst of them. He made certain it would stay, then pushed the rolling board with a clatter against the wall behind it so he could get to the map mounted to the other wall. There was a red pin on the side of Ol' Whalebones and another stuck in the location of the state park's parking lot where Higgins's car had been found.

"He can't be in here, Sheriff," Rutland said as Kaya entered.

"I know he can't," she replied. "Everett, I need you to leave. Now."

"Hang on, sweetheart," Everett muttered. "Everybody just hang on." He looked around for a writing utensil and found a Sharpie on the conference table amidst folders and photographs of the victims they had confirmed identification of—Miller Higgins, Sawni Mescal and Bethany Merchant.

He uncapped the marker and followed the lines of the mountain with his finger. He drew an additional one.

Rutland and Kaya made noises of protest. Eveline noted, "You *have* lost your mind."

Everett kept spanning the aerial distance with his hand, using the map scale. He made three more marks before stepping back. Using the marker, he pointed at what he had done. "Claymore."

When the others only stared, he groaned, capped the marker and tossed it on the table. "True and Annette. They wanted the mountain. Last year, they refiled a claim for this section." He stabbed the map over the west side of Ol' Whalebones. "And everything from that point west to their spread."

Kaya closed the door to the conference room. "Are you sure?"

Rutland gripped the back of his chair. "I thought everything north and west of the crime scene belongs to the state of New Mexico."

Everett frowned. "Fine investigative work you're doing here, Watt. How much is the government paying you?"

Eveline joined Everett, scanning the marks on the map. "Everett's right."

"Say it again, Manhattan," Everett requested. "Louder this time."

"Shush!" she hissed at him, then pointed at the map. "From here to here, everything that runs north is state territory."

"Including the river," Everett put in.

"That's how people get to Ol' Whalebones without having to trek across private property. The parking lot belongs to the state park. However, this narrow spit of land between the foot of Mount Elder and Big River Valley, right up to the edge of Ol' Whalebones is Claymore territory."

"My father, Hammond, laid claim to Ol' Whalebones and it was a bone of contention for Old Man Claymore when he was alive," Everett reported. "There's been talk of the Claymores taking it back for years. But nothing formal until my father's first heart attack."

"Which was?" Kaya asked.

"The year I left high school," Everett said. "The year my mother left for Coldero Ridge."

"The same year Bethany Merchant disappeared," Kaya said slowly.

"What if," Everett said, "the Claymores didn't want the mountain because their old man lost it? What if they didn't want it for right of access? What if they wanted it because they needed to cover up evidence?"

"You're accusing the mayor of quadruple homicide," Rutland pointed out.

"Or someone he knows," Everett said.

A shaky indrawn breath filled the quiet. He looked to Kaya who had gone pale. He reached out.

She backed off quickly. "Just… Just let me think it through."

"This could be a break in Sawni's case," he told her. "The one you've been looking for."

Rutland cleared his throat. "We're following other leads, Mr. Eaton. But we will take your information into consideration."

"That's a line of crap."

"Everett," Kaya said.

"Wait a second, sweetheart," he said slowly. He faced the agent. "You don't like me. Hell, you wanted me for these murders. Are you dismissing my information because you're on someone else's case or because it was me who gave it specifically?"

"Specifically," Rutland replied, "the investigative team is pursuing other leads." When Everett swore, he went on. "As you know, details of this case are being kept under wraps for investigative purposes. Which is why, again, you can't be in here."

"Everett," Kaya said again, "let's go."

"You want me to go?" he asked, offended.

"I'm asking you to come with me," she insisted.

There was trouble in her eyes. Scowling at Rutland, he jerked his thumb at the map. "I'll be following up on this, Watt."

"I look forward to it, Mr. Eaton."

Eveline followed them out. "Did he really try to pin four murders on you?" she demanded.

Everett stopped. "I'm clear, okay? He tried to make a connection between me and Bethany's, but it didn't stick. I'm all right," he said again. She shook her head in disbelief. "Don't tell Paloma or Ellis. It's over."

"You should have told us," she said. "How many times have I bailed you out of jail? Just once, let it be for something I *know* you didn't do."

"Next time," he promised. Then he reached for her, skimming a hand over her shoulder.

"I need to speak to him," Kaya said to her.

Eveline nodded. "Sure." She smiled and lowered her voice. "How long have you two been—"

"None of your business, *hermana*," he told her, firm on that point. "Go find Ellis. Tell him I need to speak with him."

"And Wolfe, too?"

He rolled his shoulders with an impatient rumble. "Fine. Bring the bridegroom. Tell them to meet me at the house and that Bozeman should be there, too."

Chapter Ten

"Shut the door," Kaya said.

Everett did as he was told, watching her close the blinds over the window to the bull pen. "What's going on?"

She planted her hand against the wall and leaned. He saw sweat lining her brow when she removed her hat.

"Kaya."

"I need to tell you something."

"Okay," he said bracingly.

"First," she said, "and this is really important, Everett—I need you not to go looking for blood."

He stilled. "This is about the Claymores."

"I need your word."

"Tell me first."

"Everett!" she shouted. "You said you wouldn't wind up on the wrong side of the law if we were together. Your word, please!"

He exerted a long rush of air through his nose, trying to deflate the foreboding built up inside him—the ready tension and anger. "I give you my word," he ground from between his teeth.

"I will hold you to it."

"Just tell me!"

She looked away. "I wanted to tell you before. But I've kept it to myself for years and it's hard to let go. Even with you." She wet her lips when he fell quiet, anticipating. "I told you after Sawni disappeared that I became obsessed with finding her. I knew one of the last places she was seen was The RC Resort. I wouldn't leave the Claymores alone. I didn't trust that they gave so little information about her and weren't looked into further by the authorities. The police went light on them, likely because they were The Claymores, even then. So I snuck on site and I had a look around. I retraced her actions through what I knew of her day. Then I tried sneaking into the office. True caught me."

"What did he do?" Everett asked. His hands had curled into fists in his pockets.

"He told me he had a way of dealing with 'little rez girls who liked to stick their noses where they didn't belong.'"

Every muscle in Everett's body stilled.

"He took me outside. If True had handled me himself, I would have put him behind bars when I became deputy. Before the statute of limitations was up. But he never touched me beyond hauling me out of there and putting me in one of the resort shuttles. I never even saw him talk to the two security goons who drove me back to the highway. There's no evidence he told them to do what they did."

Words raked across his throat, hot as coals. "What did they do?"

Her hands shook once. Just once. It was enough to make him vibrate with rage. She culled the explanation out in a flat tone, as if reciting the Pledge of Allegiance. "They forced me out of the shuttle onto the roadside. One of the men hit me in the stomach while the other held my arms back. They told me to say I wasn't coming back. When I refused..."

Her voice hitched. Everett wanted to move to her, hold her, but the vibrations had gone into the bone. He knew, all too well, that he didn't have a handle on himself.

"They grabbed me by the hair," she said. "I wore it loose. It was down to my waist. They made me get on my knees. The first one said, 'The boss wants you to remember what happens to little rez girls when they don't learn to leave well enough alone...' The other one held me while he..."

Everett filled in the blanks. His head nearly split. The images maxed out the capacity of his brain. Every single one of them was gunpowder. They torched his restraint.

Grabbing the first thing at hand, he flipped the visitor's chair on its head. He paced on the spot then faced the wall. It was cinderblock. It would splinter the bones of his fist if he hit it like he needed to.

With his back to her, he zeroed in on a fold of worn tape that had been left behind when a poster was removed. The anger didn't ebb. It was a restless wave pool that beat against one shore, then the opposite one until the swells met in the middle and clashed.

"I'm going to kill him," he said between his teeth.

"No, you're not," she returned.

"You're going to have to let me kill him, sweetheart," he said, revolving back to her.

She shook her head. She was steady, still and utterly calm. He was stunned by her bravery. He was awed by it. She'd had to live with this, on top of everything else. It wasn't long before she'd joined the police force, he knew. She'd come back to Fuego—to chase down her demons. Anybody else would have run from them.

"What about the goons?" he asked. "The men who did this to you. You didn't talk to the police?"

She looked away, her countenance flagging. "I was trespassing. I broke into the resort. And it stuck with me—*little rez girls.* It followed me everywhere for a time. It was my word against theirs."

"You came back," he said. "You came back to face them."

She nodded. "I wanted them to feel threatened. I thought my mere presence in Fuego in uniform would make them quiver. I learned soon after I returned that True had replaced the two security goons with others. Worse, there was no record of their employment with him. Their names weren't even in the system. They were ghosts in the wind. The first time I came face-to-face with True, he didn't recognize me. He's never put it together—the little rez girl and the Fuego County deputy."

"Sheriff," he said, moving to her. "You're sheriff now. And he should know exactly who he's dealing with. He should damn well be quivering."

"I've been waiting," she said on a whisper. "I could never build a solid case against him or Annette or the resort. Every time I got close, Sheriff Jones would shut it down. After what you said in the conference room about someone True knows potentially murdering the people on the mountain… I knew."

"The security guys." He nodded. "True isn't the type to get his hands dirty. If he'd wanted to put Sawni, Bethany and the other woman in the ground, he would have used someone else."

"They were killed execution-style," Kaya said. "One shot

to the back of the head. Mercenary." He heard the audible click of her swallow. "They were all likely on their knees when it happened…like me on the side of the highway."

He cursed and pulled her to him. He folded around her. She didn't tremor. She didn't relax, either. She was holding it all in. She'd held it in…all this time. "I want to kill him."

"No," she said, pulling away enough to look at him. "This is my fight. He's going to be my collar. I will gather enough evidence to bring him in. That's why I became a police officer, Everett. To find Sawni and to build evidence and a case around Claymore that he and his wife can never pull him out of. He deserves to rot in prison."

"He deserves to be throttled first," Everett inserted.

"I need you to listen," she said, eyes on fire. "I've waited my entire career to nail True Claymore. He might be looking at kidnap and murder charges if your theory pans out. And I will not let anybody stand in the way of putting that good-for-nothing behind bars once and for all. Not even you."

"God Jesus, you're incredible," he breathed. "But you're *not* alone in this. Not anymore."

"I'm telling you what I need and you're not hearing me," she said. "*Stay away from him.*"

"You mean don't fight for your honor," he amended, frustration stretching against the bounds of his skin.

"I'm asking you to trust me to fight for my own," she pleaded, "and the life and honor of every woman he's taken. I don't know how Miller Higgins is tied up in this. But women were his pattern. We can tie Sawni to him. I'll look for his connection to Bethany Merchant. He dated her, just as you did. We need to know the timing…"

"Rutland doesn't like my theory," he muttered.

"I'll work around him," she said.

"You're going down the rabbit hole again," he cautioned.

"I'm not alone this time," she recalled.

"No," he agreed.

"Promise me," she demanded. "Promise me you won't—"

"Beat Claymore to within an inch of his life?"

"Promise me," she whispered, holding both his arms, "you will not harm a hair on his head."

He scanned her face. Then he nodded, grimly, lips seamed tight.

"I need you to say it."

"Fine," he said. "I will not harm a hair on True's head."

She nodded. "Thank you. Now kiss me, cattle baron. I'm feeling queasy and raw and I need you, goddamn it."

He did as he was told, dipping his lips to hers in a slow motion. He kept it soft. He kept it tender. He felt the give in her muscles. He felt the release. He heard the longing report from the line of her throat and groaned in response, every bit as lost as she was.

"You're shaking," she said, running her hands up and down his arms. "I shouldn't have told you."

"Don't," he bit off. "There are no secrets between us anymore."

She searched his face. "No," she said, understanding. "No more secrets."

He made himself step back. "I'm meeting Ellis and the others back at the house. I'll have Bozeman get you copies of the Claymores' land disputes and any other legal documents they sent our way through the years."

"Everett?"

He stopped with his hand on the door. When he looked

back, he didn't read vulnerability. He saw strength. She was strong—stronger than him. Stronger than anyone he'd ever met.

And he loved her.

The realization came like a thunderclap.

He'd known it would never come to this—loving someone uncompromisingly. Men like him didn't fall, not after watching his father's heartbreak over his mother kill him slow… excruciatingly slow.

Yet here he was and so was Kaya, and he loved her beyond doubt or reason.

"I'll see you," she told him.

He felt a quaver as deep as his marrow. Dipping his head to her, he yanked the door open and left.

Chapter Eleven

Kaya cornered Rutland in the conference room after seeing Everett out. She closed the door, hemming them in. "Why are you dismissing Everett Eaton? Last I checked, this case had run into a wall. We need every possible lead or it's going to go cold again."

Rutland considered the question. He'd taken his sport coat down off the board and was wearing it. Leaning back in his chair at the head of the table, he laced his fingers over his middle. "You're seeing him."

She thought of denying it. But Rutland wasn't going to trust her or her judgement if she lied. "I'm seeing him."

He lifted his brows but otherwise didn't move. "You're trying to earn the respect and authority your office deserves, and you think fooling around with a man who dances in and out of that Mayberry jail cell you've got in the back of your wheelhouse is the way to do that? You're smarter than that, Altaha."

She was still a little bit queasy and more than a little bit raw. She didn't feel stable. She curled her hands around the back of a chair, trying to rein it all in. She would not lose her composure in front of the agent. "My personal life doesn't interfere with my ability to do my job. But you're going to tell me why exactly you're willing to throw away evidence against the Claymores."

He tilted his head. "Are you insinuating something?"

"The Claymores have bought ranking officers for well on a decade," she informed him.

"You claim your personal life has no bearing on your police work," he said. "But it's starting to sound like you have a vendetta against this family. I've read the files from your previous sheriff. I know the Eatons most certainly have one."

"That's why you dismissed Everett?" she asked. "Because he's gone after True in the past?"

"Ask yourself this," he said, leaning forward so that the chair squeaked slightly. He dropped a file on the table. "If you were thinking objectively, wouldn't you have drawn the same conclusion?"

"That's not good enough," she replied. "You said we're pursuing other leads. You lied and tossed his theory out the window."

"I didn't lie."

She lifted her hands. "Is there another lead you haven't told me about? You haven't briefed me on one."

She saw him hesitate. Moving around the table, she said, "You're the one who wanted cooperation between our teams."

"I did say that, didn't I?" He turned his chair to face her. "I was going to brief you this morning. Then the business with the festival. And I saw what Mr. Eaton is to you."

"I'm dating a man you've cleared of all charges in this case and that gives you a right to squirrel evidence away?" she asked.

He let out a breath, then reached for two Baggies on the

table. "These arrived last night in the safe haven baby box at the volunteer fire department on Highway 7."

She took the bags. One contained a standard, unmarked bubble mailer, the kind that could be bought at any office supply store. The flap was open but it had been torn. There was no address or return address written on it.

The second bag contained a small book. Kaya thought it might be a datebook until she turned it over and saw the name written in the bottom corner. "What is this?" she asked in a quiet voice.

"I need to confirm the handwriting with her mother and father," Rutland stated. "But it appears Sawni Mescal kept a diary."

The letters blurred together. "No need," she said, setting the bags on the table. "I recognize it."

"It's her handwriting?"

"It is," she confirmed. "We passed enough notes… I've reread them through the years. Have you opened this?"

"It's bagged and will need to go to the lab for prints," he said, picking up the folder he'd dropped on the desk. "But my team made copies of the pages."

Kaya opened the file when he handed it to her. She had to take a measured breath when she saw the looping strokes of Sawni's handwriting that filled the first page.

"Did you know she kept a diary?" he asked. "Did she ever tell you?"

"She did," Kaya answered. "She let me read others she wrote. This was dropped last night in the fire department's box?"

"It was."

"Someone's had this this whole time… The killer?"

"Possibly."

"Why would they do that?" she asked, flipping through the pages. "When was the last entry?"

"The night before her death," he said. "There's reason to believe some pages were torn out."

She lifted her gaze to his, then went back to studying the final page. "She talks about working at The RC Resort… Nothing seemed to be troubling her."

"No," Rutland said, standing. He riffled back through the diary. "Look at this page."

She scanned the words. Sawni's quiet voice played through her head, as real as it had once been. Her eyes seized on a name. She read through the entry again, coming to the name once more. She shook her head. "I don't understand…"

"You told investigators at the time she was dating someone," he said. "Here she mentions him a week before she disappeared."

Kaya rejected it, offering the file back to him. "That's not right. It can't be."

"Sheriff, you said your personal feelings have no bearing on your work. You're not going to let them get in the way now when the answer may be staring you in the face."

"She's not naming her killer," she said, pointing to the file. "She's naming her lover."

"Wolfe Coldero. He's mentioned no less than thirty-three times throughout her journal. I checked back through her missing person case. No one ever checked his alibi for the day of her disappearance. No one checked him out in the Miller Higgins case, either."

"Wolfe Coldero didn't kidnap or kill Sawni," she stated.

"Why not? He lived in Fuego at the time. He worked at

Eaton Edge and lived at Coldero Ridge. He's connected to Sawni through the rodeo. He was a bull rider. That's where and how they met. Why wouldn't either of them have told you?"

Her lips felt numb. She dropped to a chair. "Wolfe's mute. He's never spoken to anyone."

"Did he help with the search effort?" Rutland asked.

Kaya thought back. She combed through memories she'd gone over again and again, looking for clues or clarity or closure… "Yes," she answered. "I remember him being there. His father, Santiago, came. And Everett's mother, Josephine. She and Santiago were having an affair. They brought horses and were part of the mounted search party in the state park areas."

"I'd like to bring him in," Rutland said.

"He won't talk," she reminded him. "Not to you or anyone else."

"He can answer questions in writing," Rutland asserted. "If he doesn't, I can charge him with obstruction."

"He's getting married in a few days."

Rutland closed the file. "With a foreign honeymoon to follow, I hear. He's not getting on a plane until he's cleared."

"Wolfe Coldero isn't a killer," Kaya told him.

"Didn't he do time for shooting a man in the back seven years ago?" Rutland asked.

"Jace Decker," Kaya replied. "Wolfe shot him to stop him from throwing fuel on the cabin fire at Coldero Ridge. Josephine and her and Santiago's daughter, Angel, were inside. Wolfe tried to get them out, but he was too late."

"His record is against him," he said. "He'll be brought in at nine o'clock tomorrow morning. You can sit in."

The door to the conference room opened. Sherry peered around the jamb. “I’m sorry, Sheriff. Agent Rutland. But there’s a situation.”

“What kind of situation?” Kaya asked, coming to attention.

“It’s the mayor,” Sherry said. “The luxury vehicle he drives… It’s been vandalized. He’s agitated. Deputy Root is having trouble getting him to calm down.”

“We’ll discuss this later,” Kaya told Rutland. “Where is the mayor now?” she asked Sherry.

“On Second Street where the car was parked,” she said, trailing Kaya through the station. “He discovered the damage after leaving the festival.”

“Thank you, Sherry.”

THE SCENE ON Second Street was nothing short of chaotic. A crowd had formed. Kaya worked through it to the center. She could hear True Claymore hollering before she reached the center of the mass where he and his vehicle were located.

She stopped to assess. The mayor was without his hat. His hair was sticking straight up in places, finger-combed by frustrated hands. His hands flailed and he was on his toes, his red face in Root’s. He threw invectives at the deputy, his voice no longer smooth. Nothing about him appeared to be collected.

Kaya walked around the parallel-parked vehicle to the driver’s side. Damage had been done to more than the paint job. There was fender and other body damage. The destruction was so thorough, she doubted the vehicle was drivable.

Kaya didn’t have to ask what instrument had been used. The offending sledgehammer lay nearby. It was the kind used commonly by farmers and ranchers to drive stakes into the ground. The paint on the front edge matched the color of the car.

"Did the perpetrator flee the scene?" she asked Wyatt, who was standing by.

True whirled at the sound of her voice. "Sheriff! He's done it now! Lock him up! Lock all of them up!"

She raised a hand. "You saw who did this?"

"I didn't have to see it!" True shouted. "He was standing right there with the sledgehammer when I got back!"

"Who was?" Kaya asked, though her gut stirred, and she was afraid she knew the name already. She looked around, searching.

Leaning against one of the closest building's support posts in a neutral stance, Everett stood. His aviator sunglasses reflected the scene. The bend of his mouth showcased nothing—not even amusement.

She knew when his eyes shifted to her. His stance didn't change or his expression, but she felt it.

"Did anybody see who did this?" Kaya asked the crowd at large.

Turk Monday stepped forward. "I saw that Eaton fella there going to town on it."

"He was heaving at it like a raging bull," another man piped up from the crowd.

Other witnesses' voices followed. Kaya rounded on Everett with a glare she hoped singed the fur off his hide.

"White trash, burnout, son of a bitch!" True Claymore yelled, stepping forward.

Root caught him by the arms. "Now, mayor. You're going to need to cool down if you want to press charges…"

Kaya walked to Everett. "Do you deny this?"

"Which part?" he asked. "The white trash, burnout bit?"

"Did you vandalize his vehicle?" she asked.

"That part I'll claim."

She stepped a hair closer. "You promised," she hissed.

He pointed at the mayor. "I promised not to harm a hair on his head. His hair's fine. So's every other part of him. You said nothing about his property."

"Turn around," she ordered. "Put your hands behind your back."

He straightened. "Sure, Sheriff Sweetheart. I know how it goes."

She reached around her belt for her cuffs. "Everett Eaton, you're under arrest…"

Chapter Twelve

Kaya stayed late at the sheriff's office, long after Rutland had left for the night, her deputies had gone home, and Lionel Bozeman had shown up with Ellis Eaton to bail Everett out of jail. She stayed behind her desk with the pages photocopied from Sawni's diary.

Annette and True Claymore had been there most of the afternoon. They'd railed at her deputies and her in turn. They'd even shouted at Rutland. There was no question Everett would be charged with criminal damage to a vehicle.

They'd threatened her job if she let him out on bail.

Making threats to a sheriff in her own department was a ballsy move. She'd made a note of those who overheard and filed it away, as she'd filed so many other tidbits about the Claymores over the years.

The diary was revealing in ways Kaya hadn't expected. Sawni had dated Wolfe Coldero for much of the last year of her life. They met at the rodeo. When Sawni was forced to stop returning to the rodeo by her parents, there had been meetings with the two—on the reservation and off. Kaya read details about multiple rendezvous at the state park.

It made sense, Sawni and Wolfe, Kaya thought. It made

perfect sense, actually. Wolfe was mute and Sawni was quiet. Their similar natures would have drawn them together. Sawni had been curious about boys and men but had never found one she could trust to experiment with…

Until Wolfe, apparently. Their relationship had turned intimate. Kaya had a hard time facing the fact that Sawni hadn't confided her first time to her. They'd sworn they would confide in each other, if no one else.

There was nothing violent about their relationship mentioned in the diary. There was no evidence that Wolfe treated Sawni with anything but care.

Kaya studied the photographs of the diary itself, taken before it was bagged for prints. At several junctures, the binding was ragged. Pages had been torn out. Quite a few of them. That called to question whether Sawni had ripped them or the person who had delivered the diary after all these years.

If it was the killer, why would they hand over the diary? To throw suspicion on someone else?

Someone like Wolfe?

Some of the answers would come in the morning when he arrived for his interview with Rutland. Kaya glanced at the clock. She frowned when she saw it was close to eleven. She closed the file and locked it in her filing cabinet before switching the lamp off on her desk. She changed from her sheriff's uniform to a more relaxed set of jeans and a button-down.

She locked the station door behind her since she was the last to leave. Walking to her vehicle, she got in the driver's seat and cranked the ignition. She pulled out onto the deserted street and started to turn the wheel for home.

She paused. As the traffic light at Main Street and Second

changed, she looked down the intersecting road that reached into the black of night.

She thought about the diary. She thought about her bed and the complications she certainly wouldn't find there.

She turned the wheel to the left and followed the road well out of town.

Slowing, she made the turnoff for Eaton Edge and drove up the long, dirt drive to Eaton House. The motion lights flared to life as she parked. She noted the absence of cars in the drive.

She didn't know what she was doing exactly, but she took the path to the front door of the house and pounded on the door.

She expected Paloma to answer. When the door parted from the jamb, she found him instead.

Everett blinked at her in surprise. "Sheriff Sweetheart," he greeted.

When she stayed silent, he released a breath. "Look. I can take a lot. Scream at me. Hit me. You can bust my nuts or gouge me in the eyes. But don't give me the silent treatment. I can't take it."

She walked around him before she could tell herself not to. Beyond the foyer, she found a spartan living room he hadn't changed since his father died. There was a couch with space behind it. There, against the wall off the stairwell, she found the sideboard.

He didn't stop her from lifting the lid off its decanter. She turned an upside-down glass over and filled it with whiskey. She lifted it to her mouth and knocked it back straight.

"I'll take one of those."

She threw a look over her shoulder, quashing his attempt at camaraderie.

"Never mind," he decided.

She poured herself another, then, as an afterthought, a second. She grabbed it by the rim and pivoted to extend it to him.

He took it, tipping his head to her. "Thank you, Sheriff—"

"Don't you dare," she warned.

He took a drink, instead.

She turned her back to the sideboard and leaned. Sipping, she pointed at him, lifting one finger from her glass. "You know…call me a sucker or whatever you like…"

"I wouldn't call you—"

"But I trusted you," she added, raising her voice over his. "I understand a lot of people have died on that hill, but I thought… I actually *thought* I could trust you."

"I didn't hurt him," he claimed. "Not a hair."

"His hair's gone! It's fallen out! He's so hoarse from shouting at me and Root and Wyatt for letting you out on bail he won't have anything left when he comes at you tomorrow, which he undoubtedly will."

"I'm not afraid of him and his froggy voice," Everett noted. "Though I'm mad as hell he came down on you hard."

"You don't get to be mad as hell," she informed him. "It's my turn now."

"All right," he conceded. He set his glass down. "How do you want to do this?"

"If I was smart, I'd leave," she claimed. "I'd go on with my life and wash my hands of this."

His eyes darkened in understanding. "But you're here."

"Because there's another part of me. The stupid, impulsive part that I never could kill. It seems to think you destroying another man's property on my behalf was sweet and maybe a little romantic, by Western standards."

He chose his words carefully. "You, uh… You like Western?"

"The sheriff in me doesn't."

"What about you?" he asked. "The trick rider. Apache Annie. The real you that ran away to the rodeo and never wanted to go back home."

"I'm here," she said.

His eyes shone, making her stomach flutter as only he could. "Yeah, you are."

She set the glass down with an empty clack. With both hands, she reached for her bun.

"What're you doing?"

"Be quiet, Everett."

"Shutting up," he replied as the pins came down and her braid unraveled, falling to her waist.

She didn't meet his gaze. Not until every last coil had been undone and she'd spread her fingers through her hair to make it spill loose over her shoulders.

Everett backed up until his hips met the back of the couch. He sat and gripped the edge with both hands on either side. "What're you doing to me, woman?"

"I'm not touching you," she said.

"Aren't you?" he asked. There was a bar between his eyes that spoke of danger and longing and her heart began to quake.

She crossed to him. With him sitting, they were nearly eye level. "Put your hands in it," she instructed. "Isn't that what you wanted?"

He made a noise. His fingers lifted to the ends of her hair.

He fanned them out, letting the ends pass over the back of his knuckles in whispering strokes. Testing the weight with his palm, he wet his lips before twining one strand around his finger.

Kaya started unbuttoning his shirt. He hadn't changed out of what he'd worn earlier. She parted the chambray shirt over his front, pleased to see nothing underneath it but skin. Pushing the shirt over the hard, round points of his shoulders, she shed it.

In the center of his chest, she found the place where he'd been shot and the incisions where surgeons had opened him up to save his life. She traced the bullet wound, feathering her touch over the damage done.

His voice roughened. "I ain't touched anything as fine as you. Ever."

She smiled, in spite of herself. "Is that your way of telling me you love me?"

He cursed a stream.

"Steady there," she advised, planting her hand over the marks of his chest. His heart beat underneath them, big and forceful. "Steady on, cattle baron. It was a joke."

He shook his head slightly. "I did that earlier."

"You committing a third degree felony was your way of expressing your feelings?" she asked.

His hand came up to cradle the sharp line of her jaw. His mouth said nothing but his eyes, again, talked.

Her lips parted when she took their meaning, too. "Your love language may need a little work."

"I don't know," he considered, giving his attention to the buttons on the top of her blouse. "It's working just fine from where I'm standing."

When he removed her shirt, she stepped in the space between his parted knees. She grabbed him under the shoulders and confronted his smart mouth with her own.

He gathered her against his chest, his hands lost in the thick sheet of her hair. When he unclipped her bra, he tugged it away. Without lifting his lips from hers, he pushed to his feet.

Kaya dropped her head back, closing her eyes. Skin-to-skin, she let him feast on her mouth, absorbing the rough texture of his hands as they cruised over her in sure strokes.

When he unclasped her belt, she shimmied as he pushed the waistband over her hips.

He kneeled, tugging away one of her boots, then the other. The pants pooled at her ankles and his lips found the place on her thigh, the wound that still ached. He traced kisses around her thigh, then up, tickling the place behind her knee that was oddly sensitive.

She didn't stop him when he reached the juncture of her thighs. His mouth opened and pressed against her sex through the thin panties she'd chosen to wear that morning. It was her turn to groan, sinking her hands into his dark, cropped hair. His beard was rough, too. She felt it through the material as she had on her thigh and she shivered, bristled and shivered again as her arousal increased. If he removed the garment, he'd find how wet she was for him.

"Stand up," she directed. When he did, she yanked off his belt, whipping it free from the loops of his jeans. She undid the snap and pulled down the fly and would have reached in for him but met resistance when he took her wrist and held it. He took the other and she hissed at him.

"This isn't going to be fast, Kaya. I don't want you in fast gulps. I want to take my time. I want it drawn out. I want us both thirsty and begging. I want you in my bed."

"Long way to go," she noted absently as he guided her backward to the stairs. The promise of it all was enough to bring her up to her toes. She dragged his mouth back to hers.

Stumbling, they made it halfway up the flight before he turned her to the wall.

She found her cheek against the striped wallpaper and, as he nipped her shoulder, she sighed. "This wasn't on the list…"

"Shh…" His face was in her hair and his touch low on her navel. It cruised down, reaching the parting of her legs.

She planted her hands against the wall as his fingertips sank underneath the edge of the panties. When he traced the seam of her sex with his middle finger, she bit her lip to keep from crying out.

He made a noise when he parted her and found the cluster of nerves at the peak of her labia and the pool of arousal he'd caused. When he stroked, she drew herself up tight, arching her back.

She could feel him through his jeans. He was ready—just as ready as she was. But his touch glided slow, taking her up incrementally, stretching her pleasure to the point of affliction. "Never figured you for a sadist, Eaton," she said brokenly as she dropped her head back to his shoulder.

"You can take it," he whispered hot against her temple. "You can take all of me."

She pressed her hand to the back of his, forcing him deeper. "Don't. Don't make me beg. Not yet."

His laugh fell brokenly across her cheek. He inserted one finger, stroking. Then another.

Her mouth dropped open though she didn't make a sound.

It was too divine, this point he was driving her toward. Too bright. She burned, moving against his hand, driving herself right up to the breaking point.

He held her there in splendor. The heel of his other hand pressed against her womb, as if he knew exactly where the heat was building.

She came apart. In diamond-edged rifts and shouts, she came apart in his arms.

He turned her. When she saw his wide grin and the triumph riding high on his face, she raised her open hand.

It cracked across his face. He hissed, but the grin didn't break. Instead, he laughed. "Why you gotta be so mean?"

She placed her hands on the back of his head, urging him down. She kissed his cheek. Then the other. She kissed them better.

He hummed, boosting her up by the hips so her legs wrapped around his waist and he continued up the stairs.

The last step tripped him. The landing came up to meet them. It knocked the wind out of her.

"Sorry, sweetheart," he murmured, sitting up.

"Stay down," she ordered, switching their positions so that he was down and she was up. She yanked at one of his boots, gritting her teeth when it didn't comply. It nearly sent her down the stairs when it loosened. She tossed it behind her so that it bounced all the way to the bottom before doing the same to the other. Then she pulled at the cuffs of his jeans.

He lifted his hips so he could remove them from his waist. Once she had them off, she balled them up and threw them over the railing.

He was fine-boned, long and just dark enough to be tan instead of white. She liked the way the muscles bunched across his flat stomach, the way his shoulders flared outward, defiant, from his collarbone.

She liked the cut of hair down the center of his chest and abdomen that grew thick underneath his exposed waistline. There were other things. So many other things she liked—his long thighs, the definition of his chest and the way he looked back at her with hooded, bedroom eyes, hungry and watchful.

He wanted it slow, drawn out? He wanted them both thirsty, begging? *Fine.* That was just fine…

She scaled the length of him slowly, from ankles to shoulders, dragging the ends of her hair across his front. His knees rose and his skin tightened, and she got to watch him bite his own lip for once. When his hand came to the back of her neck to urge her mouth down to his, she held back, raining kisses over every other part of him she admired. Shoulders, collarbone, neck, pecs and sternum. She traced ribs and abs and waist, letting the dark curtain of her hair cover him as she followed him down, down…

She wanted him as sensitive as he'd made her. She wanted him wild—enough to take a sledgehammer to her enemy's car again. More.

She wanted him wild for her. There was a part of her that reveled in the fact that he'd reached that point. She'd arrested him for it. But that didn't stop the flash of pride or sparkly satisfaction that knowing brought.

She wrapped her fingers around his girth. Passing her thumb over the tip, she grinned when he jerked. "People say you're heartless."

His lungs moved up and down in excited repetitions. He

dropped his head back, rising at the bidding of her hand when she stroked. He cursed.

"They're wrong," she considered and caressed. She worked him as he'd worked her. She did it until he was breathless. Then she seated herself over his hips. She took his face in her hands. "They're wrong about you."

He took her hand and placed it over the healed wound on the center of his chest. Underneath, his pulse rocked and clamored and she dropped her lips to that point.

He sat up and grunted as he picked her up and carried her the rest of the way to his door, which was at the end of the hallway.

They made it to the jamb. He propped her against it so he could open the door. He stopped, nibbling on her lower lip before tracing a line down her throat as he discarded her panties and lifted her.

"Now," she said. "Right now."

He obeyed. She took him, all of him. Just as he'd wanted. "Oh," she cried. "Oh, hell yes!"

"I told you," he groaned. "I told you, sweetheart…"

She nodded in quick repetitions. "Don't stop."

"Bed," he grunted and carried her across the threshold, along the floor, then tipped her to the bed. "Just a second…"

She heard him fumbling in the drawer next to the bed. She blinked at the condom he found.

She'd forgotten protection. *How* had she forgotten?

He opened the packet, then fed the rubber to the base of his arousal. When his body covered her again, he uttered an oath, brushing the hair from her cheeks in sweet strokes. "I let you get cold."

"You'll fix it, baby."

His hair messy from her hands, he grinned in a quick, delighted burst. "Baby? I like that."

She smiled, too. It filled her cheeks to capacity. "Make me say it again," she whispered.

"Ten-four."

He was like a furnace. When he joined with her again, she felt like one, too.

Their bodies were already dewy with perspiration. Together, they slid, plunged, tossed. Her ankles crossed at the small of his back and he carried her up to the same point he had before, diamond-bright and stunning. When she moaned, he answered.

The flat of his hands came to the backs of her thighs and he pressed, fitful as he chased his own climax.

When he broke, she pulled his mouth to hers so that when he groaned again, it vibrated across her lips. And when he shuddered, she felt it from the toes up, just like him.

"You won't move," she told him long after he stilled.

"No. I won't."

"WAKE UP, CATTLE BARON."

"Nah," he said even as Kaya shifted restlessly. His face was in her hair, his arms wrapped around her. At some point in the night, he'd tossed the sheet over both of them, unwilling to let her get cold again. "I'm good."

"The sun's going to be coming up fast," she explained. "Paloma will be here. We both have work. Don't cowboys rise early?"

He smirked. "Which part, Sheriff?" He grunted when she

drove her elbow into his stomach. He wheezed a laugh but didn't relinquish her. "Hold still."

He growled his displeasure, turning to his back. He cupped his hands under the back of his head. Why'd he have to fall for a sensible woman? "Don't leave this bed."

She sat up, scooping her hair over one shoulder. She combed her fingers through it. He'd like to do the same once he roused himself enough, he thought.

"We need to talk."

He traced the absence of her easy smile and felt it. "You're wearing your serious eyes."

"Because I am serious," she said. "Are you up enough to talk?"

He propped himself on one elbow with some effort. "Yeah, yeah. I'm up."

"I stopped by last night for two reasons."

"Not to jump my bones?"

"That was a bonus. I stopped here so that I could pick a fight with you."

"I like the way you fight," he said, unable to hide a smile even in the face of her serious eyes.

"I'm not sure you fight fair," she considered. "The other reason I wanted to stop by was because I know who Rutland's going to target next."

He scrubbed his hands over his face and sat up all the way. "Why do I get the feeling I'm not going to like his new direction?"

"It's Wolfe," she told him.

"Coldero?"

"Two nights ago, someone dropped Sawni's old diary in

the safe haven drop box at the fire station on Highway 7. It's hers. I recognized the handwriting."

"Who dropped it?" he asked, coming awake in full measure now. "And why did they have it?"

"I don't know," she said. "There were no security cameras. Nobody saw anyone outside. It's at the lab now being checked for prints."

"What does this have to do with Coldero?" he asked.

"There are pages missing from the diary," Kaya told him. "However, the ones that remain primarily talk about Wolfe and their relationship."

"You didn't tell me she was seeing him."

"I didn't know until I read the diary," she explained.

He saw the sadness and trouble on her face. "Come 'ere."

She didn't resist much when he caught her hand. She pressed her cheek to the wall of his chest as he leaned back in the pillows at the head of the bed. "What's all this mean, Kaya?" he asked.

"Wolfe's going to be called in for questioning this morning," she said. "If he doesn't give Rutland the right answers, there's a good chance his and Eveline's wedding will be delayed."

"They're going to lock him up," Everett said.

"I thought you should know. It's your sister who loves him. And you don't mind that as much as you let on."

"I'll warn them," he replied.

"You don't think that he killed Sawni and the others."

Everett frowned and found himself shaking his head. "For the longest time, people thought Coldero killed Whip Decker. He served time for it. But he's no killer."

"He'll need to hear you say it before this is all over," she said.

He made another noise and was relieved when she let him hold her awhile longer before the break of day.

Chapter Thirteen

Wolfe arrived promptly at the sheriff's department at nine o'clock with Lionel Bozeman, Ellis and Eveline in tow. Since Bozeman was to serve as his attorney and Ellis would speak for him, Eveline was forced to remain outside the crowded interrogation room.

Kaya observed the proceedings. Wolfe confirmed his involvement with Sawni but had no memory of exactly where he was the day she vanished or where he had been during the time of Bethany Merchant's disappearance, either. Worse, he couldn't provide a witness to his whereabouts the day of Miller Higgins's death. Through sign language, he claimed he had been working at home. The only witness to that was his father, Santiago, who had moved in with him and Eveline after they built their house on a parcel of land outside Fuego town limits.

Santiago wasn't of sound enough mind to provide a statement. He'd been institutionalized shortly after the death of his wife and daughter seven years ago. Eveline had been working at Ollero Creek with Luella Decker on the day in question. She hadn't returned home until after dark.

"Can't you do something?" Ellis asked Kaya after Rutland requested Deputy Wyatt handcuff Wolfe Coldero and take him into holding.

"I wish I could," Kaya told him. "But if he can't provide an alibi for at least one of the murders, my hands are tied."

Facing Eveline was even more troubling. "How could you let this happen?" she asked, trailing Kaya through the department. "He trusts you. We all trusted you. You think he did this?"

"No," Kaya told her. "I don't think he's guilty, but Rutland believes he is and there's no physical or circumstantial evidence to fight that."

"He and I are getting married in five days," Eveline said. Her eyes were wet. "Kaya, *help him*. Please."

Kaya waited until the Eatons left and the reporters came and went. True Claymore showed up, demanding to know who they had in custody. He was only too delighted to hear it was Wolfe.

Kaya waited until Rutland left for the day before trailing Root back to the holding cells at the back of the building. "Unlock it," she requested when they arrived at Wolfe's.

Root opened the door for her and held it wide. She passed through. "You can close it," she told him. When he hesitated, she raised a brow.

Root gave a short nod. "Yes, sir."

She waited until he'd closed and locked the door before telling him, "Give us some room, please."

Root backed away at a respectful distance. Kaya crossed to the bench where Wolfe sat with his elbows on his knees and his hands together, his shoulders low.

She lowered next to him and stretched her legs. She leaned against the wall behind them, rubbing the spot on her thigh that hurt a little. Studying the strong line of Wolfe's back, she released a breath. "I knew she was seeing a bull rider. She never did say which one."

After a moment's pause, he eased back, too, until his shoulders touched the wall.

"I'm glad it was you," Kaya assured him. "I know you treated her right. She was in love with you." She swallowed because her voice grew thick. "She loved you, and you're being locked up for it."

He took her hand. The hold banked the grief and guilt, somewhat. She felt his anguish, too, in the quiet. "Did you know she was working at the resort?" she asked him.

He shook his head slightly.

"She stopped talking to me, once that started," she said. "Something happened out there. Something happened in the pages of her diary that were torn out. What happened, Wolfe?"

He lifted his shoulders. He had no more answers than she did and just as many questions, it seemed.

Kaya squeezed his hand before letting go. She raised herself to her feet. Passing a hand over her eyes, she made sure they were dry before turning back to him. "I'm sorry about the wedding." When he nodded, she turned away. Root beat her to the door and let her out. As it locked it back in place, Kaya met Wolfe's stare through the bars. "I'm not going to stop until the real killer is where you are."

Wolfe offered her a small smile before he lowered his head again, looking more than a little defeated.

EVELINE RODE OUT the next dawn to help tag the night's newborns. Everett was surprised to see her on the midmorning drive as well. She was quieter than usual, but she and her mare, Sienna Shade, did their job well.

It wasn't until they stopped near the mountains that she came for his knees. "Did you and Kaya have a pleasin' time the other night?" she asked.

He heard the bitterness behind the question and raised a brow at Ellis. Ellis shook his head and moved away to a safe distance, leaving Everett to confront his sister's anguish. "Cut the crap, Manhattan, and say what you're needing to say."

"The man I love is in jail," she stated. "Facing charges *again* for killing someone he didn't."

"He's got a bad habit of being in the wrong place at the wrong time," Everett observed.

She stuck her finger in his face. "*Don't.* Don't accuse him of this. You know he didn't do this."

"I do," he said and watched her fumble into stunned silence. "You tell me what I'm supposed to do about it."

"There needs to be a wedding," she told him. "I *need* there to be a wedding."

"You want me to bring Griff down to the sheriff's department so you can marry Coldero through the bars of his holding cell? I don't see it working out any other way by Saturday."

"Do you love me?" Eveline asked and her eyes filled with tears.

He made a face. "Ah, hell."

"I can't do this alone, Everett. We need to get him an alibi. It was his connection to Sawni Mescal that made them look in his direction to begin with. If we can provide him with an alibi for the date of her disappearance, the case against him won't hold."

"How do you expect us to do that?" he asked.

"By going through Dad's old records," she insisted. "He wrote everything down. He kept everything. You didn't get rid of any of his old file boxes, did you?"

"No." The basement was packed with them, floor to ceiling. "It'll be like finding a needle in a haystack. And that's assuming anything's there to begin with. Wolfe wasn't a member of the family then. Who's to say Dad kept anything on him?"

"Because he wanted to adopt Wolfe when he was found wandering the Edge as a boy," Eveline explained. "He let Santiago care for him only because..."

Everett looked away when her eyes turned implicating. "Because of me."

"I don't know why you rejected the idea of Wolfe coming to the Edge to live," Eveline said, "and it doesn't matter now. What matters is that if there's something in Dad's papers that can help, I need your help to find it."

"Fine," he agreed. "Come to the house for dinner. Bring Ellis and Luella. I'm not promising we'll find anything to clear him..."

"I know," she said quickly. "Thank you, Everett."

"Boss!"

Everett looked around to find Matteo riding from the north. He and Javier walked out to meet him.

Matteo slowed his mount. "Tombstone's been spotted."

"Where?" Everett asked.

"Near the mountain. Seems folks are still hanging around, trying to get a look at the place those bodies were found."

"They need to be headed off," Everett said.

"I'll do it," Javier offered.

"Take your gun," Everett advised. "And Spencer, for backup. Both of you be back to headquarters by dusk."

"Tombstone's back?" Eveline asked as she stood at his shoulder and watched the two men ride off. Fear wavered across the words.

"He never left," Everett said before turning his attention back to their herd.

EVERETT WAS SLEEP-STARVED when he entered the sheriff's department the following morning. He'd missed Paloma's fine-smelling breakfast spread with Eveline nipping at his heels to get a move on.

The two of them and Ellis, Luella and Paloma had gone through their father's boxes in the basement. Everett had stared at papers until they were blurry. Not everything had been filed or labeled but most boxes had had the year etched on them.

It had been difficult confronting his father's words, photographs, hand-drawn maps and keepsakes. Because of what had happened over the summer shortly after his death, Everett hadn't truly processed his grief. It had come in fits and starts, dragging itself out over months, not weeks.

It was one of the reasons he'd continued to sit in the therapist's office once a week in San Gabriel after he'd learned to manage the bulk of his PTSD symptoms.

He'd heard Hammond's voice again when he'd confronted his handwriting, his little notes about the day-to-day events that he'd scrawled on calendars… He'd drawn plans on paper napkins and ideas on notepads with conference labels. The low, slow sound of the man's words had filled Everett's head.

Ellis had found wedding photos of their parents hidden in one box. Eveline had uncovered newspaper clippings in another, most of them yellow and soft with age. There were ribbons and trophies that belonged to all three siblings. Hammond had kept the boutonniere he'd worn while escorting Eveline to homecoming court.

Kaya came out of her office when she heard her secretary greet him. "Everett," she greeted. "What are you doing here?"

He felt bleary and not a little clumsy. His better judgement had disappeared along with the possibility of sleep, so he leaned over and kissed her. "Sheriff."

She jumped a bit, then settled. "Good news?" she asked, gesturing to the folder he carried.

"Where's Watt?" he asked.

"Mr. Eaton."

Everett found the agent standing in the open door of the conference room. He raised what he had brought for him. "I'm here to spring my brother-in-law."

Rutland eyed the folder. "I'm afraid it's not going to be that simple."

"Why not?" Everett asked. "I can prove Coldero wasn't with Sawni Mescal or Bethany Merchant on the days of their disappearances."

"Is that right?" Rutland asked.

Everett opened the folder and pulled out a newspaper clipping. "This is from the day Sawni was taken. He was at the rodeo. He won, which is how he wound up in the *Fuego Daily News*. There's the date for you at the top. It says right here that it was an all-day event. I resented him for it, too. The events were lined up one after the other, which tied Coldero up from the early morning until well after dark when he took the final cup. There's his picture with it right there."

Rutland took the glasses from the front pocket of his jacket and placed them on the end of his nose. He assessed the clipping thoroughly.

Everett took out the second piece of paper. "This is my father's desk calendar from the month and year Bethany Merchant was taken. You can see his notation on the day she disappeared. What's it say right there?"

Rutland bent his head over the page. He tilted it to read the slanted, left-handed scrawl. "'Took Wolfe to auction. New bull bought and paid for. Stayed overnight in Santa Fe. Dinner and overnight at Renaissance Hotel.'"

"I recall that, too," Everett said, "as I wanted to be the one my father took to the auction. But he took Coldero. The man he wanted to be his foreman one day. He saw something in him. When he was gone, my father wanted me at the helm of Eaton Edge and Coldero as foreman. He trusted him. That's why I didn't need proof he didn't do what you're accusing him of. My father saw people for what they were. He saw Wolfe Coldero long before I could bring myself to do so."

Rutland took off the glasses. "That doesn't mean he didn't kill Higgins or this other woman."

"Wasn't that other woman killed close to forty years ago?" Everett asked. "I thought I heard that in the news. That's long before Coldero came to the Edge. As for Higgins, Coldero sent several text messages to my sister and Ellis. Ping his phone. He lives outside town limits. I guarantee there's no record of him being near the tower closest to Ol' Whalebones or the Edge. It'll be the one closer to his and Eveline's house."

Rutland cleared his throat. "I'll need to verify this."

"Before the end of the day," Everett demanded. "There's going to be a wedding at the Edge the day after tomorrow. I don't know if you've met my little sister, but she'll have my ass and yours if her groom is a no-show. You can thank me later for doing your job for you." Leaving Rutland with the folder, he passed Kaya on the way out. "You got a date for this thing?"

A spark of amusement entered her eyes. "I thought I was looking at him. I'll be the one in the black dress."

He winked and saw himself out.

EVERETT SWUNG THE double doors to Grady's Saloon open. The focus on the dance floor and jukebox shifted around to him and his companions. Activity slowed as the patrons came to a standstill.

"This way," he indicated, leading the way to the long line of the bar.

"You sure about this?" Ellis asked, close behind him.

"As a heart attack," Everett replied, locking eyes with the bartender.

Grady Morrison slapped his rag onto the counter. "You're not welcome here," he told Everett. "I told you that years ago. The brawl you started then resulted in over a grand in damages."

"Your memory's long, Grady." Everett had already reached into his pocket. He tossed a hundred dollar bill on the bar top. "How much for a chair?"

When Grady only stared at Franklin's face on the bill, Everett pulled another from his wallet. He flicked it onto the bar with the first. "How 'bout this, huh?"

Grady frowned at the money. Then he peeled it from

the water rings it had landed in and stuffed it in his back pocket. He set three glasses on the bar. "What's your pleasure, gentlemen?"

Everett took a seat, motioning for the others to do the same. "Whiskey, straight." He turned to look at the person who settled on the stool to his right. "That all right with you, Coldero?"

Wolfe jerked his chin in affirmation. He took the glass Grady passed across the bar. He lifted it to Everett.

Everett lifted his briefly, then drank.

Ellis tossed his whiskey back in one fell swoop. He released a breath at the burn and set his empty glass down, touching two fingers to the rim for a refill.

Grady hesitated, wary. "Who's driving tonight?"

"I know someone," Everett asserted. "Keep it coming, old-timer."

Grady grunted and fixed Ellis another drink.

Everett watched him walk away. "You think he missed me?"

Wolfe shook his head automatically.

Ellis chuckled.

Everett raised a brow and sipped. He ran his tongue over his teeth and looked around. "I fought you here that night," he remembered.

Wolfe nodded.

"What for?" Everett asked.

Wolfe thought about it. Then he lifted one large shoulder in answer.

"I don't remember, either." Everett screwed up his face. "I don't remember most of the reasons we fought as often as we did."

Wolfe tipped his glass up, swallowing the rest of his whiskey. He eyed the bottom of the glass and shook his head.

Everett shifted on his chair, uncomfortable. "I'm in a pickle. My sister is over the moon for you. And let's face it, if you were going kill anyone over the last twenty years, it would've been me. I've given you nothing but cause."

Wolfe and Ellis remained still and silent.

Everett finished his whiskey, too. "You better make her happy or I'll wipe you off the face of the earth."

Wolfe's mouth slid into a small smile. He signed.

"He says, 'It's done,'" Ellis translated. When Wolfe's hands moved again, he added, "'Thank you.'"

Everett ignored that. "I don't like surprises. Is there anything else I need to know before I let you become an official member of this family?"

Wolfe shook his head.

Everett tapped the counter, signaling to Grady that he was done. He paused when Wolfe started to sign again.

Ellis coughed in reaction. Then he began to laugh again.

"What'd he say?" Everett asked, suspicious.

Ellis cleared his throat. "He says that, come fall, we're both going to be uncles."

Everett stared at Ellis, then Wolfe and the wide grin on the latter's face. His large hand fit to Everett's shoulder and squeezed before he got up and moved to the door.

Ellis grabbed Everett's arm and shook him. "You did good, brother."

"Jesus," Everett muttered, shrugging him off. He straightened. "Actin' like I cured cancer or something."

When Ellis left with Wolfe, Everett stayed at the bar. Grady returned to take their glasses. Everett held on to his. "Another," he demanded.

Chapter Fourteen

The bride wore satin couture and carried a bouquet of desert flowers. Her elder brothers walked her down the aisle to the tune of Fleetwood Mac's "Songbird." Paloma Coldero served as Eveline's maid of honor, looking lovely in full-length chiffon and lace. The groom had been fitted for the occasion in head-to-toe black, including a new felt cowboy hat and snakeskin dress boots.

Eveline and Wolfe exchanged vows under a rustic awning that framed a stunning picture of Eaton Edge. The sun took its last gasp over the distant peak as he dipped her back for a long, satisfactory kiss to a raucous round of applause. They beamed at each other as they came up for air and the wedding party kicked into high gear.

Kaya spotted the security the Eatons had hired to block reporters and photographers—or anyone nefarious—from intruding on the pleasantries. *Smart move*, she thought, sipping champagne on the outskirts of the reception. The happy couple had chosen the wide flagstone patio of Eaton House for the party. Guests spilled down the steps into the yard, milling as far as the white barn with enchanting fairy lights trimming the eaves. She counted four guards, each wearing a spiffy black tuxedo and built like a bulldozer.

She watched the colors change in the sky. Dusk turned toward night. The hues had softened into lavender, gloaming blue and a soft touch of green in the horizon. The sound of the live band, boots slapping the dance floor and hands clapping split the quiet of the landscape with lively abandon.

“Why aren’t you dancing?”

Kaya looked around at her sister, Naleen. Older by two years, Naleen wore her long black hair to one side of her neck in a coiled side bun with a pretty, braided headband. She was several inches taller than Kaya. Her frame was curvy to Kaya’s muscly one and she wore a tea-length strapless party dress in navy. “You used to love to dance,” Naleen added, holding out her hand.

Kaya tipped the champagne glass to her sister’s fingers and watched her drink. “Why is Mom here?” she asked.

Naleen raised a fashionably full brow as she lowered the glass and handed it back. “She was Santiago’s nurse when he was transferred to the mental facility and stayed in touch with Paloma and Wolfe through the years.”

Kaya raised her chin. “Ah.”

“Is that why you’re hiding?”

“I’m not hiding,” Kaya said, but the words were lost in the echo chamber of the glass as she took another drink.

Naleen’s wide mouth curved. “If only the people of Fuego knew how their sheriff cowers at the sight of her four-foot-eleven mother.”

“I’m not hiding,” Kaya repeated because it sounded good and strong, and she wanted to mean it.

"You're going to have to speak to her," Naleen advised. "Preferably before she finds out you and Everett Eaton are—"

"What?" Kaya intercepted swiftly. "What do you know about Everett?"

"You're having some kind of fling with him and the whole town knows it," Naleen answered. She raised her hands. "No judgement. You and me—we've always had a type."

"What type?"

"The hard cowboy type," Naleen answered smoothly. "The long, tall, gritty kind of cowboy that gets under our skin and doesn't leave. Not until we've been bucked off."

"I don't know what you're talking about."

"Look who's in denial." Naleen sighed as the band slid into a slow song and the bride and groom took to the floor. "I keep thinking about Sawni. Do you think she'd be happy Wolfe moved on and found someone like Eveline?"

Kaya nodded. "If she's watching this, she's seen everything else. The way he and his family searched for her, the way he lost his stepmother and stepsister in the fire, the false accusations made against him, the time he did in jail because of it… After everything he's been through, he deserves a life with the woman he loves. Sawni would want nothing less."

Naleen thought about it. "She did want the best for people." Turning her focus back to Kaya, she added, "She wanted you to be happy, too. You have to know that's the reason she took the job at The RC Resort. So that you could continue with the rodeo."

Kaya shifted from one foot to the other and didn't meet her sister's stare. She watched the others dance. Grief and regret were close to the surface, still. She had thought there would be some resolution to them if Sawni was found. She'd been wrong. She still had to wrangle with them.

"How's your leg?" Naleen asked.

"It's better," Kaya said. "Still sore at times—especially on days I hike. But I think physical therapy is starting to pay off."

"Good. It's a damn fine wedding, isn't it?"

"They're a damn fine match," Kaya replied, happy to be moving on from the previous subjects. "Nova's got her summer job. Everett says she's a natural cowhand."

Naleen's wistful expression morphed into a fast frown as she found her daughter slow dancing with Lucas Barnes. "I keep telling myself she'll grow out of it—that she'll be burned out by the end of summer. But she's as stubborn as desert weather and just as determined. I'm afraid there's no fighting her nature. Now I know how Mom felt when you ran away to be a trick rider."

Kaya made a noise as she eyed the hand Lucas had low on Nova's waist. She raised the champagne glass to point it out. "Do you think those two are doing it?"

Naleen stiffened. "She wouldn't. She's only sixteen—practically a baby."

"You were sixteen when you lost it to Ryan MacKay," Kaya reminded her. "Then married him before you were eighteen because you got pregnant."

Naleen's jaw tightened. "That's not nice, Kaya."

"It's true," Kaya said. "I was sixteen when I lost it, too. To a cowboy with no more sense between his ears than Lucas over there. Are you sensing a pattern here? Altaha women lose their minds around silly cowboys. Nova's never struck me as a traditional sort, but Lucas's hand is well south of the mark."

"I'll be back," Naleen said, marching off to break up the festivities. Kaya grinned, dangling the champagne glass between two fingers. She hated to throw Nova at her mother's mercy, but Kaya had needed something—anything—to divert Naleen's attention from her.

She heard a growl near her ear and turned around.

Everett caught her by the waist, holding her at arm's length so that he could drink her with his eyes. "That ain't no uniform."

Kaya glanced down at the black dress she'd tried on and dismissed the night of their first date. "Even the sheriff's got to mix it up a little." She glanced over his fancy duds and was forced to take a bracing breath. "Anybody ever tell you you clean up good, cattle baron?"

He didn't take his eyes off her to examine the dark suit jacket with boot stitch that fit the long plains of his shoulders to perfection. Three dogs milled around his legs.

"Aren't you going to introduce me to your posse?" she asked.

He patted his thigh. The one that answered immediately sat at his silent motion to do so then stared, alert and sharp, waiting for the next command. It was an Australian cattle dog. "This is Boaz. She's the leader." As he passed a gentle hand between Boaz's ears, he peered at Kaya. "I have a weakness for strong females."

She smiled softly. He snapped, bringing one of the others around. "Sit," he said until the second cattle dog did so. "This is Boomer. He's four. He likes to herd, like Boaz, and he likes to play."

"Hello, Boomer," Kaya said when the dog's head tilted her way. His tongue lolled out, charming her, and she reached down to pet him.

"This other one's Bones," Everett said, snapping until Bones wound around to his front and sat on his feet. "He's still a pup."

Kaya felt her brow knit as she studied Bones more closely. "Um, Everett?"

"He's learning, still," Everett went on, rubbing Bones's scruff until the dog's left leg began to mill in circles. "His energy still overrides his decision-making. But he'll be a fine cattle dog in the future, like the others."

"Everett," she said again. When his gaze fixed to hers, she pointed to Bones. "You realize that's a coyote."

Everett quickly cupped Bones's ears under his hands. "He doesn't know that."

She rolled her eyes. "Come on."

"He's not all coyote," Everett explained. "He was three weeks old when I found him in the sagebrush. His mother had been killed and his fellow pups had been eaten, most likely by Tombstone. They were in his territory. I didn't think he'd make it."

"But he did," she considered, sizing Bones up. "Does he yip at the moon?"

"Sometimes," Everett said. He winked. "But then again, so do I."

She pressed her lips together to stop herself from laughing. "And how do I know you're not part coyote?"

He chuckled. "You don't, Sheriff Sweetheart."

She shook her head. In Apache myth, Coyote was often

depicted as either the villain or the savior. Kaya didn't think she could attribute either of those labels to Everett. After all they'd been through, she had a pretty good feeling he wasn't going to be the villain in her story.

As for *savior…* Kaya had done plenty of saving herself through the years. And Everett Eaton was hardly a knight in shining armor.

In some legends, it was Coyote who brought light to the world.

And Everett sure did light a fire in her.

When he stepped close again, easing her into his embrace, his eyes traced the seam of her lips and her cheekbones before meeting her assessing gaze. "You've got the night off."

"I do," she admitted. Her stomach clutched. His stare spread excitement in every vicinity.

He nodded. "I plan on making the most of it."

Her pulse rate doubled. They hadn't spent the night together since the evening after his arrest. Since, she'd been unable to ignore the fact that she no longer enjoyed going to bed alone.

"I'd like to dance with you, Kaya," he said. "I asked you once and you were hurting. Is your leg well enough to let me spin you around the dance floor a dozen times?"

He'd had her at the sound of her name. She slipped her hand into his outstretched one.

She'd knocked a full-grown man out with her fist once. But her hand felt small in Everett's. It even felt like it might belong there.

Naleen was right, she thought as her stomach fluttered. "Spin me," she said simply and followed his lead to the dance floor.

"ARE YOU BEHAVING YOURSELF?" Paloma hissed in his ear as the stars came blinking into existence.

Everett flinched. He thought he'd been alone at the buffet table. "Do I look like I'm stuffing crab legs down my pants?"

"I'm more worried about you spiking the punch bowl," she said with a lowered brow. "I heard your little liquor bottles clinking in your vest before the ceremony started."

"Somebody had to calm Coldero down," Everett noted. He picked up a carrot stick. "I've never seen a man sweat his bride showing up to the altar that much." He dragged the stick through the dip bowl and lifted it toward his mouth.

She knocked it out of his hand before he could shove it home. At his stunned look, she snapped, "Put it on a plate, *then* eat it. It's your sister's wedding. The least you can do is act civilized."

He took the plate she handed him and started to pile things on it, muttering, "Jesus God Almighty… I walked her down the aisle, didn't I? I handed her over to Coldero real nicely…"

"Because you know what's good for you," Paloma said, picking up a plate of her own. She used tongs to select a chicken leg from a platter. "The line goes to the left, Everett Templeton," she added when he tried to wind to the right.

"I want the chicken," he told her. When she refused to budge, he groaned. "I want the chicken, *please*."

She used the tongs again to select a breast from the platter. She set it neatly in the center of his plate. "There you are. Now keep the line moving."

"There's no one behind us," he griped. Before she could smack him again, he picked up the serving fork next to the carrots and herded more than necessary onto his plate.

"There's someone you have to meet."

"I don't want to talk to people. I want to dance." He grinned. "I'm taking Kaya onto the dance floor again, soon as I'm done." They had fallen into step together seamlessly. The crowd had split and made room as Everett had found out again how she could answer him move for move and even show him up.

"You should be fixing her a plate, too," Paloma suggested. "The way you two carry on out there, she's going to need it."

"She's already eaten," he replied. He caught Paloma's knowing look. "What?"

"I found a pair of black panties in the upstairs ficus."

He froze, trying hard to look innocent. "They're Eveline's."

"Eveline throws her panties around her and Wolfe's place now," she said, stalking him to the end of the buffet table.

"Luella's then."

"Luella and Ellis moved into the cabin behind the bunkhouse with the girls a month ago," she reminded him, keeping pace easily as he rounded the table to the other side.

He grabbed a roll quickly, fumbling it when it burned him. He caught it, flipped it onto his plate and searched for napkins.

They were behind her. He'd missed them. Cursing, he planted his feet. "I'm thirty-eight years old. I can do what I want with who I want in my own house."

"I'll take it from here, Ms. Coldero."

Paloma subsided, going so far as to smile at the woman who'd decided to intrude. "I warmed him up for you, Darcia. Everett, have you met Ms. Altaha?"

Everett glanced from one woman to the other. The new one had silver-tinged hair. She was less than five feet tall, in his estimation. But her set mouth could raise the hair on a dog's back. Her dark eyes bore into him. He could see her Native heritage in her pronounced cheekbones and her dark skin tone.

The words *It's a trap* flagged across the windscreen of his consciousness. "Altaha," he repeated. "As in…"

"Kaya and Naleen's mother," Paloma supplied helpfully. She smiled as she veered around him. Patting him on the lapel of his Western-cut jacket, she lowered her voice and muttered, "Stand up straight and take it like a man, *mijo*."

Everett cleared his throat as she cleared off, leaving him alone with Kaya's mother. He turned his head on his neck to ease the tension. "It's nice to meet you, ma'am."

She had a stare a mile wide, he discovered when she didn't break it. Everett started to itch around the collar.

"So," Darcia Altaha said, "you're the man who's currently screwing my daughter."

Everett nearly swallowed his tongue. "Ah…not currently. I mean, not right at this second." He cleared his throat louder this time when she only narrowed her eyes.

"I'm no stranger to my daughter's single behavior," Darcia informed him. "She sleeps with men. Sometimes she enjoys them. Sometimes she finds them lacking."

He tried to think of something safe to say and found a minefield instead. "Uh…"

"It seems you're one of the ones she enjoys," Darcia revealed. "You must be very impressive, Mr. Eaton."

"Well, I think—"

Her chin lowered. "You shouldn't finish that thought."

He nodded quickly. "You're right, ma'am. I shouldn't."

"Good man," she said approvingly. "Kaya seems to be enjoying you more than the others."

Everett kept his mouth studiously shut. He was sweating as much as Coldero had before the wedding. If this kept up, he was going to need a change of clothes.

"My youngest daughter, Mr. Eaton," Darcia continued, taking several slow strides toward him, "does not do what she is told. As a child, she was next to impossible."

He felt the beginnings of a treacherous smile warming his face. "Is that right?"

"Kaya is responsible for every gray hair on my head." Her eyes widened for emphasis. "Do you see my head, Mr. Eaton?"

His mouth opened, closed, opened again. "I…think it's very nice."

"It is *covered* in gray."

He thought quickly. "She has a unique effect on people."

"You like to delegate," Darcia said.

He lifted a shoulder. "Sure."

"You're the boss," she went on. "The 'chief,' I believe."

He shook his head. "It's just a title."

"Yes," Darcia granted, "but you are a man accustomed to giving orders and having them followed to the letter."

"Yes, ma'am."

She nodded. "So heed what I tell you. Kaya will not be told what to do. She will not be ordered. She will not follow where others lead. No one delegates to Kaya. She will leave your bed at all hours of the night to put herself in danger, all in the name of law and order. She won't change or be tamed. The moment you try, she will run. This you must know before getting in too deep with my daughter."

He waited for more. When it didn't come, he wet his throat. "Ms. Altaha…"

"You will call me Darcia."

"I will?" When she pursed her lips, he decided, "I will. You can call me Everett, if you like."

"Fine," she granted.

"Your daughter," he said carefully, "is the single most amazing woman I've ever met in my life."

Her arms laced over the front of the beaded, forest green bodice of her dress. "Go on."

"She's powerful," he stated. "Some people may feel threatened by that in a woman, but I find it extremely attractive. She's an exceptional police officer and a far better sheriff than that last one we had here in Fuego. As a friend, you should know she saved my life. As a companion, she's everything a man could want and more."

"Are you everything a woman could want, Everett?" she challenged.

"I hope so, Mrs…er, Darcia. What's more, I hope I'm everything Kaya wants because I'm hers."

He heard it the same time she did. He heard the confession ring with truth. He let out an unsteady breath. "Well. There it is."

Darcia's hand was cool as it twined around his wrist. "It's all right, Everett."

He looked at her, trying to fathom the satisfaction on her face. "How'd you do that?"

"Where do you think my daughter got her interrogation skills?" she asked. "Certainly not from her father."

He let out a breathless laugh. And kept laughing. He was still laughing when he spotted Kaya weaving fast through the crowd to get to them.

"Mom," she said. "Are you playing nice?"

"Of course I am," she said. She smiled at Everett. "If you'll excuse me, I have to go talk to my granddaughter's date."

Everett watched Darcia round the buffet table, still choking on laughter.

"Everett?" Kaya turned him to her. "Are you okay?"

He stopped laughing abruptly. "Your mother scares the hell out of me."

"She left you standing," Kaya considered with a shake of her head. "You must have made a good impression."

He needed a stiff drink. "How does a man survive any of you Altaha women?"

"I've yet to meet the man who does," she explained.

"Is that right?" he asked, measuring.

"Eat up, cattle baron," she said, raising herself to her toes. She brushed a kiss across his cheek. "You owe me a slow one."

I'm hers. He heard it again in his head. Caught between the urge to beeline for the open bar or to fall willingly into her arms like the besotted puppy he was, he trailed her to the dance floor, wishing he'd left the buffet well enough alone.

Chapter Fifteen

Kaya noticed Everett didn't say much after they saw Eveline and Wolfe off. Wolfe had been cleared to leave the country and would be on a plane with his new wife bound for the Caribbean in a matter of hours.

It wasn't until they were gone and the guests had slowly trickled out that Everett grabbed her by the hand and led her into the house.

He didn't say anything as he took off his jacket and toed off his boots upstairs. Well aware that Paloma and other family members were downstairs, she kept quiet, too, as he removed her dress and took her to bed.

The sex wasn't urgent, as it had been before. It felt like something else entirely—not quite soft but crystalline. His rough hands gentled. His strokes were sure but slow. He left the lights off and the windows open so that the desert breeze made the curtains restless and moon beams grazed the sheets.

She didn't realize until after they had both stilled, having rocked each other to climax, that he'd given her something finer than sex—something deeper and far more devastating.

He'd made love to her.

She lay awake thinking about it long after she was sure he

had dozed off. His back was to the window. Moonlight cast his profile into distinction but not his face. She could hear the restful sound of his lungs working. Under her hands, the muscles around his ribs swelled and released, swelled and released in long, languid pulls.

Hesitant, her touch tracked the ladder of his rib cage to his sternum. She felt the little round knot of scar tissue.

She cursed inwardly. He hadn't been touching her. He'd been touching her heart. He'd touched her soul, for crying out loud. He'd looked at her as he'd ushered her over every peak—not watchful and thirsty like last time…

He'd looked at her as if *she'd* brought light to the world.

Everything downstairs had quieted down. In the distance, she could hear coyotes yip and cows low. If she listened closely enough, she could hear the world turn.

He'd split her world in two. He'd broken it like an egg. There was no cleaning up what he'd untapped.

She was done for. It wasn't a comfortable thought. Yet it was a fact and she had to find some way to live with it.

She was going to have to find a way to cope with the strong possibility that she was in love with him.

"What have you done, cattle baron?" she whispered even as she raised her hand into the hair on the back of his head and caressed. She found her lips nestling against the underside of his jaw.

The crack rang out, its report loud. A dog started to howl a split second before the raised pane of the window shattered. Even as Everett jerked awake, Kaya closed her arms around him and rolled as the second shot echoed.

The bullet sang into the wall over their heads as they hit the floor with a jolting thud. "Get down!" she shouted, her hand locked on a hunk of his hair, forcing his head low to the ground. "Stay down!"

The third shot hit the bed. She heard the impact and badly wished for her weapon. Looking around, she saw her beaded handbag where she'd dropped it. Her dress pooled over it.

"Stay," she instructed as she shifted away.

"Where are you going?" he asked, then cursed again as another shot shattered what remained of the glass pane.

"Do as I say, Everett!" She shimmied across the floor, grabbed the bag and took out her phone. She dialed and counted the rings before dispatch picked up. "This is Sheriff Altaha. Shots fired," she reported. "I repeat—shots fired at Eaton Edge. The main house is under fire. Send all available units to this location." She left the line open as she extracted her gun. She found the clip, inserted it in the empty chamber. Using her thumb, she removed the catch and crawled toward the far window.

"Kaya?"

"Stay," she ordered, easing her back against the wall. She stayed out of the slant of light that revealed patterns in the wood flooring. Peering out into the yard, she kept her head clear, in the shadows, both hands gripping her weapon. She worked to slow her breathing, hoping her pulse rate would follow. It raced, walloping her breastbone. Adrenaline surged through her.

She could hear Everett moving around the bed. Knowing he'd left cover did nothing to calm her. Before she could chastise him, another shot rang out, hitting the windows of the room next door to theirs. "Where are the girls?" she asked. "Isla and Ingrid. Where do they sleep?"

"Ellis's house—just over the hill," came his tense answer. He was closer now. "It's Paloma I'm worried about."

She winced as more shots rang out. "There are two shooters," she determined.

"Yeah," he said, listening. "Around the stables."

"Up high," she said. "Is there roof access in the stables?"

"Through Paloma's quarters." Everett made a noise in his throat when the shooting didn't stop. "Kaya. I need to get to her."

"You need to stay where you are," she said.

"The hands. They're all going to come running. Ellis, too. We can't wait for backup. We need to get out there and stop this before my people are killed."

"I don't have visibility," she admitted. "Keep your head down and hand me my dress."

WHAT WAS WORSE than walking into a firefight was knowing that Kaya was, too. By the time they made themselves decent and had retrieved his weapon from the safe on the first floor, he realized he was going to have to let her leave the cover of the house.

Paloma greeted them at the door. She fell into Everett's arms.

He smelled her blood before he raised his hand to the one on top of her head. His fingers came away wet and warm. "Those sons of bitches," he hissed, helping her to a seated position on the floor.

"It's not bad," Paloma moaned. "They didn't shoot me. They just knocked me out."

"Put pressure on the wound," Kaya said, handing him a handkerchief.

He covered the gash and pressed. When Paloma gasped, he felt his blood run cold. "I'll kill 'em."

The gunfire hadn't let up. They were hitting the kitchen windows now.

"You go out there," Paloma said, "you're as good as dead. You can't put me through that, *mijo*."

"I'll come back," he promised.

"They've probably got night vision goggles," Kaya deduced as they left through the front of the house. "It's how they knew we were in the room upstairs."

"I shouldn't have left the window open," he realized. As they neared the corner of the house, both gripping their weapons in a two-handed hold, they tensed at the sound of running.

Kaya held up a hand and motioned him back against the wall. They waited a beat, listening.

The sound of a high-pitched whinny split the night a split second before a high-strung colt bolted past in a flurry of hooves. Another followed it at breakneck speed.

"They let the horses out," he growled.

She inched toward the corner, her weapon high. "I need backup to get here. There's light enough to see the roof of the stables, but without cover..."

"I need to get to the barn," he said. At the turn of her head, he went on. "I have to make sure the cattle are secure. Never mind the horses. If they release the herd and open the gates..."

She nodded away the rest. "You go that way. I'll look for a shot."

He gripped her shoulder. It was bare but for the single black strap of her dress. "You be careful, Sheriff Sweetheart."

"You, too," she said before she darted around the side of the house. Everett took off at a run, keeping to the shadows. He ran through the small grove of evenly spaced trees that produced fruit in summer. Grateful for their spring foliage and the cover it provided, he ran hell for leather toward the shape of the barn, hoping his long legs and speed would serve him well.

Someone ran into him headlong. "Hands up!" he yelled.

"It's me," Ellis reported. "What the hell's going on? Who's shooting?"

"Luella. The girls. Are they all right?"

"They're safe," Ellis assured him. "I had her take them into the cellar and lock the door from the inside."

"We need to check the barn," Everett barked. He could hear sirens in the distance. They were closing in. The gunfire still hadn't let up. He thought of Kaya and wanted to scream. "They let the horses go."

"I hear them," Ellis told him. "I can go around the cabins, get farther out of range and make my way around. The men should be over that way, too. They'll help."

"Don't do anything stupid," Everett said, even as he moved in the direction of the stables.

"Hang on, where're you going?" Ellis called after him.

"Kaya's out there," Everett said, pointing. "I gotta—"

Ellis waved off the rest. "Go, then! Go!"

Everett bolted, running toward gunfire. The lights of police vehicles lit the night as he broke free of the trees and crouched low, closing the distance between the grove and the house.

There were holes in the tents on the patio. They flapped, loose, and snapped in the breeze. He followed what he hoped was Kaya's path from table to table. He ducked underneath the empty buffet table. His gaze seized on the front of the house. It gaped at the windows. There was little glass left for the moonlight to bounce off.

There was fear riding underneath the beat of his blood. But anger swelled beneath it, all but incinerating. His father's house, his family's land…his woman.

Pressing his lips together, he eyed the distance between him and the open gate. There was nothing but the night between him and the truck parked on the other side of it.

He took a long, deep breath before taking off like a runner at the starting gun.

KAYA COULD SMELL ANIMAL. And not just the horses.

She found a decent position behind the water trough and near the fence in the first corral. She kept herself still as she searched the roofline. She ducked back down after counting one, two shapes against the hard slant of moonlight.

Bastards had chosen a three-quarter moon to do their bidding.

Breathing carefully, she eased her weapon around the side of the trough. She peered down the length of the barrel, aiming for the first figure…

The sound of a snort reached her ears. Her finger froze on the trigger as the hairs on the back of her neck stood on end.

She looked over her shoulder.

The bull was huge. Its head was low. She saw the glint of its horns. It struck one hoof against the ground. Dust rose in a plume.

It lowed at the sound of gunfire and shifted, restless. More scared and uncertain than anything, it was lost among the maze of open gates and fences. But Kaya knew she was the only threat it had been able to pick apart from the dark landscape.

Caught between the trough and the open corral, she had nothing but her Glock to stop it if it charged.

It pawed the ground again, bellowing.

"Walk away, big boy," she coaxed under her breath as she raised the weapon. "Just walk away..." She felt a bead of sweat roll from her hairline to her cheek.

A shout split the night. "Hey!" And another, longer. "Heeeeeey!"

Kaya and the bull looked out to pasture and saw the tall figure with arms spread. "No," she moaned. Then louder, "No, no!"

The bull charged Everett. Kaya didn't hesitate. Knowing the gunmen had heard the shout and had made Everett, she raised the gun over the edge of the trough, sighted and squeezed off a round, then another.

She saw the gunman crumple. The second ducked out of sight.

Lowering her head once more, she searched the corral for Everett and the bull. When she saw nothing but grass waving in the wind, she tried not to panic. Shouts of "Police!" and "Drop your weapons!" reached her. She wished for a radio so that she could communicate with her deputies.

Scanning the roofline, she couldn't locate the second figure.

He was on the move.

The stable doors yawned wide. She stood and propelled herself toward the opening.

A man's silhouette appeared in the doorway. She took him down on a running leap at the knees.

A shot went off from his gun before he clattered to the floor.

The man reached for his weapon, but she kicked it out of reach. She grappled with him, going right up against his cloud of day-old sweat. He was big, strong and fought well.

She was a hair quicker. She punched him in the teeth. She hit him harder in the solar plexus. The fist to the groin made him wither.

"Turn over," she instructed. "Put your hands behind your back. Do it!"

When Deputy Wyatt arrived with the cuffs, she had her hands locked around the suspect's wrists. "Second shooter's on the roof," she told him, taking the cuffs he removed from his belt. She secured the attacker's hands behind his back.

"On it," he said. Using a flashlight, he moved into the dark stables, radioing for Root to follow.

"Don't move," she told the gunman, patting his pockets. She found more ammo clips and a flashlight but no wallet or identification.

"Kaya."

She glanced up and found Everett. After picking up the shooter's weapon and unloading it, she stood. "You're okay."

His eyes raced over her. "You?"

"I'm all right," she said. "The others?"

"Ellis," he said in answer.

"He's down?" she asked, alarmed.

He shook his head. "He and the hands are securing the barn."

Relief washed over her. She took a moment to run her

gaze across his face and torso a few times. He was dirty and mussed, his hair not at all neat without his hat. She wanted to shove him back a step with both hands. She wanted to gather him to her and hold on until all the little fears…all the what-might-have-beens ceased to exist. “Stupid,” she pushed out because she couldn’t stop seeing him out in the open waving his hands and shouting like an idiot. It had made her choke with fear. “You were *so stupid*, Everett.”

His brows came together. He took a step toward her.

Deputy Root arrived. “Wyatt has the second gunman in custody,” he reported, panting from running. “Says he’s got an ID.”

“Paloma Coldero is injured inside the house,” Kaya stated. “We need to get her checked out.”

“An officer’s with her now,” Root informed them. “She’s conscious. They called for a bus, just to be sure.”

She helped the suspect to his feet. He had high shoulders and a long face. “You’re under arrest. Might as well tell us who you are.”

“Fat chance,” he grunted, then spit on the ground at her feet.

When Everett whipped forward, Root stopped him. “Take it easy,” the deputy cautioned.

“I know you,” Everett said, pointing at the gunman. “I’ve seen you—out at The RC Resort. You work security for True Claymore.”

Kaya pulled on the attacker’s arm until he faced the moon. Root helped by shining a light in his eyes. Her lips parted. Everett was right. She’d seen the man with the mayor, too.

He was one of the goons who had replaced her roadside attacker from years ago.

"He sent you here, didn't he?" Everett asked, struggling against Root's restraining arm. "This is payback for what I did to his car."

"Don't know what you're talking about," the shooter grunted, lowering his head and closing his eyes because the light in them was too much.

Kaya turned to look back at the house. True Claymore wouldn't be reckless enough to order his men to do something as drastic as this, would he?

Or had the good mayor reached the end of his rope?

Chapter Sixteen

The long drive to The RC Resort might have been scenic if not for the sick taste on Kaya's tongue. It was always with her when she made the trip to Claymore's homestead.

Next to her, Agent Rutland shrugged out of his sport coat and checked the weapon holstered on his belt. "What's the plan, Sheriff?"

She frowned as the ranch house came into view. It was resplendent against a barren desert backdrop. "You're letting my department take the lead on this?"

"As it was you Claymore's hired men nearly shot through an open window, that's fair, I'd say."

Kaya swallowed, tasted bile and lowered her head so the brim of her hat covered whatever emotions were riding high in her eyes. If she was emotional, she couldn't be clearheaded. And she needed to be clearheaded.

She'd sworn she would be the one to lock True Claymore up. She had evidence—enough that she'd been able to secure a warrant. She had the gunmen's confessions. They'd resisted questioning at first, but Rutland had looked at their banking records. A recent bonus of ten grand a piece from their employer had seemed timely.

Everett and Ellis had found the gunmen's horses a half mile away from the barn while rounding up the misplaced horses and few escaped cattle. Their saddlebags had been packed enough for a week's sojourn.

If Kaya and her team hadn't apprehended them, they would be in the wind at this point.

A breath filtered slowly through her nose as she slowed to make the turn under the arch welcoming them to The RC Resort & Spa. "He had to have known the shooting would lead back to him sooner than later. He'll be ready."

"You think he'll make a stand?" Rutland asked cautiously as she eased the sheriff's all-terrain vehicle to a stop in the parking lot. There were a dozen other cars.

Kaya frowned at the shuttle van. It wasn't the same model Claymore's goons had removed her in years ago. But it sickened her to see it, nonetheless. She unbuckled her seat belt and scanned the entrance to the house. "His wife's a lawyer. She normally talks him out of trouble. My bet is he'll hide behind her. If he's desperate enough to fight..." She heard more than saw the second police vehicle ease to a stop behind hers. "...we'll take him down."

"Sheriff," Rutland said before she could open the door.

She glanced. The lines of his face gave her pause.

He inclined his head. "We don't have proof he had anything to do with those bodies on the mountain."

"Not yet," she added.

"Be careful," he advised. "Don't make this personal. If he killed your friend, Mescal, we'll dig deeper. We'll find the truth."

How did she tell him that the anger she felt—the almost blind rage—wasn't about Sawni, for once? It was about Everett.

She hadn't been alone in the crosshairs. Everett's body had been between the open window and her. She'd learned not to think too long about what might have been if the gunmen hadn't missed that first shot.

The texture of the bullet wound on his sternum came to her clearly, as if she were touching it now. She opened the door to the vehicle. The taste in her mouth now burned in her throat. She planted her hand on her belt and waited for Root and Wyatt to join them. "We're here to bring in the mayor," she reminded them. "If you have any problem with that, I'd advise you to wait outside."

"We're with you, Sheriff," Wyatt vowed. To his right, Root nodded.

She scanned them and felt a swell of pride. As a deputy herself, she'd learned to work with them and trust them. As one of the people responsible for Sheriff Jones's fall from grace, she hadn't thought she'd earn their loyalty as sheriff—not right away.

They'd proven their loyalty a dozen times over the last few weeks. They were the best of men. "Follow my lead," she said quietly before heading them and Rutland to the big front doors. She ignored the old-fashioned bellpull that acted as doorbell and knocked in a series of raps. "Sheriff's department," she called clearly. When no one answered, she rapped again.

The sound of the latch grinding put Kaya on alert. She forced herself to relax, outwardly. As the door parted from the jamb, she felt Root tense next to her.

The round face of a housekeeper greeted them, her face riddled with confusion. "*Hola?*" she said haltingly.

Kaya responded in Spanish. "*Buen día*. We're looking for True Claymore. *Está él en casa*?"

She shook her head quickly. "*No, no está aquí*."

Kaya peered over the housekeeper's shoulder. There was no one in the foyer that she could discern. "Do you know where he is?"

The housekeeper hesitated for a brief second before shaking her head. "No."

Kaya scrutinized her. She looked worried. "What about Annette Claymore? Is she home?"

The woman bit her lip. She glanced over her shoulder, then shook her head.

Rutland shifted forward slightly. "We have a warrant. Open the door, ma'am, so we can search the premises."

At the housekeeper's knitted brow, Kaya quickly translated. Still, the woman didn't open. "*Por favor*," Kaya added. *Don't protect them. It's not worth it.*

Slowly, the housekeeper gave in. The door opened and she stepped back. Kaya swept in. She nodded to the left and Wyatt went to search the dining room and kitchen. With a motion, she sent Root to do the same in the common area and spa rooms.

"What's back there?" Rutland asked, approaching the back of the house.

"Office," she said grimly. Guests weren't allowed in that part of the house. But she'd gone there anyway once, looking for evidence linking the Claymores to Sawni's disappearance…

"I'll look there," Rutland said.

"I'll sweep the upstairs." She moved in that direction.

At the landing, she began checking doors. The guests that

had checked in were out riding or walking the nearby nature trail or shopping in town. The rooms were empty. She located True and Annette's master suite. The fur rugs and grand four-poster bed put her ill at ease. Drawers on the bureau were open. The closet, too, was open with clothes on the floor. There was no sign of a struggle. The bathroom counter was empty.

Where were the creams? The soaps? The lotions?

Kaya frowned as she traced her steps back into the bedroom, across the bear rug. Glass doors opened onto an expansive balcony.

Her radio chirped as she unlatched them. "Sheriff?"

She parted the radio from her belt and brought it to her mouth. "Go ahead."

Rutland answered. "Office has been swept. The desk and file cabinet are empty. The safe is open. There's nothing left."

"He knew we were coming," she replied. From the balcony, she could see the Claymore spread. The little chapel off to the left. The barn used for weddings and dances. Stables to the right.

She could see Root striding off to search the latter. "Who tipped them off?" It was no secret the Claymores had friends in high places. Could it have been the judge? Worse, someone in Kaya's office? "We need to put out a BOLO on True Claymore. It looks like Annette may have left with him."

Root's voice carried through the channel. "Sheriff, you want to get down to the stables."

"Did you find something?" she asked, hurrying back through the parted glass doors.

"The mayor's horse is missing."

She pushed herself forward, leaving the suite. "His horse?"

"The groom said he left on horseback before daybreak," Root replied. "He said he didn't pack light."

"Damn," she uttered, breaking into a run on the stairs.

THE MANHUNT FOR True Claymore was the biggest mounted search in Fuego County in five years. But then, it wasn't every day a mayor went missing.

Everett pulled back on the reins, urging Crazy Alice into a walk. "Whoa, girl," he murmured. "Whoa." He patted her neck before swinging to the ground. They'd been out since first light, searching the area north from the Edge to The RC Resort.

Most likely, Claymore would have headed east and there were a dozen or more riders searching the state park area for signs of the man and his horse.

Everett and his team had been mobilized in the southwest quarter of the search area. The border overlapped Eaton territory. His men were spread over the hilly, mountainous region that circled Ol' Whalebones.

Everett led Crazy Alice to the edge of the river. It was shallow at the foot of Mount Elder. As his horse drank, Everett took his canteen off his belt and did the same. The sun had been hot on his back and he'd found no indication that Claymore and his mount had come this way.

He'd been disappointed when Kaya had placed him in charge of the lower region. She knew how much he wanted Claymore's hide. Being the one to find him would have been more than satisfying.

But he was still raw enough—still furious enough—to hurt the mayor for his part in the Eaton House attack. Paloma was still in the hospital. The doctors had assured him it was just for observation purposes, but Everett's gut twisted at the implications. Eveline had come back early to sit by her bedside with Luella. Wolfe had joined the search. He'd been assigned to the team in the northeast quadrant, likely due to his superior tracking skills. And he was levelheaded enough that he wouldn't throttle Claymore when he found him.

No. Wolfe would bring him in nice and easy. Everett twisted the lid back on the canteen and sniffed, scanning the sky. No birds of prey circled. A hawk kited high on a draft, peering beadily at him.

Crazy Alice lifted her head. She turned it downwind and stilled. Her ribs lifted as she took as exaggerated breath, smelling.

Everett heard her tail swish. Her head arched high and she sidestepped toward him. He laid his hand on her withers. "What is it, girl?" he whispered, stroking in soothing circles. Her breath had quickened. He could feel the tension in her muscles. "What do you smell?"

Sounds carried in valleys. Everett strained to hear over the burbling of the river on the rocks. He heard the chirp of a bird. Then whistling.

The fine hairs on the back of his arms rose. Just like that, his horse's tension was his own. He locked his legs to keep from sidestepping, too. Under the brim of his hat, he searched the slopes of Mount Elder, scanning the sagebrush and boulders.

An eerie scream broke the quiet. It reverberated off the cliffs. Crazy Alice jumped and whinnied.

He grabbed the reins. "Easy, girl," he said, trying to stay calm. His rifle was in the sheath on her saddle. His boots skimmed across the ground as she dragged him with her in retreat. “Easy, girl. Easy.”

Her head bobbed. She jerked the reins, but she stilled long enough for him to remove his weapon.

Common sense told him to head in the opposite direction, farther upriver where Claymore lands bisected the Edge. That was where Crazy Alice would flee. She knew as well as Everett they were in the heart of Tombstone’s territory.

He clambered up rockfall, trying to reach high ground. He found a position in the shadow of a ledge. The valley spread out beneath him. He didn’t need his binoculars to see the lion or its prey.

The horse was down. It lay on its side near the point where rock met river. If it had made it to water, it had died shortly after. There was a pool of blood under its head but no discernable tears in its flank.

The big cat had positioned itself on the cliff on the other side of the water. It yowled and paced, restless. Everett reached into the flap of his shirt and lifted his binoculars. Close up, he saw the lean body lines and the grimacing face with one eye missing.

Everett forced himself to take a moment. Sweat ran from his hairline. He inhaled for a full four seconds. Then he pushed it out, letting his lungs empty. Tombstone was not the harbinger of death and despair Everett associated him with. He was a predator with greater longevity or luck than others in the wild. Sighting him wasn’t detrimental to Everett’s family, as he’d feared in the past.

That was what common sense said. His stomach cramped, however. The last time he’d seen Tombstone this close—this clearly—his mother and stepsister had come to a horrible end. In some twisted way, Everett had felt responsible.

If he hadn't volunteered to go into Tombstone's territory that day to check the Wapusa's swollen banks after a week's rain and flooding, a part of him was convinced there wouldn't have been a fire across town at Coldero Ridge and his mother and half sister would still be alive.

He hadn't been close to his mother, Josephine. They hadn't even been on speaking terms when she died. But she was his mother, and that little girl he'd barely known, Angel, still haunted his dreams.

He had to slow down his exhalations until they were twice as long as his inhales, a technique he'd learned in therapy over the last year. He did this until his heart no longer felt like a racing hare. It helped to visualize himself calm. He dropped his shoulders. He couldn't close his eyes to imagine his body relaxing but he worked to forge that mental picture nonetheless and felt his focus sharpening.

No doubt Tombstone would smell his fear over the dead horse if Everett didn't get it well enough in hand.

He changed focus, shifting his view to the horse again. Through the binoculars, he saw no saddle or bags, but the description matched that of True Claymore's mount—the one he'd escaped with in the early hours of yesterday morning.

Everett lowered the binocs to take the radio from his belt. It was slippery in his hold. Mashing down the call button, he said quietly, "This is team three leader. Sheriff, do you copy?"

It took a moment for static to hiss, then he heard Kaya's voice. It steadied him. "Go ahead, team three."

"I've got a dead horse at the base of Mount Elder where it meets the river. Over."

Tombstone's yowling filled the radio silence before Kaya answered back. "Recently deceased?"

"Affirmative," he replied. "Tombstone got here first, but something's holding him up. He won't approach."

"Are you safe?"

He heard the thread of discord in her voice and lifted the radio to his mouth again. "I'm hiding out across the valley. He doesn't know I'm here."

"Hold your position," she told him. "I'll be there in twenty. Any sign of the suspect?"

"Negative," Everett said, searching the valley again. "If it is his horse, he took the saddle and bags."

"Copy. Everett?"

"Yeah?" he said, knowing this was an open channel.

"Shoot if you have to."

It sounded better than any profession of love he'd ever heard. "I'll see you in twenty, Sheriff. Over."

Everett secured the radio, checked his rifle and hunkered down to wait.

TOMBSTONE'S FRENZIED PACING STOPPED. He leaped from the ledge and down a series of boulders, head low, body tensed, picking up speed.

Everett braced himself as the cougar charged the corpse.

A shot rang out. Between the cliff walls, it was deafening. The lion doubled back, screaming its displeasure.

Another gunshot followed, then a third.

Tombstone retreated, disappearing in the bend of cliff walls and river rocks in full flight.

Everett stayed where he was, keeping his head down. He had another ten minutes before Kaya's arrival.

Someone was protecting the horse's body.

If it was indeed Claymore's horse…

Everett used the rifle's scope to comb every inch of the valley below.

He didn't spot the shooter. But he had no line of sight directly beneath his position where an outcropping offered a respite from the sun.

Cautiously, he straightened slowly to standing. He kept his rifle up, his finger near the trigger as he crept along the slope. He veered around the rockfall. Any loose rock would tumble and alert the shooter to his presence. On firmer ground, he made his way down.

The horse's eyes were locked in a vacant stare. They had gone cloudy. There was a gunshot wound on its crown. Everett scanned its legs and saw the break in the back left. He could smell the decay. With the sun beating down on it and the blood drying, he estimated the horse's time of death to have been sometime in the night.

The gunman's position was right underneath him. Everett inched forward, easing to ground level out of the cave's line of sight. He pressed his back to the mountain, gripping the rifle in hands that were steadier now that Tombstone had retreated. He swallowed once before calling out. "How's it going, Claymore?"

A pause. Then, "Goddamn it, Eaton."

"Toss out your weapon where I can see it," Everett advised. "Don't make me come in there. I want you to walk out. Nice and easy."

"That'd be a fine thing." True's voice was tight. "But I'm

not walking anywhere. Goliath broke my damn leg when he fell on it."

Everett's brows lifted under his hatband. "What about Annette? Is she injured?"

"What are you talking about?" True barked. "Annette's not with me."

"Don't lie to me, True," Everett growled.

"I'm telling the truth. Last I saw her, she was screaming at me to man up, stay at the resort where she could protect me. Woman never understood anything. When you're licked, you're licked. That's what my daddy used to say. He left, too. When the Feds came to get him for tax evasion, he made his exodus. He disappeared on horseback. His mount wandered back to us a week later. Nobody ever found any sign of him. Authorities told me he was as good as dead, but he was as hard as iron by that point. Indestructible. He's living on some beach in Mexico to this day."

True was rambling. Everett's frown deepened. "Your weapon. Throw it out where I can see it."

"Ah, hell," True muttered. "What have I got to lose?"

Everett heard the rifle bolt as it unlocked. The cartridges clinked as True emptied the chamber. The slow repetition of the bolt clicking assured Everett that the man was checking the chamber to ensure it was empty. The gold cartridges flashed in the sunlight as he threw them onto the rocks of the riverbed where they bounced and laid still. The rifle followed with a clatter.

Everett eased away from the wall. "Show me your hands," he directed as he swung into the opening, muzzle forward.

True raised his palms obediently. They were empty.

Everett scanned him, kicking the rifle farther from the low

opening of the cave. Everett bent over slightly and watched True wave insolently as he sagged against a boulder. His legs splayed in front of him. The left turned outward.

Everett narrowed his eyes. "You got yourself in a state."

"You don't say," True remarked.

"That there's a compound fracture," Everett said. "Must be in a lot of pain."

True's face was flushed like a beet. His breathing wasn't right. It was rapid and ragged. Still, he tilted his head and scanned Everett. "I thought you'd be happier."

"I'd have been happy to find you on your feet."

"You'd have preferred *The Good, the Bad and the Ugly* with me standing on one side of the street and you on the other," True said. He let out a wheezing laugh. "You and my old man have a lot in common. He used to tell me he shot a man in Reno. He said Johnny Cash wrote that song about him. 'Just to watch him die,' he would sing when he'd had too much."

"Why did you flee south?" Everett asked. "That was stupid."

"Was it?" True asked, squinting. "I thought everybody'd be looking in the other direction. State lands. Or farther. Jicarilla territory. Nobody'd expect me to go near that mountain over there."

Everett knew what mountain he was talking about. "Did you kill the boy and those women?"

"You'd like that, wouldn't you?"

"I'd like to see you drawn and quartered after what those men did to Paloma and Eaton House," Everett told him.

"Hey, at least my guys let you and the sheriff finish first," True said. "I wouldn't have been so generous. They're the superstitious sort—assume it's bad luck to interrupt a man while he's laying his pipe."

The muscles in Everett's jaw ground against bone. He saw the horse's saddle propped behind True. He saw the saddlebags. Despite the agony the mayor was in, if True kept running his mouth, Everett was liable to get trigger-happy.

Where are you, Kaya?

"You want to kill me," True guessed. "Take your shot."

Everett found his finger inside the trigger guard. He pressed his lips together. "I won't be the one who puts you out of your misery," he muttered through his teeth.

"Don't be washed up like your old man," True barked at him. "Come on, Eaton. Shoot me!"

"No," Everett barked back. An eye for an eye was fine. He believed in such things. But before True had been his enemy, he'd been Kaya's.

He wouldn't be the one to kill Kaya's justice. He couldn't.

The sounds of horses reached his ears. He looked around and saw Ghost slowing to cross the river. He and Kaya were leading Crazy Alice on a lead rope.

"Did you lose this?" she called as the horses' legs splashed across the Wapusa.

"I got him," Everett said and watched her shoulders go high.

Kaya nickered to Ghost, bringing him to a stop on the shore. She dismounted. "Tombstone?"

"He ran off," Everett told her. "I got *him*."

She closed the distance. Peering into the cave, she stilled.

True grimaced at her. "Howdy, Sheriff."

She didn't breathe. Everett fought the urge to touch her. "What do you want to do?"

Her gaze crawled back to his. “You didn’t kill him.”

He ignored the surprise.

Her lips seamed and for a brief flash her dark eyes deepened.

He eyed her mouth. “He’s yours.”

She blinked several times. “I need to call the chopper. He needs treatment. I have a first aid kit on my saddle…”

He lowered the rifle. “I’ll get it.”

She grabbed him as he started moving. “Everett,” she whispered. When he stopped, she said, “Thank you.”

“Later,” he promised then moved off to retrieve her kit.

Chapter Seventeen

With True Claymore in the hospital, Rutland and Kaya were unable to question him until he was out of sedation.

Annette Claymore hadn't been seen in over twenty-four hours. Part of her wardrobe had been removed from the master suite closet at The RC Resort. Her suitcase was missing as well as much of her jewelry.

Other than several thousand dollars in cash, they hadn't found the remaining contents of the office safe on True Claymore or in his saddlebags. Their housekeeper had reported that she had seen stacks of cash in the safe while cleaning.

Annette had taken her own exodus. Hers didn't have anything to do with Western glory, like True's. Kaya had a feeling her idea of escape was far more comfortable than riding off into the sunset.

"She doesn't have family in Fuego," Kaya explained to Rutland as she parked in front of Huck Claymore's house. "She's from Colorado and still has family there. But she's smart. She knows better than to go to the first place any investigator would look."

"If that tracks," Rutland said as they alighted from her sheriff's vehicle, "why would she come here?"

"She and Huck are close, from what I understand," Kaya said, leading the way to the pretty two-story house on Fourth Street where the reverend had resided since taking up the position in the church two blocks away. "He may know something."

Rutland knocked over a small, stone statuette of a praying angel on her knees. He cursed and stopped to right it, then continued to the door.

Kaya's knees locked. All she could see was the angel and the others in the garden of various sizes and expressions on their knees.

On her knees.

Sawni had died on her knees. So had Bethany. Miller Higgins, too, and the oldest woman who had yet to be identified.

She fought a shiver. Hearing Rutland's knock on the door, she moved to his side.

"You all right, Sheriff?" Rutland asked, brows gathered together.

"Fine," she said with a shake of her head. "Just…odd feeling, is all."

The door opened before he could respond. Huck Claymore appeared, a look of vague surprise on his face. "Sheriff Altaha," he greeted, buttoning the cuff of his plain, white collared shirt. It was wrinkled around the shoulders, Kaya noticed. She'd never seen him anything but perfectly pressed. Come to think of it, she'd never seen him outside his robes or his pressed suit. The shirt collar was open at his throat, as if he'd just started dressing. It was five o'clock in the afternoon. "What can I do for you?"

"I'm sorry to bother you, reverend," Kaya said evenly. "I'm sure you've heard about your brother."

He nodded quickly. "Yes. Most unfortunate."

"Unfortunate that he's injured?" Rutland questioned. "Or unfortunate that he was found?"

The reverend peered at him innocently. "Unfortunate that he felt it necessary to flee in the first place instead of taking responsibility for his crimes. I was just changing so that I could visit him at the hospital. My brother may be misguided. But even misguided men need counsel."

Kaya lifted her chin. "Of course. We won't take up too much of your time. You've heard also, I assume, that your sister-in-law, Annette, is still missing."

He stepped out of the house, closing the door behind him. Bowing his head, he gave a nod. "I have heard that, yes, and I'm concerned about her. Greatly concerned."

"Why?" Rutland asked. "By all accounts, it appears that she, too, tried to flee."

"Annette had nothing to do with what happened at Eaton House. Those were my brother's men. They answer to him, not her."

"Then why would she leave?" Rutland wanted to know.

"Perhaps she feared my brother," Huck weighed. "Perhaps he thinks she knows too much about his criminal affairs and she felt she had no choice but to disappear."

"Do you know something about his criminal history that we don't, reverend?" Rutland pressed.

Huck shook his head. "The only thing I have, Agent Rutland, are my suspicions."

"Can you tell us more about those?" Kaya asked.

He glanced over their heads at the street. There were children playing on the sidewalk, a couple walking a dog and several neighbors sitting on porches or puttering around their gardens. "Now isn't the time or place. My brother's expecting me."

"Has your brother ever mentioned the bodies on the mountain?" Rutland asked.

Huck blanched. His lips trembled slightly before he pressed them together. "I don't think so."

"May we search the premises?" Rutland asked, taking a step forward, crowding Huck into his own door.

"Why would you need to search my house?" Huck asked, holding his ground. He was a big man, nearly a head taller than Rutland.

"You and your sister-in-law have a close relationship," Rutland explained. "It seems she may have confided in you. You fear for her safety. It isn't a stretch to assume that you are concerned enough—that you care enough—to let her hide out here from her husband, if necessary."

"But I told you I haven't seen her." Huck looked to Kaya for help. "Sheriff, this is superfluous."

Kaya thought about it. *He closed the door when he came out onto the porch*. Her pulse quickened. Rutland was right. "It'll only take a moment, reverend. Then we'll be out of your hair."

Disappointment tracked across his strong features. His jaw firmed. He shook his head. "I'm sorry. Without a warrant, I cannot let you in. I'm well within my rights to say so."

Kaya took a beat, then nodded. "You are."

"We'll be back with that warrant," Rutland told him as he stepped back slowly. "Have a nice evening."

She waited until they were back inside the car. "He's hiding something."

Rutland buckled his seat belt. "I'd bet my salary Annette Claymore is inside that house."

"If he's that concerned about her safety," Kaya said, pulling away from the curb, "he'll have her moved before a warrant is secure." She waited until she'd safely steered around a clutch of boys dribbling and passing a basketball to one another on the street before she smacked the steering wheel with the heel of her hand. "He knows something about what happened on Ol' Whalebones. I knew there was a connection to the murders and the Claymores."

"And I told you to drop it." Rutland's hand curled into a fist as he brought it to his mouth. "I was wrong." He met her gaze as she pulled up to the stop sign. "I'm sorry, Kaya."

She gave a slight nod. "I'll need to call the judge—the same one that got us the warrant for True's arrest."

"Getting a warrant for a small-town mayor is one thing," Rutland weighed. "Getting one for a minister may be more difficult. Say we find her. We need to hold her. She either fears for her life in regard to her husband or..."

"Or she's hiding because she has information or she had some part in his wrongdoing," she finished. "We have to take Annette into either protective or police custody before she leaves New Mexico."

EVERETT SAT AT Paloma's bedside. She was sleeping soundly, but he couldn't unsee the bandage wrapped around her head or what the wound had looked like before EMTs had arrived at Eaton Edge the night of the attack.

She looked white against the sheets. His hand held the lower half of his face as he watched the regular peaks and valleys of her vitals on the screen on the far side of the bed.

Someone touched his shoulder. He looked around to see Luella. Her smile wavered, but she gave it nonetheless. She gave so few smiles that he knew the gesture was heartfelt.

Coming to his feet, he faced her. "She's sleeping. The doctor says she can go home tomorrow. She's starting to give orders. I suspect they're eager to see the back of her."

"Her vitals are strong. She's doing well. The doctor's right to let her go home and rest where she's more comfortable."

Luella had been a trauma nurse at this hospital before false rumors of her wrongdoing had led to her firing. Everett knew they'd offered the job back to her after her exoneration at the start of the year, but she'd refused. She and Eveline had started Ollero Creek Rescue, instead.

He struggled to trust those in the medical profession and always had, but he trusted her to the bone. "So you're taking the late shift?"

"Yes," she said. "There's something you should know. Ellis told me not to tell you, but that feels wrong."

"What?" he asked, tensing automatically.

She lowered her voice. "True Claymore is being held on the floor beneath this one. He's under heavy guard but is no longer sedated and may even be transferred sometime tomorrow."

Everett took a long breath in through the nose. He rolled his shoulders.

"You can't go near him," she told him in no uncertain terms. "But I felt you had a right to know."

He nodded, then lifted his hand to her shoulder and squeezed. He looked at Paloma. "Take care of her 'til I get back."

"You know I will," she assured him. "But I can handle the morning's shift, too. If you're not going to work, you should see the girls. Have breakfast with them and Ellis. It'll be good for all of you."

He smiled. "Aside from Isla and Ingrid, you're the best thing that ever happened to my brother. You're good for his girls, too. You're good for all of us."

Her eyes widened. "That may be the nicest thing you've ever said—to anyone."

He shifted from one foot to the other, uncomfortable. "I guess weddings make me sentimental. I'll get over it."

"I don't think it's the wedding that's changed you," she considered.

"Hmm," he muttered when he saw the knowing look on her face. "Would you be willing to take the fall for some black panties Paloma found in the upstairs ficus?"

"That depends," she considered. "What'll you owe me for it?"

He laughed, then quieted himself quickly when Paloma stirred. "Don't marry my brother. You're too good for him."

"It's too late for me," she told him. "And, from what I hear, maybe somebody else I know, too."

He thought of Kaya and released a heavy breath. "I'll get back to you on that, Lu."

"Everett?" she asked as he retreated. When he turned back, she added, "You told me not to wait too long to tell Ellis what I wanted. Don't wait too long to tell Kaya, either."

"I don't know what she wants," he admitted. It sounded plaintive and he regretted it instantly.

"Still," she cautioned, "take it from someone who knows. Life doesn't wait. And these things…they slip away if you're not careful."

He stared back at her mutely before he shifted toward the door again and left.

KAYA STEPPED OFF the elevator on the second floor of Fuego County Hospital. She nodded to the guard posted there. "Officer Pettry."

"Sheriff," the young cop returned.

"Everything okay here?" she asked.

"Quiet," he replied. "No activity other than Mr. Eaton arriving about half an hour ago."

"Eaton," she parroted. "Which one?"

"The older one," he said.

Her shoes slapped against the linoleum floor in rapid succession as she rounded the corner to the corridor where Claymore's recovery room was located. She spotted the second officer, Logan, on the door and Everett leaning against the opposite whitewashed wall. As she closed in, Logan glanced over. At her questioning brow, he nodded slightly to show nothing was amiss.

Breathing a little easier, Kaya slowed. "Officer Logan," she said and watched Everett flinch out of the corner of her eye. "Anything to report?"

"Everything's good here, Sheriff Altaha," Logan replied diligently. "Though I hear the mayor's in a good deal of pain."

"Thank you for taking the late shift," she told him before pivoting to face the man against the wall. At the sight of his heavy eyes, she tilted her head. "Everett. What are you doing here?"

He glanced over her head at Logan. His jaw hardened a bit before his eyes returned to her face, weary. "I was visiting Paloma."

"Did you get lost?" she asked, letting amusement ease the question.

Perhaps he was too tired because emotions filed across

the windows of his eyes and her heart stumbled in reaction. When his mouth remained stubbornly closed, she turned back to Logan. "Five minute break?" she asked. "I can man the door."

Logan nodded. "Thank you, sir."

She waited until he'd rounded the corner and she and Everett were by themselves in the corridor. "What's wrong, cattle baron?" she asked.

He took a breath to gather himself, unable to meet her eye now. "Since I took over the Edge last summer, I've nearly lost my sister to a madman. We've had a holdup at headquarters. One sheriff turned against us. We've found four bodies on the mountain. My men have been investigated and scrutinized, I've been suspected of murder, my brother-in-law was booked for it, two gunmen attacked Eaton House and the woman I'd call Mom if she'd let me is in the hospital. It hasn't been a year, and that's what's happened on my watch."

Kaya's lips parted as she watched the agony bleed through everything else. She shook her head quickly. "There's been a wedding at Eaton House. An incredible wedding. And there will be another soon. Two new beginnings. Eveline and Wolfe will start a family before the end of the year, from what I'm told. And through all of that, your family and your men haven't gone anywhere. They're more loyal to you than ever. Every single one of them vouched for you when Rutland investigated. Did you know that? And Paloma's going to be okay, Everett. She's okay. You are not responsible for all the negative things that have happened."

"I'm head of the family," he stated. "I'm chief of operations. Of course it's my responsibility."

"You carry too much on yourself," she accused. "Your father did that, too. He bore too much and died too soon. And don't you dare try to tell me one had nothing to do with the other."

Everett didn't say anything. His eyes circled her face instead, thoughtful even if his mouth was grim.

She couldn't help herself. She touched him while they were alone in the corridor, just them two. Sliding her hands from his elbows to his shoulders, she used her thumbs to massage where tension had sunk down deep. His chest lifted with his chin and his dark eyelashes closed halfway. His brow knitted and she could see everything he carried—every burden and worry.

She shook her head. "What is it you're afraid of?"

It took him a moment to answer. His eyes had closed completely. "I can't lose anyone else. I don't have what it takes."

A strong man admitting he wasn't strong enough was a powerful thing. She pulled him into her embrace, wrapping him tight until his face was in her hair, his front pressed to hers and her hands spread across the long, warm line of his back. "It's okay," she whispered, as compelled by the embrace as she was. With his arms circling her waist and the enduring chord of strength humming beneath his skin, she felt small and soft but also like she could take on ten men.

Together, they could take on the world. The certainty was scary and thrilling. It called to the person she was underneath the sheriff's uniform—the person he'd recognized from the moment all this had started between them.

She wavered, letting her palms come up to meet his shoulders again. "I have to question True now that he's awake."

He turned his face away. "I've got to get back."

She let him back away and hated the distance. What she

wouldn't give to take him home to her own bed. "You should get some rest before work. There's still time before dawn."

"I'll keep, sweetheart," he said as he headed down the corridor, his hat brim low.

She watched him go and felt her brows arch. *Take care of yourself, cattle baron. Someone loves you.*

If she weren't such a coward, she'd shout it at his back. She'd known she loved him when she'd found True Claymore alive. Everett had wanted revenge. He believed in Old Western justice. He'd proved that many times. The mayor had Paloma's blood on his hands and Everett had needed vendetta for it.

But he'd handed True over to her, unharmed—a gift she'd never forget.

Pushing through the door to Claymore's room, she gauged the man's condition. His leg was bound in a heavy cast. He'd come out of surgery with no complications though his road to recovery wouldn't be short or easy.

How the mighty do fall, she mused at the sight of his baby blue hospital johnny and the crepey skin under his eyes that made him look fragile. His eyes lit on her, alive with pain. "You here to take me to jail?" When she approached the bed wordlessly and pulled up a chair to sit, he reached for the call button. "Hang on. If you're going to interrogate me, I'm going to need another shot of morphine."

"I've got something to say," she told him. "There's no question you're going to jail. You ordered the hit on Eaton House, and we've got the evidence to back that up. But it was sloppy. In the years that I've known you, I've never known you to be sloppy."

He spread his hands as he lifted them from the bedcovers. "What can I say? I finally snapped."

"Why?" she asked pointedly. "It wasn't because Everett Eaton dented your fender. The attacks are disproportionate. Something bigger pushed you to order your men to attack Eaton House. What was it?"

"I need my wife."

"Your wife's missing," she said, her voice reaching for the ceiling now. "Your brother claims it's because she's hiding out from you."

True frowned. "Huck told you that?"

She waited, watching.

True shook his head. "Annette. She's never been afraid of me. Hell, the only person any of us has ever been afraid of was…"

When he trailed off, she had to stop herself from leaning forward. "Yes?"

He looked toward the window. The blinds were shut tight. He shook his head again. "Annette's not afraid of me. I've never done anything to make her afraid."

"But someone else has," she guessed. "Who?"

True's lips thinned, and his eyes wavered with pain or guilt or grief. It was difficult to tell. "You think I killed those women and that boy. The ones on the mountain. You think I'm capable."

She found that she could be truthful. "I do."

"Why?" he asked, his face turning back to hers. "What have I done, Sheriff, to make you believe I'm the monster?"

She needed to break him. And she'd held out for so long. She could hardly breathe as she muttered, "Because even you shouldn't mess around with 'little rez girls.'"

He stared for a full minute. She saw the realization hit. Then the implications. His gaze raced over her, as if seeing her for the first time.

She didn't look away. It was satisfying—so satisfying—when she saw the fear sink in. He was afraid of her, of what she'd experienced. What she knew and had always known about him. "Tell me," she demanded. "Tell me why you had Sawni Mescal killed. I'd like to know that first. Then you can tell me about the others."

Air hissed through his teeth as he braced them shut. He closed his eyes. "I didn't kill her. I didn't kill any of them."

"Not by your hand," she said. "But you gave the order."

"No," he said, shaking his head frantically now.

"True." Kaya stood up. She gripped the raised railing of the bed that caged him in. "Annette's not here for you to hide behind. There's no hiding. Not anymore. You're going to be booked. If you tell me how it all went down—if you tell me the truth—the judge will soften the sentence. You know that."

"I know that!" he shouted. "Damn it, you don't think I know that? But I'm trying to tell you! I didn't kill them! I wasn't the one who gave the order!"

She narrowed her eyes. "If it wasn't you, then who did?"

He took a fortifying breath. "For you to know that, you have to know who my father was and what he did."

"Your father's been dead a long time, True. You can't hide behind him, either."

"My father died the same year Bethany Merchant did," he added. "He was alive for her death and the first's."

"Who was she?" Kaya asked, needing the identity of the first woman. "Who was the first victim?"

"My stepmother." He seemed to wrench the truth out of

himself. “Or, the woman who was going to be my stepmother. She and my father were engaged. Her name was Melissa Beaton. She was twenty-two years younger than him.”

“He had his fiancée killed?” Kaya asked. “Why?”

“I didn’t know how or why until later. I didn’t know until Huck told me…”

“Huck knew?”

He didn’t so much look at her as through her. “Of course Huck knew. He was the one who did it—who my father ordered to kill her.”

Kaya’s mouth gaped. She closed it. “You’re saying your brother, the reverend, killed the first victim, Melissa Beaton?”

“I’m saying,” True said, rounding the words out slowly, “that you found those four bodies on the mountain because Huck killed them there. Because my father programmed him to do so.”

Chapter Eighteen

Programmed?

Kaya tried to make sense of what True was saying and wondered if he was speaking nonsense. "Your father couldn't have ordered Huck to kill all four of them. He was dead before Sawni Mescal worked at The RC Resort. Long before Miller Higgins went hiking on Ol' Whalebones."

"My father didn't fight in Vietnam. Do you know what he did instead, Sheriff?" True asked.

"No."

"He was part of a training initiative for special forces," he said. "It was experimental. The theory was that a man could be trained to kill on command. Like Pavlov. If a dog can be programmed to salivate at the sound of a bell, then a man can be trained to execute a command—no matter how ruthless—at the sound of a 'kill word,' as he called it. After the war was lost, he was sent home to New Mexico. He had orders never to talk about or reveal what he did before he got there. He disobeyed orders. Not only that, he kept the program going. He knew Fuego County was rough country. 'Lawless,' as he used to say. He needed a soldier to do his bidding. Huck was born first. If he hadn't been, it would have been me. From the time he could walk, my father started programming him to kill."

The information was hard to take in. Kaya stepped back from the bed and moved away to roam the section of floor between the door and the window. She roved back to the foot of the bed and stopped. "So your father gave Huck the word to kill Melissa Beaton."

"Yes," True said, unable to meet her eye.

"How old was Huck when this happened?"

True's bottom lip shook once, then stopped. "Twelve. Just twelve."

"Why would your father want Melissa killed?" Kaya wondered.

"He said it was because she strayed," True revealed. "I always thought it was because he needed to see if his programming had worked. It's not like he loved her or needed her. My father wasn't motivated by those things. He was motivated by anger and greed. Growing up at RC was like the worst episode of *Survivor* you've ever seen. He made sure I knew what he could make Huck do. It didn't matter how much my brother loved me. If my father gave the word, Huck would kill me—without even thinking, he'd kill me. I couldn't run away and I sure as hell couldn't tell anyone."

"Why is there no record of this?" she asked. "Someone must've noticed a woman was missing from your ranch."

"People who worked there looked the other way," he revealed. "My father bought their silence."

"She didn't have family?" she asked. "Friends? Someone who would have asked questions when she disappeared?"

"She was a stripper from San Antonio. We thought somebody might come looking for her. Nobody ever showed up."

"What about Bethany Merchant?" Kaya asked. "And why did so much time go by between the killings?"

"Huck got away," True said. "Killing Melissa destroyed him. He left school, started drinking. Then he ran off and got a job as a ranch hand somewhere in East Texas."

"Why did he come back?" Kaya asked.

"My father's men found him," True explained. "They dragged him back. He paid for it. Believe me. My father made him pay. He took his pound of flesh. He made Huck bleed."

A shiver went up Kaya's spine. She went to the window again. "This was when?"

"About six months before Bethany Merchant turned up missing," True said grimly.

"Why did your father order Huck to kill Bethany?" she asked. "She was just a girl."

"She wasn't just a girl," True said resentfully. "That son of a bitch made Huck kill her because I loved her. Because I got her pregnant."

When Kaya stared, True nodded. "You know I'm telling the truth now, don't you? The ME would have told you she was a couple months pregnant when she died. The baby was mine. She was hung up on Everett Eaton, but I loved her. I would have gone anywhere with her if she'd have asked me."

"She didn't." Kaya put the pieces together. "She asked him."

"She asked Eaton, and it shattered my heart," True said. "She cornered him at the rodeo because she wanted to meet him at the motel that night she disappeared. She was going to tell him there—that she was pregnant, that the baby was his and he was trapped. He would've had to go east with her to college the way she wanted him to. But Huck met her at the motel instead. My father found out about the baby. After she was gone and I saw how broken Huck was again, I knew he'd given the order. She died because he couldn't abide his line being plagued by the potential of a bastard."

Kaya didn't know if she could hear any more. But she had to. She had to know everything. "Legal records show the first land dispute between your family and the Eatons was around this time," she noted.

"The lines between the RC and Eaton Edge are fuzzy," he explained, "at least when you're out there in the mountains. My father thought the mountain was on our side. After Bethany died, he realized he was wrong. He didn't like lawyers, but he hired one to file a claim before his death."

"Sawni Mescal." She forced the name out. "I need to know why Sawni Mescal was killed. If your father was dead, who was controlling Huck if not you?"

At this point, True raised a hand to his brow. He lowered his head, looking broken himself.

"True," she said gently. He may have kept his family's secrets. But it had haunted him every bit as much as Sawni's disappearance had haunted her. "Please."

He sniffed and lifted his head again. His face had turned red. The words quavered slightly when he spoke again. "I, uh… I met Annette, at college. She was prelaw, from a good family. I didn't want to bring her home. I didn't want her to know what…who I came from. But Dad was dead and I thought maybe everything died with him. Everything but Huck. So I took her home. And she and Huck… They became close. Closer than I expected. I didn't know he'd told her. Not until after the rez girl… She said her name was Kaya."

"You know her name." The response was punchy, but she was no longer in control. She was beyond it.

"Sawni Mescal worked for us for a while without incident," True said. "It was summertime. That's why we needed the extra help. Annette and I had a few months off school and her, me and Huck… We spent it on the ranch. We talked about what it was, what it could be. For the first time, I saw it as something to be redeemed. Something that Huck and I could be proud of. Together, we could make the RC something special. Annette and I even talked about getting married, which thrilled me to pieces. I thought if she and I got married, Huck and I could start over. We could forget everything that happened before—just sweep it under the rug and start clean. But then Annette started to think something was off about Sawni."

"What exactly?"

"Annette thought Sawni wanted Huck," True said. "The girl and Huck were friendly. I didn't see anything deeper than that. There was an age difference, and Huck was friendly with everyone. The girl kept to herself, though, and didn't respond much to Annette's questioning. Annette felt protective of Huck. She seemed jealous, even. I tried not to dwell on it. If she was jealous, it was because she loved him as much or more than she loved me, and after everything that happened with Bethany and Everett Eaton, I couldn't let my mind go there. There were too many ghosts. So I let it be. For weeks. And her hatred toward Sawni festered and whatever she felt for Huck… She became *possessive*. I didn't know until after the girl disappeared and everyone started looking for her that Huck had told Annette everything—about our father, about him, Melissa and Bethany. And she was angry enough…obsessed enough…to use my father's kill code—the one Huck had trusted her with—to snuff Sawni out. Like she was nothing. Dust in the frickin' wind."

Kaya breathed through her nose. Her eyes burned. "So you *married her*, True?"

True turned his eyes down to the hands twisted in his lap. "She knew our secrets. There was no getting out of it at that point. And once she saw how much it destroyed Huck again, she was sorry. She used the trust fund from her parents to send him to a specialist. Someone we could trust. She paid for his therapy. She paid for him to go to some monastery in California where you're forbidden to speak. It was supposed to be healing and he did heal, somewhat.

"When he was done there, he wanted to go to seminary school. He wanted his slate wiped clean. He wanted to be cleansed. The only way he felt he could do that was to become a shepherd of God. So she paid his way. Anything he needed, she sponsored him—on one condition. If he became a minister, he had to return to Fuego. After everything, she felt we had to keep an eye on him. If he'd told her everything, he'd tell anyone else he felt close to. He could have married, Sheriff. Started a family. Started over, finally. But Annette… She couldn't let that happen. If he loved her enough to spill his guts, he'd do it all again for another woman."

"Who kept Sawni's diary and why?" she asked.

"That was Annette. I told her it was foolhardy. Dad burned everything of Melissa's. He didn't take anything from Bethany, either, when she died. He didn't believe in leaving traces. Like I said, though, Annette was obsessed with the Mescal girl. She kept everything in the girl's bag."

"Was it her, too, who turned it in?" Kaya asked.

"Yes," True answered. "She had a row with Huck about it. She showed us the pages she'd torn out—the ones that mentioned her and Huck and me. It was the only thing belonging to Sawni she ever burned."

"What was the point in turning in the diary to begin with?" Kaya asked.

"She thought you and the FBI were sniffing too close in our direction. She got paranoid. She knew Wolfe was mentioned in the pages she left in the diary. She thought you'd start looking his way instead. It worked, for a time."

Kaya spread her feet apart and wrapped her arms around herself. "Tell me about Miller Higgins."

"Higgins was an accident," True said regrettably. "Despite Annette's warnings, Huck started spending time with a woman he met in Taos. They became close. Too close, to Annette's thinking. When he wouldn't listen to her and let the woman go, she took him to the mountain as a reminder why he couldn't be with anyone. They got into a heated argument. Higgins heard everything. Too much. Annette had Huck catch him…"

"She gave the kill order again," Kaya said with an unbelieving shake of her head.

"It was too much," True moaned. "And then the bodies were found, and I knew if any of the three of us made a mistake…a single mistake…you'd know. The Feds arrived and we started to scramble. I started to unravel. Huck talked about leaving, disappearing again, taking the Taos woman with him. Annette wouldn't let him go. I couldn't ignore how much it all hurt—how much she'd come to love him when it was supposed to be me. If she was going to be obsessed with anyone, it should've been me. All my spite and anger came to a head when Eaton did what he did at the festival. Finally, I had somebody I could pin all my frustrations on without hurting anyone I loved."

"If you hadn't ordered the hit," Kaya told him, "you'd still be at The RC Resort. And your secrets would still be yours."

True shook his head. "And none of us… We'd never be free. We'd carry it on our backs for the rest of our lives. To hell with what my wife wants anymore. I can't live like this anymore. And my brother can't, either. His spirit has been traded away by others for too long. If I want him to remain the man he is—the one he should've been—I can't let this go on. If I've got to do time to save him, you can be damn sure I can live with that. My father's sins—his ghost—have been alive in this world too long."

"I need to find Annette," Kaya said. "Agent Rutland and I think she is—or was—hiding out at Huck's house. Do you think that's where she would have gone?"

He hesitated. Then he passed his hand under his nose. "She'd have gone there. But enough time's passed that she's probably up on the mountain or on her way there now."

"The mountain," Kaya repeated. "Whalebones?"

He nodded. "That's where she told me to hide it before I split town. She left me enough to get to Mexico and told me to hide the rest."

"Hide what, True?" she pressed.

"The money," he said. "My father's money. Everything the Feds came looking for when he took his exodus. We saved it for the day we'd need it to do the same. I hid her and Huck's cut on the mountain where the bodies were found, as she told me. If that damned cougar hadn't startled us, my horse wouldn't have broken his leg or mine. Secrets would still be secrets. We would've gotten away with everything. Everything except our souls."

Chapter Nineteen

Everett had Huck Claymore in his sights. The reverend had no idea. Still, Everett kept his finger outside the trigger guard as he followed Huck and Annette's progress on the trailhead of Ol' Whalebones.

As soon as Everett had returned to Eaton House from the hospital in the early hours before dawn, Kaya had called. She was mobilizing the mounted search again. There would be another manhunt—this time for True Claymore's brother and wife. And the most likely place they would be found was the mountain.

The other members of the search party would take time to get into position, but Everett, Ellis and their men were closest.

If you find them, I need you not to engage. Call in your coordinates and wait.

Waiting didn't sit well knowing he was looking at the man who'd killed four people and the woman who had ordered him to do so.

If Annette's with him, Huck Claymore is expected to be armed and extremely dangerous. Do not engage, Everett.

Everett didn't understand Annette's hold on the reverend.

But he had understood the urgency in Kaya's voice—the fear behind it.

Something about these two had her spooked. His promise to Kaya was the only thing tethering him from stopping them before they reached the summit. Once they did, they would be out of Everett's line of sight.

"Should we follow them?" Javier asked at his right shoulder.

Ellis, on Everett's left, made a discouraging noise. "Orders are we hang back."

"We'll lose them on the ridge," Javier reasoned. "We could find another position…"

"Sheriff Altaha told us not to approach," Ellis told him. "Right?"

Everett frowned. Annette and Huck were gaining ground too quickly.

"Everett?"

Everett lifted his head, staring across the muzzle into the distance. "You two wait here. I need to get closer."

Ellis gripped him. "What?"

"If they escape on my watch, I'm the one who has to live with it."

"What do I tell her when she gets here?" Ellis asked, not having to say her name for Everett to know who he spoke of.

"She knows I'm a man of my word," Everett returned before he left the small circle of boulders where the trio had been hiding. "Tell her I've got her back."

KAYA COULDN'T HAIL Everett on the radio. She didn't enjoy not knowing where he was or what he was planning to do.

He told me to tell you he's got your back, Ellis had said when she'd located him and Javier in the canyon below.

She and Rutland picked their way over rocks as they approached the place True Claymore had described—close to where the four victims had been found over the edge of the cliff. Root and Wyatt weren't far behind. She raised her hand when she heard amplified voices on the wind. Her team slowed. No one had eyes on Huck or Annette anymore. In the canyon below, Ellis and Javier had lost sight of them close to a half hour ago.

"That's Annette," she muttered to Rutland, recognizing the voice if not the harsh tone reverberating off the rocks around them. She glanced back at Root and Wyatt. "Silence your radios. We don't want to alert them."

They obeyed and Kaya reached down to twist the dial on the radio on her belt, muting it.

Rutland leaned toward her. "If they see us coming, you realize Annette could go ahead with the kill code."

"Huck is used to enacting it against a single person," she said. "He never shoots them on the spot. He gets them into position, executes them all with the same shot to the back of the head. He's never faced anyone that was trained in combat, much less four. Root and Wyatt approach from the north, us to the south. Unless you'd rather hang back."

He shook his head, his standard issue already braced between his hands. "I'm with you, Sheriff."

She nodded, then gave the motion for the four of them to spread out.

EVERETT LAY BELLY-DOWN on the canyon wall, barely breathing. The wind was against him. Any shot he took, he would have to take it into account.

He was alone across the wide gap between the top of the

canyon and Ol' Whalebones. The river ran between, its rush audible even at this height. He could see the ledge where Huck and Annette had hidden the bodies. He could see the pair arguing on the cliff edge above it.

His finger tensed near the trigger when he saw Kaya creeping toward them from the south, Rutland closing on her six.

The shovel in Huck's hand waved as he gestured wildly. There was a mound of dirt at his feet. Annette didn't cower. She grabbed him by the shirt, pushing, inching him back toward the ledge.

Kaya's crouching walk quickened, her feet moving swiftly across the ground, her pistol in a two-handed hold. Rutland followed. When she stood, the wind carried her terse command to *freeze.* Annette pivoted. Huck dropped the shovel. Everything inside Everett did freeze as he watched it tumble end over end over the cliff's edge and fell in a silent arc to the water below.

KAYA WATCHED ROOT and Wyatt crowd Annette and Huck from the north side. She was aware of the wind teasing her hair and the brim of her hat. She was more aware of the long plunge down the cliff wall to her left. She felt more than heard Rutland behind her. Her eyes moved over Huck's face, trying to gauge his expression.

The debate between him and Annette had reached screaming pitch by the time Kaya had given the order. She'd seen Annette nearly shove Huck off the cliff's edge and had decided to move in.

"Sheriff Altaha," Annette said. Flushed, she was not the polished mayor's wife people in Fuego knew her to be. She swallowed, reaching down to straighten the sand-colored vest she wore over her front. "This is a surprise."

"Show us your hands!" Rutland shouted when Huck's began to reach around his back.

Kaya stiffened even as Huck's hand lifted into the air along with the other. He looked miserable, she thought briefly. He stepped a hair closer to Annette, his toes inching over the edge of the hole they had dug. "You're both under arrest."

"For what?" Annette challenged.

"Huck for the murders of Melissa Beaton, Bethany Merchant, Sawni Mescal and Miller Higgins," Kaya informed her. "You'll be charged in the deaths of Mescal and Higgins."

Annette's eyes widened. "Those are serious charges, Sheriff. Are you sure you have the right people?"

"I have your husband True Claymore's detailed statement," Kaya replied and saw Huck waver like a blade of grass over his feet.

"True says we did this?" Annette laughed. "That's ridiculous. He'll say anything at this point to get himself out of trouble. He's accustomed to talking his way out of sticky situations."

"A search and seizure of Huck's residence turned over Miller Higgins's cell phone. If True's guilty, then what are you two doing at the murder scene? Why are the horses we found at the foot of the mountain packed with a week's worth of rations?"

Annette's mouth fumbled.

Kaya lowered her chin. "Come forward quietly so that we can bring you both in for questioning. Resisting arrest won't work well for you if you're innocent. You're a criminal attorney, Annette. You know this."

Huck's feet shuffled forward, but Annette's arm snapped up to block him. "No."

"Annette." His fingers closed around her wrist in a gentle bracelet. "It's over."

"No!" she shouted. "Not like this! I will *not* see you rot in prison for this!"

"You won't see it," he assured her. His front buffered against her back and his other hand came up to meet the line of her shoulders. "I'm tired, Annette. I can't do this anymore."

Her gaze fused to his. "You can't live with me anymore, Huck? Is that what you mean?"

His shoulders lifted and his expression grew helpless. When he lowered them, his posture caved. "I'm sorry," he whispered.

Annette nodded slowly, jaw flexing. "You won't have to." In a lightning move, she reached around his waist.

"Don't!" Kaya yelled when Annette's grip closed over the butt of Huck's gun. She pushed herself forward. "Hold it!"

Annette threw her shoulder into Huck's chest.

His heel caught on the mound of earth. His hands windmilled as he tipped over the ledge and fell into the open air.

Annette whirled, her gun hand trained on Kaya. "Tell them to get back!" she cried, pointing at the deputies behind her. "Tell them or I'll shoot!"

Kaya lifted her chin to Wyatt. He and Root shuffled backward. "Any chance you had of talking yourself out of murder charges is gone. You realize that, don't you?"

"Not if you let me go," Annette told her.

"You pushed him off the cliff." Kaya shook her head. "Why did you have to kill him?"

"I gave him the easy way out," Annette stated. "He

couldn't have sat in a cell for the rest of his life thinking about all the things he's done. He's not built for that. Yeah, he killed those people. But he isn't a killer. He never would've hurt anyone—"

"If not for his father," Kaya finished. "If not for you."

"This doesn't have to end badly," Annette argued. "Huck's gone. He can't hurt anyone anymore. Just back off and stay back and you'll never see me again. I'll leave what's in that hole for all of you."

Kaya's eyes jumped from Annette's right eye to her left and back. "I can't do that."

Annette tilted her head slightly. The sheen over her eyes caught the light. Kaya saw the grief and guilt wash over her about what she had done to Huck.

Kaya lifted one hand from her weapon to motion Rutland back.

"No!" he hissed.

"Just do it," she shot back before repositioning her hands on the Glock when the rocks under Rutland's feet crunched under his careful retreat.

"That's typical," Annette muttered. "My husband disappointed me. Even Huck disappointed me in the end. Now you. I expected more of Fuego's first woman sheriff."

Kaya wasn't going to be like the reverend. She wasn't going to apologize. "I don't think Huck disappointed you. I think he did everything you ever told him to."

Annette's voice broke. "Except run away with me."

"He has run," Kaya told him. "In the past, he ran to get away from all of this. But it followed him. He knew if he ran again, he'd never be free of it. And neither would you."

"The truth wouldn't have set him free, either!" Annette cried. "Don't you understand? That's why he had to die!"

Kaya nodded. "I know what it is to love someone—to love all of him—the good side of him and the bad. I know what it is to live without someone you love—to feel responsible for what happened to them. It tears at the very fabric of who you are."

Tears tracked down Annette's cheeks. "Lower your weapon, Kaya. Please…just lower the gun."

"In order for me to do that, you have to lower yours first," Kaya said evenly.

Annette shifted onto her back foot. The gun lowered by a hair.

"Slow," Kaya murmured, watching Annette's gun turn sideways and her knees bend. She edged forward. "That's it, Annette. Nice and slow."

The gun came to rest on the rocks between them. "Now you," Annette said.

"Step back," Kaya advised. As Annette did so, Kaya released one hand from her weapon. She set it on the ground. Stepping over them, she reached for her cuffs.

Annette backed away, skittish. "You didn't say you were going to restrain me."

"It's procedure," Kaya reminded her. She stepped forward again. When Annette retreated toward the ledge, she stopped, holding up both hands. She didn't know if Annette was desperate enough to follow Huck over the cliff. "All right, look. If you promise not to resist, we can walk out of here together. No restraints."

"Until we get to the bottom of the mountain?" Annette said with narrowed eyes.

Kaya measured her and realized she had no intention of making it all the way to the bottom of the mountain. Not without running. "Yes," she lied.

Annette stilled. She let Kaya close the distance.

Kaya took hold of her arm. "Come on," she said, nodding in the direction she had come.

Annette twisted, attempting to break the hold. She forced Kaya back a long step.

Kaya caught her breath. She felt open air behind her. Annette drove an elbow into her gut. Kaya felt her heels slide back over the ledge.

On the wind, she thought she heard the sound of her name.

EVERETT DIDN'T HAVE a clear shot. He hadn't had one since Kaya laid down her weapon and crossed to Annette.

He watched helplessly as Annette tried to drive Kaya back over the ridge. For a second, it looked like she would go over, crashing to the same ledge where Huck lay.

Kaya lunged, grabbing Annette as she did so and shoving her to the ground. She tried to restrain her.

Annette was fighting for her life, arms and legs flailing. She kicked, punched, bit. Her fist closed over a rock and swung it up to connect with Kaya's temple.

"Son of a bitch," Everett breathed as Kaya's head snapped back. Rutland and the deputies rushed to break up the fight. "Hurry up!" he yelled. Why had they left in the first place?

Kaya tried to overtake Annette by pinning her in a reverse hold, but Annette rolled out of it, away from the edge. She scrambled for something on the ground as Rutland lunged for her.

A shot echoed across the canyon and Rutland fell. Kaya

had brought herself to her feet, grappling for the Taser on her belt. Annette pointed the gun at her.

Everett felt the trigger, placing Annette in the center of his scope. He remembered the wind at the last second, adjusted his aim.

The rifle kicked against his shoulder as he squeezed.

KAYA WATCHED ANNETTE slump in a limp sprawl on the rocks of the cliff edge. Her Taser was in her fist and her deputies were behind her. Rutland was still down.

Blood pooled beneath the line of Annette's throat. Her body had jerked sideways. Which meant the shot had come from the north…

Kaya looked wildly across the empty space of the canyon to the cliff side a hundred feet across.

She had to squint. The rock to the head had made her see stars and her vision double. She watched a figure and its carbon copy unfold from a sprawl on the flat top of the canyon. As he stood up, she recognized Everett's long lean form. He lifted his hand, waved.

Ellis's words came back to her.

Everett said to tell you he's got your back.

A sob worked against her throat, and she braced her hands on her knees as they loosened. Root grabbed her arms, preventing her slide to the rough ground, while Wyatt sailed by to check Rutland's condition.

As Root asked if she was okay, Kaya's gaze fell on Annette. For a second, she thought their eyes locked. It took a delayed second for her to realize the other woman was dead. She had tried to kill Kaya. And Everett had been quicker.

She looked across the canyon again and saw that Everett

had picked up his rifle and was running for the sloping side of the cliff face he'd somehow shimmied up to get to his position. Shrill ringing pierced her ears. Blinking, she struggled to stay conscious—at least until she had a chance to kiss the cattle baron when he arrived.

Chapter Twenty

"True Claymore is in custody. Reverend Huck Claymore and Annette Claymore are both deceased. Agent Rutland is in surgery but is expected to recover. Sheriff Altaha was injured, but she is doing well and should be back at work next week..."

"He's doing fine," Naleen commented at Kaya's bedside. Deputy Root's face filled the screen of the television high on the wall opposite the hospital bed.

"He's doing great," Kaya granted. "But I still could've done the press conference."

"The doctor says you have to stay overnight," her mother, Darcia, said as she fussed around the room, straightening the curtains, adjusting the blinds. Turning the chairs so they were angled just so with the bed.

She was driving Kaya crazy. They both were.

Nova breezed in with a large grease-stained paper bag. "I brought reinforcements."

Kaya sat up in bed too quickly and winced when her head split open with pain. She saw little white lights and leaned back on her elbows. "Damn it!"

"You might be the world's worst patient," Naleen considered as she received the bag from her daughter and rattled the paper as she opened it.

Kaya's teeth ground at the noise. "Nova, get out. I'm about to say more bad words."

"You go ahead, Aunt Kaya," Nova invited. "After spring break at the Edge, I feel like I've got them all memorized. Did you know there are over fifty different ways to use the word fu—"

"Do you really think finishing that sentence will convince me to let you work there all summer?" Naleen questioned.

"Do you really think talking at this volume is making me any friendlier?" Kaya drawled.

The door opened again and two people walked into the room. Kaya's jaw came unhinged when she saw Sawni's mother and father.

Mrs. Mescal carried a vase full of flowers. She looked small and kindly behind them as she smiled hesitantly. "How's the patient?" she asked in her familiar quiet voice.

When Kaya remained speechless, Naleen stood up from her chair. "Indignant."

Mr. Mescal chuckled. He was not a tall man, but his presence had a habit of filling any room he was in. That effect had dimmed after Sawni's disappearance. Kaya had noticed that at the funeral as well. But his shoulders were back, and his smile was broad as he scanned the bandage on Kaya's temple. "The headache's to blame, I'm sure."

"It's the captivity," Kaya found herself saying. She glanced at Naleen. "Can you…"

Naleen patted her arm. "Nova and I will step out."

"Leave the bag," Kaya said, snatching it from her before Naleen could escape with it.

Darcia sat down in the chair closest to the window, signaling that she intended to stay. Kaya didn't have the words to tell her to leave, too.

Mrs. Mescal waited until Nova and Naleen closed the door before placing the vase on the bedside table.

Kaya reached out to touch a delicate spray of petals. "Lilies," she said. "For Sawni."

"Our Sawni did love lilies, didn't she?" Mrs. Mescal asked, tracing the shape of another. "The lilies are for her. The peach roses are for you."

Kaya met her eyes and noticed the veil of wet over her dark irises.

Mrs. Mescal turned the vase slightly, fidgeting. "Do you still like peach roses—or do you prefer something else now?"

"Peach roses are fine," Kaya said, her voice breaking up.

Mrs. Mescal's hand found hers. "I'm sorry we didn't keep in touch through the years. I'm afraid you might think it was because we blamed you for what happened. That wasn't the case. Not at all. Seeing you…reminded us of her. So we cut ties when we should have gathered. Nothing heals like community. You needed that as much as we did, and we denied you."

Kaya shook her head. "I denied myself."

"Nonetheless…" Mrs. Mescal patted her hand. "When I saw you at the memorial, you looked so guilty and ashamed—still, after all this time."

"I was afraid I disappointed you." She lifted her eyes to Mr. Mescal who stood now at the foot of the bed.

"Why would you disappoint us, Kaya?" he asked. "You've risen. You've made your people proud."

"You found her," Mrs. Mescal muttered. "You found our

Sawni and brought her home. But even if you hadn't, you should know we're proud of you."

Kaya looked to her mother who sat quietly. Darcia nodded in quiet agreement and Kaya had to look away. "Thank you," she said. She reached up to swipe at tears. "Sawni used to get so mad because she'd cry at the drop of a hat and I didn't. Now look at me."

Mrs. Mescal released a sobbing laugh.

"We bend," Mr. Mescal stated, "so that life doesn't break us."

Kaya sighed at the wisdom. "I think I get that now."

Mrs. Mescal leaned down and pressed a kiss to the center of her brow. "Bless you, Kaya Altaha."

Kaya mimicked Mr. Mescal's wave and watched him and Sawni's mother file out. She raised both hands to her head as the door snicked closed. "Did you know they were coming?"

"I didn't," Darcia said, rising to smooth the covers over Kaya's legs. "But I'm happy that they did. You needed that. So did they. Our families have needed each other for some time. Maybe now things can go back to the way they were."

It would be bittersweet without Sawni there, but Kaya found herself wishing the same.

The door crashed open, knocking against the wall. Darcia jumped at the sudden noise and the man that charged into the room. "Are you all right?" Everett demanded to know when he found Kaya lying in the bed.

Her heart stuttered. The wash of her pulse made her head ache in time with it. Still, she hadn't seen Everett since the rescue chopper had arrived to transport Rutland to the hospital. He, Root and Wyatt had insisted she go, too. She cleared her throat and tried to sit up straighter against the pillows stacked behind her. “I’m fine. Why wouldn’t I be?”

He swept an arm toward the door. “There’s people crying out in the hall like there’s somebody on their deathbed in here.”

“No one’s on their deathbed,” Darcia assured him. Her tone dripped with both frustration and amusement. “You silly man.”

“You’re fine,” he repeated, eyes drilling into Kaya, hands propped on his waist.

“Yes,” she insisted. “The doctor wanted to keep me for observation through the night as a precaution.”

“There’s nothing wrong with you?” he stated in question.

She pressed her lips together because she was very close to smiling. “No.”

He nodded faintly before he flicked a glance at her mother. “Darcia.”

“Everett,” Darcia volleyed back.

“Nice to see you again.”

“Is it?” she asked mildly.

He shifted, uncomfortable.

Kaya took pity on him. It was nice to know she wasn’t the only one who withered in her mother’s presence. She lifted the bag from the bed. “Do you want a burger?”

“I could eat,” he weighed. He looked around. “Do you have a drink?”

“I don’t,” she realized. “Nova forgot to grab one.”

“What do you want?” he asked, sidestepping quickly to the door. “I’ll get you something.”

“A coke is fine,” she replied.

He grabbed the handle of the door. "Darcia? Can I interest you?"

"You interest my daughter enough for both of us, thank you," Darcia retorted.

He grimaced, then pinned his gaze again to Kaya. "Do you need me to do anything else?"

She started to say no, then stopped. "I need to get out of here."

He lifted his chin and a mischievous grin lit his eyes, turning the corner of his mouth up in a crooked smile. "Oh, I'll get you out of here, Sheriff Sweetheart. Don't you worry."

Kaya didn't realize how wide her smile reached until she looked at Darcia. She shrank back into the bed. "What's with the look, Mom?" she asked bracingly.

Darcia's half-lidded stare was more incisive than usual. Her lips parted a moment before she spoke, as if she were weighing her words or whether to say them. "You've been waiting."

"For…" Kaya prompted.

"For redemption," Darcia said with a wag of her chin. "The Mescals have given it. You always had it, but it took them visiting here today for you to believe that."

"Okay," Kaya said, unsure.

"You've been waiting for something else," Darcia continued. "Something you've probably never been aware of. I've always found it so curious how Naleen could fall so fast and dive into relationships with hardly a second thought and you never could bring yourself to do so."

Kaya had to fight the urge to roll her eyes. She fought it hard. "Mom. Naleen and I are hardly the same person—"

"Very true," Darcia agreed. "But I know now—what you've been waiting for."

Kaya narrowed her eyes. "Care to clue me in?"

"You've been waiting for a warrior."

A laugh burst out of Kaya. "A warrior? How Apache princess of me," she said derisively.

Darcia looked at her until her amusement faded, and Kaya was left to contemplate the seriousness of her expression. "He's a warrior like you," Darcia continued. "You've never found your equal—until now." She stood. "If he's returning, I think I'll take a walk. He won't want me staring daggers at him while he mashes food into his hairy face."

"Why did you tell me all that if you don't like him?" Kaya wondered.

Darcia closed the flaps of her long sweater over her front. "I don't mind him. But you'll allow me to resent the man who's stolen the heart of my youngest daughter. You may be the sheriff of Fuego County, Kaya Altaha. But you are still my child." With a nod, she left the room, leaving Kaya to grapple with her thoughts.

BEFORE DAYBREAK, THE kitchen at Eaton House stood silent and still. The rest of the house lay quiet, too. The boards over the windows blocked the faint stain over the mountains, buttes and cliffs that heralded another long day of working cattle. The windows would be replaced later in the week. Repairs were still going on at Eaton House, off and on, but it was slowly coming together again. Soon, the ambush would only be a bitter memory.

In the dark, Everett pulled on his boots. He didn't bother to button his shirt as he crossed to the counter and the cubby where Paloma kept the coffeepot. He took down mugs. Pouring the coffee, he left it strong and black and lifted the mugs by the handles. No sooner had he turned than he hitched at the sight of the figure hovering in the doorway.

"Jesus Holyfield Christ!" he exclaimed, touching the mugs safely down to the counter next to him as the liquid sloshed over the rims. He grabbed his heart like it was going places. "You can't do that to somebody who's had his chest opened up in the last ten months."

Paloma clicked her tongue, tying the belt of her quilted, scarlet robe as she entered the room she'd ruled for the last three decades. "You're jumpier than usual. Not that that's a wonder." She grabbed the hand towel draped across the handle of the oven and tossed it to him.

He dried the piping hot liquid that ran in between his fingers.

"She's upstairs," Paloma said, eyeing the pair of mugs.

He tossed the towel onto the counter. "She fought me tooth and nail about not letting her go home. But I couldn't sleep. Not without knowing she was okay."

"You stole her from the hospital sooner than doctors advised," Paloma reminded him.

"I did it because she asked me to," Everett responded. "I'd do anything..."

She lifted her chin knowingly when he trailed off. "You'd do anything for her," she said, laying it out for him.

He pressed one hand to the countertop. Paloma saw everything. She saw him better than most.

She sighed. "Oh, *mijo*—"

"What are you doing out of bed?" he intervened smoothly. "You shouldn't be up."

"I feel fine," she assured him. "I'd feel a sight better if you children would stop fussing over me and let me get back to my work."

"You don't need work," he argued. "You need rest."

She grabbed him by the open flaps of his shirt. "Look at me, Everett Templeton. Look *here*." When he obeyed, she widened her eyes. "I am fine. Paloma's fine. *You*, on the other hand, are a basket case."

He sneered. "Now you're just being mean."

"You're not blind," she said gravely. "Nor are you stupid. You know what it is to love someone. What it *means*."

"How do you know?" he asked, uneasy.

"You love your brother," she told him. "You love your sister, despite what you have to say about her. You loved your father more than any son has."

He frowned but couldn't argue.

"You love your men," she went on. "And you love me. We've had our spats. But you were my child long before Ellis and Eveline decided to be. You chose me first."

He dropped his gaze from hers. Yes, he'd chosen her. Like a lifeline, he'd reached. She'd answered. He wondered if she knew, by doing so, that she'd saved him. He shifted his feet and cleared his throat to block the emotions building in the back of his throat.

She waited until he stilled. Then she said, "I never thought the day would come when I would have to point out to you that you've chosen someone else."

"Yeah," he whispered because his voice was somehow lost. "Me neither."

"She's worthy of it," she told him. "She's worthy of your heart."

"That's not what I'm worried about," he admitted.

"What are you worried about, *mijo*?"

He shook his head restlessly. "I don't know if she wants it."

Paloma nodded, drawing a long breath. Lovingly, she gathered the flaps of his shirt together. "You watched your father get his heart broken. It broke when your mother left. It broke a little more when she married my brother, his friend. It broke when she had another child—someone else's. It broke every time he saw either one of them in town. They say people don't die of a broken heart, but in the end, there was no doctor in this world who could fix it, was there?"

Everett was unable to contemplate the lengths to which his father had suffered. "We buried him with it. Why did we do that? You don't bury a man with the gun that killed him."

"The heart defines the man," Paloma insisted. "The same heart loved you and your siblings with every beat. It forgave your mother and my brother. Every betrayal, big and small."

"He was a fool for that," Everett stated.

"He could have been bitter," Paloma spoke over him. "He could have gone off like a demon—like that Whip Decker—and killed them both for it. He could have shut out what remained of his family, given up your birthright and fled. He didn't do those things because he was no fool. He did them because his heart was strong."

"Why're we talking about him?" he asked. Talking about Hammond hurt. Would it never not hurt?

"Because now you're the one who has to decide how your heart defines you," Paloma asserted. "Starting with your woman upstairs." He opened his mouth, but she stopped him. "She's your woman, Everett. There's no denying it."

"I'm hers," he granted. "She hasn't told me yet whether she wants to be mine. Not in the long run. She hasn't told me whether she wants this life with me. And it was me that told her I wasn't easy to live with. She knows all too well that this life is hard."

"Life's hard with or without the person you need most in this world," Paloma explained. "What do you want?"

"I *know* what I want," he said through his teeth.

"Does she?"

He hesitated long enough for her to pounce. "Tell her," Paloma told him. "Tell her, *mijo*, so I don't have to watch you live the rest of your life with regret. Never mind your heart. Do you think mine could stand that?"

He ran his eyes over her face. A smile grew on his. "You like kicking my ass, don't you?"

"What do you think gets me out of bed every morning?" She laid her hands, one on top of the other, over the center of his chest. "Be a good man and try not to plague us both to death."

"No promises," he replied, then added "*Mami*" and watched her eyes grow damp. She drew him into her arms and, for once, he went quietly.

KAYA WOKE FACEDOWN in a bed that was not her own with her head about to implode. She rolled slowly to her back, reaching up to hold her head on her shoulders.

She felt like she'd been hit with a rock much bigger than the one that had concussed her.

Going back to sleep seemed like the safest option. If she slept through the headbanging, she wouldn't have to learn to live through it.

As she tried to slink back into the deep, empty chamber she'd just climbed out of, the aching in her head crescendoed and she realized there would be no respite until she took something for the pain.

Groaning, she dug her elbows into the flannel sheet and propped herself up part of the way. Her neck muscles screamed, and she wished for a hammer to knock herself out with.

A hand gripped her shoulder, preventing her from rising further. She angled her head back.

“Stay down,” Everett instructed.

“I have things to do,” she grumbled at him.

“Such as?” he asked, lifting a single brow.

“Where’d you put my phone?” she asked. “I have to call Root and Wyatt and check in…”

“Nope.”

She sighed, dropping her chin to her chest because her head felt heavy. “Not this again. I’m sheriff. I have responsibilities…”

“Not today,” he informed her. “Not tomorrow, either. For the next few days, you’re not the sheriff.”

She frowned. “I’m just your sweetheart?”

His hand slid from her shoulder as he stepped away. “No. You’re Kaya. And that’s enough.”

She raised her hand to the back of her neck, trying her best to ignore the pancake-flippy feeling his words placed in her stomach. “Do I smell coffee?”

He thrust a mug into her face.

She grabbed it like a lifeline.

Everett piled pillows behind her. “Slow,” he told her when she began to scoot back.

“I’m not an invalid,” she informed him. Clutching the mug

in both hands, she let the heat seep into her fingers and closed her eyes, breathing in the aroma. “That’s nice.”

“Drink,” he said as he sat on the edge of the bed with his own mug. “It’s been sitting for a minute.”

She did and found the temperature to be just right. Scanning his profile, she swallowed and waited until the warmth spread to her belly. “How long have you been watching me sleep?”

He drank in answer.

“Hmm,” she muttered thoughtfully. “Just so I know—how long do you plan on doing that?”

He lowered the coffee. His voice delved deep. “Until I’m certain you’re going to keep waking up.”

“I’m fine.”

His eyes roved over the bandage on her temple and what she imagined were bruises starting to color her skin. “I nearly had to watch you go over a cliff and get shot again. You’ll let me worry about you.”

He’d come close to watching her die again. He’d saved her life—again.

She closed her eyes. “Thank you.”

“It’s just coffee.”

“Not for that.” She shook her head. “For having my back.”

“Always,” he said softly.

She looked away because it was too much. He was too much.

His mug clacked onto the bedside table. “I’ve got things to say to you.”

She wasn’t sure she was ready to hear them.

“Right now, though, you need something to eat. You can’t take those pain meds the doctor sent you home with on an empty stomach. Paloma was making you a plate when I left the kitchen. I'll go see if it's ready. When you've taken something, you can go back to sleep and rest some more."

As he moved to the door, she wanted to call him back but saw the stubborn line of his shoulders and forced herself to stop. When he closed the door, she slunk back down into the covers and pulled them over her head, overwhelmed by all that was inside her.

KAYA COULD ONLY take so much coddling. On the second day, by the afternoon, she was out of bed and wouldn't hear refusal from Everett, Paloma or Luella—who Everett had brought in to do regular checks on Kaya as a nurse.

That evening, close to sundown, she ventured out onto the patio, settled into one of the wooden Adirondack chairs and wouldn't hear a word spoken from any of them about returning indoors until the bugs started to bite and the cool night air began to nip.

Upstairs, Paloma drew her a hot bath. Soaking felt divine. Parts of Kaya ached from the skirmish with Annette—not just her head. She didn't mind so much when Paloma lingered nearby, as if she were afraid Kaya would drown if she left the room. She even helped Kaya wash her hair without getting the bandage on her temple wet.

"Thank you," Kaya murmured as Paloma helped her dry and dress.

"It's no trouble," Paloma replied. She handed Kaya a fresh stack of clothes. "Your sister brought these for you."

"It *is* trouble," Kaya argued. "You've all gone to way too much trouble—"

"Kaya Altaha," Paloma snapped, "out there you may be

the sheriff and you may have to care for everyone else. But under this roof, you are in our care. It's my duty to care for Hammond's children, his grandchildren and the ones they choose and that pleases me. You've done enough. Our troubles are over because of all you have done. All we ask is that you let us take care of you now. *Por favor*."

Kaya held the knot under her collarbone that kept the towel closed around her and the clothes Paloma had given her with the other hand. "*Si, señora,*" she murmured.

A smile touched Paloma's eyes but not her mouth. Reaching up, she brushed the hair back from Kaya's face. "*Buen*."

Kaya responded by taking her hand. "Paloma?"

"What is it, *niña*?"

"Does it take as much strength as I think it does?"

"To do what?"

"To..." Kaya pressed her lips together. Then she closed her eyes and made them part again. "To love him the way that you do...for as long as you have..."

Paloma blinked in surprise. "It takes strength to love anybody." When Kaya bit her lip, she straightened her shoulders. "But he isn't just anybody. Is he?"

Kaya shook her head silently. She felt open and tried to make her expression unreadable.

Paloma squeezed her hand. "I have loved him—even when I thought he would never change. But he has changed. Do you know why?"

"No," Kaya replied.

"Then you are blind," Paloma said simply.

Kaya searched the woman's face. She started to shake her head again, then stopped when Paloma eyed her in warning. She released a breath. "I haven't changed him."

"He did some of the work himself," Paloma admitted. "He was forced to open himself—to grief. To acceptance. That is how love found him. But we do not love him because he has changed."

Kaya thought about it. "No," she stated.

Paloma nodded. "That is how you know it is strong. That is how you know this has what it takes. Do you think he is strong enough to be your man—through everything, good and bad?"

"I do," she realized with no hesitation. She could see it—him and her, through thick and thin, together. She heard herself gasp. That was the answer, wasn't it? To all her questions. "Do you do this every day?"

"What?"

"Change people's lives," Kaya said softly. She jumped a bit when Paloma laughed in a loud, genuine burst. Then she laughed at herself and pressed her fingers to the center of her brow. "I'm sorry. I'm a mess."

"If this is you at your lowest, Kaya, may I just say," Paloma said, "you handle yourself with more dignity and strength than anyone in this house before you."

"Never meet me when I'm sick or hungry," Kaya asked and laughed much more easily with Paloma the second time.

EVERETT HAD FINALLY gone from watching her sleep to sleeping beside her. The bags under his eyes had started to pop. He'd come to need rest as much as he said she did.

Kaya found herself sleepless. The pain had slunk back to an irritating level. She was no longer buried by it. She hoped tomorrow it would be mild enough that she could manage a trip into town. The desire to speak with her deputies had only escalated. She'd checked with the hospital to hear Rutland's status. Surgery had gone well, and he was recovering.

The fallout for Fuego would be long. The mayor was facing charges. The reverend had killed four people, at the behest of his father and sister-in-law. He and Annette Claymore were dead.

Kaya had to get back on patrol, if only to show the people of Fuego some measure of assurance.

She just had to get past the big tough cattleman first.

He looked soft when he slept. His breath whispered across her face. She lifted her fingertips to feather across his lips. They parted at the motion and she licked her lips to stop from kissing his. *Let him sleep*, she told herself, despite the need. It kindled, insistent.

She knew what flowered with it. She knew what she felt beyond need and want. And she knew how loud that voice screamed whenever he looked at her. Like she was still on that pedestal he'd put her on at the beginning of all this. It didn't matter how broken or bruised she was. He looked at her, and she believed—in herself. In him. Everything.

True to routine, Everett stirred near dawn. He raised one arm over his head and opened his eyes to find her sitting up in bed.

"Thirsty?" she asked.

"You have no idea."

He sat up slowly, letting the sheet fall to his waist and he took the drink she handed him. Together, they drank in silence.

He judged her constitution. "You're stronger today."

"I think so," she said. When he raised one knee and drank again, she bit her lip. "You said you had things to say to me."

"When you're ready."

She waited until he'd finished his coffee before she admitted, "I think I'm ready to hear them."

"Better be sure, Sheriff Sweetheart," he warned.

"I'm sheriff again, it seems," she observed.

When she didn't break eye contact, he took the mug from her. "You think you can handle getting dressed?"

"Why?" she asked as he got out of bed.

"Because we're going for a ride."

THE HORSES SHAMBLED. He wouldn't hear of them going faster.

"We could've walked faster than this," Kaya informed him.

"If you'd stop complaining for a few seconds at a time, we could do something crazy like enjoy the sunrise," he stated.

She didn't so much settle into silence as bristle at it. The light coming into the world did draw her gaze, however, and hold it. Day broke the grip of grim night, painting Eaton Edge and its river, hills and mountains in nature's watercolors, one after the other, until the sun's golden fingers grasped for its first hold of the sky.

Kaya had no words, so she let Everett and Crazy Alice lead her and Elsie, the gentle, sweet Haflinger he'd put her on, down a dirt trail a mile to the west of Eaton House, past Paloma's vegetable garden, past the orchard with its neat rows of trees, beyond the bunkhouse where the hands were beginning to stir and the cabin Ellis and Luella shared with the girls... They rode until the buildings were far behind them.

Finally, when the sun had rounded over the top of Ol' Whalebones, Everett tugged on the reins to bring Crazy Alice to a halt. Kaya did the same. "Where are we?" she asked, frowning at the ponderosa pines surrounding both sides of the trail.

He walked around Crazy Alice to grab Elsie's bridle and ran a hand over her long neck. "Attagirl," he murmured. Then he reached out a hand for Kaya's.

She ignored it. She'd gotten on the horse without his help. She could get off it, too. To prove it, she nudged her right toes out of the stirrups and swung her leg over Elsie's back. Gripping the horn, she lowered smoothly to the ground.

The change in altitude made her head spin. She stumbled as she brought her other leg down.

He caught her, gripping her upper arm. He cupped the back of her shoulders to keep her off the ground. "You said you were ready," he said near her ear.

"Stand me back up," she instructed, gritting her teeth. "I'm ready, damn it."

He made a noise in his throat but helped her steady herself. After several long seconds in which he watched for signs of weakness, he asked, "You good?"

She jerked a nod. He didn't let go of her arm, she noted, as they walked off the trail and into the trees. "Where are we?" she asked again.

Winding his way through the long shadows of the ponderosas, he hooked a right and guided her into an open glade.

The headstone gave her pause. It was centered in the safety of the dell. She opened her mouth to say something, then stopped because Everett released her and moved closer to the stone.

She watched as he crouched in front of it and tugged weeds from its base, then tossed them away before standing again. "This is where we buried him."

Kaya walked around the stone to stand at his side. It rose out of the ground to the height of her shoulders, coming to a point. The shape of a ten-gallon hat was etched just beneath the crest, followed by the name "HAMMOND WAYNE EATON" and the dates that marked his birth and death. The words "LOVING FATHER, GRANDFATHER & FRIEND" were carved in the center.

She read the words by Virgil inscribed in small italics below. "'May the countryside and the gliding valley streams content me.'" It felt sweet and so sad. She twined her fingers through Everett's and felt his hold tighten.

"He stands alone here," he muttered.

The breeze rustled the leaves. A hawk called from the distance. Otherwise, there was nothing here but the stone. It felt lonely. She made sure her eyes were clear as she raised them to his. "Why are we here?"

"Because that's not what I want." He paced away. Tracing an unseen path around the glade, he lowered his hat with one hand to drag the other through his thick hair once, twice and again, mussing the waves thoroughly.

When he ceased the restless roving, he faced her, planting his feet. "Until he died, I didn't give dying alone a thought. Then something happened." He pointed in accusation. "You."

Her lips parted, but he spoke again before she could. "I don't need much in this life. I never needed to be the boss or the man everybody looks to when the day's starting. Before last summer, all I wanted was to know that my family was going to be okay—that we'd survive because life keeps swinging at us. I thought that was all I needed. All I'd ever need."

Her pulse was high, she realized, when he paused. She

was starting to feel heady again. There was nothing to grab but the headstone so she crossed her arms over her chest. "Until me?" she asked.

"You're damn right until you," he muttered, holding his hat in two hands.

She watched him bend the brim, misshape it. "Why does that bother you so much?"

He stopped and quashed the hat over his head again. Planting his hands on his hips, he looked at her long under the shadow of it. "Because I need you to marry me."

Kaya realized after half a minute that she was gawking at him. She looked around—at the circle of trees, the empty glade—and shook her head. "You're proposing."

He made a face. "The hell did you think I was doing?"

She held up a hand, trying to get a grip on the situation. "You're…proposing to me…in a graveyard." And she started to laugh.

She laughed herself silly. She laughed until it hurt and she was bent over double, her hands on her knees, eyes tearing. "Oh, Christ," she hooted, swiping the back of her hand over them. She raised herself back up to standing, throwing her head back to peer at the sky. "That's good stuff."

"You 'bout done, sweetheart?"

She saw the deep-riddled scowl on his face and sighed at him. "Oh, I'm done. Believe you me."

He smacked his lips together unsatisfactorily. "Fine." He turned sharply on his heel and walked away.

She tailed him. "Wait a minute. Where're you going?"

"I know when I'm licked," he tossed over his shoulder.

She sprinted to catch up and grabbed her head when it protested. "Stop, please!"

He whirled back around just as fast as he'd left. "Look, I'll get on my knees."

"Everett—"

"Is that what you want, Kaya? You want me on my knees for you?"

"No!" she shouted when he started to kneel. "Get up!" Grabbing him by the shoulders, she yanked until he straightened to his full height again. She hissed when her head sang an aching tune.

He cradled the side of her head gently.

Who knew he could be so gentle? Yet another reason she loved him. "I don't want you to kneel for me," she told him. "Life's brought you to your knees one too many times before." Before he could open his mouth, she clapped her hand over it to make sure he listened for once. "And my answer isn't no. It was never no. It's yes."

As she lowered her hand, he blurted, "Yes?"

"Unequivocally yes," Kaya breathed and beamed at his utter confusion. "It may kill us both, but I'll be your wife." She framed his face in her hands and stroked his bearded cheeks. "You won't have to walk this world alone anymore—or the next one."

He lost his breath. His hands met either side of her jaw and he lowered his brow to hers. "It's a yes."

"Yes." She would've closed her eyes if he had. But understanding started to gleam there and she saw relief riding behind it. She threw her arms around him and buried her face in his shoulder. "I told you, didn't I—that I was your woman?"

"Christ," he breathed in disbelief. "Mine."

"I didn't think I was strong enough," she admitted.

"You're the strongest person I've ever known," he said.

"I'm in love with you—and have been for a while. Sorry it's taken me so long to say it. I guess I wasn't strong enough, either. You make me stronger."

She sighed, taking a moment to savor it all. He loved her. He wanted to be with her, always. "I love you, too." She swallowed. "I love you so much, I'm overwhelmed by it. You're not walking away, and neither am I. This is it."

He nodded. "This is it," he whispered in agreement.

"I'm in, Everett—all in. Do you see that?"

"I see you," he assured her. He swayed with her over the grass. His arms gathered her against his chest. "I see us." He touched a kiss to her cheek, then the high point of her brow and her other cheek. He grinned and she felt his happiness and her own radiating through her. "To the very end."

In the quiet glade, in the shadow of the trees, she felt Everett's warmth and for the first time in her life, she knew something beyond life's uncertainty. She was certain they would be together. She was certain they would love each other truly, uncompromisingly.

To the very end.

* * * * *